LEAVING RUIN

Jeff Berryman

LEAVING RUIN

a novel

New
Leaf
Books

ORANGE, CALIFORNIA

PUBLISHED BY NEW LEAF BOOKS
ORANGE, CALIFORNIA

This is a work of fiction. All characters and incidents in this novel
are the products of the author's imagination. Any similarities to
people living or dead are purely coincidental.

Cover painting by Dan McGregor, Abilene, Texas.

Text from *The Essential Tao*, translated & presented by Thomas Cleary
Copyright © by Thomas Cleary.
Reprinted by permission of HarperCollins Publishers, Inc.

For information, contact New Leaf Books
12542 S. Fairmont, Orange, CA 92869
1-877-634-6004 (toll free) / www.newleafbooks.org

ISBN 0-9700836-5-3 softcover
0-9700846-4-5 hardcover

Printed in the United States of America

02 03 04 05 06 / 6 5 4 3 2 1

for Jody

Acknowledgements

As I have learned, a book does not arrive at the whim of the writer, but as a grace bestowed by God at the hands of a community of people. For the appearance of *Leaving Ruin*, there are many people to thank. First of all, my thanks to Beth Amsbary, Sandy Freeman, Martha Heady, Adam and Donna Hester, Faith Russell, Sam and Candace Vance, and Nikki Whitfield for their willingness to wade through the early drafts of *Leaving Ruin*, as well as for their helpful and insightful suggestions. Thanks to Terry Moore, whose generous work in copy-editing the first draft was extremely helpful in approaching the later revisions. Thanks to all those who sat through readings of the early drafts of the stage adaptation of the book, and to Conrad Hild and Stephen English for their faith in booking the opening of the play, keeping the story alive. Thanks to Thom Lemmons, a writer and editor whose ethic and perseverance have both challenged and inspired me; to Curt Cloninger, whose early enthusiasm for both the book and the play were a great encouragement; to Milton Jones, who first introduced *Leaving Ruin* to New Leaf Books; and finally to my editor, Leonard Allen, for his friendship, his faith in the book, his insightful suggestions, and his willingness to see it through. My heartfelt gratitude, of course, to my family—Anjie, for all your love, faith, and patience (and for being my patron), and to my children, Amy and Daniel, for your willingness to let Dad do his work.

These days
the quiet is a curious thing
as if a cloud
a mystery
is not only out there
down the road
but coming
coming now
rolling slowly over dust
toward me
and I'm afraid . . .
afraid if I speak too loudly
ask too much
know too much . . .
the mystery will retreat
pass me by
leave me in the lonely place
and I'll have nothing . . .
nothing to hold when all things
are truly known
save the banal
and blatant, empty rules
and an empty soul besides

If I miss the mystery of God
I'll die.

August 17

I think he's odd, don't you?

Edna Johns, told to Roland Minor
Administrative Committee

My name is Cyrus . . .

Last night, Sara and I talked.

We talked of Gunney Sax dresses she wore to proms and banquets, and I said I especially liked the Victorian, the yellow one with the long white sleeves and lace. Her eyes narrowed. The high collar, with layers of lace at your throat, I said, and those loose, pearl-white buttons running down your front framed your sassy youth with elegance, and it was a memorable frolic in the wee hours of that long ago morning. Brighter days in the lost glory of youth, I told her, and she snorted, and accused me of having selective memory. I grinned, and said you loved it.

That was over twenty years ago—our senior year in high school. Twenty years. With those years, I feel warm in my belly. Oh, she's no savior, but she's a partner, a silky brunette who once chipped a front tooth, adding a crazy off-kilter charm to an otherwise average, but smoky, smile. Years later she fixed the tooth, but her charm remains, and her beauty still sneaks up on me, slaps my heart into beating. Her dark and lazy eyes rest on strong, hard cheekbones, and I savor her kisses, petal-soft and ripe, always longing. These days make such sweetness imperative, and those kisses last 'til we can't breathe, pulling me up, toward eternity, but sadly, the deep taste tells not so much of what is, but of what is to come, leaving the full truth for another time.

Last night, facing west, settled in the old-fashioned pine glider we bought for our ninth anniversary, we slid back and forth, no sound, looking for Jesus in the clouds, knowing he could come today, but probably won't, so we talked of other things—things that had to happen if we had to leave Ruin. Richard came out and asked if we were going to have to. You're not supposed to be up, young man, and when you're seven, bedtime's at eight.

"Do we have to move?"

I thought of Jeremy Dotson, Richard's best friend in the whole, wide world, and how best friends change and forget when you move away. I felt sorry for him, and said not to worry, but maybe. He said Ty Potter said his dad said we have to, because you're not a very good pastor, and you make people nervous.

Sara walked him back to bed, and when she came back, she snuggled into my lap, and too afraid to look things full in the face, we whispered our pain into the night, giggling mostly. The porch light was off, and it got dark, and the Manning's occasional courtship on the front porch has always been part of what make the good people of Ruin nervous about the preacher.

∼

My name is Cyrus Manning, after a great-grandfather on my mother's side, a circuit preacher who kept switching from Baptist to Methodist and back, so I guess my bent toward ambiguity, what my detractors would call irresponsibility . . . well, I guess it comes naturally. Like I said, I'm the preacher, or the pastor—depending on what denomination you go to—here at First Church; the guy in front on Sundays. Call me what you like, except "Father" Manning. There's only one Father, in my book, though I do have a good friend in the clergy over at St. Joseph's in Odessa named Rosey Peterson, and I call him "Father" some. He makes me laugh. A round, salty priest from St. Louis originally, he's constantly reminding me I enjoy a good woman's bottom sashaying by way too much to ever be a superior man of the cloth, and late at night, at the alley snack bar, he describes despair and grace as if they are twins, the only difference being a sparkle in the latter's eye. Father Peterson and I go bowling together the first Tuesday of every month, and more and more, I've come to believe that whatever I call him is probably fine.

Besides preaching, there's Bible class. No one at First Church pays the slightest attention to what Bible classes are called what, and Sara and I, we still attend what's labeled "the young marrieds." I like the class, mostly because I teach it, I guess. And then there's counseling, and elders' meetings with ambitious deacons, and worship planning, and midweek service, and putting out fires, and lighting them, and weddings and funerals and it's enough to make 90 and 100 hour work weeks, and I do the best I can. But sometimes, my mind wanders, my shoulders slump, and I go for long walks or runs, all the time wondering if my best is worth all the effort it takes to get it out. But my mom always wanted me in the clergy—said I wasn't fit for much else, and Mom was usually right about things.

And, by the way . . . so am I.

That's a joke.

Did you hear the one about the preacher who lost his calling?

I don't tell jokes very well, and once, back at my former congregation in East Texas, I stood up on a Sunday morning and tried to preach on the comedy of the cross, because in the classical sense, of course, there is one, and Frederick Beuchner does it beautifully, but he's Presbyterian, and I'm not. That afternoon, the elders called me into their office and said there was nothing funny about it. I lost my job then and there. Which I'm glad of now, cause now I'm here, at the First Church of Ruin, Texas, where me and about 276 other folks from around the county come to try to make sense of things. That was the membership at last count, though with visitors, lots of Sundays, we have over 300. It's my 11th year of thinking maybe I'm not cut out for this, and I have that peculiar disease that's mostly fatal called they-don't-want-me-here-any-more.

∼

I didn't believe Ruin could be the name of a town, but when I saw the land, I understood, and I imagine its founder, back in July of 1837, standing here on the plateau over his one dead cow, with his covered wagon uncovered and its axle flat broke, lamenting he ever left Boston. But being out of ways to go anywhere, he figured he might as well set up shop in the dust, and call a spade a spade—Ruin. Why anyone came to join him is the question. The stark landscape depresses passers-by, but my boys enjoy the tumbleweeds, racing them from one end of Curtain Street to the other. The water's oily, or tastes that way, though it's worse in Midland, and some kid told me that first week we were here, don't fall in the grass, when you can find it, or the stickers will eat you alive. Now a sticker is a little ball of thorns, sharp as needles, she said, and I said, Yeah, I know, and she said like a lot of things in life, no matter how you pick one up, it's gonna stab you. And it'll hurt when you pull it out. Then she waited for me to be impressed, and I said where did you read that, and she grinned one of those grins only 16-year-old girls with small noses can grin.

Ruin is a good Texas town, she said, over 26,000 now, and I thought, 26,000 people stuck out in brown desolation, by their own choosing, somewhere between Odessa and El Paso. Kim was the 16-year-old's name, and she brought us some pecans later that month—there were lots of pecan trees around—and she pointed out the elms, and the oaks, and her mom came along and said it's really lovely if you look at it right. Sara thought she'd try to look at it right, but it's always been ugly to her. Our yard's pretty bare, no oaks or elms, and we make do with one lonely mesquite tree whose trunk rises off the ground at a sharp angle, then mosies up toward the sky in a lazy curve that makes me think of an old grandmother's bent back, finally tapering into nothing about fifteen feet above the earth, as if it just lost interest and decided to sleep. Spreading branches at the top look like wisps of hair on a bald head, and in a stark sunset, that old mesquite can be austere and iron-strong, and on those evenings, I imagine it to be a giant, haggard old settler, a desert lady wandering, searching, for her son, her life, or maybe—just one last piece of bread.

But that's just me, my mind wandering—again. Wishing I were a desert monk, shrouded in a mystic veil, cloaked with God.

Kim's mom also told me that I could probably grow some tomatoes, and maybe some beans, and didn't I think I wanted a garden? I listened politely, but I hate tomatoes, and gardens, too, and Sara smiled at me, and said that would be lovely, too, if you looked at it right. Sara's sleeveless tee shirt was dark with sweat, front and back, and later, watching Kim run off down the street like it was a breezy 65, Sara licked her lips, smiled a cool smile, and didn't complain, but headed back in the house. The screen door closed, and she asked me if I wanted some iced tea, and though I couldn't see her eyes, her voice mocked me a little, as if she couldn't believe she'd been dragged off to the bottom end of the earth. She spent most of her youth in the Pacific Northwest, and when I told her iced tea would be nice, thanks, she stuck her head back through the door, said she used to wear sweaters on August evenings, and heading back to the kitchen, she kept mumbling, but there was a smile in it, and I think I heard the word "annulment."

I joke about Ruin, but Sara doesn't always laugh.

~

The church itself is old, and driving in, I catch the steeple peeking over mesquite trees and neighborhood houses. It's the tallest in town, but the cross on top leans, and swivels in a good wind like a weathervane. Built in the early part of the century by an optimistic group of Church of Christers that moved over to Highland street in the '30s, it's little more than an ambitious box, ugly, with sienna walls, and tall paned windows, with one small stained glass window installed years later just above the massive front doors. The box stood empty through WW II, and was a funeral home painted green for about a decade before eighteen people who were starting a church got together and bought it in the late '50s, some five months before I was born down in the hill country.

In recent years, two additions created classroom space and a gym/multi-purpose room where four or five teens hang out on Friday nights in winter. The sign out front simply says:

FIRST CHURCH OF RUIN
WELCOME!
A Church of the Bible

(They added "A Church of the Bible" after a series of inquiries wondering if the church of Ruin might be a satanic cult.) As a Bible church, its beliefs are non-descript, not easily defined; one of those amorphous flavors that pop up when people get tired of creeds and traditions, and decide to split, and divide, and innovate—all to the glory of . . . well, you get the picture. The initial founders—the first eighteen—were a mixed bunch; a couple of Baptists, two Church of Christ couples, and at least five Presbyterians, and the others I don't remember, though "Spirit-filled" is in there somewhere. They wanted to get closer to the Bible, they said, and maybe they did, maybe they didn't, but they tried, and we still do, but people fight over interpretation, wondering what's essential and what's not, and the unity Christ prayed about in John 17 must be mystical, cause I sure can't see it. The pine racks in the lobby used to be full of tracts telling why heads should or shouldn't be covered, and how God likes one style of music, or worship, or prayer— but not the other, and who ought to be baptized and when, and what kind of cracker should be used at the Lord's table, but I cleared out a lot of that when I got here, cause there's a lot of haggling over stuff that doesn't matter as much as we think, while love goes ungiven, and I can get really red-faced talking about non-essentials. I tend to err on the side of judgment. Independence and autonomy can be foolish, and lonely, and though our theology runs straight back to Jesus through Calvin and Luther, mixing with medieval mystics, saints, and 6th century Catholicism (whether we know it or not), my little congregation tends to believe the straight and narrow is the Main Street in Ruin, and there's no other street like it in all of Texas, or anywhere else.

I disagree with that basic premise, and that's another part of why some folks around Ruin grouse about the Mannings. Seems like the grumbling gets louder every day now, and truthfully, I may have only a few short months left. I just hope it's long enough to teach one more series of classes.

∼

This morning, before the sermon on the fear of rejection, a ceiling fan turned slowly, rocking slightly, and I watched it, cause there were lots of eyes to avoid. Probably a screw loose, I guessed. "Glorify Thy Name" was the last song before my turn, and as it began, I noticed Jack sitting right underneath the fan, and I wondered, if it fell, would the blades decapitate him, or just crack his skull, like any old falling object? My worry moved on to medical insurance, cause if the vote went against me, there would be no retirement, little savings, no pension, but suddenly the chorus, the part about "Glorify Thy Name" came around, and my heart snapped into place, moved by the music, but more by the thought, and I had to stand, deliberately, and unannounced, which I knew seemed pretentious and theatrical, irritating to people when I did it, but instantly my soul was rising, and my body had to follow. Life gets up and goes when such music wanders in, and there are moments when God arrives, and I hold on, because, though I know I'm not exactly charismatic, or maybe I am, I know the air is changing, growing thick with Presence, and I expect that stained glass with the dove at the back to just burst into shards of flying shrapnel, but it doesn't, and the air thins again, and suddenly, normal is back, and it's time to preach. But I know I must look wild-eyed, if not loony, hair sticking in all directions, but mostly straight up, making me look like I just enjoyed a tumble in bed, but suddenly, I find myself standing before the eager people of God, daring to say what he would say if he were there.

So to speak.

～

The fear of rejection, I began, comes from knowing full well what is being rejected.

As I opened my mouth, I remembered that as a kid I wanted to be a pilot. Or maybe it was just to fly. Just to lift off the roof of the old house and rise to 2500 feet and barrel roll in my stocking feet, shirt flapping hard enough to cut flesh, and diving for earth at terminal velocity, finishing with low flying over water. Flying comes in music sometimes, or movies, or occasionally when the Spirit's voice

takes over mine, and it's a high that feels like God reaching through
the curtain and reminding me heaven may seem far, but it's part of
the bargain. How did I end up as a plodder, I wondered, going on
through sermon points three and four, and I considered saying I quit
right then and there, and even as I wound toward the climax, inter-
nally, I ruminated on whether we would move up north or just go
back home to Austin.

I grew up in the hill country of Texas, and I first met God wandering through my uneventful childhood, spending lots of time walking among trees not far from our home. My parents were faithful, if
not boring, but lured by a druid's need to honor the mystery of things,
I walked and thought, and read Ecclesiastes, and knew instinctively
that there was indeed, nothing new, and that knowledge and wisdom
were paid for in pain. God called me, but said little, and my family
left me to myself, to the visions they saw me lost in. By the time I
went to college, to UT just up the road, I felt like the odd man out
most everywhere I went. Or maybe not so much odd man out, as odd
man—period.

Still true, I thought this morning, still odd, and at this point I
was fifteen minutes into my twenty-minute sermon, and my forehead
was shining, sweating. I was way in over my head, talking right to
crossed arms, saying that when you are no longer wanted, no longer
respected, no longer trusted, no longer loved, it is not a set of actions
or words or postures being rejected—it feels to us like the identity
itself is being turned away. It is the "I," the knowing part of you, the
emotional seat that weeps at sappy movies and good-byes, and feels
longing deep in your bones. It's the you made up of the way you spend
a Saturday off or the extra $50 you got for your birthday. The you that
has a style in your days, a way of holding a fork, or doing foreplay, or
getting the house clean, or reading the books you read, and the names
you would name your kids, and the little things like what you believe
about abortion, and marriage, and missions, and your mom, and
there's all this stuff that's being stepped on and trashed when you are
ignored, or flat pushed away. You slave to get the word out, the word
God has placed inside you, the word that will build, maybe contribute
to his making, and if you say no to me, and if I say no to you, then we

crumble, and cringe, and melt like the witch in the water, go into hiding, and fear leads to walls leads to isolation leads to depression leads to no hope, and much is lost. I was embarrassed because I stole some of this from a tape I listened to a couple of weeks ago, but it was in my body today, and I said what you lose is a sense of worth and meaning, and what a black pit that loss is, and that I hope none of you face it, but you face it every day, don't you, and I face it every day, and I almost asked them, "Love me, please," . . . but I stopped.

I couldn't breathe. A void opened. Swallowed me. I had lost my place.

I had lost my place.

Confused, I took a drink, and a breath, and wrapped it up with saying God should be the audience of one we cared about pleasing, and don't be afraid, but live, and think of being accepted by God, and that he did accept us, because of Jesus' blood, and riding home in the car, Sara didn't speak.

~

Lunch was the familiar roast and baked potatoes, and the clink of silver on plates made me lonely. Richard went to take a nap because his stomach hurt. The Cowboys are on, Sara said, and Wayne and I turned it on. There was Emmitt Smith, faithful Emmitt, running, bulling his way to a first down, and I thought, now there's a man who knows what to do. Give him the ball and he runs. He knows he's going to get pounded and gouged, but he runs, because he knows that's the game, and my life seemed absurd, surreal, and for a long moment, just the length of a dying sigh, I had to close my eyes, and press them, working them over so they wouldn't explode, and I thought, I could've been a player, a good player, and is that what you wanted, O God? O God, I said. Then . . . I'm sorry.

Sara stood in the door drying a cup with her apron, watching Wayne absently scratching the scab off the cut from yesterdays's fall from the porch. His knee was bleeding again.

"I won't pity you, Cyrus. You should stop it . . . . You through with your cup?" She lifted the cup from my hand, and I turned my face to her, but like God, she was gone, and I was disappointed. She turned on the dishwasher, and the clinking was over, and the Cowboys lost, but it was only an exhibition, and I think they'll probably win it all this year.

∾

I know she's right, but there's meaning in the silence of God, and when I can't find that meaning, my balance goes, and I end up drifting, wanting nothing but to rock myself to sleep. Sleep comforts me, and I need it, true enough, and it's late besides. The night came quickly, but more than rest, I need this alone time to orient myself, count the losses from the previous week, set some goals, get my head straight, order my private world—all that stuff that's over in the get-it-right-or-you-don't-have-character section of the bookstore, and it's all good stuff, I know . . . but these days are granite hard, like a quarry, and monstrous, like a tomb, and I pick up the phone to call somebody, but why call if I don't know why, and besides, I can't think of anyone I trust, and besides, it's past midnight, and I chew the receiver, the *enh-enh-enh-enh* finally reminding me to put it down.

I used to be a good guy, well liked, and how I came to a place in the world where I call no one friend is another branch of the mystery. What do beatitudes have to do with me, with their "blessed be you" given to this one or that?

∾

How does Jesus come?

I can't help it. I ask questions. Always have. Clear answers may sooth me, but I'm wary, suspecting them of hiding layers of truth under the comfort of assurance. When I take the worth of an answer at face value, I remember the Pharisees were fools, and that his ways are far above mine, though not utterly unknowable, and I walk a tight rope between awe and doubt. The idea of true religion being the care of widows and orphans, and keeping myself unstained by the world, is simple, but inhabits a profundity that leaves me gasping for air, and the implications of stupidity buried in my daily life habit are crushing, humiliating, enough to break a man's soul in half. The one thing I know, and freely confess, is that I, like Paul, am the chief of sinners.

Confession, of course, opens the door, and the Lord comes.

But . . . how?

Shamefully, perhaps, imagination calls me. I imagine worlds of sparkling dust, whirling hair, where birds speak angel languages, understood by idiots and commoners. Imagined worlds where God laughs, and his laughter is water, nourishing the poor and unknown of planets undiscovered, where God will one day send the Savior, but the timing is not yet right. Where suns are blue, but the blue has no meaning physics would understand, and is merely pretty, and so the people of this pale cast world are filled with the blue ache of a beauty that penetrates even the dullest of rocks. Where Jesus would carry me on his back to watch as he spread healing across clouds of stars.

I long for his coming. I wait for it.

I dream of having been prepared like the Israel of old, and I hear a distant shouting, full of locusts and honey, and a wildness, a holy wildness that is so stark, so blindingly full of sun, that I can feel my will wanting to shear away, and open to the coming of the One who baptizes with fire. Perhaps that fire, and his coming, will not be surprising. Not shocking at all. But will I accept him? I mean, of course, I accept him, in that my-personal-Lord-and-Saviour fashion that counts me among the Christians of the world, but when he visits me on my porch, someday, perhaps in imagination, perhaps in fact, and we talk, I wonder if I will listen, or will I simply write it off as another silly game.

~

O, Cyrus.

My faith is fine. I'm fine. Just drifting a little, needing a little rescue, a little help.

~

My pressed wood desk cost me 99 dollars at Sam's, and it's too small, so I tore off the upper shelves, and they're out in the garage holding an old lamp shade and a few tools now, and as I sit here, trying to focus, I'm thinking I should be thankful for what I do know, not grousing about what I don't. I grab a legal pad, open my Bible to Matthew 5, and Sara often tells me that it's not hard to see why my thinking, and my preaching, makes people squirm, and makes them mad too. They like *to know*, she says, and because I'm the pastor, I'm supposed to know, and if I don't, who does, and what are they paying me for? I always say you're right, but what they don't want is the trouble of wondering why smart, educated, loving believers in the world say *they know*, and say *this is what the Bible says*, and then spout doctrines of varying degrees of reasonableness and insanity, many of them unrelated and in flat out conflict with one another. I'd like to know, too, and I too believe in simplicity, but standing in the presence of the vast array of God's worshippers in multiple cultures and histories, thinking of our stumbling attempts at knowing him, it all seems a bit crazy to wave a flag over anything except the fact that Jesus is Lord.

I used to care about all the conflict, and trying to figure it out, but honestly, I don't much anymore. It's hard enough trying to do unto my neighbor as I want him to do to me. Hard enough not to look at every pair of sun-tanned legs in shorts or flip skirts going by. Hard enough not to amble my way through life appreciating little but what gives me pleasure, without ever stretching myself to give away the one cup of cold water, the last one I have, the one I think I must keep to survive.

~

The hard thing is, I tend to work out all the stuff I don't know in places and ways that, as my son said, make people nervous. Sara has heard the word "disgusting" and "Cyrus" in the same sentence more than once, and she heard Beatrice Thomasen going off one day after I preached on the will of God. I'd been reading a Catholic monk named Thomas Merton who says everything is the will of God, or in the will of God, and I think if you know what he means, I'd agree, and I used lots of scripture, but oh, what about the suffering babies, and deaths in earthquakes, and random violence, Beatrice said, and I'll be hanged if I'll listen to preaching about Catholic doctrine, and she stormed off to see Elder Jack right after services, and I actually called U-haul to get prices on a truck first thing the next morning.

Once, over coffee, I told some college kids who were home for the holidays—I think it was Christmas—that the *Tao Te Ching* was kind of interesting, really beautiful in places, because they'd been reading it at coffee shops with names like "The Last Exit," and I told them I especially liked

> *The Way of heaven*
> *is like drawing a bow:*
> *the high is lowered,*
> *the low is raised;*
> *excess is reduced,*
> *need is fulfilled.*
> *The Way of heaven*
> *reduces excess and fills need,*
> *but the way of humans is not so:*
> *they strip the needy*
> *to serve those who have too much,*

which sounds a lot like Jesus, but of course, I know it's not Jesus, and I cringed when Elizabeth Pourer cornered me for teaching Eastern writings to her daughter Xan, who was at the University of Illinois, and didn't I know she was struggling, and who did I think I was. And right there in the video store, while she screeched, I tried to convince her that I read other things besides the Bible because I'm not afraid, and the Bible is the essential truth but that other truth might poke its head out if we were watching, and that I was trying to get on Xan's side of the table. But Elizabeth stood there with tears in her eyes, as if she'd just received news of her death, and that night, as I watched my video (Gerard Depardieu in a fantastic performance of *Cyrano*), I thought, just like I'm thinking now, what am I doing?

Then there was the Sunday when a visitor in Bible class asked me what I thought about the gay question. I wanted to ask what question he had in mind, but I knew what he meant, and in Ruin you don't joke about this one, and you can barely say homosexualty without getting crucified, so I took a breath, and paused, and it was the pause that made the trouble. I said all the right things, and I know the old Law and the words of Paul, and that God is the same now and forever, and I believe all the right things . . . essentially . . . see . . . there's that pause . . . *because it kills me.* The whole thing kills me, I said, and it was risky in a damning sort of way, but I went on to say that again, I don't understand. My heart dies a little as I understand God's command about it because a good, good friend of mine from college is a gay man, out of the closet, HIV positive, but he's kind and loves Jesus, or says he does, and he grew up believing TV was a waste of time like me, and so he works, and spreads a kind of love around, because that's who he is, and it keeps me awake at night, his sin, and I pray and hope, and I know what my conclusion is on that one, and I give it to God, and I suppose he aches worse than me. But the pause put fear into a few of them, and Roland saw me at Burger King and obviously I'd been squealed on, because he mentioned a couple of evangelical books that would help, he said. Help me get clear, he said. I chewed an onion ring, and got an extra order of fries.

Then there's the race thing. One of my dad's cousins used to tell me—*I was six years old*—we should line up Hispanics and shoot them, and even then, I was appalled, and now, still, I'm ashamed of my family heritage. I remember starting out a sermon with the statement "The black man is a friend of mine," and the air conditioning seemed to go out of the place. I went on to say I'm sorry for what we whites have done to them, and though I didn't do it, and though you didn't do it, maybe, we did it, and we do it everyday, and how I wanted to repent, and didn't know how exactly, and if anybody wanted to join me in that, we could pray, but nobody did, and I prayed, "Lord, forgive our prejudice, seen and unseen," and there were no amens, and in fact, I saw several people flatly refuse to close their eyes, and though most times that doesn't mean anything, those open eyes burned, and they'd have risen with a shouted "no" if they thought they could have gotten away with it. In the silence of the aftermath, I decided maybe God hadn't called me to say that after all.

But Brother Collins over at the Hillcrest Fellowship, Ruin's largest black church, got wind of it, and he called me, and invited me to lunch, and I was tense that day, and a little scared, but confession, especially of this magnitude and awkwardness, is always that way, and I was determined to get it out. And Brother Collins—call me Harold, he kept saying—helped me, and we prayed together, and in the middle of that prayer, the tension broke, and he laughed a laugh like the shouting of an angel, so high and loud, a growing crescendo, so without pretence, so without fear. I need to hear that laugh at least once a week just to remember the power of freedom. We have T-bone steaks down at Ron's Steakhouse together a couple of times a month, and Harold and June have been to visit our home, and Sara and I have been to theirs, and I love their church, and got to actually speak there once, and the amens and shouts were an ocean I could walk on, and though there's a long way to go to bridge the chasm, I'm thankful for the hope. It's more than what was before.

But at First Church, just the other day, I heard a guy I won't call by name say nigger in the parking lot, and I was reminded that when I was five there was a rhyme with that word in it, a white child's game, and I am ashamed that it lives in my mind like a canker. I told the church about it last Sunday, and said racism is still in us, and a sin before God, and we don't want to see it, and I could see Roland shaking his head, wishing he had a pastor with some sense. Or some tact, at least.

I am a Republican, though, which means a little. But Sara's a Democrat, and lovingly calls me "politically deficient."

And there's other stuff, worship "issues"—issues is a word that raises the ridiculous to a serious level of debate—but I can't get too worked up over this one. I like the old gospel hymns and the new praise songs, and again, I don't care really cause I figure God likes music and variety, and praise is in the heart, and Jesus can change channels when he gets bored with one style or another. Worship styles 101. In spirit and in truth, and walk humbly, and I want justice and mercy rather than sacrifice, and maybe Evangelicals and Mystics and Charismatics and the High Liturgicals should just trade places once a month. I look at the entrails of my body, and the ecosystems of the planet, and I get diversity, but I also get truth, and the great evidence of God's presence, and if he'd wanted to cross the t's and dot the i's he could've and would've, and on and on I go, just talking, talking, and a person starts to get the picture after awhile.

I get in trouble all the time.

~

My boys were born here, and it was here that Sara learned to love Jesus, and me besides, and I hope we can stay.

We'll see.

~

Back to Matthew 5. I need to get ready for next week, for what Roland told me may well be my last chance to teach a class here at First Church. I could do what I wanted, he said. A class on the beatitudes, I decided, and some other things that I like from the Sermon on the Mount, because I guess, in Matthew's mind at least, that's where Jesus started in his thinking, so it's where I want to start in mine.

But, I have to remember, I'm one of the ones without authority, an old-style scribe, a teacher of the law, one of the ones Jesus was not like.

~

Jesus. Come to me. Fingering the yellowing paper of my Bible, sipping the old, burnt coffee left over from the afternoon, listening to Sara's easy breath coming from the living room, I lean over the book, and pray to find you.

~

He came to the people on the mountain, on the plain, wherever, and taught them, and I imagine Matthew writing furiously as Jesus spoke, although of course, it never happened that way, and the people hanging on his words like rock climbers to a cliff. The carpenter friends of Jesus, who bid the same jobs he did, and his buddies from when he was a kid, and the Israeli girl he maybe liked when he was 14 but he knew that path would never be his. Maybe a Shylock character, a grubby money-lender turned a talent in his hand while the Master spoke, and over there a man and a woman who were doing it on the sly, and next to them a couple of courtesans who wish they didn't have to do it at all, but there was no other way to make a buck for the baby at home. And good families were there, too, probably, kind men with faithful wives, but maybe they lived tempted lives, and they regretted, and sinned in an addictive kind of way, with hidden bottles, hidden thoughts, and though the kids obeyed them and honored God, there were fights, and brow beatings, and cryings in the dark, and occasionally a suicide happened, or a fortune was made. I will tell my class that I suspect those Matthew 5 people were like the people here, in this town, in this class, and it won't be hard to imagine them, and though the multi-purpose room next to the gym isn't a mountain exactly, it will be hot, and it's as good a place as any for the people to gather to hear the words of Jesus on a Sunday morning.

And who knows? Maybe he'll show up. Before it's all said and done, maybe he'll come, like Sara said. He could, you know.

I close the book.

He probably won't.

∼

Dear God,

You are holy, and great, I know, but I don't feel it much tonight. The written words of Jesus are old, and good, and he is still here, I know, but I need a new word, somehow, new like your mercies each morning, and on nights like tonight, days like today, I long to know your presence like I know the taste of sweet bread in my mouth, like I know Beethoven's Ninth, with clarity and power, like the ringing of cathedral bells in this sanctuary I call my life. Roll into me, O Lord, like a warm front coming down off the plains, and say my name.

Forgive me for the deep sin I keep. I have no goodness, no nothing, to offer.

Does triumph ever look like barely hanging on?

Show me Jesus walking among the people of the mountain, and Lord, I'd like to walk behind him. May I listen as he speaks? Love as he loves? May I ever talk with him at the end of the day?

Thank you for the quiet . . . but feel free to break it anytime.

Give me your voice.

In Jesus name,
Amen

~

I work for another hour, close the book, shut off the light, and head to bed. Richard threw up about 9:00, and he's still awake as I peek in. How's the tummy, I ask him, and he says okay. Go to sleep, I say, but his eyes ask me to stay. I walk to his bed, pull him from under the sheet, and hold him tight against my chest, his thin legs wrapping around my back, and as his head cradles into my neck, and his arms go limp, I think why not, and we slip by Sara asleep on the couch. My seven-year-old and I walk out onto the porch, and for him, and for me, as I invite him to the comfort of stars, and the anniversary glider, the night becomes a soft meeting ground where fathers and sons might find in each other the strength to move on through the night.

August 24

I don't care what he says as long as he doesn't say it here. Sorry, Jack, but that's it for me. It may be wrong, but I can't help it.

Sam Cooser, told to Jack Simons, Administrative Committee

... the silent counsel of eternity ...

I often dream of lone violins, and time turned around.

Violins break my heart. The soul of a violin is the tautness of string held softly between a strong wrist and shoulder, and if I listen carefully, maybe with headphones on, maybe early on a Lord's Day morning, as I am now, I can hear the itching, the scratching sound behind the note, and whether it's quick or mellow slow, my heart wants to lean over and rest with the effort of it all. Put a rich guitar with it, with a tapping rhythm that runs along behind, underneath, that same top note over and over on the upbeat of three, and I get a rush of hope, hope like I knew the day I first came to Ruin, way back when, a little joyous, a little off balance, a little in love with God, knowing his grace could pull music out of anything, even an old box of wood and catgut, and maybe my broken frame as well.

∼

The big, blue Chevy truck was a flatbed with sideboards, coming from East Texas to West, and it wasn't all that full, cause we were younger, and just married—well, maybe four years, and I remember the one good piece of furniture we had. A huge, early 20th century, antique cherry sideboard with a white marble top. We picked it up in the Oklahoma panhandle when Sara's college roommate's mother passed away. We got to town early, and had to kill some time in an antique store . . . but again, another story. The movers, a small local firm we got dirt cheap, were thrilled to get a long distance run, and they set the sideboard on the side of the truck and were trying to tie a blanket on it when the sideboard got away from them, and the boss, balding, wearing a long sleeve white shirt, yelled as it dropped, and the impact barely missed the youngest boy's foot, who had been holding the antique from the bottom. The boss yelled "You dumb sh—!" at everyone, and the poor boy's eyes teared up, but he was tough, and he took it. My face was red, I'm sure, cause the boy looked at me, scared, and blurted I'm sorry, and it took them half an hour just to clean up the broken marble and mirror glass. The tag that said $1900 was still inside one of the drawers, and with one bottom corner busted, caved in, and it sitting there in the street crooked, uneven like a restaurant table with one leg too short, I spat, and muttered at least one shameful thing, and said just throw it out, but Sara said no, silly, keep it, that we need the storage, and maybe I could repair it (like I was a handyman). But we threw it back up on the truck, and it came to Ruin, and my Bible sits on it most days, leaning, open to Psalms or Galatians, but Sara had it yesterday (my Bible, that is) and when I first got up, I hunted for awhile, but couldn't find it, and decided to give up rather than coat my day in frustration.

But my nose is running, and I want my Bible. I unplug the headphones, grab some toilet tissue, blow my nose, and get to digging through a tall stack of books by the phone.

I bought my Jerusalem Bible not long after college. It's thick, with a flimsy paper cover, hard to miss, and I remember my interview at First Church, how they asked me about this Bible, Jack and Roland and Everett Collins, who was an elder here, too—but he had cancer at the time—tumors, I think—and he died the week before I got here. They wanted to know about this unusual word of God, and I showed it to them, a brown and orange paperback, filled with red markings. I read one of the Psalms—132, if I remember right—and said isn't the language gorgeous, but Roland asked about the use of

"Yahweh" and I said it was published originally in French by the Catholics. Roland shot me a look, and I said but the language, and that I used them all—King James, J.B. Phillips, and the New American Standard, but I knew lots of people had the Revised, or the NIV, and now that Eugene Peterson had finished his new translation, I found it accessible for many people, and I finished by quoting a little Greek and assuring them I relied heavily on original languages in all exegesis.

I got the job.

Truthfully, my Sunday mornings aren't right without my Jerusalem, but Sara must have put it somewhere, and it's 5:55 a.m., and I have to read and pray now, before my sons interrupt the quiet. Reluctant, I go to the shelves I put in the south wall of the little den that doubles as a home office. I'm not a carpenter, and they're a little crooked at the top, but I brought almost 60 boxes of books to Ruin, and that was then. Sara bought a maple stain, but I never opened it, saying I preferred naked, unsanded wood, and Sara said I just preferred being lazy. Snooping through the few stacks, I get a little perturbed, because that may be a tickle at the back of my throat, and I refuse to have a cold, and . . . there's a Bible. An old one I haven't seen in a long time. I get my cup of coffee, but it's lukewarm. I hope the microwave doesn't wake Wayne—he's a light sleeper—and now I'm sitting down with my life and my worry, ready to face this ancient word of God.

But the couch feels wrong, and I beat the cushions, and twist, getting comfortable, or trying to. It's a great couch for naps and guests, but it doesn't sit well, and I look through the blinds. It's a clear sky, and now I'm gliding on the porch, where it's cooler, and more hopeful, and not quite full light. Sneezing twice—those silent kind where you hold it in and your head blows up—I open this book in my hand, and get to laughing at the little boy it brings to me.

This Bible was my Dad's.

There are no pictures, I think, and it's comical, really, that this book has made it this far. It started falling apart about the time I graduated from high school. In fact, our baccalaureate service was held on a Sunday when, coming in from morning services, most of the minor prophets broke away from the binding and landed on the pristine kitchen floor Dad had just mopped the day before. He wasn't mad, really, and I remember him humming "Time in a Bottle" while he picked up Nehemiah and Zechariah and Habbakuk and the others. He tromped over to the rotary phone and dialed it, saying he had a friend who could fix it, old Freddy.

"Hey, Freddy, hows it going? I've got an old Bible that I need put back together, can you do it?" It was one of those phones where you can hear the guy on the other end like he's screaming, and he sounds like he's on the moon, and I heard Freddy holler back, "Hell, yes, I can do it. You know me, Mr. Manning, I can do anything. How hard can it be to repair a Bible?" Now that worried me, cause I knew old Freddy, a retired tinkerer of sorts (though no one knew what he'd retired from) who piddled with any junk he could find, mostly to get his mind away from his regular life, which hadn't turned out *at all* the way he planned. Truth to tell, he was much loved, but not much of a fixer of things, if you know what I mean. So, I wondered, as I hunted for the tassel to my cap and gown, what kind of Bible would emerge from this old con man, this inventor of distractions and junk art.

I guess at the process, looking over it now. Freddy must have stripped away the old binding, and taken the old pages and chopped the headers and footers off, and the side margin, and then, to be artistic, cut the top and bottom outside corners at an angle. Then two 1/4 inch thick pieces of masonite, cut to maybe, 8" x 6 1/2", which was about the size of the pages after he chopped them, and he covered the masonite with a really awful imitation wood contact paper, which of course, is ripping now, and the masonite's fraying as well. How it's all glued together is beyond me, but it's hanging on. It lies in my lap like a memory. Dad's smooth hands are here, his average fingers that never learned piano, but turned these pages countless times, searching for answers to questions he didn't know how to ask, and his musings are marked in pens of all colors—his scribble and his griefs all here for his son to see.

I open the cover, and my dad's short, squatty cursive spreads across the first page in a kind of soul's graffiti, and thank God it's here. In black felt — "The silent counsel of Eternity." In blue ink — "The most beautiful and profound sermons of this book were often preached to only one person." Again, black felt tip — "Breathless bosom of Eternity." Black pen — "May God give me only enough time to finish whatever divine purpose I . . . and wisdom to let God decide when that purpo(se) is finished." Pencil — " . . . the joy of the hills, cradled in the valley of peace." Bold Black — "If any nation would concern herself more with the human rights of her people than with her human responsibility to her future generations, then that nation finds herself courting the fate of Babylon." Small pencil, can barely make it out — "If I ask God to give me the things I need; then I must assume that I have the fulfillment of my prayer in what-soever cup he gives me to drink."

That last sounds a little like Merton, and I wish my Dad had said more. But one thing he did say was that I might not last in Ruin. He didn't know me well, but knew enough to know I was peculiar, and that any call of God was more peculiar still. But Dad, eleven years is pretty good, isn't it . . . and suddenly—I'm sobbing.

It's been happening a lot lately. Like a slow leak, growing under pressure, my emotion presses on my chest, and after years of steadiness, am I finally caving in, teetering on the unknown brink of who knows what? Last Wednesday, after my nursing home visitation, and a long run, I locked myself in the bathroom, turned on the shower, and wept until the hot water turned cold.

I turn back to my Dad's Bible, but I can't see it.

Dad baptized me, and thought deeply maybe, but I can't ever recall us praying together. He wanted me to go to law school. Why didn't I? He never did the right thing with his life either, or so he said, and maybe such doubt is inherited. When I told him my plans for ministry, his hope for me changed, and he was laughing, but his face fell, and his wrinkles extended, and he seemed to go gray in a matter of minutes. The next day, on his way to work, he stopped at the door and asked me what I meant by "a call," and said he'd prayed all his life and God had never said one word to him, much less called. He was a gentle man, and kind in his way, but a loner, and I knew my distant posture was his own, and how lonely he must have been. He said he was glad for me, but his face mourned, nothing more than sad on my behalf, and after that day, all his smiles resonated with that dark knowledge that all the people of God face crucifixion, that his voice comes only to the ones he chooses.

Is it false, this "call" of mine? Have I missed my life? I'm supposed to be an attorney in New York, probably, or Iowa, or a pilot, or fireman, but not this evangelical, protestant, preacher-teacher thing where old women get ugly and spiteful and old men just go to sleep, and sometimes there's this deep anger that rises because nobody knows what I really am, except maybe Jesus, and what about when it doesn't feel like he's around, either, and maybe it's not too late to go to school again, and make my way the way I want . . .

The way I want. What might that be?

Maybe that's the mystery. The one that's coming.

∽

Every once in a while, usually on a Monday, last Monday, for example, in the late afternoon or early evening, that mystery sneaks up on me, and I amble off to a tavern.

The Down Under stands on the outskirts of Odessa, an hour and a half away, and I've been known to meet my Maker there, and others less congenial, when my thought gets dark, my reason lazy. Its obscurity gives me room, though it's scary, and over the course of eleven years, I've been enough times to average out to maybe three, four times a year, but over this past summer, my average has increased, as has my anxiety, and my visits have been more regular. In my early twenties I discovered that remote bars occasionally make for fertile thinking, though I have to fight through a fear of being seen. As I said, Sara and I drink almost no liquor, but the sweat-lined air of the Down Under stimulates me, and this arid, smoky room, where clarity gives way to the easy buzz of a slightly drunken haze,

shocks my system, removes me from the dull stupor of that depress-
ing notion that I am significantly wasting my life, and nothing at all
like God intended. Don't misunderstand—I still don't drink. Mostly
ordering two-dollar cokes and spicy buzzard wings with extra napkins, but the loosing of the strings is in the air, and I invariably drive
home a little under the influence of something slightly relaxing,
slightly intoxicating, though no highway patrolman could ever
measure it in my blood.

Bud Light neon greets me, and all its partners besides, and neon
mixed with hidden florescents glance off the hundred or so bottles of
mixers and liquors lined up against the glass of the bar-length mirror,
making a soft glow on the face of a cowboy who's at the bar almost
every time, and his girlfriend sits on the edge of her stool, facing him,
knee against his, tracing his sharp jawbone with her stubby hand, and
then kisses him, but on the cheek only. Last week, an old widower
with long ears bought them a glass of wine, which they didn't like,
but they toasted him, and chased it with beer, while Long Ears nib-
bled at a mound of nachos, sticking his old forefinger on the rim of
his margarita, sucking the salt in a pucker. I wondered if his life was
spent picking cotton, or working oil, but it was too dark to see the
clue his hands no doubt gave.

Folks come and go, slow or loud, and two young kids often play
pool on the one table in the back. The felt is torn, glued back down,
and the side pocket baskets have holes, the noise of a six or nine ball
bouncing on the hardwood floor punctuating the passing time like a
slow, erratic clock. The thin guy wins mostly, though one night, a
short, brisk woman with cropped brown hair and the eyes of a crow
came through with her own cue, and won over a hundred dollars from
him. The jukebox plays Bonnie Raitt, and Garth—90's country mostly, with an occasional Hank Williams, and it rarely blares, but hovers
just at that decibel level that makes it hard to talk, hard to be heard.
But I don't want to talk anyway, or be heard, and the only woman who
ever tried to have a conversation with me was looking to pick me up,
but she swallowed and buttoned up her cleavage when she saw my
open Bible, and she soon slid from the table and headed for the door.

There's a 6 x 8 dance floor, and why not, I don't know, but on Mondays, no one dances, though the cowboy and girlfriend usually do one slow turn before they head out. He puts his hands in the back pockets of her low hipped jeans, and their knees lace in that slow way, and I wish I knew them, but they never speak, to each other or to anyone else, and I've never wanted to intrude on the magic of their lives. I imagine that dance is a movie, perhaps after a long, brutal struggle to stay together, a Romeo and Juliet tale with bodies of enemies strewn in their wake, and this moment is the climax, the end of the film. Music (Trisha Yearwood) swells, and they walk out hand in hand, cowboy hats bent over eyes in love, strong bowed legs silhouetted against evening sky, and when the door closes behind them, I want to see credits scrolling up, and wake up to see I'm in a theatre, and this bar, and my life, is made of that unreal quality that makes us dream of all things being possible, and peace.

This past week, I stayed for just over two hours, from seven to a little past nine, thinking of . . . what? That call. Where it started for me, where it might go, this call of mine that feels like it's slipping away, slipping off my shoulders, though once it was as comfortable as the old threadbare overcoat given to me by Dick Marler back home in Austin. He bought that coat in Detroit in the late 50's, and gave it to me because every year when it got chilly we'd see the Marlers out at the mall or at church, and Dick would have on that long grey tweed and a matching fedora, and I would tell him he looked like Tom Landry, or a gangster, and only needed snow and a gun. I love that coat, but I'm losing it now as well, losing it to age, to memory, and to the need for warmth. It hangs, alone, at the edge of my closet, just beyond the camel hair blazer, and Sara, again, tried last Saturday to take it to the Salvation Army, but I caught her, and put it back, saying I still get comments when I wear it, that it stays with me. She says I should give it up, 'cause the backside is worn through, and the cold doesn't stay out anymore.

The call.

I wonder. What else could I do with my life? Marci, the waitress, in a short but tasteful skirt, brought me a new coke, and sitting there with spicy sauce on my face and napkin, I realized and said out loud that I have no skill of economic worth. She didn't respond and went back to the bar. If I could turn my thoughts into a commercially viable product like a video game or theme park, I thought, or even one of those bad boy/bad girl graphic comic novels showing up in bookstores these days; if I could write a book and draw out the forms of my mental twitches, give them names like Dwirly or Dindo, and make them palatable, even tasty, for those Disney imaginations; if I could somehow learn to simply fix something, like a car or a hairdryer or a VCR, or if I could go back and learn to sing or dance, and spend ten or twelve years alone, in deep, disturbing discipline, emerging again at this age to be a maestro, a master craftsman; if there was some way to escape my mind, rewrite the past, and choose the future differently, perhaps I would find what I seek.

But no. It's preaching. I do preaching.

I speak words that haunt me. Words that burn my chest when they go unsaid. Could I ever learn to not say them?

What did he want of me?

～

It began in the middle of a lake, one hot August, an August not unlike this one, down around San Antonio. The lake was near the home of a peripheral friend of the time, one I think eventually lost his way, and last I heard he was in Huntsville—the state prison—for an unknown crime—a robbery, I think. But Cam and I—his name was Cameron—had gone swimming for the day off a dock belonging to another friend of his, a guy I didn't know whose family had gone to Spain for a week, or maybe France. But there was a little rowboat at the dock, and, tired of lying on the fat inner tube, just burning, tired of the nonsense of splashing and doing cannon balls off the little three foot platform serving as a diving board, I decided to row out a ways. The sun concentrated on me, warding off high, bulbous clouds on the horizon, clouds that said thunderstorms might make it by nightfall, and the water stilled. Cam slept under a tree, and I paddled slowly over so-small waves, until I sat about 300 yards out from the dock. The paddle clanged as I tossed it to the other end of the boat, and my feet stretched in front of me, and I waited.

For an hour I waited.

I wasn't thinking. Trees I didn't know names of sat in clumps of five or eight or eleven, along the northern shore, drooping drought-brown leaves toward the water. I didn't know such names were important at the time, and the idea that *trees were* was far more interesting than the idea of one particular tree having the name of elm or live oak or whatever. There were two other boats, both with fishermen, looking for catfish, I supposed, or perch—God, I didn't know the names of fish either. Nor did I care.

But suddenly, it came. I sat up. The air ruffled my hair, and my skin chilled. Goosebumps all over my forearms and neck. I heard. I knew. My fate, my destiny, my call. But that's not right, exactly. To say fate or destiny is to run away from the idea of command. The idea of responsibility. I had to answer. There was an answer demand-ed. This was not the word of some sloppy, incoherent, impersonal universe dropping clues to guide the awakened soul, but of a God who, in one theologian's simple words, *is there*. As there as I was, and it was indeed a call. A spoken word, almost, but in no language that needed ears to hear, and madness seemed just on the other side of the word—as if to say, if I ignored its meaning, the boat and my being would capsize, and I would drift ever down until all my flesh was gone, and nothing but bones would greet me at the last day. I took that word into my body, and we spoke a bargain over the vast space between my earth and his heaven, and I had to stand up in the boat to keep my sanity. I wasn't looking up exactly, but the sun grew brighter, hotter, with the wind picking up, and I sailed way beyond the lake, to a place only angels know. I was aware, but en-tranced, and hokey as it seems, I know in my bones God gave me a gift that day, a small peek at a heaven only seen by saints and sav-iors, and the occasional madman he mistakenly chooses to entrust with his words.

I have been that madman, clinging to my lake vision, but last
Monday night, in a tucked away corner of a tucked away bar, the
whole thing looked pale, and fabricated. Made up, dressed up to look
better than it was, and God seems so quiet these days. So utterly gone.

As I pulled away from the Down Under, I had to admit this
absence of memory and God was nothing new. It was, and is, in fact,
several years old, and now I speak because I believe and obey, but
God—what I wouldn't give to journey back to the lake, to the bright
coming of God. Maybe I should go back to the water, and stand in
the boat. Maybe he would come again, show me again.

No.

Face it.

He'll have to come here, to the morning porch . . . or not at all.

∾

A big *whump* drifts out of the house. Richard fell out of bed again.
But there's no cry, and he's asleep, face scrunched against the throw
rug, and there'll be a creamy color drool-stain there by afternoon.

This morning, the silence of God seems not only reasonable, but
the only possibility. I could drop off the edge just now, but I resist, and
my mind—surprisingly—empties. I think, wiping my eyes, someone
must be praying for me. Must be. Probably Mattie. Mattie Mae Jones,
in her bed, just waking up, praying for the preacher she says she's not
crazy about, but her eyes always say she loves me. I know because my
heart beats slowly again, the drama of a grown man breaking is over,
and self-pity will not be my breakfast after all. But now anxiety takes
a turn, creeping up on me, because I know privacy is leaving, and it's
time to shower, time to go by Tastee Donuts and head to the office.

But not yet. Another a minute or two, just this once.

∾

It's quiet, holding my Dad's old King James.

You know . . . I think I'll stay. Not go in early. Just be with my family this morning. Cook some Bisquick biscuits, scramble some eggs, pour the Trix for the boys, and watch Sara dress, maybe even zip the back of her skirt. I miss her this morning, though she's just inside.

Jesus.

~

My, my.

Look at the clouds.

. . . *a gossamer palace* . . .

I poured the Trix and the milk, but didn't get to zip the skirt. The phone rang at 7:30, and once Connie and Sara start to talk, you might as well grab a book, because it's going to be awhile. When we left Connie and Dirk Jackson back in East Texas, it was hard on the girls, and Sara has yet to find the friend to pick up where Connie left off. They call each other once a month or so, but intimacy wanes with distance, and Sara has an ache that is Connie missing. When I finished my breakfast (toast and butter, with honey), I poked at Sara in mock frustration, and kissed at her, trying to weasel her off the phone, but she wouldn't play, and waved me off with an irritation way out of sync with the moment. Disaster on the other end of the phone, it looked like, and I hit the shower, and got my stiff white shirt just back from the cleaners, but now Sara was talking to me, saying that Dirk moved out again, just 10 minutes before the phone rang, and Connie was going to call back in about an hour. I wish he'd make up his mind, I said, and she said that wasn't funny, and would I mind if she didn't come with me this morning.

She grins, snuggles up to me, says I love you, honey, and I say, no way.

~

I'm headed for First Church now, and it's only seven minutes to get there, but at the first stop sign two blocks from the house, the car isn't warm yet, and it dies, and I can't get it to turn over. I'm pumping the pedal, but it's slowing down, sounding like it's flooded. I stop pumping. Richard's quiet and Wayne's playing air guitar, singing some wierdness about a suicidal cocktail waitress, and I ask him what he's singing. He mumbles the proverbial "nothin." I make a mental note to have that conversation later. I twist the key again, and again it won't turn over. We sit, looking at the street sign marking this as the intersection of Curtain and Mesquite streets. I look in the rearview mirror, and unexpectedly, day changes to night, and I see my house back there, but eleven-years-ago rises in me, a home glowing at midnight, and I remember first coming to this small Texas town.

∼

Our first night in Ruin was, at least, well lit.

The moving guys, the same ones who dropped the antique, hoped to arrive by late afternoon, but they were lousy planners, and Sara and I and the truck arrived just after 10 p.m., exhausted, sick of listening to *America's Greatest Hits*, which was the only cassette we didn't pack. We were both testy, because I said we should get a hotel, and get a fresh start in the morning, but no, she said, I want to be in my own home tonight. I knew she meant it, because she said it at least four times during "Horse With No Name" alone. The boss in the long sleeve shirt concurred, but cursed about it, and he said he had to get back by 11:00 the next morning for another job, and we have to unload now, at which point the young kid wilted, and again, almost burst into tears.

The boss yanked the truck forward, and I knew he couldn't see, because it was dark, with no moon, and only one streetlight about a block away, but he threw it into reverse, arrogantly backed up to the curb, and gave it the gas. But the truck rebelled, refused to climb, bounced off, and we silently cheered, rooting for the truck. The boss grunted, and gunned it hard, and the truck bounced again, protesting, but this time it landed on the lawn side, trampling the only bush we had. I waved my hands to stop, but he didn't, lumbering instead toward the porch like a tank. Sara screamed, and he jumped on the brakes, gears grinding, and the truck lurched forward about a foot, and died. The boss jumped out, short legs pumping, grinning as if to say I know exactly what I'm doing, and in less than two minutes, the first load of boxes came rolling down the ramp.

I unlocked the door, and Sara said carry me over the threshold. I felt foolish, and everyone stopped to watch. A wolf-whistle softly cut the air, and I remember being flustered by the notion of this old man and this young kid both leering at my wife. I looked at Sara in what little light there was, and sure enough, there she stood, weight shifted, hip swung out, making that familiar sweet curve of waist and back, boldly flirting in floppy tee shirt and jeans. I laughed, and in the slant of the shadows, her tired smile was sexy, indeed, and she said, carry me, cowboy, and I said, we've been married for how many years, and she said, *Cyrus.* We crossed the threshold, and I was surprised at the strength in her arms as she held on.

I couldn't get the lights on. I talked to the lady at the electric company, I said, and gave her the 25th as the day we needed it on, but Sara said it's the 24th, and I said no, and we looked at a calendar, and I couldn't believe it. I felt bad, and she knew it, so she didn't punish me, but headed out the door to rummage through the car, looking for a flashlight, I thought, but what she was really looking for was the box of candles we kept close for those romantic longings that crept up from time to time. She found the box, and soon the house was from another age, an older time, when light was gentle, and dark, and Tom Martin, who was only 16 at the time, but had shown up with his dad to help the new preacher unload, said later that the house all lit up with candles looked like a place the Holy Spirit had landed, and that he knew Sunday was going to be special.

Two hours later, it was done, and the flat-bed lumbered out of Ruin headed east, and what had been crisp, newly filled boxes on the other end of the day were now crumpled with corners bashed, but the house didn't look full, really, because, like I said, there wasn't that much, and 1320 square feet seemed big back then. Sara said she was tired, ready for sleep, and I started looking for the bedding, and in the first box I opened, full of old school yearbooks and torn track and field ribbons, I found a tarnished, silver-plated picture frame. There we were, Sara and I, standing hand in hand, at the senior prom, in a silly back-to-back pose, and though the dingy glass in the frame was cracked, her beauty was still there, in the picture and in the person, especially in candlelight. She yelled from the kitchen, did you find it yet, and I didn't say it, but I knew I had "found it" at that dance, at the age of seventeen, years ago, and my hunger for her woke me, made me forget the fatigue of the day.

We brought a bottle of wine with us, a $2.99 California Merlot. We picked it for the cool bottle, just to toast the new house. Neither of us are drinkers, but we always look for ritual, that gentle mixture of headiness and romance, of holiness and/or heat that might seal a moment in our lives, make it distinct in the barrage of forgotten days constantly swirling. The candlelight made the old house a gossamer palace, a Tennessee Williams place, and I could feel the walls breathing with barely being there, and it seemed like the stars would come falling through the silence at any moment, like the return of Jesus during a deep sleep. We got out the Waterford goblets from the wedding, poured the wine, and wandered out onto the front porch. What time is it, she asked, and I said 1:15, and it was cloudy, maybe 75 degrees, and the moon wasn't to be found, but here and there lights would show themselves in the sky, saying welcome to West Texas, and a new home, and perhaps a calling that would make a difference to a soul new born, or someone lost.

And we talked, Sara and I. We've always talked. Built our lives there, on glasses of tea and water and cups of coffee warmed in microwaves. Early morning hours of nodding off while the other unloads the burdens of the heart. We're quiet, really. We seldom yell—a handful of times—but we're fighters nonetheless, and lots of times there's space between us. That space reminds me of my essential loneliness, that constant pull—temptation, I should say—toward isolation, but it makes me remember that only God knows me truly, though most days I wish Sara knew me truly too. But, like I said before, we're partners, and after we fight we often end up dancing in the living room, without talking, and somewhere in the music we find that together place, and a word comes out, coffee gets brewed, and we sit down, talk again, make our way back home.

My watch said 1:30 a.m. The conversation stalled. The stereo was packed, and no music touched the quiet. Sara stood up, and rubbing warmth or comfort into tired muscles, she wrapped her arms around her waist. Leaning on the post at the corner of the porch, looking out on the bare field to the south, she claimed my adoration without a word. I knew she felt lost, missing old familiarities, old habits, old paths. And she missed Connie. But there was something else, too. Her slender fingers pushed hair back, away from her eyes, and when she glanced at me, those eyes blurred, and slid back around to the field.

"You better take care of me, Cyrus."

"Okay." I whispered in her ear, and though she was afraid, she believed me.

We walked out on the lawn in our bare feet, picking our way slowly to miss the burrs and stickers, and though the breeze helped, we felt the heat, the dying grass still warm from the day. Out by the curb, we turned, looked at the house, windows open, candles flickering fast. Some had gone out, and it was darker, and we clinked our goblets, drank the wine, and made faces at the pungent taste. Sara took a second drink, but spit it out, and we laughed, kissed a long deep kiss, then, perhaps in faith, perhaps in doubt, we prayed. Prayed that this house might be a kind of temple, a kind of refuge. A home where lives were lived simply, with kindness and joy, with love well made. A home where good things were said to good people, true words, and lasting, and honest, and we hoped that God would deem to join us, and live in all such words.

We danced on the lawn, and there was quiet, all the candles finally gone out. No electricity, but a warm fire appeared anyway, making a magic beginning, and as we walked on the dark side of the house, as we wrapped ourselves in a wilding moment of daring, dreams crushed our timidity, lifted our hearts, and in the midst of the thrill of her body with mine, the magic made a child as well. That night, Ruin was home.

~

"Is the car gonna start, Dad?"

It does, and I'm running behind now, it's past 8:00, and I hate to hurry. But there's a holiness in memory, and I mutter a thanks for a moment of sweetness. It will sustain me, and the six minute ride goes fast, and I'm getting out of the car now, calling out hey to Jan across the parking lot—she just started as part-time office secretary—and I panic.

I left my Bible, with my notes on Matthew 5, at home.

∾

Seeing the crowds, he went up on the mountain,
and when he sat down his disciples came to him.
And he opened his mouth, and taught them . . .

Jesus didn't use notes.

8:17. Class starts at 8:30. I'm usually here hours ago, so I can pray, or cram, but I'm late, flustered, unclear with worry. I could go back home, but that means I'll be late for sure, and if I'm slick, maybe they won't notice I'm rambling, and who knows, maybe the muse will show her face. It's an art, this preaching and teaching, as is the early morning posturing with classmates, and friends, and visitors, knowing what to show them, what to hide, and I wish I was transparent.

My nose is dripping in earnest now, but it's clear, and it's gonna be a scorcher today, lots of shirt sleeves, but I know Bill Buber's dad'll have on a jacket, and he'll look away when I roll up my sleeves, because God only wears suits, but that's a fading attitude around here, and three weeks ago, a new member named Ron Stern served communion in his overalls and nobody called the office. Progress.

I'm glad Sara stayed home, because I'm sniffing, and I can't decide if it's a cold or allergies, but I'll sniff all the way through class, though I'll try not to. It's a habit I got from Dad. I watched him snort and blow for years. Sara hates it, but she's not here, so I won't worry. But as I go through the lesson, I know I'll notice all these noises—coughs, sniffles, the shuffling of knee over knee, and scratching, clearing throats, and gurgling stomachs and wheezing (the wheezing is loud because Will Sorendon has asthma and punctuates the lesson with an occasional pull on his puffer), and of course, Mrs. Eric, who hiccups at least 5 minutes every week. She's not one of these petite hiccuppers, either; it's all or nothing here, every hiccup a loud bang, and the whole class bounces in time, like third graders on a school bus . . . you know the way their heads all bounce at the bumps . . . I like these noises. I like percussion, and scraping sounds, because they're human, and such noise lets me know I'm like them, and they're like me, and that's when I teach best, because I'm just talking, heart open, and those are the times I feel most apt to get it right.

I walk into the gym, and it's thumping away already, echoing the dull thud just waking in my temples. Some grade school kids are playing basketball in good shoes and short ties, and Richard and Wayne run over to join in, and most of these kids can barely get it to the basket. My class meets in a room just to the right, and the ball caroms off the wall next to me. I grab it, make a run for a lay-up, and I jump, but at the last minute I flip it back over my shoulder to Buster Eager, the seven-year-old trailing behind, and it hits him square in the mouth. He stops, and we lock eyes, breathing hard. A tooth is missing, and he's teary, but Wayne says his tooth was already gone. Is it bleeding, I ask, and he touches his lips, and quivering, says no, and I notice a short blonde with curls walking over, and she's Buster's girlfriend. He grabs the ball from another kid and runs for the basket. I say good man, Buster, and hurry on in to class. I'm surprised to see I'm the first one, and as I look at my watch, I think, I must be in the wrong room, but I'm not, and wondering if I should know something that I don't, I realize I'm sweating more than I thought, and a little chilled.

My eyes itch. It's gotta be allergies, and taking off my blue jacket, I throw it over the chair in the corner. Rolling up my sleeves, I watch it slip onto the floor, hating the sweat sticking to the middle of my back. Where's the air, I wonder, as big Reggie Appleby barges into the room. Richard and Maxine Bauser slip in right behind him, but I barely notice, because now the walls tilt slightly, and I have to sit.

Maxine says hi, Cyrus, and asks if I'm okay. Sure I say. She's excited, bubbly, and Richard, shaking my hand hard, says it's about her new job as a legal secretary. She gets the ice water every week, so she takes off for the kitchen, but turns at the door, giving Richard a final swing of the head, and he's watching her, in quite a lascivious way, really, and I remember they've been married some two years. His eyes make me glad, and I poke him. Turning three shades of red, he asks if Wayne is going to play football this year at the junior high. I poke him again, saying don't give me that, and I stand, making sure

the walls have righted themselves, and as I go to get one of the gener-
ic red Bibles we keep on hand for visitors, I am reminded that mine
is not the only drama being played here. In the next hour, tragedy,
comedy, romance, and farce will all make appearances, and each
moment is a little opening night. The Sermon on the Mount is like
that, I try to reason, but there go the walls again, just a bit, and arriving at the podium, I lean, and open to Matthew. Energy floods the
room, though no one enters, and it's the Mitter's outside the door.
Brett is obviously upset with Mindy, and even as my head slowly
spins, I can tell her jaw is set, hard, and I worry she'll get her TMJ
going. Without warning, this greeting time can get scary, a dangerous
place to be, and truthfully, it's only by corporate agreement we all act
civilized. People like Brett and Mindy and the Bubers (not to mention the Mannings) drag in their up and down lives on gurneys, hoping that the hospital is open, or at least the morgue, because they
don't want to do life like this anymore.

None of us do.

The others trickle in. I wish Jesus was here to talk, instead of me,
and who knows what I'll say this morning. No notes, a rising temperature, walls out of kilter, wife at home, and people wondering why,
afraid for my future. As I bow my head to pray—it's pounding now—
for this assembly of twenty-some-odd friends of mine, I am overwhelmed by the fact that I love them all, though there may be several I don't particularly like.

Maybe soon, I'll hope to stay another eleven years.

I don't know what I hope.

~

As he stood on the bright plain, Jesus must have known. Known
what we forget he knows. What I forget he knows. He must know
that Cyrus is a fake, a liar, and a fool, and that I am the disciple who
trusts no one, and could easily betray him if offered the right deal. I
am the woman with five husbands, though the man I live with now
is not my husband. I am the dog at the Master's table, looking for

scraps, the servant cutting the throat of the Vineyard Master's son, and the soldier wearing the sandals Jesus lost on his way to the grave. I am Pilate and Nicodemus and Thomas, one of the doubters, in fact, and there are moments when I think how can he be the Christ?

How can he be the Christ?

My knuckles go white, and the faces, and all my world, are swept away in the swift blackness of an anvil-hard wall.

∾

I sit on the mountain, on the plain, among lost friends, but I recall no names.

Jesus is coming, moving among us. He brushes by, and how do I know him? I can't answer, but without hesitation, I steal after him. We walk for months. Time falls away. Finally, he stops, looks at me, and speaks in no language I know.

"I know. I know you, and Ruin, and how your children will die. I know what happens when you are wet with temptation, and sin, and I know part of you is disturbed, and uneasy, but you love beauty, don't you, and I wonder if you might accompany me while I walk? God is walking today, and I have people to talk to, things to say, and I wish for a friend in the lonely places, and you have been following me, haven't you?"

I nod.

"You are a teacher of the law?"

I nod again, ashamed. He looks away toward the crowd.

"What would you tell them?"

I would tell them, listen to this man.

"But I am not the Law, nor am I here to tear it down."

But you are the Christ.

"Who told you that?"

I tell him I'm not sure, but that I read my Bible.

He smiles, and says these people on the mountain have no Bible, that they are simply hungry, and that he wants to feed them, and would I hold a basket, be a basket of food or a flask of water? Would

I walk among the people and simply repeat what he says to those who are just out of reach of his voice? Just speak alongside me, he says, and he is walking again. I walk, too, and gale forces blow, and though his voice is average, it's strong, but in the howling I can't capture the sense of it, the nuance behind the words; the ache, and the love, and the stark revelation that he is who he says he is. But I tell what people I find, over here, and further, still no names, but one by one, they all lean in, straining to hear.

Listen, I say to no one. Calmly, I am screaming to no one there. I hear nothing but the roar.

Jesus.

∾

My knuckles release their grip, and faces rush back into the room. I step away from the lectern, the smell of dust in my nose. Only a heartbeat has been lost, and as I drag a breath down to the bottom of my lungs, heads are still bowed, though several have begun to sneak a look, wondering why the long silence. I open my mouth, wishing for water.

∾

Dear God,

We sit, and wait for your words. Carve the words into us, Lord, let us know your words as we know the heat of the desert, in our pores, and don't forget to give us water when we forget to drink. We are foolish, we know. But we want to listen, we want to walk on the mountain with you, but we are stuck down below, and our hands cannot reach high. Will we hear you today, O God, or will we only talk to hear our heads rattle, empty pots of pride and boasting? Speak, Maker, and with a God's war-hammer break the stern fortress, and march around our stupidity and rage seven days, and blow trumpets and shout, so that we might fall to a gentler rule.

I wish you were here to speak.

Walk among us. Amen.

≈

It's nightfall, and my temperature is 103. I missed the evening service. I am hovering in the between place—can't sleep, can't wake up, dreaming of absurd couplings of people I've never seen, and an ugly face hangs in the air for a moment, and I swat, and bat the air, and Sara told me later I laughed out loud, and now, still dreaming, I 'm brushing my teeth, and a spider the size of a plate crawls over my bald head and sits down, and now it's turning white, and it's gone. And a great Queen of England sits with me in my delirium, stroking my face, and her ruff is made of prickly steeples that poke me as she leans over to kiss me goodbye.

≈

The fever breaks, and it's midnight. I'm weak, too weak to get up, and the room spins if I turn over too fast, but I'm fine, in that sickly way. Sara brings me a coke and I somehow lean against the wall while she changes the drenched sheets, and as I sip the coke, I run the chilled glass over my face and arms, relishing the coolness, especially on my lips. Sara tells me Dirk—was he leaving Connie?—hasn't gone after all, but he's thinking about it, and could I call him. Okay, I say, but I don't want to.

Did you go to church tonight, I ask, and she says she did. Several commented on my lesson from class, but I protest the conversation, moaning tell me tomorrow, falling into the fresh pillow, and the dry sheets are so comfy. Okay, she says. I should sleep, I know, but I can't remember what next week's lesson is, and she climbs in to bed, says go to sleep, and as I drift back, I hope to avoid the dark dreams of the afternoon, and slipping away, I wonder—in fact, mumble a prayer about—what dreams I might find if I went looking for those poor in spirit Jesus mentions, and off in the distance, in the approaching dark, a dog is howling, lonely, and I am gone.

August 31

He doesn't know the people here.
After all these years, he doesn't even
try with me. I've always cut up with
preachers and elders, but I can't with
him.

My daughter says he's all right,
though. And I think he likes her.

I suppose that's one good thing.

Francis Moore, told to Roland Minor
Administrative Committee

. . . *inside the most inside place* . . .

Sons are naive warriors who wrestle Dads fearlessly, but of course, they don't understand the strength—or the danger—of what they're dealing with.

Wayne and Richard hide, and circle me, stalk me, these blue and red Rangers, like I was once Mighty Mouse, ready to jump on my head if they can catch me turned around just right. I move cautiously, Peter Sellers looking for Kato, and then—aaaahhhh!!—kamikazes from all sides, arms and legs hacking, swirling, and it's a wonder the boys don't throw shoulders or hips out of joint, although Wayne did put his hand through the glass of the antique stackable bookshelf not too long ago, and took six stitches. Dr. O'Keefe was quick and the glass was only $10, and soon we were back at it. They scream at me to pretend I'm Mr. Ooze or Mr. Freeze, or some other maniac, but that kind of pretending embarrasses me, and I just can't go that far.

But I love to fight, and Sara will often come in from her Monday Night prayer group to find us all in a heap, not quite ready for bed, like we're supposed to be. Oh, we've bathed, and combed hair, and brushed teeth, and we even read a chapter out of the family book of the month, which this month is a story about an old dog named Pot Likker, but she pulls in the drive, and we don't hear her, because if we did we'd sit pristinely on the couch with our book open and blandly smile when she walked in. But the storm door opens to screaming and pounding on the floor, and I imagine her stopping, looking for keys in her purse, wishing her life was lived in the house next door. She's tired, needing to relax, and there we are, splayed across the carpet, looking up at her, guilty, sweaty, wide-eyed, panting with the chase. They've been choking me, gouging playfully, and I'm usually sitting on top of Richard, holding his arms, waggling my mouth, tongue, and eyes into funny faces, my body shaking with the force of his laughter while Wayne beats on my back like a jackhammer.

Occasionally, straining against the force of little bodies pushing against my chest, their spindly muscles flexing with all the faith and effort of the blindly optimistic, an odd urge enters, surging in me, and in my imagination I break my sons in half, leaving them limp on the floor, lifeless, killed. But I breathe, and it passes, and I shudder to know in another life I could have been a murderer, a killer of children and weak women.

∾

Last night, Sara and I fought well past midnight. I know Wayne was listening, and he cried, I think, but I heard it, too, when I was a kid. I remember the Sunday morning when I woke to sounds of shouting and a door slam and a car pulling away, and my heart was fully awake, pounding like it wanted to pump enough blood to make a small boy into a full-grown man *right now*, and I was up, watching Mom bending over, crying, frying the eggs and bacon. Mom was tough that way, just going on, serving meals and cleaning bathroom floors. She handed me the plate, put her hand on my shoulder, and I ate, and they were good, my eggs and toast, as always, but I couldn't see them, and swallowing was hard, because I didn't think Daddy was coming back. But he did, and later he said he just went to find his sanity, and when he found it, he packed it back in his head and came home.

I'll talk to Wayne, and we'll be all right.

∾

I didn't marry a theologian—who would want to? Metaphysics, epistemology, hermenutics—meaningless terms to a woman whose wisdom I will never claim to understand. My inner life does not, strictly speaking, bore Sara; she graciously listens to my rambling for hours, calm as a tea-cup, mostly quiet. But she rejects the conceptual in favor of the concrete. She is deep, but her depth is the earth's, not the philosopher's, and her questions are rooted in the constant, unabstract demands of meeting the actual and imagined needs of a minister-husband and two freckled boys. She prays often, but rarely meditates, though she tells me she tries to meet God in the quiet, but her quiet is mostly interrupted—*turned off*, she says—by children rising too early, complaining of homework and clothes no longer cool, their whiny voices clamoring for milk, when there's not any, because she didn't have time to go get it. She loves these guys, but tires of bad jokes and dull tales of girlfriends, sports, and the absurd difficulties of sloughing off childhood.

What do boys need, she wondered out loud, to no one. She was in the kitchen, blandly finishing up the pans, miffed because the dishwasher's busted, weary from the ordeal of trying to settle the boys enough to get through our bedtime read, and more than a little tired of what she perceives as my mousy, noncommittal approach to our looming crisis, our money, and our future.

Her future.

The phone rang. I picked it up in the room with the books. It was Roland. We spoke briefly—a tight, curt conversation—and as I put the phone down, Sara was standing in the door, heavily, her edginess silhouetted against the brightness of the hall.

"What'd he say?"

He said he met with Francis Moore this week. Francis, an unsuccessful Amway dealer in her middle fifties who works at the Eckard's drug store, and Beatrice Thomasen, a white-headed older widow from way back, and a whole gaggle of good Bible women, studiers all, meet over at the Bar-T truck stop on Wednesdays for a weekly chicken fried steak before evening service. Francis is the daughter of one of the original 18 members, an opinion maker, a woman who's disliked me from the beginning. Roland said their conversation was animated and vocal, and that if it was up to Francis and the ladies, it would pretty much be over. He said that the old guard is nervous, unhappy, and on cloudy days, downright hostile. According to them, anything attributed to Bhudda has no place in the church, in any context, quoting King Lear just makes people feel dumb, and Rumi . . . well . . . Rumi was just too much. I was uppity, Francis told Roland, and she said she heard me say a swear word, *and then laugh*, as I was walking to my car, and I said I don't guess searching and reading and being human belong in church, and Roland said well, maybe, but not in this pulpit anyway.

Sara turned back to the kitchen without a word. I stood rock still, knowing it was coming, and soon she was back, angry, but trying to rein it in as best she could.

"They don't want us, Cyrus."

She said she saw Francis at the drug store on Tuesday, and said hi, and Francis didn't speak. Literally. And that she was in the bathroom at church Wednesday night, and heard Tina Cooser say Sam met with Jack and Roland, and that Sam said if we weren't gone by Christmas, he knew of 30 families that would leave and start a new church, where they taught the truth, instead of this damn junk. She said she came out of the stall, and Tina looked at her, and didn't even stop to take a breath, but just kept going on and on about Sam and Jack and Roland, and how they told Sam it was all going to be okay, *that things were in the works*. It's getting old, Cyrus, Sara threw at me, and I didn't sign up for this. Wayne didn't get invited to Carl's birthday party, and he cried about it, and I don't know why you won't do something, Cyrus, and I said I know you didn't sign up for this, you didn't sign up for being alive, either—none of us did.

Sara stood there, rag in hand, swaying slightly, tapping her foot, as if being still would shatter the illusion that I might one day be able to do the one thing she wanted. Her face was flat, stone, but I knew she was pleading, maybe demanding, asking me to wipe away the uncertainty.

I went to the sink, and for no good reason, washed my hands. I knew the hours ahead held tensions and muted shouts I'd just as soon avoid. Finally, I turned off the water, grabbed a towel, and managed to turn around. Her eyes told me nothing. A quiet obscenity rose in my throat, but I squashed it before it escaped.

Sara had barely moved. But her breath labored, and the tap had stopped.

"What are you going to do, Cyrus?"

I walked past her heading for the den.

She followed.

"*Cyrus.*"

I sat down, buried my eyes in the books on the bottom shelf. A row of unread Harvard classics stared back at me.

I told her I didn't know.

~

In sixth grade I knew enough to hit Pepper Bailey, my best friend, and the best athlete in town, coming out of the backfield with the soft touch pass, and he'd get a touchdown, and everybody would like me. And most times, I did, he did, and they did. In 8th grade, I knew to keep my mouth shut and my hands in my pockets when Andy Lynn was around, because he was an I-won't-say-what, and bow-legged, and always bragging about his sexual conquests even then. He was always after me, teasing me about my ears, and my religion, and my clothes, because my parents had no fashion sense, and unbeliev-ably, one day he actually hit me full in the face. Andy had a great body with big shoulders and biceps, and I regretted it later, but I just stood there, looking at him like a moron. I remember his slitty eyes, his fat tongue cocked on the side of his mouth, and I walked away, mostly because I was scared of my mom's belt, which I would get on my backside if I was expelled. And I knew in Mr. Dollar's 11th grade English class that the Romantics moved me, and that I could some-how stand in front of people and speak, and an energy would emerge right in the center of my chest, inside the most inside place, and my

eyes would focus, and link with *that place*, and a challenge would
come running out of me, and I could get an audience to hold their
breath, and that I needed to run for class president. (Amy Casella
won, but she was pretty, and we dated, so I didn't mind.)

And at UT, I knew that there was more to this God thing than
met the eye, and that I needed to bring all these yearnings and longings and gifts and curiosities to bear on this life of mine, and that
God would take care of the future. And I knew Sara Barber had great
boobs (why lie?), and wasn't thin, exactly, but her smile bit me, and
I made a bet with a college roommate that I would marry this girl
who said I was fun on the first date, and I knew the first kiss would
be made of movie magic, and it was. I knew what to do, and I held
on to her for dear life, and said I'd take care of her, and didn't mean
to lie, and when it came time, I knew enough to be gentle and
patient, and I knew that these boys of mine would change my life,
and they did, and I know enough now to know I should probably see
a therapist because I wonder—have I lost my ability to know anything at all? And not knowing that—scares me.

As well it should.

It's the first day of the week again, I got my donut, and now I'm
printing 40 copies of my resume. I told Sara I spent the week working
on it, though in truth it took me about 30 minutes of a Friday afternoon. A torturous process I loathe. Hawking myself on an evangelical
midway. The religion business irritates me, and though I'll gather the
stomach to face it, I'd almost rather let it all go. If I could let the words
of God go, and just sell bread or postage stamps or gummy bears,
maybe it would be better. But I don't think I can—let it go, or sell
gummy bears, either—so I made 40 taped copies of a successful sermon on the Resurrection that seemed especially hopeful to the people who heard it, though I remember nobody got saved, but if anything can get a foot in the heavy door of a church looking for a
preacher, it's a dynamic sermon on hope. "It'll preach" as they say,

and I suppose I'll send those tapes out as soon as leaving Ruin becomes official.

The light of the printer makes shadows on the Holy Spirit section of my bookshelves. I open the shades and think of what he's doing right now, and what he's going to do with all the lousy, unused preachers of the world.

The phone rings.

"Cyrus? This is Connie."

Connie's having trouble with Dirk again, and Sara's been monitoring things all week. No doubt part of the growing tension at my house. And though I rarely think about it anymore, Connie's voice this morning, intruding on the lazy melancholy that usually follows my battles with Sara, strangely reminds me of a soft autumn weekend my senior year. It's no big deal, but then again, I've never told anyone, either. Years ago, I fell hopelessly in love with the woman my wife calls her best friend, this woman on the other end of the phone.

"Hi, Connie."

Connie and Sara and Dirk and I knew each other in Austin, in high school, though none of us were close at the time. I was a book nerd, Dirk was a jock, and Connie and Sara ran in different crowds. I found Sara when we were seniors, and Dirk and Connie didn't match up until a couple of years later down at Southwest Texas in San Marcos, apparently falling for each other in the midst of a roaring drunk. They got to East Texas about five years after we did, and that's when the girls began their rituals of morning coffee, the constant testing of baby names, and a monthly night out sans the boys. Their love for each other is surprising, a grace in the oddest of places.

But back then, Connie was dark, tall, and shy, too embarassed of what she thought of as a gangly, sickly body—I just called it lean—to be bold, or engaging, but secretly, I found her slight frame endearing and sexy, especially when she danced. She'd had ballet and jazz early on, and she knew how to move, and every school dance over those three years found me sitting more often than not, watching the tall girl with the thin, ribbon-fine black hair, watching her dance with various suitors, none of them impressive. She finally ended up dating a short, burly guy who rode a Harley to school every day, and he was outrageously possessive, and terrifying, but one Friday night, at a late September dance after an in-town football game, he wasn't there.

Rumor had it Connie and the burly guy broke up. Thrilled, I watched her all night. She wore jeans, I think, faded blue Levi's, with a short sleeve half-tunic, or maybe it was sleeveless, and her stomach was flat and smooth, and I thought, as perfect as a waist could be. She was sitting with Stephanie Stewart—the real prize for most guys— blonde, friendly, curvy, chesty—but Connie held my attention easily. Leo Sayer's "I Need You" came on, and even now my body remembers going blank, stuck in a kind of stasis, protecting itself from the prospect of absolute humiliation, but miraculously, I fumbled over to her, and by the second chorus, there I was, dancing with this shy beauty, my right hand on her lower back. We swayed a bit, and the song was over. But a second slow dance followed, and we began that tight circle again, this time legs closer. Her skin was cool, and her blue eyes amazed me, because there was an interest there, an interest in me, which I never expected. Her lips were never full, a little too red for my taste, but they were smiling at me, and for an instant, in the last moment of the song, as our bodies leaned into each other with an intent unknown to me at the time, I was stunned to know that I was going to kiss this young woman right then and there. We hardly knew each other, but that kiss is another of memory's sweet moments, and after it ended, the disc jockey kicked into "Taking Care of Business," and she started rocking, and though I was terrible, we danced 'til we were drenched. Still, we didn't speak for a long time, but we didn't let go, either, at least not with our eyes, and for the next three days, we were inseparable.

∿

"Connie?"

"Dirk left me." Again? Is she crying? "For sure. This morning. I just got off the phone with Sara."

Connie always wished too hard, praying Dirk would be a Christian man in the way she wanted him to be a Christian man. Truth to tell, Dirk wasn't much of any kind of Christian man, though he was a good guy who grew up in a religious home. He lost his faith, he said, and Connie came to Sara when she and Dirk separated the first time.

"Are you okay?" It's all I can think to ask.

Dirk and I wanted to be close, but ended up less than buddies. He often said he'd like to believe, but couldn't, and when he'd say that, he'd get a queer, misty look on his face that always reminded me of a kid who just found out Santa isn't exactly real.

"Can Sara come for a few days? Is that okay? . . . Cyrus?"

I blink. Two boys. The first week of school.

"Cyrus?"

Pain can cement relationships as surely as it can tear them apart. Connie and Sara are blood sisters. They chatter in that heart way men only see at a distance, covering everything: disappointment in husbands who are never what they seem, the hope for children (Connie and Dirk have tried for almost three years), and the fading possibility of being adored the way they'd dreamed of at tea parties. Sara says their companionship both heals and makes most things possible.

"That's fine. Sure. What can I do, Connie?"

Connie thinks I failed her, probably, because I never backed Dirk into a corner about Jesus. She watches Billy Graham crusades and reports of the Promise Keeper conventions and cries that her husband can't be like that. I don't blame her, I guess, but I always tried to discover how God might show up sometime if we just walked along with Dirk while he did his living. Look at *him*, I would say. Love *him*, and see what happens. Maybe he's not a crusade or convention kind of guy, and maybe a poem or a painting or a play will spring itself on him, and open him to a place where he can meet who he doesn't believe in on new ground.

"Just let me have Sara for a few days. And talk to Dirk, maybe? I wish you would."

They got back together, and it's been back and forth for years, though I sure don't know the whole story, and as far as we knew until last week, things had been better.

"I did. I talked to him last week, Connie. He didn't like what I had to say."

〜

Tuesday morning, after Monday off, rising from my sick bed, or whatever it was, I called Dirk and asked him what was up. He said Connie didn't satisfy him, and I asked what did he mean, and the phone got quiet, and he said, you know, and I said, no, and he said, it's a sex thing. Said he recently slept with a redhead, and he didn't love her, but boy, did she ever give him what he wanted. Said *it was great*, laughing, with this bravado. My anger caught me napping, and I put the phone down to keep from throwing it through the window. Whether my burn was righteousness or envy—or both—I didn't know.

Dirk liked talking about sex, which was unsettling, and he was constantly in heat, and walked accordingly. But I wanted to know him, be his friend, and truthfully, where else could I hear such stories? So we shared experiences, and choking, I'd tell a little, very little, and wouldn't you know it, God always walked in on the conversation, which was embarrassing. God never said much, and Dirk didn't want to hear it, so I'd let it go, and when the talk was over, I'd feel unclean, and shower immediately. But once in a while he'd open up, and we might drink a root beer in the window booths at T and R Hamburgers, and he'd tell me stories of lost dreams, of wanting horses and farms he would never have, and how there were no friends, because all Connie's friends were believers, and he wasn't. He'd sit in his loneliness, and I'd look at him, praying, eyes open. Now that he was getting older, and more tired, and the thrills were less, his distance from all of us was growing, and I think he, like Sara, like me, gets more frightened with each passing day.

〜

I tell Connie I'll try to call him.

"Thanks, Cyrus. Bye . . . and . . . well, thanks. . . bye."

Sitting on the edge of my desk, printer still whirring, my senses flood, remembering the excitement of being newly eighteen, the pain of an early love, an early mistake.

I've slept with two women in my life. Connie was the first.

The memory of it wraps around me, but, not unexpectedly, there's little warmth. Sara knew I wasn't a virgin when I married her, but I never said more than that, and she never asked.

~

Gathering my notes for class, I'm wondering if Jesus was human—as human as Dirk, or me. Did he ever have . . . well . . . a . . . *longing* . . . for a woman? I know the verse about his being tempted in every way, but secretly, I doubt it. But I hope so. I hope he wept bitterly—at least once—over the human love that he would never share with that Israeli girl, over his emotional and physical desire for her, over the girl whose eyes were for him as beautiful as the lily more gloriously robed than Solomon. That would make me feel better. But I'm chuckling now, amused at the prospect of having this conversation with Francis and Beatrice, who would no doubt scream pornography if they knew I thought such things. But you are my Lord, I say out loud, digging in my desk drawer for a pencil. And if you are my Lord, I continue, then I must bring all I am, and let you decide.

I grab a pencil off the floor, and cross to the door. But I stop where I am, hand on the knob, and ask him again to check on my poor friend and her husband, and to soften the blow of what I told him. I told Dirk that forgiveness is possible, but faithfulness is the deal. Promises are hard, and weaknesses can be brutal masters, and mercy is everywhere, but in the end, if he wanted his life, his marriage, and his heart to survive, he had to stop it. Oh, that was helpful, I thought, as he promptly hung up.

I didn't get anything done the rest of the day, but when I got home, Richard and Wayne were squatting in the backyard, watching the ants build those little red mounds they build when it's about to rain. Sara was thawing lean hamburger, and her hands were stained, but I turned her to me, and held her, and made her hug my white shirt with her red hands, and we stood there for at least two minutes, silent, and I was thankful.

Then we danced, and ate medium-well hamburgers with red onion and cheese.

Blessed are the poor in spirit,
for theirs is the kingdom of heaven.

Blessed means happy, I'm thinking, and I blow my nose, looking at Sara, and she smiles and I stuff the hanky in my pocket, which I know . . . I know—it's gross.

Blessed means happy—so says modern translation. My spirit is poor enough, probably—am I happy? What is it to say that a spirit is poor? Good morning, old Mrs. Eric, and yes, I like your new green suit (it's the same one that was new last week, and the week before that) and her false teeth are blaring a smile like she doesn't know the vacancy of her mind, and I guess she doesn't. 72 years old, she's a fixture in the young marrieds, though at first I couldn't figure out why. But Mr. Eric taught this class for almost twenty-five years, and when he died 10 years before I came to Ruin, Mrs. Eric sat home and wept every Sunday morning for a year. But one day her daughter brought her back to the class, and she didn't cry any more. I shake her hand, I feel the rise of her blue veins sticking up on the skin, like little mounds of past life looking for attention, and as I give it a gentle squeeze, poor in spirit comes to mind. I walk Mrs. Eric to a seat, hold her elbow as she gently lowers into the chair. I smile.

Without meaning to, I'm thinking of Connie.

A loud, high pitched "yup!" brings me back.

Oh, great. Mrs. Eric has the hiccups.

~

The opening prayer is over, we prayed for rain, and cooling off, and healing for Gwen's little boy—that's Gwen in the blue dress with the combat boots. Her little boy's got the mumps, and will miss his first grade first day of school tomorrow. And for Dexter Smith's new job, a praise for that one, he's been out of work for about 8 months,

but he's not always . . . well, . . . we'll see. "Amen." "If everybody's got
something to drink . . . somebody get Mrs. Eric . . . thanks, Dennis."

Here they sit, all eyes, all ears, hoping to hear something good—
or at least interesting. But they've heard this all their lives, and they
know it by heart. Can this stuff be vital and alive, and I guess that's
my job, or are we doomed to memorize and spout, turning out three
point sermons full of alliteration, like

> The poor in spirit:
> 1. They know they need sustenance.
> 2. They know they need support.
> 3. They know they need salvation.

not that such things aren't true—they are—but I'm not a good three-
point guy, nor do I want to be.

The poor in spirit. Should they memorize blessed or happy?

Tom Martin is here this morning. He's sporadic these days, and
just had his twenty-seventh birthday, but he didn't tell anyone, and,
unbelievably, we let it slip, and I think I heard he went to see
Mission: Impossible at a cheap matinee, alone, and didn't leave the
theatre until after midnight. Now he's in the corner, leaning his
metal chair against the wall, balancing without thinking, chewing a
straw and watching the morning sun playing tag with a cloud. He's
trying not to imagine his wife's mouth buried in the face of another
man, trying not to imagine the bed, and that's like saying don't see
the white mountain, which of course, you always do. She left him
and their four-year-old daughter not three months ago, and went
north to Virginia, and Tom thinks it's for good. I haven't seen him
break, but he showed a picture little Meghen drew, and I had to suck
air, because it was mommy with a suitcase. The class helps out, but
he's wounded, tearing his soul apart, probably, looking for the right
piece of gut to graft into the wound. But no salve cleans, and no
suture can repair, and he is face down, eating dust, crying to Jesus,
and he must qualify for poor in spirit. I would say the kingdom
belongs to him.

And there's young Skip and Lacey, both under 25, no kids, holding long hands, forearms wrapped tight, right in front of me, all smiles, but there's a cloud there, and I know Lacey is too thin. She's changed her hair this morning, with long, tight ringlets that frame her smooth face, and her legs are stretched out in front of her, and her eyes are tired, fixed on nothing 'til she catches me looking at her, and she makes me think of a Greek, a twiggy-like Aphrodite. She always turns heads, mine included, and macho guys go nerdy just trying to talk to her, and Skipper McKinnon is the envy of the entire men's south-end softball league. Her eyes are to drown in, and her deep laugh is as bright as a summer snow, and she is slowly starving herself in a vain attempt to be okay. Skip's not too in touch, though, or he's in denial, but he doesn't seem to know yet. Anorexia and bulimia are french to him, words that bring Karen Carpenter to mind, and weird, sick teenagers, and death-camp looking girls on the fringe of things. Certainly not his Lacey. She was in my office a week ago, and told me she throws up at least once a day, sometimes as many as four, and is amazed, and upset, that Skip hasn't noticed. She's done it since high school, and I know as I talk of the contextual background of Matthew 5, and Matthew's desire to set the teaching of Jesus against the backdrop of rabbinic traditionalism, Lacey is thinking of dying, maybe, because it would seem a relief to the madness of binge and purge. Skip leans over to her, gives her a peck on the cheek, flicks one of her ringlets with his little finger, and her bright smile is coy, sexy. That's what he likes, she told me, what he wants.

Then there's Roman, 230 pounds, and his size 14 wife Serena, at a table to my right, each on their second cinnamon roll, and Roman just spilled his cup of coffee on Will Sorendon's Jerusalem Bible. (Will borrowed mine one day, then bought his own.) They're laughing, cutting up, yellow-gold crumbs spilling out of their mouths and onto the table, like 16-year-olds constantly flirting with the rules, always walking the line, but innocent as doves, a little slow on the uptake, and irritating in that juvenile kind of way. But Roman is a carpenter, raised by an angry sharecropper of depression days, but his mom was the rose in the garden, and her son knows nothing but

work, saving, and giving of himself. Just last week I ran into him in
the hardware store. I was looking for a paint brush to maybe do the
stupid stain on the bookshelves, and he was getting supplies for putting in a new roof for old Mammie Griffin, a poor old white trash of
a woman who hasn't darkened the door of the church in over a year,
and she's as mean as a cornered coon, and I said how did you get
rooked into that, and he just said that he overheard someone say (he
wouldn't say who) Mammie Griffin's house was a disgrace and ought
to be condemned, and have you seen the roof, and the sagging corners, and that house is gonna fall in on that mean old lady, like
Dorothy's on the witch, so Roman had gone over on Wednesday
evening after work to check it out. Any pay, I asked him, and he just
looked at me with a grin that said absolutely nothing. And then he
farted out loud, and we laughed our way out the door, waving at the
air, and somehow I knew he was getting nothing out of that old mean
leather-skin-bag, and that in ways only God knew, it made him happy.
Next Saturday, he and four other guys are gonna put up a new roof, and
they are the poor in spirit, and to them also, belongs the kingdom.

There are others. Much of this class is made up of baby poop and
throw-up, and not much sleep, and mothers neglected as they sit in
the boredom of day in, day out, mothers who cry when their husbands won't talk to them night in, night out. The Bubers went out
last . . . I think they said Valentine's, on Bill's Christmas bonus
money, which wasn't much. To the steakhouse out on State Route
216, where they had sirloin and wine (but nobody saw) and Bill said
let's get a video, and they did, and went home, and Bill fell asleep on
the sofa. Roxie said she found a way to amuse herself. I didn't ask
what that meant and she didn't offer, but this is late summer, and her
eyes look a lot darker than they should.

And there's the Andersons. Their teenagers, Kari and Darren,
are the prize leaders of the youth group, and seem to do everything
right, including winning Bible bowls, leading Bible studies, and
going to Young Life, and the annual June campaign into Mexico, and
several of their friends have come to Christ, but a wake-up call just
came, and Goose (that's the Dad) has been spending a lot of time in

the Ruin city library in the nonfiction, looking at L's and C's, trying to see what his eighth-grade daughter's chances are with leukemia.

~

Maybe understanding poor in spirit is like understanding quality in that old book from the '60s about Zen and motorcycles. No one can define it . . . but everybody knows it when they see it.

~

The class seems empty, and I have the vague sensation I'm not saying anything. Reggie is asleep, and Lacey is staring at the table in front of her. Brett and Mindy left a few minutes ago, several others have followed. When does sanctuary duty begin?

It's quiet. The sun pours in the window. I wipe at the streaks on the glass. They're on the outside.

Jesus says the sun is hot out here on the mountain, so let's walk. I turn. There's a mountain, and it's hot. I walk.

His robe is light and airy, and his strong thighs stride through miles of people asking him will their prayers be answered. I can't keep up—though it's not fast exactly—but I'm lagging behind, like a kid behind his Dad on a downtown shopping day, scurrying, scurrying, but never able to stay with him. Jesus goes on, hair flapping, running occasionally, turning his head, laughing at me, but pulling me on, and there are all these people, yards and yards of bodies, and faces crowding, and I fight my way through, tearing through togas and chitons, and I hear centuries of Chinese Opera and Wagner all growing up through the very ground. I rise into air, and chain suits of war-armour clank, and there are howls and flashes of blades making blood. Jesus pushes on, reaching into this free-falling tidal wave of arms and legs, and severed eyes, and those are Elizabethan ruffs, again, steeples, and, funny—a whole row of Gibson Girls, and Indians, Indians on the plains, on a cliff, silhouetted for miles and miles and miles, Apache,

Cherokee, and Choctaw, chests painted, skull lances, and aboriginal blues and reds, and the quick boom-boom-boom of runnng feet, pounding out the hunt, the kill. But there's another face, a thousand million faces, with eyes slanted, and yellow skin, and the Goths and Visigoths sacking Europe, and all those babies pitted on pikes, crying, babes of all colors, stacked up, piled high, gurgling that same gurgle with the sound of exploding stars, and the slaves, and Jesus, Jesus, where are you, and I've lost him in the sea, and ships of Vikings are ramming me, and I drown, and the great, golden Aztec King lifting high sacrifices, and I am on the stake, and burning, and hear me, God, and colossal vessels of city-size carry black men and women to dung-pits, and earth is throwing up its dead, and the slave chains, and guilt, are train-heavy, and tons of lashes and blood, and is there no song for these, O Jesus, Jesus—is this how the name became swearing—where are you Jesus, and all the concubines of all kings with harems are dancing, gyrating, undulating with the rage of being used, and cast off, and on, go on, go on, and the piles of Auschwitz people, and my God, all the Henrys and Richards and Princes of Wales, and God, Tom Cruise, and—is that another Gibson Girl?—and Marilyn, and Sara, Edwin Booth, and poor John Wilkes, and Jihads and holy wars, and a cross sears across the sky, burning the night, and the dawn, and finally—

"Cyrus?"

I'm in the class, and I have—indeed—stopped talking. Tom Martin asks a question.

"Don't you think we better pray? We're running out of time."

Reggie raises his head off the desk. A final prayer, I say, and bow my head. And as eyes close and heads droop to bow, Jesus drinks from his flask, his eyes holding mine.

~

Dear God,

Poor in spirit confuses us, and your Son is raking our imaginations with his greatness, and if I see your face I will die, and I must see your face or I will die. Come to us, Lord, gently, and teach, and set us right, and shield us from looking too hard into the core of sin that is too, too much to bear, perhaps even for a God.

Who are the poor in spirit? And how are they blessed? If we understand this Jesus on the mountain, there is a terrible comfort for us, or is it a comforting terror, because there is mystery here, but let us not hide from its simplicity. Reduce us, Lord, let us be as those who do not sow or reap, but who know you will sustain, support, and save.

If I come to the mountain to sit at his feet, let me listen. Strip distraction, and help me hold each thought, each word, each wisdom as tightly as light holds the day, though my breakfast was not what I wanted, and I hate the grime under my fingernails. I long for the blessing of Jesus, but, too often, I'd rather have what I'd rather have.

I am not poor in spirit, but I long to be. Forgive, and make again.

In the name of Jesus,
Amen.

∼

It's evening, and school starts tomorrow, and Sara has decided not to take off for Connie's until Wednesday morning. Richard's pumped. He can't wait for second grade, for Mrs. Craig's class, because she's easy and nice, which is a lousy combination, I think. Wayne, on the other hand, is pretty down, because he makes mostly "D's" in language arts, and we've been working on it, but it doesn't click with him, and he avoids it, and though he's bored to death with summer and TV, he knows Mrs. Schrieder will be tough on him, and he's afraid.

So I decide to treat after church, and I'm licking my chocolate sundae, sucking at it, liking it, except that it's sticky, and we're at the

Baskin-Robbins down on Third Avenue, and the boys can't decide. Sara does Rocky Road, because she likes nuts, and in the car headed home, I wipe my mouth, chew on the aftertaste, and flip on the radio. It's oldies, and I hear that old Carpenters song about every time I listen to the radio and memories and every sha-la-la-la, and Sara reaches over and turns it off. Her window is down, and she's pretending her hand is a featherlight, and she's cupping it, letting the wind blow it back, and she tosses her hair back, and with a voice that reminds me of the easy curve of a badminton bird's lazy drop from the sky, she wants to know if I have any new ideas, any new plans.

I look at her, but she's waving in the wind, and Richard is leaning up between the front seats, listening, and a car honks, and I wave at Roman driving by with a french fry lolling out of his mouth, and he's holding a Jumbo Jack *with both hands*, laughing. I say I don't think I have any plans, any good ones, at least, and Sara says, you know it's going to happen, don't you, and I say, no, I don't *know* it's going to happen, and she says, it is going to happen, Cyrus.

Silence and wind, then a sigh. Richard sits back.

I'll get my resume together, she says, looking away from me.

I turn the radio back on.

September 7

You think he loves Jesus enough?

Cole Abbot, told to Roland Minor
Administrative Committee

. . . *if only God'd let me* . . .

Sara got up early Wednesday morning, before 5:00 a.m., during the first hard rain of fall. She crept down the driveway in the dark, leaving us boys asleep, mouths ajar, hair askew, alone. We spent the back half of the week fending for ourselves—unsuccessfully. Second and fifth grade homework forgotten or done poorly while getting by on skimpy meals of peanut butter and jelly, microwave hotdogs, and spaghetti with Ragu—twice. I cleaned the kitchen once in four days, and Richard ran out of underwear Thursday, but didn't tell me 'til Saturday afternoon. I tried to sort it all out, but colors got in with whites with predictable results, and the household absolute musts got mostly ignored, and I was testy all day yesterday, what with no one to talk to, and no sex since last week.

Last night, about 6:00, we panicked, and the boys and I spent the next four hours undoing the damage.

~

Wayne had the roughest week. Mrs. Tucker, our regular reading specialist, a kind woman Wayne finally learned to trust, was forced into early retirement by cataracts in both eyes, we learned, so a new woman did Wayne's evaluation, and she called me with news that's no news at all. This gal's voice irritated me, grating out the words with low tones and rough consonants, sound dragging over chords with ragged edges left by years of no-filter smoking. She described his difficulty with phonics and word recognition, concluding that, yes, he was behind, and special tutelage was needed, probably year-round. Did I read to him, she wondered, or with him, and of course I had to say "no," and felt like a sorry father. Wayne watched me as I held the phone, his face drooping, waiting for the verdict.

I hung up.

"Still behind?"

I hated to tell him. "Yep."

"I'm sorry, Dad."

~

I forget that ten can be every bit as tough as twenty, or thirty-eight. He's moping more often these days, and maybe I don't blame him. He's a mopey kind of kid, a particular boy who, at six, worried about getting his cowlick to stay down, so he'd stand at the bathroom sink, drenching his head, sopping his clothes, his comb slapping away, unsuccessfully. At seven he moped about his chores, and that year he had the kitchen; unloading the dishwasher, putting away breakfast dishes, sweeping the floor, cleaning the counters and stove-top—all before school. At eight, he got cantankerous, moping more often, with intent, and now it was the living room, returning books to shelves, vacuuming, folding various quilts and blankets, *slowly*, watering the ivy, dusting, straightening the arm covers on the green chairs and couch—but he's just *so slow*. And at nine, still thinking I should tie his shoes occasionally, always begging for frosted flakes in the afternoon, pouting when he didn't get them, and now at ten, Sara and I are always on him, pushing him to go on and get it done, stop wasting time, stop moping.

Yesterday, Wayne was wandering around the house, nosing around in that mopey way. I asked him what he was doing.

"Nothing."

I asked him what he'd like to be doing. I got a series of shrugs, and I said, okay, and he shuffled off to the bedroom, where I think he looked out the window, and wondered if what he wants really matters.

∾

I hated being ten. I remember wanting to go to the library or the movie, or maybe just out to play, and my Mom would tell me no. I'd pout, or throw down my mayonnaise sandwich, and she'd leap like a lioness, and slap my face, hard. *Don't you dare get that way with me,* she'd say, the words razor sharp, and though I could never look her in the face after a slap, I knew her eyes were killers. You don't always get what you want, she'd holler, so get used to it, and I'd watch her stalk off, vowing to prove her wrong, if not a fool.

Once, after I'd grown a little, maybe fourteen years old by then, I caught her off guard, calm, reading an old romance novel called *Love's Vengeance* (I'm making that up, I don't remember the title), and I was putting another teaspoon of sugar in my iced tea, and I asked her what she wanted. She said what do you mean. I said, you know, you say you don't always get what you want, and . . . well, I was looking at you in the black and white picture when you were young, and you and Dad were standing in front of that old blue car he had, and you were bending back and your hat was falling off, and Dad was kissing your neck, and I was just wondering what you wanted, that maybe you didn't get? Little did I know the power of such a question. If I'd known then what it meant to grow up, I would never have asked.

"I don't know, Cy."

She laughed, obviously pained. A tight, weary laugh, hiding, perhaps mourning what she knew I'd never understand.

"I dunno. We didn't want much. Just wanted to be happy, I guess. And I am. I'm happy. I'm happy enough. Doesn't matter anyway. That's the way I was brought up. But a front porch'd be nice one of these days. I always wanted a porch. And a plum tree, since I was little girl. Dorothy Johnson used to bring us fresh red plum jam her grandma made. But I never did, never did have a porch or a plum tree. Now I just like to sit and watch TV of an evening, with your dad, not too worried about things. Play with a grandkid or two."

She stopped, staring.

"That's all."

I had an urge to hug her, but I couldn't, and she put her foot up on the chair next to her, went back to her book. I drank my tea, went outside, and walked in the heat for a long, long time.

~

I never knew what my father wanted. And I never asked.

His name was Jim, Jim Manning, Jr., and he used to mope, like us, and I'm sure that's where I get it—Wayne, too—although Dad was sly, a skillful moper, adding tired jokes and pretended laughter to the usual sagging face, but I always knew better, and I'd think, you can't fool me—you're moping. His shoes were huge, heavy black things, and he lugged them around on his feet like dead weights. He had never been in sports or student council, and certainly wasn't ever voted the most likely to do anything except get through it all, and he did have that—perseverance. But he was slow, too, like Wayne, and ponderous, infuriating while he was at it. The only time he ever kicked into high gear was when he was angry, and then he would almost self-destruct because "fast" was a whole new world, a parallel reality that didn't exist unless some cosmic event forced it into being. Like the time we were turning the last corner before getting to the church one Sunday night, and his coffee, which always sat on the dash making the little cloud of steam on the windshield, came flying off to the right, into my church-clothes lap, and it was hot, burning, and I yelled, and Dad swore, one of the only two times I heard him say damn. We were late, and it was ten miles home, ten miles back, but back we went, and I thought we'd die for sure, going eighty-five in the twilight.

He and Mom would fight, some, and she was intense—downright scary—and he'd just get slower, more deliberate, like a bank teller counting out ones with twelve people in line. After it was over, and she cried, he'd go to the bathroom and shower, fading into a dead standstill, and I always imagined him standing there, steam and soap smells rising, with shampoo on his nose, hoping the world might decide to quit, so he wouldn't have to.

But he'd dry off, and they'd hug mostly, and go bowling. Or he'd go walking, me always wanting to go, and he never let me, and I was always mad about it. But once, after Mom died, I got to go. She was 54. It was February, around Valentines, and we were having one of those Texas ice storms they usually get further north, and the funeral was the week before. Mom had an aneurysm burst, and we buried her out in a farm-to-market-road cemetery. Dad was going walking that night, about a week later, and I said can I go, and he said not tonight, it's too cold. But I said, please, and I thought hard, *please*, and he looked at me, and when he said yes I knew I might yet become a man. I ran for my tennis shoes, struggled with the laces, scared he'd change his mind, leave me behind, but in a jiffy I was ready, tugging along next to the man who, slow or not, would always be my hero.

He said to lock the door behind me, and I did.

It was dark already, and cold, like he said, but the air was beautiful, my breath expanding over my head in a mist, but blank, saying nothing. Dad crunched through patches of ice, leather gloves wrapped around his coffee cup, but I didn't have any gloves, which was bad, because I scratched my hands when I fell, and they bled, and with the emotions running hard, it was a strain not to cry. But Dad set his coffee in the ice and picked me up. He took off his gloves—a ponderous task—and gathered up my hands, rubbing my fingers between his lukewarm palms, and though my hurt still hurt, I hardly noticed, cherishing our closeness, his smooth, big mitts holding mine, and us blowing on them together. There wasn't much light, and I was looking for his face and what it might tell me about how he was, but now the moment was past, his gloves back on, and picking up his coffee, always looking at something away from me, *over there*. I started scrunching up my nose, getting a little fun out of the numb feeling in the muscles when you let it go, when Dad spoke. The icy world muffled the sound into a whisper.

"Take care of things, Cyrus. You got to take care of the things that need taking care of."

I didn't know what he meant.

He said feelings weren't much good, and now that Mom was gone, the feeling part of our family wouldn't be the same. But not to worry about it, because he knew how to take care of things. His dad taught him that, he said. We stopped, as if he couldn't walk and talk at the same time, and the sleet came a little harder. Our coats weren't waterproof, and his chin quivered, and I knew my Dad's need for comfort was a thing I couldn't take care of. I couldn't make him warm, but I put my short arms around his soft waist, and his shaking surprised me, because he was sobbing, but I was glad for it, and I cried too, and to this day I'm thankful for one walk on a night of sleet, and a quiet moment under a street lamp in a time when fast didn't matter, and slow meant we might find peace.

Maybe that's it. Maybe that's what he wanted. Peace inside his mourning.

∼

My thoughts are dark today. Appropriately mournful. Even so, I'm praying, trying to, early Sunday mornings being what they are, an office appointment with God on whatever terms I can give him. Just now I'm on my knees at the window, leaning my chin on the sill, crazy enough to hope it'll all turn out fine. September/October is easily my favorite time of year, crisp, strong winds and cool evenings, and I'd love to live in a north country where leaves were heavy with color—gold, brown, orange, red—and bigger than my hand, where, when they fall, they leap toward the earth like ballerinas in the sky, settling in grass, as if snuggling into down comforters on a cozy, chilly Christmas afternoon.

∼

Sara got home just after eleven last night. She looked beat up, her eyes dark and swollen, exhausted from what she said seemed like endless bouts of Connie keening. It's official, she said. Dirk filed for divorce on Friday, and why haven't I talked to him, she wanted to know, to which I replied I haven't been able to reach him, which I haven't. (I tried once on Thursday, once on Friday.) Sara said he moved to Ft. Worth, and plans on staying with a friend there, hoping to get work with UPS or FedEx, but for now he's living off savings. Connie didn't sleep, couldn't eat, and Sara came home whipped, close-mouthed about their conversations, and Connie's plans, but right before her breath leveled out into sleep, she wondered if Connie could come stay with us for a few weeks. I said, fine, and tossed and turned for at least three hours while sleep hovered just above my head.

I left the house before Sara got up.

~

My clock reads 8:05. Cars pulling in. Sunlight pouring through the glass, steps picking up in the hallway outside my door, and I'm looking in a hand mirror I keep in my upper right drawer, picking at my face. It's breaking out again, and there's a tiny scab underneath the line of my left jawbone. I rub my eyes, digging in the corners, fighting sleep, giving way to a huge, back-breaking stretch, arms out, mouth and nostrils flared wide. I glance out the window, noticing Francis and her daughter, Joy, sitting in their old Buick, nobody talking, and it looks like they're both staring into my office, silently damning me, as if it's my fault they have to occupy the same space. I close my mouth and collapse my arms, embarrassed, but they can't see me, and I take the time to watch them a moment, absently fiddling with the blemish again, wondering when I last saw the clear look of happiness on anybody.

Joy came to see me this week. Francis' girl, at 34, is gaunt, pretty in an awful way, her brown eyes set deep, creased with aging too fast, shading toward black with liner, fatigue, and depression. She's a smoker who pretends she's not, pretends nobody knows, but I told her go ahead, and offered her a light. She looked shocked, probably wondering if I was a mind reader, and I said everybody knows, so go ahead. That shamed her, which I didn't mean, and it took her at least five long drags to finally get a breath and settle down. The smoke made my throat dry, gave me cotton-mouth, but she kept on, and I opened a window. She talked for an hour, revealing nothing, but as she pressed on, she got more comfortable, and I could tell she was checking me out, wondering if this office was a place she could trust, making an early decision about coming back. I noticed her rubbing her right hand off and on, and near the end, I asked her about it, and she said most days it hurts, bad. Arthritis, she said, and she laughed, said she was too young for that, but would I mind to just listen a little, and though I'm ashamed to have to be here, she said, and I don't like the idea of therapy, you seem like a normal kind of pastor, or man, and I thought I might could talk to you.

She's coming again next week.

Francis won't be happy about it.

∼

I step out of my office, smiling broadly, squeezing a visitor's hand, asking where're you from, and what do you do, and are these your children—the questions of friendliness, but I'm thinking about Dad, how he used to pity himself, regretting things. I never heard him complain, exactly, and in the teeter-totter of how-dee-dos and wishing I still had my chin on the sill, it's hard to tell where resignation and acceptance meet. Moping is little more than complaining, and the Apostle says don't do it. Attitude is everything, I know, but sometimes moping hangs in the air like a mist, and my feet have to go slower, and my shoulders have to droop a little, and it's okay, even if it lasts a few years, and thinking of all the people I know on antidepressants, I believe Jesus may have been looking into the late 20th century when he spoke of the mourning and the blessed.

Blessed are those that mourn,
for they shall be comforted.

Bible pages rustle as the class turns again to Matthew 5. The morning chatter's all about school starting, the rising cost of day care and baby-sitters, mothers reclaiming houses from summer-bored adolescents, and the whole language approach to learning. Children's education sets people off, and we need more drills, and no we don't, we need more relevance, more connectedness, and surprisingly, shockingly, in the doorway, there's Donna McCowen—nervous, gutsy, scared-out-of-her-mind. I think it's her, the same Donna McCowen who hasn't been through that door in a long while, in eight or nine years. She's smiling, too big, a Barnum and Bailey smile, but it's frightened, disoriented, like she is.

She left her tough home, her drunk husband and her unhappy children, some eight years ago, armed with her Visa and some man she probably didn't even care for. As far as I know, no one's seen her since.

Even as I say hi, and it's good to see you, Donna, my first thought is for poor Tom, and I know he remembers this woman, and the mess she made, and he's thinking about his own wife, his own pain, and though I suppose I'll be glad that Donna's here, for now, I'm hurting with my young friend in the corner. Donna is saying hi back to me, though, and as I turn, I notice she's thicker now, though she was never small, but her face is still shiny, puffy on the edges, full of living alone, I'd find out later, and dying too. The smile hangs on, lips pressed together, tense, and the moment hangs, empty, and suddenly I realize she may not remember me. I extend my hand and say my name.

"Yes, Cyrus, I remember you."

Everyone now knows what they didn't then; Donna's then-eighteen-year-old daughter had a baby, and sadness on sadness, it was a Down's child, and that broke the daughter's spirit, and Donna's. Donna's life was hell, with her husband and all, drinker that he was, her best friend said later, and the baby episode sent her over the edge, and she gave up, abandoned her life. I'm not sure I blame her. Few knew about Donna's bastard grandbaby, that it was given up for adoption, and the secret was laboriously kept for several years, but finally the tale lost its tawdry value, and eventually, the news muddled out, and everybody buzzed for about two hours, but after that, as is the way of old news, nobody cared, nobody cared.

I say welcome, and with that, chatter resumes, the crowd idling noticeably away from Donna, leaving us alone, and we are twins, we outcasts, both seemingly unrepentant—one coming, the other going. Wary eyes follow her, peeking out from under heavy shaded eye-lids and lashes, and though she ignores them and we try to talk, I know those rolling eyes touch her, wound her, and I can see her courage wilting slightly, though it's obvious she's long prepared for this sort of reception. I take her hand, and it strikes me how like a disease she must feel, a virile carrier, as if her sin will kill us all. True enough, perhaps, but I carry the sin virus too, so I come closer, and awkwardly offer an embrace. She accepts it, returns it firmly, says thank you, Cyrus, and turns to look for a seat toward the back. But I see her change her mind and continue on out the door, pausing only long enough to say excuse me to the Bubers just coming in.

I'm shocked, frowning, or is my mouth hanging open, and I become conscious of all eyes on me. I close my mouth, and beginning with Tom Martin, I point my scowl around the room, silently confronting, feeling an anger, a scarlet embarrassment wanting to rise. Now the eyes scurry, run for cover, searching for walls, floors and ceilings, gaping out the door, toward the morning, watching one delinquent fifth grader shoot free throws. His dribble slaps our ears while we shuffle homeless-like to our places, me standing, the tiny congregation sitting down, knees together, hands folded, like children just shouted down, and settling in to talk about grief and blessings, it strikes me that our laughter has turned, if not to tears, to self accusation, and at least there's enough of Jesus in us to know when to be ashamed.

I don't know if she'll ever come back.

Even as I take prayer requests, my mind escapes, traveling its own path, toward the afternoon, and a cup of coffee I will get alone, down at the Nickel Cup, and maybe a chicken fried steak and fries will

sooth me, lift me, and an odd thought hits me just as I bow my head
for the opening prayer. Would Jesus like such a meal, and would he
like brown gravy or white?

≈

The mountain is gone. The sun's out, but no question—the rain
is coming in sheets. Jesus takes a roll from the basket, stirs his tea.
The gravy is brown—definitely brown.

I know you didn't say blessed are the depressed, for they shall be
comforted, but the depressed are who we are, and there is much to
mourn. It's about loss, isn't it, and he nods, but I can see he's relishing the tough meat, the heat of the spices. Smiling at his pleasure, I
say but what did you mean? I know it's a call to something. Let your
laughter turn to mourning, he quotes, wiping the gravy off his extra-
large navy blue tee shirt, and yes, I say, I know. Things are not okay,
and I'm-okay-you're-okay is a parlor joke. We are all asses, broken
people with little good, I say, and we should admit it, and Jesus,
mouth full and trucker tough, sputters true enough.

≈

Depression is a sin, I've been told by more than one well-mean-
ing Christian, a tacit declaration of unbelief. It offends the stronger
brother, the happier brother, the brother who sees nothing but high
mountains and crosses full of glory and heaven's bright coming.
Rejoice in the Lord always, Paul said, and that statement haunts me
on deep nights when "night knowledge" shows me nothing save long
stretches of unknown desert, and worry.

I'm depressed, I tell him, and he says he figured that already.

It's just that with all this change coming, I've been poking
around my life, like I did at the old house after my father's death years
ago, going through the attic, opening brown boxes with ancient tops
held shut by rotting tape. I didn't like what I found. My Pooh
emerged from the second box, its one eye lifelessly staring past my
left ear, its seams split with age. I stuck my finger into the stuffing,

but learned nothing. My HO trains were all in a heap, and Dad never liked helping me put the track together, or anything else besides, and there in the attic I made a small circle of track and pushed an engine. The attic ceiling must have lowered through the years, and I found my back hurting, and the fun of it all gone. It was a furnace up there that day, sweat dripping inside my clothes, and an especially ratty box caught my eye, dusty and forgotten, and inside were all the old books—Mike Mulligan, Curious George, Paddington. Wendy and Pan were there, too, and the Bobsey Twins, the Power Boys, Hardy Boys, and young Miss Drew. And the Black. Walter Farley's Black Stallion, who ran like fire in a dry wood, and so did I, I thought, every time I got a new pair of striped running shoes, the flimsy black and white kind with no support and three racing stripes.

A lament psalm, he says. It's a lament psalm. Jesus closes his hands over his cup of coffee, and I notice their smallness for the first time. Such slight hands he was given, such slight fingers to grasp the edges of a cross.

My parents loved me, I guess, but they're gone, and I would have wished for more, I say, plowing on. Those simple blue collar people, both profound in that way all such family gods are profound, unwittingly placed into my heart the very shape of the self I now rail against, a shape full of holes, a shape bent in straight places, and somehow warped in against itself, a self in which I find little comfort. In the boyhood home—sold the month after the attic adventure—I was anonymous, unnoticed, and praised insofar as I was able to keep out of trouble and out of the way, and at the end of teenage years, I was glad to leave. But now, again, anonymity returns, and I feel I am fading into transparency, into a fear of never being seen again, like the stuff in the boxes.

Friends help, Jesus offers.

Friends are miracles, I spout back. Few and far between, and connections are rare. We so rarely touch. I go to pot luck dinners at the church, and wonder at the pressure of standing alone in the ocean of easy words pouring through the room, chock full of edification and joy, some pretended, some not. Feeling my cheeks smiling, my hands pumping hands, and my chest heaving with forced laughter over absurd stories of in-laws, vacations, and buying stuff, my private side quivers in fear, fear that my melancholy, my lack of faith, will turn to disbelief, and I will walk away from it all, from you, O Jesus, and there will be no way to save me again, nothing left save hell, and the end.

"Nobody wants to die." Jesus, as always, hits the nail on the head. His eyes bore into me.

I can't look away.

He didn't want to die, either.

He takes a deep breath, leaning toward me, and again he says, slowly, blessed are those that mourn, for he shall comfort them. I ask again what it means, what comfort looks like when days come and go and the same pain, the same hiding, the same refusal to live gets up to greet the day and meets me in the shower, just like it met my Dad? Wanting to smile now, coaxing me to find his meaning, he looks toward the rain, misty eyed and open, and says it again, blessed are those that mourn for they shall be comforted. What, what? I canvass my knowledge, turn to his other words, and still can't find it. What is this comfort? The comfort of knowing? Of feeling? The comfort of companionship or love? I think of Paul and his rubbish, all things rubbish save Christ. Paul was content, comforted in all things, rich and poor, alone or in community, and he says renew our minds. His Lord said the truth will set me free, and that I must be holy, that his yoke is light, that his burden is easy, and that those who mourn will be comforted. His face turns back to mine, and I drink it in. He laughs a little more, softly, a whispered warmth playing along his lips, repeating the words again. His smile breaks out, a dawning light all for me, and I sigh, thinking it's slippery, but I may yet be on the right track.

Finally, like a partition crumbling, blackness breaks, and as we sit, my rebellion comes apart (for that's what it is—rebellion), and there, in his presence, an unnamed . . . what's the word? . . . *wholeness* . . . asserts itself. A wholeness in all these words of his. Suddenly, these are no longer verses, no longer Matthew five whatever or John this and that. Jesus is talking, speaking to me, of life and living, like my Dad and I talked, the way friends and I talk. *This is Jesus*—his thought life, his scars, his loneliness, his companionship, his memory of Peter's lie, and Judas' hanging, and his shattering experience in the tomb—and my God—I think . . . *is it possible to know him?* He's teasing me now. He can see I am getting a new thing here, and it is so joyous to him, and now he is urging me on, go on, grasp it, take it in, lets get another coffee and know me some more. He starts to tell me a joke, a joke about a dinosaur who got to the pearly gates, and Peter was there, but he can't get to the end of it, and we are laughing, together, and those that mourn will be comforted. Yes! *Those that mourn will be comforted!* The waitress is perturbed at our ruckus, and I am shocked at his roaring voice, high-pitched and loud, but his humanity is deeper than mine, and he is a God, so why be surprised that his laughter at absurdity runs wild and unexpected, a delightful thing, like a southern snow at Easter?

∾

I am . . . comforted.
"See, I told you."
"Oh. You mean, you are the comfort."
"I am."
We look out at the rain.

∾

I ask him if my Dad ever found the comfort he was promised. And if Wayne would always mope, or would he ever be one of the ones with joy's fire in his eyes, one of the real warriors. He says, your dad was real, and loved you, and as for Wayne, we'll see.

The waitress hands me the check. There's no one across from me, and though my loneliness is real enough, for a few days, I'll refuse to believe it. Digging in my pocket, dragging out a couple of fives, I watch Jesus take a last sip of coffee, this king, and wonder of wonders, he is my friend, my hope, the one who knows. It's time to go back, back to the class prayer, and I am mourning still, because pain is never far, but I see it soften with hope, and I am borne up not by the comfort of religious words, but by the comfort of a man who may yet travel with me always. There's a new command perhaps being revealed here. *What he wants me to do.*

God help me, I do not want to turn away sad.

~

Dear God,

Mourning is heavy, and I don't want to carry this load anymore. Why be born, why lift the bother of living, it's just going to hurt mostly, and even the best of moments are stained, and my children have to see it, and learn it, and learn to go on in spite of it? I know this is darkness talking, that you indeed are light, and joy, and hope, and that in this paradox, there is a mystery called faith being revealed. The sun always rises with or without clouds, and Lord, wherever I need to walk today, to see your face, to lift the bother of living from another shoulder, let me walk there, and as I mourn, comfort me. Let your comfort flow through me like a fount, running over the tired feet of friends, and may we speak comfort when we stand in the hall and talk.

Bless our secret lives, and may we love your ways, and not our own.

In Jesus,
Amen

~

It's night, and though I feel better, I'm still moping.

It's been awhile, I tell my wife, and she smiles, knowing it's bed time, but she gives me a blank look, and I say, since we've talked. So we get our coffee, but I change my mind and pour iced tea instead, adding a teaspoon of sugar, and we leave the news on, and totter out to the porch and the glider. It's unusually chilly for September—a relief—and while Sara grabs her sweater, I'm thinking about Donna's grandchild somewhere, the Downs baby, but I can't—I can't afford to think about it now. Sara's back, and she wants to talk about Wayne, and school, so we do, and now it's the jobs she might be able to get, and how will we decide where to live? The TV's on, droning at us, wanting attention, but the stories it tells always fill me with impotence, stories of towns destroyed by floods or a tornado, and kids killed in their sleep, or by their mom's boyfriend shaking their brains out. A congressman had sex with his aid, and now the government in Zaire is changing again, refugees piling up, starving, wandering the earth, and who's a hostage this week? Sports final about Cowboys and Bulls, and there's been suspensions, fights, steroids and hemorrhoids, and my God, the planes and trains are going down, and another record falls, cause it seems there's more ugly in the world than ever before. I get up, almost running to the set, flipping it off.

But as we talk, back on the porch, as 10:00 becomes 11:00 and rolls on into midnight, ugly seems to move away from Curtain Street. My hand holds hers, and now it's just back and forth, back and forth, wind picking up a bit, and the ancient woman in the mesquite tree starts to roam again. A distant truck horn drifts out from the highway, and Sara says it's late. I ask her to dance, and she says you have a one-track mind, and I say fine, and we're okay . . . aren't we? She says she loves me, but she doesn't give me the look I want, and I'll see you in the morning is all I get as she stands. I pause, my heart pounding, and decide on silence. She eyes me, touches my shoulder, and it's awkward, but she bends at the waist, and gives me a dry kiss. "Is it okay if I go on to sleep?"

Okay.

The door closes. Lights out. It's me and the moon.

I get a weird urge to howl like a wolf, a pagan, a lover.

September 14

Jesus saved my life, and Cyrus saved my marriage. I'll stay either way, but Cyrus is my pastor. I don't want to lose him.

Brett Mitter, as told to Jack Simons
Administrative Committee

. . . gaining strength in the middle miles . . .

I got mad this week. I'm too much of a coward to be angry in public, but alone, out of harm's way, I'm a devil, a demon enraged—
stomping and spitting, throwing things, panting and cursing—and
when reason returns, damage can be extensive.

My eyes blink open in the dark beginnings of the five o'clock
hour, and I know this will be an angry Sunday. My temples thud with
a dull cadence. My eyeballs ache, a rough film covering their con-
nection to my soul, and I lay still, working to fend off the gathering
passion. I jerk, kicking off the covers, hard. My jaw slips out of joint
on the right side—*damn*—and I panic. Locked. Slow down, slow
down, breathe in, get hold of the chaos, make it subside, better, better, calming, and sitting on the edge of the bed, I wait, furiously, willing the jaw to pop back into place. Sara turns in the bed, moaning,
grasping for the sheets. A minute passes. Another. I'm a Rodin in
underwear, stone still, dark shadows striped over flaccid muscles,
pointy bones. My right eye closes, but my left refuses, instead hanging on, concentrating. Gingerly, I drop my chin a half-inch, now
another, and the joint finally clicks over, back into place. My body
sags, releasing its tension, already tired, and though the shower washes away the sweat, it can't stop the tremble.
     I'm afraid for the day.

~

Harry Johns is a big cheese, a big man of 52, and he called me up at 11:30 Tuesday morning and said he was taking me to lunch, at which point I said tomorrow would be better, and he said he wasn't asking when it would be convenient—he was telling me now. So . . . he took me to lunch.

I'm a wuss. He has oil wells.

That juxtaposition of fear and power gives men an appalling right to say outrageous things, I suppose, though thinking about it now, I find the whole episode ridiculous and absurd, patently hard to imagine. We sat down at his country club, ordered tea and three-bean salad, and as the waiter stepped to the next table, Harry took a big slug of water, and promptly announced, with precision, that it would be better for everybody if I resigned this Sunday.

My salad fork froze just under my mouth as I checked to see if he was serious. He was.

Stasis set in. I had no reply. I chewed while he talked, but my computer was down, crashing out of sheer disbelief. Suddenly Harry was a ghost, a blurred face producing a humming sound I couldn't decipher, and I woke up a minute or two later to catch him in the middle of a sentence about my brand of compassion, saying that what I called compassion was a piece of rhetoric, a fancy synonym for lib-eral, a good word kidnapped and used in a way God would hate, and that true compassion was in telling the truth.

Dumbfounded, backpedaling, trying to recover, I quoted Pilate's evasion of Jesus, my voice no more than a whisper.

"What is truth?"

His fist hammered the table, and the water glasses jumped. He shouted that's what I'm talking about—and it started again, that animated humming, that it was time for this church to get serious, get new elders, get new programs, and when was I going stop mealy-mouthing the gospel. I needed to preach the truth, to tell it like it is, and for God's sake, man, the truth is right there in the Bible, like for example that a fag is a fag is a fag, lazy people shouldn't eat, and welfare breeds bums, simple as that. The waiter plopped down sixteen-ounce prime ribs in front of us. Medium rare, mine bled on the white plate, running into the garnish. I wasn't hungry.

Why hadn't I been to Promise Keepers yet, he demanded, vigorously chewing like a cow with a cud. Harry wore glasses, expensive wire rims sitting on top of fat, hairy cheeks. They kept slipping down his nose, and each time his wormy finger pushed them back up, fork in hand, I secretly wished he'd poke his eye out. He hadn't been to PK himself, he confessed, not yet, but he said leaders like me should have been three or four years running by now.

With as much vicious calm as I could muster, I attacked my plate, chewing my meat right back at him. His glasses slipped, and his head tilted back to compensate. I tried to smile, but failed.

"Harry, how's your family?"

He stopped. He put down his fork, wiped his mouth, stared me down. Finally, he picked his fork back up, stabbed another piece of flesh, and just before it popped into his mouth, he said, fine.

His son had been to see me before he went into drug rehab, and his wife was a recovering alcoholic. Sara didn't normally gossip, but she knew how to keep her ear to the ground when serious news came around, and Sara tells me that when Edna recently discovered she was married to a man who kept a business bungalow in the mountains of Colorado with a mirror above the master bed which she had never heard about, seen, or stayed in, her drinking began again. I also wanted to ask about the IRS suit against his company, but he didn't know I knew about that, so I was quiet, my discomfort taking on a more agressive tone, moving toward seething, and he started on me again.

After awhile, the cherries jubilee showed up, and he told me he'd been at First Church since he was 12, and in all that time, I was the worst investment the church had ever made, the biggest mistake, and if I had any integrity, I'd find a way to give back every penny of my salary from the past 11 years of service. He said admit it. Not that many people had come to Christ anyway, had they? He placed his elbows on the table and leaned over them, his paisley tie dangerously close to the red sauce. Dropping his voice even as his face pushed across the space, crowding me, threatening me, Harry produced a low, but distinctive, unmistakably manipulative tone, saying that if

my family didn't vacate the pulpit within the next three months, the
First Church of Ruin *would not get one more f——ing penny from Harry
Johns, Inc.* I'm sure my eyes watered, as blood flooded my face. He
sat back in his chair, wiped at his mouth, his chin, his tie, then put
down his napkin. He asked me what I thought I would do.He pushed
his dessert plate away from his waist, and picked his teeth, waiting for
me to fold.

≈

Wayne came home with a busted lip that same afternoon, and a
tooth loose, and a one day suspension from school, all over a game of
keep away with a football, and some simple foul language. I told him
anger was almost always expensive.

≈

I didn't fold. I waited. I hadn't touched my dessert. I was offend-
ed, my mind white with anger and disbelief, and I had nothing to say.
Harry leaned back in his chair. Without thinking, I got a foot
under one of the front legs, and he roared as he sprawled, grabbing at
the tablecloth, and he escaped with dumping only one glass of tea in
his lap, and a couple of plates on the floor, but flatware clattering on
china made quite a ruckus, and the restaurant came to a halt. Harry
was, of course, livid, and he was up and on me in a heartbeat, shouting. I'd guessed he'd be willing to hit me, and had jumped out of my
chair, but I was surprised at the ferocity of his lunge. He swung at me,
just as the maitre d' got there, but I was ready, and ducked away from
him, but the tables were crowded, and with nowhere to go, he got
lucky, catching me with the next shot just under the ribs—a hard,
clumsy uppercut. Some people stood up, a couple yelling at Harry,
and as I got up from the floor, gasping, Harry started at me again. But
I heard my voice shouting (which startled me), threatening him,
telling him I'd have him arrested if he touched me again, that there
were lots of witnesses and he really didn't want to push me, because
I knew his life. He looked surprised, and I got up in his face, shouting

I KNOW YOUR LIFE! I KNOW YOUR LIFE!, and I came within an inch of adding a string of obscenities, but there were no less than thirty hotsy-totsy men and women staring at us, some in shock, others in rapture, everyone open-mouthed. I backed down, stepping away from him, and felt a rude crunch under my right foot.

In the scuffle, Harry had lost his glasses.

The left lens was busted, and the frame resembled a paper clip. I picked his glasses up, threw them on the table. I should've said sorry, or thanks for lunch, but without a word, barely masking my rage, my shaking, my fear, I turned away, stumbled over a chair, and left.

≈

As I stood in the shower that afternoon, trying to get the grime of Harry Johns off my soul, I hit my fist on the tile, drawing blood. I covered my mouth with a wet washcloth and yelled until I was hoarse, and both hand and voice hurt until yesterday, and I thought, I am mad, insane, and what are these demons sitting on my head?

≈

When I was sixteen, after the last football game of the year, I stood at the mirror in our second bathroom, staring, grappling with those same demons. I pulled at the porcelain pedestal sink, leaning hard, gripping the edges, knuckles white and red, fighting to corral my anger. My girlfriend Paula, my first car-date girlfriend, broke it off with me, and had been with Terrell that night. Not with me. I had to watch them dance, her smiling, resting her hand on his close chest, his hand playing along the bottom of her back. Her skirt was way too short, and he kissed her, and by the time I hit the house, fury was in my mouth, a raging tension, my muscles heaving, straining, my eyes wine red, burning into themselves. I swore I wouldn't curse, and prayed not to, but I failed, and leaning on the ancient sink, swearing, I tore it from the wall. The clamps on the pipes were old, and water was well into the laundry room and kitchen before I could get it shut off. This fed the rage, and though everyone was asleep, I took a bar of soap and shattered the glass, and was grateful that at least I could no longer see my stupidity staring back at me. But standing in the water, with glass at my feet, remorse hit me, and my panting eased. I was picking up the glass, lost over how to repair the damage, and I heard mumbling, feet sloshing through water. Dad stuck his head in the door, and said what happened, and I told him about Paula, determined not to cry. He nodded, respectfully, and ran his hand around the jagged holes in the sheet rock. He got the mop, and handed it to me, telling me to get old Freddie's phone number. And by the way, you have to pay for it, he said. It cost me almost $150.

～

Years later, I'm brushing my teeth, remembering I forgot to get milk yesterday, remembering that Paula married that Terrell guy, who was such a slob, really. It still irritates me, and now Richard's coughing, and there's another fifty dollars if he goes to the doctor, and why anger is crawling over me this morning, why this dark mood makes me think night is just beginning, I don't know.

～

It's cold out. I left my coat at home, and gasoline's gone up a nickel, and I don't want to preach today, or be a husband or a father or anything good. I'm fumbling for my keys, standing out in the barely light morning, trying to get into my office, holding my precious cup with my thumb, balancing. It's sloshing over, and with about nineteen keys on my ring, I never get the right one until after trying seven wrong ones, and now the coffee is spilling on my hands and pants, and it's hot, and I'm alone, so—GOD—I let it fly. Literally jumping up and down, my legs kicking, the demon takes over, my neck coiled and rolling, the cup demolished at my feet, my foot screaming from kicking the wall, and there's a gash in the toe, the shoes are wet with coffee, and I slam the door shut, and churn down the hall. I rip the office door open, kick on the light at the desk, and lean on the back of my chair, heaving as if I will throw up my guts, and over and over again, through clinched teeth and locked jaw (it's out of place again), I'm shouting . . . *WHAT DO YOU WANT WITH ME?*

⟿

Two hours later, I face a classroom filling with happy Christians. Great.

My pants are khaki-colored, or used to be, before the giant coffee poured down my right leg. It'll stain, and Sara'll be perturbed, because they're new—$79.95—and this things gonna happen, but . . . I can deal with her. My prayer time was mute breathing, gaining calm, listening to John Michael Talbot, the monk, trying to agree with his adoration, but mostly frustrated that he gets to feel so close to Jesus, while I feel like a mongrel dog following a gypsy wagon. I'm rational again now, though strained, standing here at the podium, the class trickling in. My pulse is high, and I can feel a fever standing in the wings, waiting to enter my blood, and all I have to do is give it permission to come.

Tension is here, and I'm embarrassed about the Harry Johns incident. It made the paper. There was a small write-up (PASTOR DECKED) about First Church in the process of deciding its future— *local oil baron and pastor come to blows*—but in this class anyway, sympathy is on my side, and their eyes tell me go on, go on.

The announcements begin, a weekly who's who among the sick, the poor, the afflicted, and the Andersons have taken Kari to Houston for a round of chemotherapy. Goose is down (an old joke at which we usually chuckle, but nobody bothers today), and has anybody heard what happened to that family in Abilene who lost their house in the fire? A new couple wanders into class. They stand at the door, awkward, hunting a place to sit, obviously pleased to be here at the threshold of a new bunch of supposed brothers and sisters in Christ. Someone is challenging us to really believe God answers prayer, but I'm watching the pair in the door. The new husband is a chubby fellow, with a broad, nervous smile, and the wife, petite in a tall kind of way, is roughly five months pregnant, proud to be showing, and seems genuinely excited, almost giddy. In fact, she's stifling a giggle, as if she's just hit the midway with fifty dollars in her pocket, her best date at her side, in love, and taken care of. Now everyone's turned around, and she says hello. We all say hello. Her husky voice reminds me of Carly Simon, and the Bubers make way in the front row for this newest pair of young marrieds. The chubby man is speaking now, and I peg him for a singer immediately, his squarish head producing sounds that make me want to hear him do Shakespeare, or Job. He says his name is Jeff, which disappoints me; with a voice like that I was hoping for Mercutio or Lysander, but hers is Cassandra, and I am redeemed. Their baby is due in early January. It's a girl—they just had the sono-gram—and her name will be, and is, Judith Miranda, and the class is giddy over saying hi to the unborn.

Early January. Going through the remaining litany of listing and praying, a thought bearing bitterness sweeps along, lodging itself squarely in that space between head and heart, at the throat, and I know I'll never have a daughter, and when Judith Miranda comes to class for the first time, I will be gone. How do I know that? I don't know, but I know it—I *know* it—and my fever breaks out, like a splash of hot water, and we close our eyes to pray. I'm fighting, unseen, gripping the podium like the sink of old, and it seems I am victim of chasing truth, of holding on to God, of holding on to the idea he might yet use me. But in this moment, I see that everything will not be all right, and my jaw is set to pop out again.

God, it's hot, and I notice the window is closed.

Blessed are the meek
for they shall inherit the earth.

"Meek." An elusive word. Rhymes with weak. Milque-toast, sappy, soggy, weak back-bone, another word that, misunderstood, saunters up next to depression. It implies a vulnerability that's a little disgusting, like the nursing home.

~

I'm saying to the class that the Greek term "expresses that temper or spirit in which we accept his dealing with us without disputing and resisting," and there's a dog barking—I bet I know which one—outside the window, barking like a screen door flapping. The air's warming up rapidly now, and this dog's been at it for ten minutes, at least, and it's getting old. He's distracting my flock, being, as he is, more interesting than me, more urgent, more arresting, and in my fever, I say to the class, excuse me, but let's try to ignore the dog. Tom ignores me instead, keeps looking out, and Roman and Serena just stare into space, hypnotized by the warm and the day's low hum. Jeff and Cassandra—I dislike her name after all; it's pretentious—they're already confused by what I know they must recognize as a deep tension in me, and wanting to vent, I stop dead in the middle of a sentence explaining the meekness of Jesus, waiting to see if anyone bothers to notice. They don't. I walk to the window. Yep—it's that same dog, and I can't help but smile. I glance back at the new couple, and I soften just a little, and in a flash of absurdity, I give up the lesson, motioning to Jeff and Cassandra to come here and check it out. I do it because . . . well, I don't know . . . because this familiar dog is a silly friend of mine, belonging, as he does, to all the people of Ruin.

Let's take a short break, I say to the class, and Jeff and Cassandra come to the window, asking me about the dog, and my tension is easing. Out by the parking lot, a mix of black fur and blue/black eyes with a nice baritone voice is barking furiously at a parked red Nissan just

minding its own business. He's a dumb dog, I think, always barking at
nothing, and I wonder what he'd do if the Nissan decided to bark
back, or chase him. But I know this dog, cause he's been around for
several years, and he's much more bark than bite. A short-hair, a per-
manent stray, I see him mostly around the downtown park when I'm
there with one of the boys. There are swings with long chains and
rubber, half-circle seats, and the Black and Blue (the Black and Blue's
what I call the dog) likes to entertain himself by jumping through the
swings and occasionally landing on one in such a way that he is actually swinging for maybe two or three seconds, and there's always a
kid, sometimes young, sometimes old, there to applaud. But mostly,
the Black and Blue just sits down by the courthouse, asleep, or looking sad, and it's only every couple of weeks that he catches my eye.

I met the Black and Blue on a back road running one day. He was
shadowing me for about a half mile when I turned, and he strode up
to me, simply, and I rubbed his head, noticing blood on his right
flank, the bruising on his chest, and that one eye was black and the
other was blue. The Black and Blue ran with me the rest of the day,
and off and on again for a year or so, but never regularly, and he did-
n't want a home. Over time, I noticed that he ran with lots of folks,
played chase and fetch with most anyone who called, and enjoyed
jumping in the rain if the drops weren't hard enough to hurt.

And here he is, interrupting my lecture, as if he knows what I
don't. His feet spread, he's staring straight into nowhere, barking,
barking at me, I'm sure, and as I look out at him, I think, you get
along pretty well, don't you, boy, and you don't spin or weave or
worry about tomorrow, and yet I bet God knows about you, and likes
you, doesn't he boy? Mrs. Eric goes into her hiccups again, and several people can't help but bust up laughing. I join in, released again,
and I'm ashamed to be talking to these good people in this frazzled
state of mind. But what an odd way out of it, conversing with a dog.

∾

Break is over, and I start in again. I have to stop. I confess that I
can't go on with the lesson, and they nod, feeling sorry for me, and I

say that I need mostly to pray. The room gets quiet with knowing there's only a few weeks left. We all bow, and after the amen, I shake hands with Jeff, and head to the office. Standing at my window, I watch the Black and Blue run away from me for the sheer joy of speed.But he makes a long turn around the far end of the lot, and now heads back, looking right into my eyes. I pull up the blind, and twenty feet away, he stops, dead in his tracks, and sits, looking at me, now looking away, and now back at me, panting, tongue hanging out, and I know he wants to play. I feel my life slowing, slowing, and breath coming in, and I don't know why, but I feel the Christ smiling.

~

Dear God,

Meekness is beyond me today, and I cannot pretend. Pain on every inch of my skin makes me swell and pitch, like the ocean, and I curse the gods inside that want to take me from you, who want to take up residence in your hall, in your place. God, my neck hurts, and my back, and my mind, and my foot, and I am so mad—just so mad. Forgive my rage, and my curses. My mouth can't be tamed today, unless you do it, so please move your hand this way, and thank you for dogs and good friends, and new faces, pregnant with hope, and protect their innocence, Lord, their naive belief that all will be well when it seems like it won't all be well at all. Speak in me, through me, and kill the rebel, kill the demon inside, so that I may one day find what it means to stand before you, meek, and loved.

In Jesus,
Amen.

~

After the sermon, Jeff, Cassandra, and Judith said they loved First Church, and wanted to join, and five other people chose Jesus. They wanted baptism, and now, driving home, Sara takes my hand, looks at my stain, and my busted shoe, and I can see it coming, but instead she looks back at Wayne and his lip, looks back at my scared eyes, and wonders out loud who is more pitiful. Wayne's laughing, and Sara, too, and Richard, and my morning is melting into afternoon, and healing is possible, even in that scary hell called change-I-didn't-choose.

≈

The afternoon weather turned nasty, and channel 12 says it might rain all week.

Sara's brushing her hair, and it's night, just before midnight, and the sound of that long stroke of the brush, coupled with the rising wind outside, makes me sleepy. We always go to bed late, and I stack my pillows up behind my back in good reading position, squirm my way into comfort, and pry open a new book on grief I picked up over at the Open Way bookstore last Thursday. Chapter One is called "The Loss of Grief," but I hear a sound, and it's Sara squirting some unnamed scent, and she's humming, and I regret I didn't shave this afternoon, and I think I'll get back to the book in a minute. She kicks off the light. Sara is a meek woman, a humble woman, whose embrace is like being touched by a cloud going by, tingly but smooth, and as my fingers trace the goosebumps on the back of her arms, I hear rain on the roof, and her rhythms are mostly unnoticed, but here, in this, our secret, sacred world, hers is the rhythm of a long run, settled and powerful, gaining strength in the middle miles, and resting in all the right places.

≈

Sara turns over, but before she succumbs to sleep, she mumbles, and her last words are whatever happened to that man. I say what man, and she says the Black and Blue always makes her think of that man. Again, I say what man, and she says you know, that man who used to come on Sunday nights. What did you call him? Did you ever find out who he was? And she's drifting off, not really wanting to know, and the rain has stopped, but I hear the boom of thunder in the distance, and I know the storm's not over. She pats my thigh, and says, you know.

Suddenly (will it never end?) I can't sleep. I wait for her breath to even out, and then I sneak out of bed, trying to keep the weight even because the bed squeaks. I grab the grief book, and slip out the door, but I have to stop and look in on Wayne. His hamster's running, and he has his hands in his pants, snoring without a cover. I kiss him, knowing things only fathers can know about their sons' hearts, and now I'm out on the porch glider again, trying to read, but the wind is wet, and I hate this light anyway, so I throw the book inside, and flip off the light.

There's thunder, and distant barking underneath.

I'm wishing I'd known more about *that face.*

I never got his name. When I contemplate the word "meek," his face shows up, like a dream from God. He only came to church in winter. I looked for him after many services, but I never had the chance to ask him his name, or where he lived, or how he earned his money. Word was he was a drifter, not homeless exactly, but a kind of transient, making his home with family that lived in different parts of West Texas. A wanderer you could count on, if that makes any sense, a man who someone said someone said had once lived on a farm about 8 miles out on highway 47, but there's no house in sight there now, and no one can remember when anyone lived there, ever. The first time he came was on a Sunday evening in late December. I remember it being cold outside, bitter temperatures— probably in the teens—ushered in off the plains by a silent, but insistent wind. Most Sundays, the 6:00 evening service is scarcely half-full, and this night was worse. I remember that night because the regular pianist was on vacation, and the normal back-up had an arm in a cast, and so we decided to do the praise a cappella. Risking understatement, the singing was weak, a soupy chorus time. The song leader was a tenor who mostly sang *around* the pitch, now flat a little, now sharp, and his tempos were an abomination before the Lord. But one bad soprano worked hard at keeping us interested, randomly attempting to sing the tenor line up the octave. Boredom sat like a hat on most folks, and I think Rhonda Blotter, a ninth grader with the most beautiful eyes and the most ugly teeth I can ever remember seeing, actually lay down and went straight to sleep even as I stepped up to preach. I opened my mouth to speak and the back door opened.

The air in the sanctuary shifted, and the silent wind opened its mouth and moaned. The room expanded, and as he slid in the door, necks craned and eyes narrowed. His coat was hobo brown, a khaki color, but muddy with time and hope-busting work, and couldn't have been warm. An old, crushed Fedora came swiftly off his head, and that face appeared. Soft, blackened eyes returned the curious gazes of the people with a solidity unexpected in a transient. Simply—he looked like a bum. Unshaven, dirty like a potter's hands, he was too far away for me to smell, but as he slid into the back pew, the reactions of Jason and Betty Carpenter were pretty grim. Finally, the congregation turned back to me, and silently, collectively, told me to get on with it.

I preached on Ecclesiastes that night. My text was from the 1st chapter, verse 18. As I spoke on the price of wisdom, and the pain that would come from increasing knowledge, the wind seemed to lose its quiet and began to roar around me in a burst that made me wonder why everyone else didn't cover their ears.

Even now, this man's face burns into mine. He was gaunt, as you would expect, and looked a little like the thin guys in all those Norman Rockwell paintings. High cheekbones, shallow eyes, lines carved into skin. He never smiled, but sometimes nodded as if he simply agreed with my latest opinion, and that nodding gave me the impression he was not unhappy, or bitter, but that he knew who he was, and had somehow learned to be okay with it.

I did see him one other time, away from church, asleep on a grassy hill over in the park. The Black and Blue was running around in circles, chasing a mockingbird over by the bike racks, and I was in a hurry trying to squeeze in a quiet time, because I had to be over to the potluck to set up tables before 5:30. I had to pick up Richard from a party before that, and he was there, the Sunday Night Only Man, like a baby, breathing that easy breath that sleep brings. It was summer, and the heat was tougher than usual. He had his shirt off, and his muscles rested, but were hard like a miner's. I wanted to wake him, but it was hot, and I had sweat in my shoes, and had to go. His face held me. It wasn't a pretty face, exactly. But not ugly, either. Savage almost, I thought, a simple monument to perseverance and humility. And it was still, not agitated, but in repose always, as if his dreams were a mulling over of peace, and the defeat of cruelty that awaited the rising of the next sun. There was one long scar that ran from his left temple across his forehead, then arched up into his hairline, but I got the feeling it was a reminder of some paltry, senseless moment, and that the real battle of the Sunday Night Only Man was fought in a landscape no scar would ever see. His theatre of war was unassailable by those who can kill the body. Circumstance was master, and brutal, but his slavery left him lean, and tough like a bullet. A sudden gust of wind woke me, and as I walk-ran to my car, I kept looking over my shoulder, and sure enough, as I turned the engine over, rolling down my window to get one more look, he was gone.

When I walk on the mountain, or like tonight, out on the sparse lawn by the bending mesquite, *that face* is the face I give to Jesus, or maybe it was him, and is, and I imagine him in that coat and fedora, unshaven, stinky, looking out past me at the continents as if they are mere puzzle pieces. *That face* speaks to me, and like he and Satan once did, we see all the kingdoms of the earth at once, as if from the clouds.

Teach me "meek," Lord, and the wind is from the northwest tonight, and dark storms are moving away to the east, and he says the meek will inherit the earth. But I want to know what meekness looks like, and he says read scripture, taking it for what it is—his breathing. I open my mouth, and *that face* opens, breathes into mine, and an unseen world enters, his words rolling through me, like water. I hang onto the tree, wind whipping, and I'm suspended between heaven and earth. The kingdom of God hangs in the air, with saints from millenniums past piling on stars for better views, and my Dad and Mom, and Moses, and Martha all sit together, and watch.

≈

The saints begin to speak. All at once, but without confusion. I hear the voices of martyrs, and housewives, patriarchs and judges, the sons of god, the daughters of men, the heroes of old, the Jews of death camps and Sabbaths, and all the lion-eaten believers of long ago. They speak unknown words, and I tell him I don't even believe in tongues, really, and he says you may have things to learn. I ask *that face* what are they saying, and he says listen. I listen, straining to obey, and the noise changes to song, a collection of verses bursting in my chest like so much thunder, so many symphonies, and I'm sure I will not survive. I await unknown truths, like a converted mystic, hoping for new prophecies, new scripture, new sayings to make glad my heart, and the words are becoming clear.

But there are no new words. The life of God is pouring into me from the heavens, and like separate notes of glory, I feel seek-first-the-kingdom running in my arms, consider-others-better-than-your-self knocking around my middle, turning into song, and ushering in a host of God-realities that the world holds banal and foolish. If someone strikes you on the cheek, offer the other one. Go the extra mile, they will run and mount up as eagles, seek peace with others if at all possible, submit to the authority of the elders, restore sinners gently, and all fall short of the glory of God. Deny yourself, take up the cross, true religion is the care of widows and orphans, walk humbly with your God, the Lord is my shepherd. Better to be poor and innocent than rich and wicked, and become like little children, wise as serpents, innocent as doves. Have faith as of a mustard seed, and my son was dead, but now is alive again. God, have mercy on me a sinner, and this woman is very poor, but she gave all she had. Lord, where would we go, for you have the words of eternal life, and oh, ye of little faith. The hosannas, the beaten Christ before Pilate, Joseph caring for the Christ body. The weeping of Peter, the death of Stephen, the eunuch reading Isaiah on a lonely road. Paul crossing Asia, working, writing, spreading Jesus, and the exile of old man John on an island where in his punishment, Christ came to him, with comfort, and gentle, frightening glory.

The book is alive, all at once, and my spine watches, and the truth of God crushes my spirit, my sin, my stupidity, and meekness is the only choice in the presence of heaven. My day's anger melts into silence, and I watch as the saints return to invisible, and *that face* and I sit at the mesquite, our backs to the bark, and I hadn't noticed the rain, but I'm wet, and muddy, but how can I care when I am holding the hand of forever?

He says, it's a simple idea, when you think about it.

~

Barking drags me to my feet, and the Black and Blue is a mess at the end of the driveway. I slosh to the garage, and my feet are cold, but this afternoon, on a lark, I decided I wanted him with me, even if I was losing my job (or is my job losing me?), and couldn't afford it. He's my friend, has no home, and I have a vague idea that he can remind me of holy things when I forget. I grab the collar I picked up at Sharon's Pets, and a worn red leash from my last dog, over 12 years ago. The sky flashes, and his outline against the horizon excites me, and I think, maybe I won't be as lonely anymore, at least there'll be someone I can talk to unafraid. The Black and Blue can't help me, really, but if he would sleep in front of my fireplace, or out on the porch while Sara and I sat silent together, our uncertainty might be warmer, and Richard and Wayne might someday understand.

He's not exactly ugly, I think, approaching him, and he thinks it's a wild game, of course, even in the storm. His body instantly crouches, ready to spring. I always wanted a beautiful dog, like a Siberian Husky or a Samoyed, but this guy's scraggly, a true mutt, with mud and slime hanging on his short black hair in a cute kind of I-don't-know way. Now he's on his toes, leaping away in a huge bound toward the house, then stopping on a dime, like a cat, transfixed, eyes locked with mine. I jump, and he jumps, and I run, and he chases, nipping at me, and after I'm winded, I'm sitting on the steps of the porch, arms open, daring the night. The Black and Blue trots up just close enough for me to scratch his head. He shakes himself, and he smells bad, and I grab him by the neck, and we wrestle, but again, he knows it's a game, and scratches at me, bounding away, into the night. But now he's back, sniffing the collar, and suddenly he lays his face in my lap, and his black and blue eyes tilt up, wet with rain, with a comical what-about-it look inviting me to do my worst.

But I can't.

I can't put a collar on this friend of mine, not in any weather. He belongs to Ruin, and in the cold of the downpour, I accept that uncertainty isn't supposed to be warm. It's not time for a puppy, and the blessings of God always come, even in the storm, and the face of meekness is his face, and if we ask enough, with enough persistence, with enough faith, he may yet make it ours.

The dog took off when the hail came, but it was small, pea-size, and I went back to bed. My last word was thank you, and I was asleep, playing in unknown fields and waterfalls with a tall Arabian black horse with blue eyes. I wrote it down the next morning, that he and I had ridden out past Alpha Centauri, and found a wedding chapel, and ridden in, and *that face* was there, and we rode on, across water, and were free.

September 21

I saw him eating by himself over at the cafeteria the other day, but I didn't speak. I always figure it's better to leave him alone.

Maybe he'd rather be doing something else. Maybe he's in the wrong line of business.

We've been gone, and besides, he doesn't hold my attention, doesn't give me what my family needs. Mine's nay.

Johnny Spann, told to Roland Minor
Administrative Committee

. . . Jesus took his own sweet time . . .

Harry and Edna left for Europe yesterday, and in six weeks, when they return, it'll be over.

~

I should fast.

Fasting interests me. It seems like a good idea. I've read books about it, read discussions both theological and physical, and at various times in my life I've decided to make it part of my discipline, but I'm not good at it, and anymore the only time I fast is when I'm bargaining with God. It's stupid, I know, but I always think maybe I'll get his attention, and maybe he'll meet me halfway. So I spend a day not eating, like yesterday, drinking water and my usual coffee, never quite sure if coffee counts. But the whole ordeal leaves me cranky, a bit angry, and there's a determination growing in me, telling me I need to do something, not just roll over. But I can't think of what to do short of getting with each member and begging.

I decide to skip the donut shop, and just do toast and butter at home instead. After five pieces, two with strawberry jam, I drive on in to the office, fire up the coffee pot, and rummage in my desk looking for ideas. There's the church directory, and I grab my yellow highlighter. Starting with the As, I start marking through the names of families who are anti-Cyrus. The ones in cahoots with Harry, the ones who want me gone.

I guess I should talk to them. Yuck.

I resolve to contact each of them today—in person, on the telephone, in writing—somehow. Then, sometime in the next two weeks, I'll follow-up with a personal visit in their home. Go to the lion's den myself, since there's no king to throw me in. Counting the yellow marks. Thirty-seven families. Thirty-seven out of seventy one.

Jan's here, and I tell her the plan, saying cancel everything for the week. She frowns, wondering out loud if that's a good idea. She's suspicious already, having seen my compulsive side several times in the last few weeks, and I say, it's the only idea. What about Wednesday, she asks, and I say oh, yeah. Cancel all my appointments—except that one.

~

Wednesday is my day out at the Shady Oaks Retirement Center. Shady Oaks, a glorified old folks home on the north side of town, houses four of our members—three elderly women and a man in his thirties, one Adam Collingsworth. A single man who worked at the meat plant, Adam fell in the shower at home, banged his head on the hot water faucet, and now he can't walk, or play checkers, or swallow. He has a tube to keep him alive, but his stare is vacant, and he'll probably never know, or say, his name again.

Wednesdays are hard for me. I complain to God on Wednesdays, saying that to fade to ruin in full view is awful—no dignity, no beauty, no teeth, no nothing. He agrees with me, but tells me to remember that that's not the whole story, and invariably, he walks me over to room 207 on the west wing, and I think of the old man, and the promise.

I promised Geyser Meredith that if I was well and in town, I would never miss a Wednesday.

In the ten years since Geyser died, I never have.

~

Maybe I can get in one call before class.

The phone sits in front of me, stoic. I look back through the yellow marks. . . . *Meredith* . . . *Meredith* . . . there . . . Clarke, wife

Barbara, four kids. I cradle the receiver, consider the number. Clarke wasn't kin to Geyser, but he met the old man on one of the rare Sunday mornings Geyser felt strong enough to make the trip to church. Barbara and the kids fell in love with Geyser, made him an honorary grandpa, and the whole family was standing by his bed when he died. Years later, Clarke and I had a falling out over plans to build a new education wing. Design was a hobby of his and after the planning committee rejected his proposal, his level of involvement went from connected to hardly at all.

672-9034. I think . . . *do it.*

It's ringing on the other end, and adrenaline rushes in. I'm following a hunch, sensing that this call is a good idea, done in good faith, following a prompting of the Spirit—well . . . maybe. I close my eyes, and wonder if Geyser's watching me, telling me this is a good place to start. He's probably giggling, wanting to help.

∾

Geyser was 102 years old, bald and lean, with one leg shorter than the other, though that didn't matter, because I never saw him walk. He hadn't walked in over twenty years, not since the early sixties, he said. Most of the time he dragged himself up and down the halls, wheelchair-bound, bent-over, looking at the floor, offering slow good words of blessing that went largely unnoticed.

For Geyser, conversation was work, his face stretching to unbelievable proportions as he fought consonant after consonant, vowel after vowel, but I relished his words and his company, so I never hurried him. Perhaps my contemplative life began with him, as I sat through the long minutes he took to get sentences out. His room was quiet, and I'd sit there for an hour, sometimes two or three, while we got in maybe a good fifteen minutes of talk.

Geyser had been a wild thing, in his teens, he said, and had at least two bastards (his word) running around, but he'd never met them. He'd been estranged from his mother, said she'd keeled over in the middle of a square dance back in 1919, while his father worked in the fields raising watermelons. He told of living in Oklahoma, getting married late and having three daughters, of heading west for California after the crash, and that he was Tom Joad. He told me about Faith, his wife, and that she was a good woman, and loving. But his face would cloud over, and I wondered what happened to her, but he wouldn't say. But about three weeks before he died, he confessed he'd been a drinker, and that he loved scotch and wine. He must have been a mean drunk because he said he always got a kick out of fighting, out of stomping a man in the head. He beat Faith one day, he told me, the only time he ever did. It was 1934, when the girls were teenagers, and they watched him do it, and they all took her to the hospital, and she lived another five years, but was never the same. And he told how his daughters left, one by one, and after 1946, he never knew what happened to them. They hated him, he thought. He'd come back to Texas around '48, and for the next fifteen years or so just hung around, working odd jobs for the highway department or the schools, and bussed dishes at a restaurant for five years. He especially liked serving popcorn in movie houses. And how in 1963, at the age of 78, he'd had a stroke while passing through Ruin, and no one knew what to do with him, and somehow, he ended up there at Shady Oaks.

But then, he'd get this twinkle in his eye, and say I was 71 when I found out about this grace business, and Jesus took his own sweet time in finding me. He said it was back in 1957, at a tent revival, but he'd only gotten a Bible after coming to the home in '63. But by the time I knew him, he could quote most of the psalms, and I remember his slow, lovely treatment of Psalm 51. *Have mercy on me O God, according to thy loving kindness, according unto the multitudes of thy tender mercies, blot out my transgressions.* I always knew he was confessing, and that he'd never really forgiven himself for his life. He'd said he'd been hanging on to grace for 25 years, but wondered if he hadn't done a little too much bad, too much damage, and his voice would be asking me, reaching for me when he said it. But I'd hold his hand, and we'd laugh, and I told him over and over that I didn't think that was the case at all, that with God, nothing was over 'til it was over.

~

"Is this Clarke? Clarke Meredith? Cyrus Manning here."
There's quiet on the other end. I'm saying I'd like to talk to you Clarke, but he interrupts and says though it's good to hear from me, he's in a bit of a rush, and that he guesses I should know that after the vote, he and his family will be going over to the Second Baptist church. Well, that's okay, I say, but maybe we could have lunch next week anyway, maybe trade old Geyser stories. Another time maybe, he says, but good to talk to you.

~

It was early April of an evening when Geyser went on home, and I bet he found out what grace means for sure, and I bet it blew his mind.

~

Jan's gone on to class, and the parking lot came to life 20 minutes ago. I sit leafing through the directory, perusing those yellow marks, twisting the phone cord.

It's quiet, and Geyser wasn't watching after all.

There's a quick knock, and I raise my head and the door opens. Cory Allen is grinning ear to ear, and Molly Reigns is right behind him, waving a paper, holding Cory's hand. We all giggle, and as we hug, I almost break, because I love these kids. But they can't see me, can't see my pain, because they're getting married Saturday. I'm preaching the wedding. She hands me the order of the service, and though I choke when I see "We've Only Just Begun" on the program, I thank God they've asked me to do it. Molly's rattling off how she can't believe the cost of the cake, and wait'll you see the dress—it's off the shoulder—and Mom's been crying all morning already. I silently thank God, so glad for this fresh open window in a stuffy morning. I first taught Cory in junior high nine and a half years ago, and he's a good kid from a good family, and as much like my own child as any student I've had. He's overweight, and at 24, is balding already, and Cory's been a cut-up and practical joker for years, and rumor has it that *he is going to get his* on his wedding night, which makes me worried for Molly, who has a monster nose and saddlebag thighs, and is more than a little pigeon-toed. But these guys are beautiful, and marriage is truth, and at least I have something to look forward to besides being rejected. As I grab my Bible and the three of us walk out the door, Geyser comes to me one more time.

Geyser loved to come to First Church, prayed every week to be strong enough to come to worship. Called us his family, just about the best family he'd ever had.

I feel the same way.

∾

But here's Beatrice Thomasen at the water fountain, and I take a deep breath and ask her if I could maybe take her and Francis to lunch this week, maybe Thursday. She looks me over. Time passes, and it's still quiet, and I stammer and say maybe we could talk, you know, about our differences, and she smiles, looking at the floor, and what a horrific moment, and she says it's a little late for that, don't you think? I say no, I don't think so, and she says, firmly, that it is, she was sure it is. That God has things well in hand, and she's just gonna trust him to the end. She's putting her hand on mine, and I'm thinking get your hand off me, and she says I should have faith, cause she and all her friends are praying for me.

I head for the gym, shaking with rage.

Blessed are those who hunger and thirst after righteousness,
for they shall be filled.

The little coffee can marked Benin is going around, and I dig in
my pocket and find a five dollar bill, and move my hand to lay it on
the podium, and I notice I'm still shaking, and I need to breathe, and
I do, deeply, and long. Tom walks by, and I shake hands, and there's
solidity there, and strength, and I'll put the five in when the coffee
can finishes going around. I'm better at tithing than fasting, though
I don't really tithe either, but this morning it all seems so dumb, this
doing religion, and I know I have that familiar glaze over my eyes
that's me in retreat.

∾

I'm looking for prayer requests, going over the sick list in the
church bulletin, and wonder that I'm not on it. I see Francis Moore's
at home, that she went to the hospital complaining of stomach pains
Thursday, and will be having tests this week. Joy was in my office on
Tuesday, and, among other things, I remember her saying her mother
rarely felt well. But I saw Francis on Wednesday, in the Eckerd's drug
store where she works, and she was curt, and unusually tense, and spit
her words out, and was huffing, and her bra straps were showing, and
I knew she knew I knew. Joy talked too much, she muttered, taking
my money for the deodorant, and smiling my best, I told her I liked
Joy, and was glad to get to know her. Francis looked at me like don't
insult me, don't talk to me like you're my friend, I don't care if you are
a pastor. I know you know my secrets and I'll rip your head off if you
even think you know me. I said thank you, Francis, and I'm sorry, and
awkwardly mumbled something incoherent about maybe she could
come see me, and we could talk, and I could almost see the blood vessels going off like little rockets inside her skull as she smiled her best
and turned away. But regardless, she looked like she felt fine, and I
wonder what the trouble is. And . . . why don't I already know?

I also notice a reminder that the next church business meeting will be held on Tuesday, October 28. That's when they'll decide.

~

I need some time. Tom, would you lead a couple of praise songs, and we stagger through "As A Deer Pants For Water So My Soul Longeth After Thee" and with 20 people singing, it's not too bad. Then "I Will Enter His Gates with Thanksgiving," but nobody wants to clap, and as the song winds down, it's my turn. I take my *Jerusalem Bible* and my notes fall on the floor, and I stand at the lean-to podium at the head of the center aisle and listen as the last notes die away.

I launch in about hunger—unclear, and coming apart—and I wonder about skin and bones, and being thirsty. Bug-eyed kids with beer bellies jump to mind, stark images of emaciation, I say, in both fashion and Rwanda, and I hate those pictures, which I don't say, and I don't know if we want righteousness anymore. I think we want what we want, and if righteousness is part of the deal, so much the better. I'm rambling, but I notice a little banging sound, and I look, and there's a small, useless, rectangular window looking out onto concrete, just to my right, and there's a bee banging its head there, wanting to come to my class—backing up and taking another run at the light, and bouncing off, and flying like a drunk, and again caroming against the glass, and finally dragging itself away in defeat—little bee tail between little bee legs, and who knows if he's in despair or not? He needs a flower, and the thought of madness again rears its head.

I'm lost again. Looking at my notes, the sweat bursts out on my skin, and the mysteries are overwhelming me. Breathing deep doesn't always help, but I steady my hands, and look up, and in the awkward pause, I notice Doug and Sue Goods. I haven't seen them in . . . oh, what—three months? They've been looking for a new church, too, a new place to fight the battles. They're tired of me, said so to my back, and they wished it were all headier stuff. He's a Ph.D., a fiction writer, as boring as summer school, and the wife's a thoughtful runner, 20 miles a week, and she meditates, and they have Maggie, 14, who is going to finish high school next year. Faithful Christian family, kind of, but listless, and over the years they've turned down no less than five invitations to come to my house. But they look perfect, and as I gather steam again, I think they look fat and happy, anything but hungry, but she'd like some romance, they say, and he'd like more money and tenure, but that's looking iffy. And Maggie . . . well, Maggie. Baptized into Christ at 12, she knows as much Bible as I do, seems like. She's not too sure about this Christian business anymore, because she's read Camus, alongside Paul and Peter, and selections from a condensed Levi-Strauss. She's decidedly something called postmodern, she told me, and I smiled that day, because I kinda do, kinda don't know what she means.

The post-modern world is a hungry world, I'm saying, but I'm thinking of Maggie, and how I told her that what I know is that it's hard not to know anything, as in not being sure. No God for sure, no love for sure, no beginning or ending for sure, where's the seat of identity? What's the place of origin? Are unborn babies alive or can I kill one? Is sex sacred or should I sleep with the quarterback because I really love him, and I can see it in her eyes—Maggie's scared about all the stuff she doesn't know. The moral universe is no more, she said, and Zen is more applicable to her life, and she doesn't really think Jesus got out of the grave. Can't imagine the physics of the thing, her dad tells her, although he's still Christian because he believes the metaphors of this not-so-applicable religion are so strong, so rich.

The problem is the hunger and thirst. We can say we don't know, but how do we stop the desire? The need that wakes us in the night, the place between the stomach and the heart twisting with an ache that reaches into the back of the thighs, and no food, no sex, no drug, no companionship can slake it? I hear it in the heartbreaking pulse of a night rain. I see it in the face of the pet being put to sleep, or in the eyes of the lover betrayed and lost. The simple, dimply face of my gummy seven-year-old, crusty with mud and dessert, stretches my heart, his eyes looking clean into me, turning me toward something more, something unseen, something hovering in the air above my soul, and I reach, reach, and the night of not knowing offers itself, and if I take it, I leave the God of my father just on the other side, reaching, coming up empty, just like me.

The hunger and thirst can be filled. What a joke. Don't mock me, smart people say. Don't mock my pain by telling me there is an answer to the complexity. My degrees are good, my midnight conversations—fights, wars, really—over the pre-eminence of this moment, and the antique idea of history and linear cause and effect, and I have a career and $25 bottles of wine, but I have to be better, more accomplished, and we lived together for 4 years, and that's better, and I have to keep in action, get my kids and convince them to have integrity with themselves, that their heart is the guide, the moral compass, and be pragmatic, and I'm sorry, Daddy's leaving now, and now that my new house is 2400 square feet, and I traded my Lexus in today for the new one, (that's it in gold, have you seen it?), and she's 21, and I'm young again, but that was yesterday, and why am I so jaded anymore, and the possibility now is of stock going down, and energy going down, and I'm sagging in body and soul, and cremate me please, and sing the old religion songs at my funeral, and God, I thought I could retire and be happy, and the hunger and thirst is still here, though I've lived good, and well, and isn't it enough to try, to try to do the best you can, and there's nothing matters anymore, I hurt so much, just help me die, help me die, this suffering is inhuman, and I'm incontinent, my bed is wet constantly, and just help me die, and God, if you're there, I've done the best I could, could you let me be with you, though I never really bought you at all?

∾

I just said all that, I realize, and I thought I was only thinking it, and the coffee can is on the chair on the front row in front of me, and I take the five and drop it in. I notice Skipper's intensity as he is listening, and Lacey's head is down, and I'll bet she told him about her retching.

∾

My head is clearer now, and I've been talking for thirty-five minutes, and my mouth is dry, and it's almost over. I say up front what fools we are, for abandoning the idea that we can know, and I realize that's not the topic, so I tie it back in by saying the love affair with not knowing is the particular form hunger takes in our age. That our thirst is naked, on display, and hanging on virtually every billboard in America, and that the hunger and thirst of the culture is obviously for something other than righteousness.

But righteousness is the forerunner of all hunger, and I'm talking straight at Maggie now, because I probably won't get another chance, and we are all hungry and thirsty, you and I and the world, and I say there is something to know that you know that you know, something true to fill the need. How do I know? The empirical evidence is solid, reasonable, though not ironclad, but regardless, it is my faith that leads the way, my faith not in faith, but in God, and Jesus, and the Spirit, and how can I say there is a knowing that is different than what physics or psychology can teach us? Mysteries are deep things, and God comes, and the pool that is my hunger, my thirst, is the eternity placed in my heart, and there is nothing save he who is Holy who can fill that empty place in the pool.

We will explore righteousness next week, I say, and Doug and Sue and Maggie, I'm smiling at you, as I sit down, and there are a few more announcements before we're dismissed, and it's good to see you, but don't sit there and look at me with blank eyes, and tell me that sensation, stimulation, pleasure, self-actualization, or existentially responsible action can do it. It can't, and I am too lost, too much in pain, to fall for such pitiable lies.

∾

And again O God,

We are hungry. We are thirsty. Famished for what we cannot name. Jesus, you spoke, and gave that longing a name. Make us righteousness, give us righteousness, lead to understand that the hunger is for you, for your food, the will of the Father, the body and blood of you— the Christ. Bless us in the search, in the digging, planting and harvesting of lean truth with which to feed our starving, shrinking souls. Make us both food and the fed in these churches, and do not let us merely drift in the knowledge of our need.

In Jesus, Amen.

. . . *He keeps making me laugh* . . .

Sara majored in elementary education, with an emphasis in art, but she's never had to work full-time. She did some tutoring in East Texas, and she substituted—saving money—before we went to New York for a week, and substituted again when Wayne first started playing tennis, so he could have all the right equipment and clothes and lessons, but other than that, she's been able to be home all these years, which is important to her, and she doesn't want to work, she's telling me now as we sit on the porch on yet another warm September evening. She's on the steps, head down, crying, trying not to, but she's tired, and the boys both have colds, and hated dinner, and fought bath time, and Wayne's still struggling with compounds and tenses, and Richard got mad when Pot Likker, the dog hero of the book we're reading, got killed, saying sad stories are terrible and he never wanted to read another one.

It's been a nice evening.

∾

I called them all. All thirty-seven families. I was on the phone from 1:00 until 5:15, and from that, I have 3 appointments for the week. Sam agreed to meet me over breakfast Thursday morning, and I appreciate Sam because he's up front in an unoffensive way, and who knows, we might even be friends after I go. The two other families I'll visit with Tuesday evening—the Firestones at 5:30, the Middletons at 8:00. Major Middleton is a retired military guy who likes me, but his wife doesn't, but Mike and Emily Firestone are the only true seekers in the lot. They acted thrilled to hear from me, and invited both Sara and me for dinner. They came several years ago, and have opinions, and Mike and I had one major run-in not long after he came. But they're relatively young believers, trying to stay pliable, and I'm thankful for their openness. What I didn't tell them was that they were my thirty-fourth call, and that what they thought wouldn't make a practical difference.

Maybe I should fast again.

≈

I'm looking over Sara's sparse resume, and turning the pages of the Rand-McNally, and I say the good thing is we could go anywhere, and yes, I've got a list for the tapes and resumes, and no, I don't know when I'll get them out, and yes, I know I'm putting it off, and no, I don't know if anyone'll want me. I'm sorry I can't just claim the power of God, and no, I don't believe he's a gumball machine that spits out what I want if I say it with my mouth, because he is God and bound to no one.

But praying would be good, and we do, briefly. I cite the usual requests, the usual acknowledgements of sin, and Sara interrupts with the needing guidance line, and I suddenly realize that Jesus hasn't come today, like other Sundays. Not 'til now, he says, and I glance out in the yard, and he nods. How long can a person sit, not being able to think of anything to pray, and for Sara, the answer's not very long, and she gets up and goes in the house. Soon I hear the shower. I amble off the porch, noticing there aren't any stars tonight, only clouds.

≈

What did you used to talk about, I ask him, and he says, what do you mean, and I say what do you mean, what do you mean? You know exactly what I mean. He laughs at me, and I don't know how he always gets me feeling easier about it all. We used to walk for hours, he says, and John and Peter and James were always serious, and I would drift back to see Thaddeus, who liked to sing, and Silas, who knew how to enjoy a joke or a riddle, and the three of us would enter-tain each other while others fought over first rights in the kingdom. I say, could we walk? He says, sure.

And we traipse off, Jesus singing, and I'm surprised he's a tenor. I don't know the song, though it's lovely, and it makes me want to join in. But I don't know the language, and I quickly give up the idea. He notices me, and the singing stops, and as we walk up the road toward Mr. Javonovich's place a quarter-mile to the west, we're both silent, and I know he's waiting on me, but I don't want to talk.

~

As I called those families, my hands shook, and my heart pounded with every punch of the numbers. I'd hear a voice at the other end say no thanks, or we're busy, or they're not here, but don't call back, or the dial tone at the end of an abrupt hang-up, and my arms hurt even now—I can feel the blood backing up in my forearms, thinking about it.

I have to stop.

I sit, leaning against the fence. There's no breeze tonight. It's still, calm, and Jesus is standing across the road, looking at me. I notice he has jeans on, and it's still *that face*, and I get so tired of almost crying, and I'm almost crying again. I don't know where to go, what to do—was I born for this? Have I failed, I ask him, and will my life lose its meaning now? I want to swear, but I'm not stupid. His head's turned, as if he's looking way off, at a coming car or plane, or event, and he's making me curious, so I stand, too, and look. I see nothing but scattered houses, distance, and empty fields.

I could show you, he says, and his eyes slide around, light, laughing a little, daring me.

What great eyes, and they're all there is in the world when they hold you, when they lock on yours. I always thought his eyes would fill me with meaning and destiny and love, but he keeps making me laugh. I've tried for years to find the color, but it's shifty, and always turning, like planets of soft clouds, so that the change is subtle and calm, not the startling dance of the kaleidoscope but the ease of the changing sky at twilight. I know he's challenging me to think, to see beyond this moment, to hold faith in a new light, that there is a new thing to be seen if I will but see it.

It's a game he wants me to play, and I look to the horizon again, and still it's dark. I wonder, and he watches me wonder, and it's tempting, because he knows exactly what I want, and what I want to know, and he could tell me. The offer is on the table, but I decide to hold my ground. I let go of the real, and imagine.

I think death is coming, and I will live somehow, and enough money will be there, just enough, and I can keep meeting him (thank God!) and Sara will grow old with me. Wayne will marry, and Richard will discover he's a writer or a singer or that he doesn't have long to live, and we will grow and change. There'll be college, and weddings, and perhaps grandchildren, and the funerals of friends, and who knows where my descendants will travel? Are the heavens open, and how do I know that in coming centuries there will be newness in the world because I lived believing? But I do know.

What is the loss I call you to, Jesus says, other than a call to live simply, in this fool's love the world calls naive. Life not trusting is a choice to make, Cyrus, and you die today if you make it. I laugh again, and I like this game with God, and I say I didn't know what life was when I was born, did I? But you came anyway, he says, and terror is just part of the deal. But hanging on by a thread has other meanings than fear, *if you can trust me.* He pauses, looks away again.

Then he smiles, and says they don't sing "Great is Thy Faithfulness" for nothing, you know.

Wisecracker.

∾

I wander back toward the house, and Sara's standing on the porch, waiting for me. The wind has picked up a bit, blowing her dark robe around her bare legs. She's saying it's okay, Cyrus, I just get scared. I come to the steps and look up at her, and her eyes are swollen, and I say how about Washington? Washington, as in Seattle, she whispers, and I say, that's the one. It might be fun, I tell her, and there'd be white Christmases, and green and freshness, and the ocean, and the boys might like it, and closer to your folks, and as I hold her, I tell her how much I love this man we follow, how much I love Jesus. You sound like you've seen him, she said, and I look out at the road, he's almost out of sight now, and I laugh again, and confess that lately, it almost seems that way.

≈

We turn to take our moment, our love, our need for each other, to a dark, soft place, when the sound of a truck coming from the east catches us just inside the door. We watch headlights bounce up to our drive, and the wind blows them to within a foot of our Taurus. The rusty door of the white pickup squeals as it opens. Sara groans.

Connie's timing has never been good.

September 28

Cyrus? Don't be silly.

Lacey McKinnon, told to Roland Minor
Administrative Committee

. . . the inevitable always comes . . .

Days are getting shorter. I go to bed late every night, and it's catching up with me. Old age once seemed like a distant country, but not anymore, and the passage of time has no mercy, wrinkles coming willy-nilly whether I'm interested or not. I was bald years ago, and standing here, at the morning mirror, bleary-eyed after a long night split between driving and fitful sleep, I stare at my bare torso. Love handles, skin sagging on ribs, little muscle to flex. I flex anyway, and laugh, though what there is to laugh about escapes me. The joust with middle age goes on. It's inevitable, I suppose, and mercy must not be about missing the tough things.

My laughter subsides, and I stare in silence. But . . . I just can't be somber today. There's light in that eye, *ar-ar-ar-*, I say to the image, bulging one eye as big as I can and doing the best pirate I can muster. I bite hard on the toothbrush and attack my molars, glancing back into the bedroom toward the alarm clock. Two minutes to brush, I think, and I smile again, surprised again at how a simple wedding can change things.

∼

Late Friday morning, Sara and I drove over to Dallas for Cory and Molly's wedding. From Odessa on, it rained hard, even by West Texas standards, and 45 and 50 mph was the best we could do. We passed the slow hours with an old game we call Sara/Cyrus Trivia.

We've played it for years, thinking why not remember us, asking questions and playing out memories of our own, about our own lives, rather than about dead presidents, geography, and pop culture. It was a giddy pastime at first, but as we got closer to Dallas, memories turned down darker alleys, and Sara got quiet, even cried a couple of times. I knew better than to say much, and opted to hold her hand and hide behind the steering wheel. I was hoping she'd talk to me. She kept her distance, but squeezed my hand a time or two, just enough to remind me that even in moments of strange, repressive silence, I'm thankful for her, glad to belong to someone's love.

When we got to Dallas, we got lost, began circling, and after an hour and a half of trading curt questions and bogus directions, we finally rolled into the parking lot of a spectacular building that in no way resembled a church. Austin Reigns, Molly's dad, who owns several clothing stores in the Metroplex, swanky places pitched at executives and wealthy wives, had rented a couple of floors in a mammoth design center. When we walked in the huge glass doors, Sara stopped, and gawked. The lush, towering, north downstairs lobby had been transformed into a stunning sanctuary, albeit a secular one, decorated in shades of fall burgundy. Eye-popping floor arrangements of autumn flowers were being set throughout the space, and tall beeswax candles on gold candleholders were beginning to carve out lengthy aisles. The next day, Sara counted at least 150 candles on the stage alone.

This wasn't going to be a wedding. This was to be a festival, a pagan love-fest. Ironically, the whole thing was being thrown for and pastored by a small band of wandering Christians.

The rehearsal was stressful, due to the Reigns' recent divorce. Austin, a raucous man with an unabashedly blue way with words, says it was his fault, and it's too bad, because—and this sounds a bit absurd—he has a good heart. But Molly's mom Wendy, a kind and strong woman, had no tolerance for Austin's affair, and called for the breakup as soon as she found out. But two years later now, she's on the mend, engaged, and came to the rehearsal, new fiancée in tow, determined to gamely celebrate what she no longer trusted. Wendy only broke down once; I think she was looking at Austin's latest blonde thing, a severe looking 30-something who neither spoke nor smiled.

Molly and Corey just kept their eyes on each other, and we got through it with minimal damage, though the vows were hard on everyone.

But the next afternoon, the tension had been pushed aside. Though the sky turned cloudy, the glories of wedding regalia, two-tiered chocolate groom's cakes, and miles of champagne and truffles swept the losses into the corner. The ceremony was lush, Corey and Molly radiant, and amazingly, during the sermon, everyone seemed to listen.

Including me.

I reminded us all of love's origin. Of love's meaning. That it has little to do with the burn in the loins for the dark of the wedding night, although I didn't say it that way. Passion fades, sex has to be cleaned up, and the living is day to day. I told them that love can be a war inside, and that there are enemies in the battle. I wanted to say that hell will chase you down, and try to destroy you, and that in our world, hell seems to have the upper hand at the moment. But I said love never dies, always hopes, always believes, always forgives, and is not quick to condemn. I said for richer for poorer, in sickness and in health, and 'til death do us part and let no man separate, at which point I paused and looked at Molly, then Corey, then Austin, then Wendy, then Sara.

Why I did such a thing, I don't know, but each of them returned my gaze, and didn't look away.

∼

I pronounced them man and wife, Mr. and Mrs. Corey Allen, and the party began.

As the day wore on, my cheeks began to hurt. Smiling constantly, laughing at the endless goodwill, bravely shaking hand after hand in the receiving line—I was nothing less than giddy. Food was everywhere, all of it exquisite: mountains of finger-size cucumber sandwiches next to cascading layers of sliced ham, turkey, and beef, and exotic cheeses complimenting fresh French bread, and melons and grapes and kiwi and watermelon, and I'm sure I wandered the hall bug-eyed—I couldn't imagine the expense, or my good fortune in getting to partake. Molly skipped from table to table, saying thank you, thank you, and people applauded, and then the dancing began, and conversation grew more quiet and simple, lots of it between strangers caught up in the rare goodness of it all.

Then it happened.

Austin Reigns and his ex-wife Wendy found themselves alone on the edge of the dance floor. A word, then another, and more. The fiancée was nowhere to be found, and the severe 30-something was in the powder room or on the phone, and my eyes got cloudy as Wendy took Austin's hand and walked to the dance floor. I saw Molly watching, absolutely still, her hand to her mouth, trembling. They danced, and even found the grace to smile.

∽

I spit into the sink, and smile. It's going to be hard to be somber today. I slide down the hall toward the kitchen, anxious to get to my morning quiet and coffee. I think I'll use Dad's old Bible again, and see what God might say today. There's a vague itch on my back, just above my right shoulder blade. I take a whack at it, even I as drag the coffee canister across the counter.

Ah, coffee.

The canister is empty.

∽

One of the first fights of my marriage came on a Monday morning in grad school, with a paper on Revelation due at 9:00 a.m. I'd worked most of the night, writing until 2:15, and after that, waiting for the old style daisy wheel printer to slowly spit these sixty-four pages out, *tat-tat-tat-tat*. I had to hand feed each sheet, and each page took exactly three minutes to print, but it was better than typing and carbons. I was standing in the bathroom the next morning, about 7:30, head draped over the sink, buttoning my shirt, asleep, and Sara, as she wandered by, said there was no coffee. And I was awake in nothing flat, and Sara found out right then and there that she'd married an irrational man.

∾

Who didn't get the coffee? I find a Folgers can, and there's hope, but I pick it up, and I can feel emptiness anytime, and somber may be easier than I thought. I close the cupboard door, but it gets away from me, and slams. I freeze, thinking, breathe, breathe, and I'll just go get some, cause I think it was me that forgot in the first place. I hear Sara stirring, and I know she can feel my irritation from there, and so she'll just play possum and stay in bed, but I have to get coffee, and I don't want to wait for the stop at Taste Delight, so I'll have to go shower at 5:45 in the morning, put on my pants, and head for the store.

∾

"I'll get it."

Connie looks like she didn't sleep much, either. She's standing at the kitchen door, eyes puffy and hair awry, already dressed in jeans and tee-shirt, holding her white tennies in her hand. I ask her what she's doing up, and she shrugs and sits, unlacing her shoes. She mumbles.

"I meant to get some. I forgot. Food Lion's open. I'll be right back."

I asked Connie if she wanted company, and for a moment she didn't answer. She obviously wanted her privacy, but I said wait for me, and she finally said whatever. I threw on some clothes. I was hoping she'd talk to me, but she's stubborn, and we rode in silence. But I like that about her—no false chitchat. I turned off the ignition, noticed the sun wasn't up yet.

Neither of us opened our car door.

My heart started a loud pounding, though I didn't know why.

"I can't talk to you."

I said okay, and she climbed out of the car. She crossed the parking lot in front of me, strong, head high, black hair blowing, messy. I watched her body—a body all too familiar—moving with tension, hidden pressures, a subtle panic. Her walk was fast and hard, but uneven, a near limp.

They say divorce is worse than death.

~

I feel funny in my tennis shoes with no socks. I'm a socks kind of guy. The floor feels squishy, and I'm wondering if I should make the leap from Folgers to the $6.99 a pound stuff in the fancy bag. We can't afford it, but why be rational? Espresso Rhumbo—a rich, acidic bean. *The right morning kick to make you feel smooth and secure in the warmth of a kinder world.* Maybe that's for me.

But as I scoop out almost a pound and go to the grinder, I'm aware of Connie standing at the end of the aisle, looking at me.

What, I say.

She doesn't answer, but keeps looking, and suddenly I am reminded that in all the years of friendship between she and I and Sara and Dirk, we have never talked about our short, intense—dare I use the word?—*affair*.

I care about this woman, but I don't know how to begin.

I turn back to the store's coffee grinder—it's broken. I don't have one, and wouldn't want to go to all that trouble anyway, so I throw back the Rhumbo and grab the Folgers. Connie's still there, ten feet away, but now she's staring at the pocket cameras on sale when I yell think fast, and toss the coffee can at her, a bit too hard, chest-high.

~

Why am I nervous?

Driving back now, suddenly, I can't escape her presence. She sits next to me—like before—staring straight ahead, legs crossed, fingers idly drumming on her left thigh, chewing the inside of her cheek. But the air has changed, the wind blowing from a new place, uncomfortably sweet.

She caught the can without flinching, and she didn't move as I cruised by her shoulder on the way to the check out stand. When I got to the register, the early morning crew must have been stocking, because no one was around to take my money. Connie came up beside me and set the Folgers on the counter, and her arm was against mine. I said pretty good catch. She inhaled, paused, thinking it over, inhaled again.

"Why did you do that?"

Her voice was pointed, direct, and a new energy suggested I wasn't up to speed on something, wasn't paying attention. I turned to her, trying to catch on, and when she faced me, we were closer than I'd intended. Her eyes took me back, took me back to years ago, and I suddenly became aware of that shift in the air.

I didn't step back. I didn't move my eyes. I just said I didn't know, just following an impulse. Then another impulse.

"When did you get so strong?"

Her eyes smiled, and kept looking. Connecting, my body flooded, so easily, and I was screaming to step back, step back. Thankfully, or not, she did it for me, because the checker showed up. Connie walked to the car while I waited for my check to clear, and when I got to her, she was leaning on the trunk. I didn't look at her. But I felt her as I went by. I unlocked her side, and held the door open. She slid into the seat without a word.

∽

Stopping the car in the drive, turning off the ignition, again, I don't touch my door. The sky's opening, taking on light, and neither of us can talk. What do you want, I want to ask her, but I can't possibly ask her that, because I don't want to know. And I can't look at her, but just now I'm dying to look at her, and I didn't even see Sara at the door, coming out to get the paper. How long have we been sitting here?

"Connie, I . . . ."

But my door is opening and Sara sticks her sleepy head in, saying good morning, and where have you two been? I show her the Folgers, and Sara says did Cyrus tell you about the wedding, and you should have seen the groom's cakes. Connie gives in to a quirky smile and looks right at me, saying no, he didn't tell me, and as the two of them chatter into the house, I slowly get out, close my door, my heart still banging away.

I stare at my mesquite tree. After a moment, I relax, knowing this too shall pass. Strange moments happen between people, I theorize.

She'll be gone soon.
I hope.

~

What time is it?
My office clock has stopped. The strap's off my wristwatch—I left it on my dresser. I wish for a world where big hands and little hands don't dominate, but I got in here late, and I wish I knew what time it was. It's time to pray is what time it is, but it's hard to focus.
I wonder why.
I think, I read, I sit quietly, I turn on John Michael Talbot—again. I kneel and prop my chin on the window. A moment passes. I stand up again, walk. Around the desk, to the shelves, pacing, gazing at books, back to the window, back to my chair at the desk. I sit, prop up my feet, take them down, stand up, change my mind, and sit again.
Oh, well.

~

The phone's ringing.
Hi, Sara, and she's telling me Joy Moore called the house and is on her way up to the church to see me, and that she seemed pretty upset. How was I doing, she asked, and she wanted to know did I get a chance to talk to Connie. I said not really. Sorry about the coffee, she said, and she complained that the boys were doing their best Cyrus imitations, mad at her for being out of Trix and Cinnamon Toast Crunch. They had to settle for Bisquick biscuits. I fake a laugh, but Sara doesn't bother.
I hang up the phone, and notice the sun climbing out of its hole. Shouldn't this room be brighter?
I wander into Jan's office to check out the clock. It's almost 8:30, time for class.
I guess Joy's not coming after all.

~

I run into Sam Cooser in the hall, and as he shakes my hand, and as we say how are you, all I can think is, I'm sorry.

I hate being in trouble.

〜

Sam and I met at the pancake house Thursday morning before I went to Dallas, and we talked for half an hour. It was awkward. Uncomfortable. That made me sad, because when I first came to Ruin, Sam was a good friend. He and I sat at that booth at that pancake house once a week for two years. Maybe that's why, on Thursday, I had trouble swallowing my silver-dollar pancakes.

Sam's a man of few words, an old cowboy, though these days he manages a grocery store—the A & P out on Fifth. But he grew up on a farm—still has dung on his shoes, so to speak. He spits out his words and never has learned to chew with his mouth closed, but Thursday morning, sitting there watching him chew, teeth sticky and gums red with strawberry syrup, I thought, I've always liked this hard man. The few times Sara and I have played dominoes with Sam's group—eight couples who've been playing together for two decades at least—it's been cordial, even fun, and I remember when his then four-year-old grandson Joey got his pants zipper stuck, and stood right on the front row of the red-carpet sanctuary, struggling to get it up while we sang "When Peace Like a River." Sam and I laughed 'til we cried, and for a moment, felt like brothers.

Sam's over sixty now. He was one of the 18 who started First Church back in the late 40's, and he's seen too many changes, too many things he thinks are going to get this new generation damned. He's a solid Bible man, which I like about him, and he can quote with the best of them. He thinks women ought to still wear hats— that's a small thing he says—and he hates to see people at the Lord's table with no ties, and no coats, and people ought to look their best before God. The worship upsets him every Sunday, cause it's too fluffy, and confused, he says, with no meat on its bones. And when was the last time he heard the idea from the pulpit that anybody at all was going to hell, and that's a part of the gospel. And there's other things, he said, things involving baptism, and that the teaching of children shouldn't just be about God's love, as if God didn't have a temper when a man sinned. And there's not enough information, not enough getting kids to know Bible verses, and why weren't there any more debates like in the old days, when people really knew Bible, and really wanted to know what it said. He didn't have anything against anybody, he told me, but people ought to marry their own kind, and he couldn't follow my sermons very well, and what about Acts 2:38, and this Holy Spirit stuff—it's just too much, and that he wanted to ask me a question. He'd heard I'd been praying in tongues, and was that true? And he heard I swore a lot, too, and was that true? Sam said he just didn't know what to think about me anymore, that I'd changed, and all the promise he'd thought I'd had years ago was just down the drain, down the drain. He felt betrayed, and I marveled as he almost wept, lapping up the last of his sausage and syrup.

As Sam and I stood at the cash register, Sam insisted on buying. I thanked him, and he just nodded. He and the cashier had a mumbled exchange and we wandered out toward our cars. Finally, he put his hand on my arm, and I stopped. I waited for him to say something, but he never did.

He climbed in his car, pulled out of the parking space, and stopped next to me. He just looked up at me, cheeks puffed out, like he was holding his breath.

I'm sorry, Sam.

He exhaled, and drove away.

~

Sam lets go of my hand, and tells me he knows he was rough on me the other morning, but that he doesn't know any other way to be. But that he wants me to know, in spite of all he said, he still thinks a lot of me. See ya later, he says, as he trundles off down the hall.

~

My mom would slap me at the drop of a hat. My Dad was slower to come around, but he could be tough, too, and when I was twelve, he caught me lying. Previous to this, I remember being maybe seven or eight, about Richard's size, climbing up a brick wall at a nearby elementary school, clambering onto the roof, and my dad coming around the corner just as I swung my leg up. He was mad because he told me not to climb on the roof, and I got to the ground in a hurry. After that, it got pretty chaotic, him dragging me the couple of blocks home, and wailing on me, scolding me through gritted teeth, his hand busting my backside. Literally. I was thankful it wasn't his belt. I was bawling, fighting him, and I remember Beth, the blonde girl with freckles I was always chasing, she was standing by the school flagpole watching me, and I was embarrassed, humiliated. Why he spanked me for two blocks I never figured out. But now that I'm a Dad, knowing what it's like to adore a kid and want to take his life all at same time, I think I wasn't the only one in trouble that day.

But he caught me lying when I was twelve, thirteen. Dad wasn't above spanking me even then, and he always used my own belt, which I thought was mean, but it worked. Modified my behavior. But it was hard on him, and on this day, knowing I'd lied to him again, he was tired, and disappointed, and all out of that mad energy that parents use to fuel their discipline. So we sat out behind the house and talked.

The lie itself was idiotic, as all lies are, about taking the trash out, when I didn't, and I don't even know what kind of lie you could tell about the trash, but he wondered what we were going to do about it, and in the end I was given mercy. It was a passage of a kind, and I never got spanked again. I wish I could say it was the end of lying as well, but that wouldn't be the truth, though I did reserve all future lies for big moments only.

The only problem is that when I grew up, I realized all moments are just that—big ones.

~

I'm late for class. Maybe it'll be good for me to talk about mercy. Or at least to pray for some.

Blessed are the merciful for they shall receive mercy.

Connie and Sara sit in the front row, next to Donna McCowan.
Three brave souls, I think, and though my short breath is due to
Connie, my mind is actually full of Donna. She came back, after all,
and in the craziness of the week, it seems like our session last Monday
afternoon was years ago. Now here she is, dressed up, anxiously looking around, almost as if someone was coming.

I smile at her, ignoring the other two, trying to anyway, and
Donna beams back at me.

∼

Katy Teller McCowan, Donna's daughter, a tall, plain girl, with
long, stringy hair, and long spider legs, went to our old high school,
but she was younger by almost ten years, so I never knew her. They
say Katy fell for an English teacher named Mr. Pullen, which I never
understood cause this man was forty by then, had a mole on his chin
with a hair sticking out of it, and he didn't exactly smell "fresh," as
my wife would say. Katy apparently got old in a hurry giving birth to
a baby just after her eighteenth birthday. She'd gone to stay with her
grandma in Alabama during the pregnancy, didn't graduate, and gave
the child up for adoption to a couple who lived in Florida. But most
people in Ruin didn't hear the full story until years later, and it was a
scandal even then. The fact that the unwanted child had been born
with Downs syndrome made it worse, and the whole affair made
Donna's decision to get away from her life more reasonable, more tol-
erable, though no more forgivable. The teacher left town—without
Katy—and the young girl sat down on her parent's couch, though her
mom was gone, and stayed there almost five years.

Donna found her spiritual side, her soul, and her calling that year
after the baby came and went, so she said she had no choice but to

abandon the McCowan name and house after 22 years. She left in honor of a deeper life, in search of someone who could help that new-found soul grow. I think the guy's name was Custer. Katy, and Thomas and Landon (Katy's two younger brothers) stayed with their dad Carroll, and he worked hard at one of those shoe repair places, and drank beer like water, and though he was never an alchoholic (so he said), he raged around that couch with the cutting skills of a saw. While the boys ate cereal watching late night TV, Katy caved in, crawling to a place inside her head so far away she might as well have moved to Rhode Island. The boys left, came back, and Thomas served time for driving while being like his father, while Landon divorced and remarried, and now his second divorce is in the works. Katy's been in therapy for several years, and though she comes to class once in a while, sitting here with her Bible open, her eyes tend to drift and shut. Her skin's worn paper thin, and the scars of these poor souls sit just under her closed eyelids. Carroll's liver quit this past winter, and the doctors couldn't coax it back to work, and a December warming softened the walk to the grave. Donna came to the funeral, and wept, and wept, and at the graveside, after the service, standing next to Katy, she tried to lay her face on Katy's shoulder, but Katy flinched and moved away. Donna stood there, bent over, sobbing, as Katy climbed in the limo and shut the door.

This past Monday, months later, Donna walked into my office, unscheduled and unannounced, and we talked. A bony, bent woman of 54, she looks 70. Custer's gone, and she hates the north, and after being away almost ten years, she wants to come home, if there is one. But her soul's tired, she said, too tired to jump through religious hoops. Just talk with me, she said, and she spoke of her son Thomas as a boy, his easy way with sports, and how his kindness seemed to come out of thin air. She didn't understand her other son Landon, either; his self-absorption, his constantly failing relationships. It was all such a mystery to her. Carroll lost himself somewhere in his 30's, she said, and she said that Katy frustrated her, so bright and so stupid all at the same time. She herself had always wanted to be more than she was—smarter, prettier, better with conversation, especially with her husband, but none of that ever came. She said she woke up the morning after Katy came home from Alabama, home from the baby scandal, and Katy shouting at her all day, screaming at her, that Donna should have taken the baby, that she should've done something.

But when she woke up, staring at the ceiling, at 11:52, almost lunch, she realized she hated them all.

She said it seemed honest, and right, embracing that hate, because it was clean, and manageable, and gave her a course of action that was simple enough. Five months later, she lived in another state, with another man's legs on hers in the night, and now . . . my God . . . she said over and over, what will I do, Cyrus? What will I do?

I thought, prodigal son, and I started in, but the prodigal son story doesn't always help. It's one thing to squander your money, and your own soul, and sit in a pig pen with slop in your teeth, but her life was no Bible story, she said, and to squander a family, and a Katy . . . it's not the same. Where's the Downs baby I should have accepted as my grandchild? I've killed all my home's possible goodness and sent my children to hell. She put her hand to her mouth. Oh God, she said. I sat looking at her, watching her body break. Her eyes were stars burning out, and I wondered what Jesus was going to say. Where would mercy play out here? Who would forgive, and how would it begin? And what difference would it make?

The years are gone.

And here I stand, Sunday again, to speak the mercy of Jesus.

Donna asked me if there was any hope. Any mercy in the dark, any let-up in the pain.

We prayed. Sometimes it all seems absurd. Sometimes, the hard steel-edge of reality seems to mock the God of simple sinners like Donna and myself. How can we hang on to love, when the storms of hell come against us? Donna McCowan lay before God, and it seemed absurd that he would speak. But he does speak, and she prayed, and he heard, and on Monday afternoon, in my little cramped office, full of books and sermons, and philosophies and theologies, this woman's ravaged life was redeemed again. Seventy times seven is the promise, and in her brokenness, in her weeping, in her lost soul, somehow, the God of the prodigal son story came to a prodigal daughter and there was mercy given.

Donna called Katy, and they talked, shortly, and to the point.

Forgive me, sweet girl. I forgive you, mom.

～

And now, it's Sunday, and Donna turns her head, and Katy is in the door. The class barely breathes. Donna is standing and walking toward her girl, and coffee cups are still, no ice tinkles, and a hush covers the room. Donna and Katy hesitate, then slowly embrace, holding each other in that tight grief-laden hold-me-up-please hug, and others are there now, and we're praying, laughing, shaking hands all around, wiping eyes. The electric buzz of grace is in the air like a fire, and I can barely speak. Jesus sits on the front row, too, next to Connie, next to Sara, next to Donna and Katy. His mercy spreads like the proverbial ripple in the pond, and for the McCowans of the next century, if there be any, there is hope yet. There is mercy yet.

～

Dear God,

Somewhere, a man hits a woman, and a woman dies, and the man's life is severed, and a child is dropped from a killing height, and papers are signed, death certificates and warrants, and sin rolls through the earth like a wave of hell, and that anyone smiles is a miracle of humility and grace that only you can author. Lord, how forgiveness begins is absurd, and hidden, a mystery that I run toward, and from, and you are that mystery, and I stand dumb, mute, astonished, like a brick cut in half, chiseled into a begging shape by the rough hand of time, and discipline, and love. Oh, Lord, leave me, for if I see your face, or its shadow, or even if I sit with your word in my lap, I die, for I am sin, I am wrong, I am pride, I am lust, I am the seven deadly sins, and they are tattoos on my soul, full of spikes and piercings and skull's bones, and how can you stand the hate hidden within? Is love this deep? Is blood, even the Christ's, enough to clean, enough to slake even my deadly thirst, and praise is due the one who replies to this accusation, and says, yes, it is enough, my blood is enough, and my love is that deep, and there is nothing that can separate me from you, for you are mine, and are mine forever.

An unworthy servant, I bow.

Thanking Jesus, and in his name,
Amen

. . . *the soft hem of grace* . . .

I rarely take naps, especially in my own bedroom, but I need to hide. Lunch, like the rest of this day, was bizarre. Connie cooked, and we feasted. Ham cooked in pineapple and coke, with creamy french green beans and onions, fresh rolls and butter, smooth mashed pota-toes without so much as one lump, and a great corn casserole with just a touch of jalapeno. During the meal, Connie sat at the end of the table, across from me, passing food first to Richard and Wayne, then back across to Sara, constantly asking me for whatever I had at my end, and I couldn't help but notice her depression lifting. She looked happier, prettier, than she had all week, and from the way she treated Sara and the boys, I began to think our morning had been a trick of imagination, a hang-over of sorts, left over sexual energy from the wedding.

Who has energy for sex? Lying on my bed, the apricot pie still settling in, I can hear the guys outside, fighting over whether Richard was in bounds or out when he caught the ball. The girls ran up to Wal-mart, and I'm drifitng, dozing just a bit, when I catch myself thinking of how long it's been for Sara and me, since we last made love. I can't pin it down exactly, and I start wondering whether Connie has changed in bed, and how it would be to make love to her now, after all these years. I hardly notice that the current of my thought is shifting, running the wrong direction, and I'm surprised that I remember the feel of her lips on mine, and I have to smile, even after twenty years.

∾

Grace is bigger than you think, Jesus says, and my bedroom is gone. Instead, he and I sit at the bank of a river, about 20 or 30 feet across, with water unlike any I've seen. Flowers grow deep below the surface, at least twenty feet down. Yellow and red roses, and white lilies, and bunches of bluebonnets, which I take to be a joke, and he laughs and says, you like that? And I say, yeah. This gold water moves like blonde hair in the wind, framed by the sun, but it glints, and sparks fly, but gently. It's wet, and cool, and I take a drink, and he says, that's fine, go ahead. I wait for the colossal God-things he will say today, but he is strangely quiet.

The air is blank in this place, and brilliant, and there is no need to breathe, and something like heaven is poring into my skin, and my heart is slowing, slowing, and where are we, but beyond, beyond, but here, so much here, so alive. I'd swear Jesus the Christ is weeping beside me. I can't fathom how weeping might exist in such a place as this, which must be a dream, I guess, but there are no words, no words, just sheer beauty, like dew on new petals, like first kisses from sons, like colors crying love in the night, and beauty like nothing defined, everything known. *All* paradigms are shifted, banished, and new is all, but full of old goodness, and poems, and memories like soft beds, full of companions lost and loves never found, and here is home, and even the soft, crying sound of a Christ is music in this place, which must be the palace of God.

The weeping stops, but he still hurts, and I can see it is a deep thing, a grinding in his gut, and he says he can't show me all he'd like to, but that Sam is right, in some ways, you know, about that hell thing. Such an idea is horrific, profane in the presence of this glory, this vast lushness, this towering beauty. You can't know how hard it is, he says. Cyrus, you can't grasp my love for you, for your deep, true being, the one I birthed and shaped in your mother's womb. How deep that being is, and ever deeper is my love, and my Father's. It's an old story, but take all the love, all the love you've lost, and I interrupt, and say, is that a lot? Jesus tells me all love lost is hell, and I say, true enough. He makes a ball with his hands, and begins to slowly turn the imaginary ball round and round. Take all your grief, Cyrus, he says, and roll it into a ball, and throw it down a tall Everest mountain, and imagine that that ball will pick up other grief, like a simple snowball. It grows. The mountaintop is a universe wide, and all people of all nations of all times stand together, hurling lost love down the sheer cliffs of time. All these balls of grief and loss become worlds, which become galaxies, which become infinities and forevers unimaginable, and they grow without end. That is my grief, that is my loss, in knowing that the end must come, and the enemy will take his share of my people. Each death brings the day closer. He closes his eyes. Goosebumps rise on the skin of his arms. Tell me, I say, and he shakes his head, once, quickly. There are horrors you cannot know, he says. If I told you, your soul would be no more. Trust me. Cyrus, pray, and give my grace. Listen to me. Be merciful, Cyrus, and make that mercy known, for not all will touch the soft hem of grace.

A kiss wakes me. A gentle kiss, from a princess, a fairy tale, and as the bed takes on her weight, creaking, she kisses me again, fully, open mouthed, and I am suddenly afraid to open my eyes.

. . . then he took a breath, and told the truth . . .

It's late now, 11:15 p.m.

Wayne just got to sleep. He got hurt playing football this after-noon, and we spent a good hour taping his sprained ankle. It's swollen, and he's proud of it, but I know it hurts. I heard him crying in the shower. He told me it was okay, though, because he'd never had to use crutches before, so he was looking forward to tomorrow. Maybe at school he could get Mary, the cute 12-year-old (you know, Dad, the one with the hair and the dresses—his description) to carry his books. I said I hope so. At which point he started asking me about my junior high days, and girlfriends, and given the kind of day I'd had, I said no way, and goodnight.

~

I never heard from Joy Moore.

Sara and I are sitting on the porch, watching Connie walking in the field across the street. Sara's half-heartedly punching my leg, try-ing to get me to talk, but I don't want to. She and Connie spent most of the evening with Emily Firestone. They got home about 10:30, and when I asked how it went and what they talked about, Sara said don't ask.

Who can tell about my wife? She's irritable and touchy, almost angry. On the other hand, her lovemaking this afternoon was ardent, and strong, or to put it another way, lusty and hot, which, truth to tell, is not our usual way of doing things, especially with the boys in the vicinity.

Do you and Mike (Mike Firestone, Emily's husband) get along at all now, Sara asked me, and I said well enough, that when we had dinner this week, didn't you think it went well? She said, I guess, but that Mike seemed nervous around you, and I said well, Mike and I talked in the back yard, and it was iffy . . . but things are okay. He's struggling with his job; sales are down. He told me there's never enough money, and that Emily wants to have kids, but he's afraid they're not secure enough. Sara wants to know what I told him. Nothing, I tell her. I just said you can never afford kids, so you might as well have them now anyway. He told me one might be okay, that he might be able to make that work.

"Is that all you talked about?"

I look at her, at the focus in her face, like she's digging into me. What is with the intensity running through my house today? I say, yeah, that's all. That's all we talked about.

She knows, of course—I'm lying.

Mike and I had a terrible falling out several summers ago. He and Emily got involved with a group of people I didn't approve of much, a parachurch group that taught and advocated a high degree of accountability, which is good—in most cases. As a result, Mike decided to confront me about some things. About my giving for one. He wanted to know if I tithed, because he was sure I didn't. (He had a friend on the finance committee.) He also had questions about my kids, and my discipline, and wanted to know what my problems were with lust, and how I dealt with it. Who was keeping me account-able—that sort of thing. The rumors about my behavior with my wife on the porch were shameful, he told me, and then he moved on to evangelism, and wondered if I took Matthew 28 seriously, because he didn't think the church was growing nearly fast enough.

Good questions, I guess, but it got old.

Mike's a big, handsome guy, well built at 6' 3"; the kind of man people listen to. How our relationship got to be the big stink it was I can't remember, but a few families ended up leaving the church. It sounds absurd thinking about it now, but it was a harsh time. He was on fire for the Lord, he said, and Emily's a strong woman, and loud, and one Sunday morning, after the final amen, he jumped up and shouted that he thought this church needed some confession and purging and he was calling on the elders of the church to make things right. Things on both sides had been building for awhile, and several families shouted back, and I was dumbfounded and horrified. I'd never seen people out and out yelling in the sanctuary, and that afternoon, as he and I talked, he got hot, and I got hot, and I think that's where my reputation for swearing got started. I'm just embarrassed about it all now. The cultish folks are gone, and we're still here, and my giving still isn't quite 10%, and I thought I was okay with the lust thing—until today, that is. Things have thawed some between Mike and me—we say hi and how 'bout those Cowboys, but until Tuesday night we'd said nothing of substance, nothing that might recall those days of open hostility.

~

When we got to their house, Emily immediately dragged Sara into the kitchen, and Mike and I stood in the living room. He was cordial, and smiling—and obviously unnerved. It was odd. He seemed upset, skittish, as if he was afraid, downright scared, but hiding it, and I knew this wasn't going to be just about dinner, or us leaving, but that there was an unknown here. I wasn't sure I was glad to be the one to land in the middle of it.

After Mexican food—burritoes and chalupas and tacos not nearly as hot as I like them—Mike and I wandered out in the backyard, and I commented on the new swing set, and Mike said he bought it last year for Emily, as a kind of symbol, a promise that soon they'd begin to try. We heard Emily and Sara continuing their conversation about the evils of child birth, moving to the front of the house, and Mike turned and looked me dead in the eye and said he had a problem he needed to get right with God, and for reasons he didn't understand, he knew I was the man he had to tell. And I thought, oh boy, and the next 15 minutes were intense, like Mike could be, and his eyes burned white hot, not with anger, but with shame.

It began when Mike finally stammered out that he liked to look at naked women, and I smiled and thought who doesn't, but then he went white, and started shaking. I lost the smile, and kept looking him in the eye. He was close to tears, so I made sure he saw in my eyes that I wasn't going to damn him right then and there, and finally, he went on. I knew he was in new territory, and though I had heard confessions of this kind before, our history together, our hot and cold wars over rules and behaviors added the shame of hypocrisy to the deal, and I was, in my own way, frightened for him. But I listened. I held my ground, and told him to go on, tell me, and he said the naked female body was amazing, and that as a young man, he'd justified it as looking at an art form, and that he still thought there was some truth to that. I said yes. But he started shaking again, and turning red. The silence worried me after a minute, and I wanted to prompt him, start taking guesses at what his problem was, 'cause I figured it was a variation on a theme. But I decided to keep still, to let him tell his story. I waited, quiet, like Mike.

He told me that in the past three years—then he took a breath, and told the truth—that in the past nine years, he'd been to Dallas alone, perhaps a total of fifty or sixty times. Business trips, sales trips, and that on every one, on every overnight trip, he'd . . . used (what other word is there—consumed?) pornography. He'd also always managed to slip off to a gentleman's bar, usually a topless place, though he liked it better when the girls were completely nude, in different parts of the city, and he said he always thought of Jimmy Swaggart, and he always half expected television cameras to find him. But then he figured nobody was really that interested in him, in some sales guy from Ruin. But he always wore a hat, he said, and dark glasses 'til he got in the door, and he never talked to the girls who wanted to dance for him in the corner, on the couches, and usually, after realizing what an absurd thing he was doing, he'd somehow manage to keep his wits about him, watch for maybe an hour or two, and leave, sweaty and shamed, but—and this was the weird part—strangely calm.

I sat like stone, and he went on, telling me he couldn't keep it up, that he could feel his desire escalating, wanting more, and that it had to stop. That the last time, he'd been to this place out on 635, late at night, past midnight, and he'd gotten in a conversation with one of the girls, who told him her name was Lisa, and I thought, man, the last thing I want to know is this girl's name—*do not tell me her name*. She did a table dance for him, then another, and I thought *I don't want to hear this*, and that after she finished, she whispered in his ear, said she was about to get off work, and would he like to . . ., and he said okay. He said he gave her a hundred-dollar bill, and she said wait here, that she'd be back. But that when she'd returned, fully clothed, and they walked out to his car, he'd panicked and said no, he couldn't, he just couldn't. But she kissed him hard, pushed him up against the car door, and he had to shove her off, too hard, and she'd fallen and scratched her hands in the gravel. She started yelling at him, at which point he said he jumped in his car, and bar-relled out of the parking lot as hard as he could go, taking out a trash can, throwing dirt and rubber, praying he'd make it home without killing himself.

He said he drove 90 miles an hour all the way to Ruin, and couldn't explain to Emily why he was home at five o'clock in the morning, or the dent in the fender, so he lied. She'd never know about the hundred dollars.

He knew God could forgive him, but that he was afraid he was going to lose his life, his sweet Emily, and that it felt like a demon. He wanted to know did I believe in that sort of thing. I said we'd bet-ter pray, and we did, hard. His shaking finally stopped, and he want-ed to cry, but wouldn't, he said because he wasn't ready for Emily to know. He said he wanted to come to my office and I said, fine, how about Monday, and he said, fine. His face cleared a bit, and the ground seemed to take a breath, and he and I stood silent for five minutes, knowing this was holy ground, this place of confession. Thank you, he said. I said, you're welcome, and we went back in the house, back to our wives.

◞

I saw Mike this morning after worship, and he couldn't meet my eyes. I worried that he might wonder if he'd made a mistake telling me, and as I touched his shoulder, I could feel his strain. I took him into my office, and we prayed again. Afterwards, we talked. I assured him nothing he told me would be repeated, and for the first time, he released his pain, and wept, wept like a baby, and I wanted to join him, but I couldn't. I prayed while he cried, and after a minute, he started taking long breaths, settling down, his body letting go. A quiet crept in, and there seemed to be no shadows, only sunlight. But when we left the office, it was starting to sprinkle outside, and the air was unusually cool, unusually clean. Mike said he felt clean, for the first time in years, and when he held me in his arms, I knew that whether I stay or go, a deep thing was beginning with this man. A friendship, a bond born of a lonely, lonely pain, anonymous and terrible. It's a gift to me, perhaps a parting gift of healing, and joy, and maybe Jesus will come again to both of us in that office tomorrow. Mike's scared to come, but he wants to, and he'll be here at four.

I forget sometimes how brokenness destroys hate. How it makes barriers crumble. How it sets foolishness aside. Such cleanliness as Mike felt today is rare as desert rain, and I praise God for the occasional chance to see the redemption of Christ up close.

I will miss them, if such chances go away.

We had the porch painted this week. I guess we're getting the place ready to sell, if we need to. The smell of the paint in the dark spoils the evening air, I think, and Sara can't sleep. She often falls asleep on my shoulder out here on the porch, and she's leaning on me even now, but she's restless. Oh well, she says, and now she's up walking in the yard, pulling a weed here and there, bending down in the dirt, the wind making her pull her robe close. Connie joins her, and they hunker in the dirt picking goatheads. Sara's long fingers pull at the stalks while Connie talks in a low voice, again wanting privacy, and as I watch them, there is no doubt that Sara is by far the most gracious woman I know. If not the most beautiful.

She's convinced that leaving Ruin is a foregone conclusion, a done deal. I think she's excited about the idea, though she hides it like a pro. She's hoping we go north—to Washington, or maybe

Idaho, and who knows? Maybe I'm hoping, too. Maybe I'll stop preaching for awhile, learn to cook Italian and Chinese, do wood-working, take up writing. It's an appealing thought, starting a whole new life, but it scares me, and I don't think that's what God's telling me anyway. I also worry about Richard and Wayne, all the transition, the new school, the toughness of finding the right kind of friends.

The truth is, I can't say it yet, can't get the words out of my mouth. I can't say I'm leaving Ruin, mostly because I'm starting to see that if I do, it will have little—if anything—to do with a congre-gational vote. Forces are at work here, forces I can't predict or con-trol, and not knowing the outcome, not knowing how the mystery turns out—*a month from now . . . or less . . . well . . .*

It's getting harder to take by the day.

~

The thought of not unfolding the word of God to the people makes me want to die.

October 5

He always ends up where he shouldn't be . . . saying things he shouldn't say.

It's shameful.

Wanda Pursival, as told to Jack Simons
Administrative Committee

. . . *the wrong tie to preach in* . . .

Ours is a sick house this morning. I should hang an old-fashioned quarantine sign on the door, but nobody's coming over anyway. It's just past 7:00 a.m. and the house is quiet, sleeping, even Connie. I'm up to see how I feel, cause I spent most of yesterday in the bathroom, throwing up or with the runs. I don't know if this stomach bug will let me get through a Sunday's schedule or not. I called Jack yesterday and said I'd try, but so far, my legs are wobbly, and the room doesn't want to sit still. I'm propped up here in my tee shirt and shorts, coffee in hand, trying to be steady. A dry piece of toast just popped up.

Wayne and Richard both have fevers, low-grade, up and down. They complained all day that their bodies ached, and Richard coughed all night. To top it off, Sara's got the cramps, and though she can't say why, in recent months, they've gotten worse. She's beginning to spend at least one day of her period in bed, and since she made it through yesterday, it looks like today's the day.

≈

The dry toast is awfully dry, but maybe it'll settle my stomach. I need to keep something down. I'm bent over in the chair, elbows on knees. Toast crunching is the only sound.

If I didn't preach, I wouldn't have to get out of bed on sick days, or well days either, for that matter. I stop chewing. There's a new thought, and the sheer joy of being unemployed for a few weeks makes me consider turning in my resignation on my way to the doctor's office. A happy, fleeting notion.

I wander out to the porch to grab the paper, and have to lean on the doorframe for a minute to keep from falling headfirst into the yard. I'm feeling pretty iffy about being able to do it all this morning. But I told Jack I'd call by 7:30 and it's just ten after, so I'll give it a few more minutes.

Richard's cough is back, and it's barky, so I check on him. He's still asleep, and when I mosey back into the kitchen, Connie says hi, how am I feeling, and would I like another cup of coffee. She's wearing a short robe, tied at the waist, but loose, and I say sure, and good morning, doing my best to avoid noticing her legs.

Good sense returns to me, and I hide behind the paper.

It's all bad news, she says, pouring black into my cup. So it is, I mumble back, but I want her to leave me alone, so my reply sounds like a final word, the end of a long conversation. I think, just let me read about OJ and Whitewater on my own. But persistency is one of her character flaws. She's sitting down now, kitty-corner from me, wanting to talk. She asks me if I'm feeling better, and I say I'm okay, that I'll live, and we go back to the quiet game. I turn over to the sports, looking to see what time the Cowboys play. Now she asks me if I've talked to Dirk lately. I'm tempted to ignore the question, but I give her a simple answer, that I've tried to call him several times, but no luck.

"Do you want me to leave you alone?"

The answer to that is of course, yes, but I put down the paper. I'm sick, I'm tired, and I find myself looking at her, guard down, openly admitting with my eyes that a strange thing is going on between us, and that it's almost time to speak it out loud and deal with it. I say the words simply.

"You probably should."

The air thickens, a tangible shift. Her eyes get teary, and they have a question in them, and an answer, and she flushes red, turns her face away. I instantly realize I've made a mistake. She's seen what I didn't mean for her to see, and didn't mean to say. I've spoken the attraction between us, and now it has a life. In this kind of moment, a ringing phone sounds like a bomb.

∼

"Jack, I said I'm okay. I feel fine. I'll be there. . . . okay . . . yeah, thanks."

Sara wanders into the kitchen as I replace the receiver.

"Liar."

I know, I tell her. She heard me tell Jack it was probably food poisoning, that I wasn't contagious. I want to make all the Sundays I can, I say, watching Sara rub Connie's shoulders, while Connie wipes her eyes, saying thanks Sara, that feels good. Sara yawns, and says so you think God'll forgive you, huh? I can tell she's wanting to feel okay, too, wanting to fend off her cramps, but as she leans over the cabinets, I'm sure her day is going to be rough.

I help Sara back to bed, and Connie stands in the door. Connie says not to worry about the boys today, that she'll take care of them. Sara says thanks, and rolls over, pulling the covers close under her chin. I sit on the edge of the bed, stroking her cheek, watching her frown in concentration, watching her fight off the tight grip of her insides. I say I love you.

Sara smiles, eyes still closed. She snuggles her cheek against the back of my hand, whispering.

"Now go away."

∼

I walk back to the kitchen to get my coffee. Connie's scrambling an egg, buttering her toast.

I tell her I'm hitting the shower, that I've got to get dressed. She nods without speaking. I linger, and finally, she looks up, eyes blank. I glance at the floor, and head down the hall.

The hot water feels like baptism, makes me think I can be clean again. I'm a fast dresser, and frankly, I'm trying to get out of the house as quickly as I can. I've got my pants and shirt on already.

They're clean and pressed. The shirt's stiff, and that rich, heavy-starch rigidity makes me feel classier than I am. Helps me feel better. I like ties, too, and this one has Gene Kelly on it, in black and gray, and he's singing in the rain. It's probably the wrong tie to preach in, but it perks me up, so here goes.

~

It's blustery, and the mesquite leans away to the south, courtesy of an easy cool wind. Clouds pile along, and I'm surprised there's no rain. Pulling out of the driveway, nausea rolls over me, and thinking I'm going to throw up, I stop the car. I open the door, hang my head out the side, but nothing's coming up, so I close the door and go again, heading down Curtain, praying for God to do some simple healing here.

Now it's raining. I lean over the wheel, push a tiny lever, and drive on, the wipers slapping at the rain.

Blessed are the pure in heart
for they shall see God.

My hands steady as I lean on the podium, but my stomach is still in the car.

It's a small group today, and I guess sickness is a guest in more homes than one. Of course, the Andersons are in Houston. Bill Buber says he got a call from Goose, from MD Anderson, and that little Kari is pretty sick with the chemo. Losing her hair, the whole bit, but Bill says Goose sounded hopeful, and that the doctors there say her cancer can be beaten in some cases, but no guarantees. We immediately bow our heads and say a special prayer for Kari.

After the amen, I take stock of the class. Looking around, I see the McCowans aren't here, and I doubt the Goods will ever come back. Reggie Appleby is out of town, and Richard Bauser says Maxine isn't here, says her back is out again, and she'll be seeing the chiropractor several times this week, so if we could pray, it'd be good. To which Will and Roman reply they wouldn't pay good money to see one of those guys, and Cassandra Smith, the new girl pregnant with Judith, calls back that she swears by her chiropractor, and as the banter gets more heated, I notice Skip and Lacey aren't here either. Cassandra's husband Jeff comes in wiping his hands, and so it's the Smiths, the Mitters, the Bubers, and Will and Roman and Serena, and Gwen and Dexter and Richard. I remember Mattie May called me yesterday, and said Mrs. Eric had another of her spells and fell. She didn't break anything, though, and they think it might have been a third stroke. Tom Martin's in the back, leaning back in the chair, watching the sun create one of those rare moments in Texas when it shines and rains together. I glance outside, and the Black and Blue's out there, but there's no bark this morning; he's just walking, headed downtown.

I read the text out loud and just as I finish, Mike and Emily Firestone stick their heads in, wondering if they're not too late. No,

not at all, everybody says, and they take chairs about halfway toward
the front. Mike smiles at me, sighing.

~

A man needs a friend. And surprisingly, I may be in the process
of finding one.

Mike and I met on Monday. We talked of women, and pornography. I told him that when I was five, I saw my first Playboy magazine,
and was honestly amazed at the beauty. He said he was eight when it
happened to him, but he thought it was mostly gross. And he said
when he was ten, at a relative's in Missouri, he came across some single black and white photos, small shots of naked women in curious
positions. He thought they were ugly at the time, but perversely fasci-
nating. I came back with a story about being seventeen, getting into
a peep show place, and the first image on the screen was so shocking
and disorienting I literally ran from the place. I tried to describe the
image, but I couldn't get the words out.

We chuckled as the conversation stalled. His face was taut,
straining. I'm sure mine was the same. It's not easy to talk about.

I told him I didn't know any man who hasn't struggled with this
stuff at one time or another. Mike described his hidden life of buying magazines, and hiding them, and how one time he was up late,
and had several magazines spread out in front of him, and Emily
had walked through the next room, half-asleep. Thankfully, she'd
hardly glanced up as she went by. She'd asked him what he was
doing, and he'd said, nothing. She never came in the room. Mike
said he'd always been afraid, but that God had been good to him,
more gentle than he deserved. He quoted to me about the Spirit
convicting men of sin, and said he guessed that was the deal, and I
said, yeah I guess so. He said he felt lucky he'd been spared any public embarrassment, and that the incident with the dancer had
scared him, scared him out of his mind. He said it was time to be
done with it.

Oh, if it were only that simple.

That's when he broke.

A man weeping his guts out over moral failure—a wonder seldom seen. I guess they get it at AA meetings maybe, but in my years
of counseling, too many men like to be tough confessors. They pray
to God for forgiveness, stuff it in their front pants pockets like so
much petty cash, and walk out ready once again to take on the world.
Maybe it's an American thing. Pioneers, and self-sufficiency and all
that. But often, these guys drop into the same old patterns that
brought them to their knees in the first place. And then they pray
the same prayer again. And then they're surprised when they wake
up and find their lives are gone.

Mike wept and wept. He hates his guilt. We talked of this faulty
thing called being a man. How the promise of youth didn't exactly
work out, did it? Why wasn't Emily enough, he wanted to know?
Why wasn't prayer enough? And why did he not want a child? It did-
n't seem to be okay to not want a kid. But he was afraid of losing his
freedom, he said, losing the special time, the alone time he had with
Emily. They fought about it constantly, he said. Two years ago, she'd
skipped her birth control for several months, without telling him,
which led to an early-term miscarriage they'd kept quiet. He'd found
her sobbing in the bathroom, bleeding on their new blue and white
tile. He carried her in his arms to the car, and in the emergency
room, all she could say was she was sorry, she was so sorry.

He was angry for a long time, and their sexual lives became part
of the battleground. Sad, huh, he said. They'd even gone to therapy
a couple of times, but frankly, he said, we both have issues we don't
want to deal with. Now her period brought it all on every month, and
that strain, month-in, month-out was killing him. She cries a lot, and
now their sex life is dull, rare, and he's lost. I love Emily, he said, and
then he had to stop and cry some more. Finally he went to say but I
have this hunger, this hunger, it's a wanting something I thought I
would find in her. But now, I don't think I will. I don't think I'll find
it in Emily, he said. He wanted to know if that made sense to me.

Unfortunately, it makes perfect sense, though I might not admit
it in a conversation with Sara.

Mike's work isn't great, either. Sales is okay, he said, but selling
time seems absurd. The radio and television world all seems that way,

he said, people doing commerce in fabrication, falseness, selling lit-tle but personality and sex. I asked him what he really wanted to do. He shook his head, laughing, but his laughter got cut short when it almost turned into a sob. He sucked in a deep breath, and looked out the window.

"I used to want to be a pilot."

Mike said he had a buddy in high school named Todd, and Todd's dad had a biplane. When they were seniors, he'd taken Mike up in the old ragwing—that's what Mike called it—and he'd fallen in love with flying. He told me about trying to pull the money together for flight school, and that far-off, familiar, I-used-to-have-a-dream look came into his eyes. He talked about the pictures he had in his dorm room, old planes built in the 30's and 40's, Veronica Chiefs and Champs, I thought he said, but he laughed and said, no, it's a-e-r-o-n-i-c-a, Aeronica. He said those old planes, if they had high-time air frames, which just meant they'd flown for lots of hours, could be gotten cheap. If they were rebuilt right, he said, they could go for years. (I could tell by the way he said it he still wanted one.) But his folks didn't have the money for the school, and the banker he knew wouldn't lend it to him. Said there'd be a glut of pilots soon, so it was a bad risk.

He said he didn't want to be an airline pilot anymore, but he couldn't think of anything better that to just be a Sunday after-noon guy with an old Champ or a Cessna, with time enough to bore holes in the sky, and maybe take his kids up when it was "severe clear," and you could see forever. Mike said he thought if he could get good at sales, maybe he'd make enough money some-day to have a Cessna, maybe a 150, and learn to fly it. But that the money he and Emily have saved so far needs to go to the baby, if there ever is one.

So he said he knew that these days, he'd probably never get to do it. And what makes it hard, he said, is that it seems like none of the dreams I used to have will ever even come close to coming true. There's that wanting something again, I said, and he said, yeah, exactly.

~

I asked him if he had any friends.

Oh, guys to hang out with, he said, guys to get a beer with occasionally and maybe play cards or dominoes. He said he likes Brett Mitter and they talk sometimes, but that no, if he knew what I meant, he didn't have any of those kind of friends.

He took a breath, and said by the way, I've gotten into a bad habit of swearing, just by myself, but that he didn't even care anymore, didn't give a damn, in fact. He paused, waiting for me to react.

I grinned.

His shoulders dropped, and his voice opened a bit, saying he felt bad about that day in church when he yelled. He still didn't think those people were a cult, but he knew he'd been way out of bounds. He just felt like he failed constantly, and that Emily didn't see him the same way anymore, that though she loved him, she was losing respect for him, because he didn't always do what he said. Little things, he said, but he was starting to think this was the best he could do.

What do you think, Cyrus, and I told him I was hungry, and we got lunch together, and talked for two more hours, and I can't remember when I've felt closer to a man than that day with my new friend Mike.

When we got back from lunch, we prayed, and it was a good thing, a special thing, to not only know God's forgiveness, but to see it as well, to feel it deep in our bones. Mike and I decided to meet once or twice every week from now on, just to check up, to talk, to play a little basketball or catch, and as he drove away, I felt thankful and glad to know him. But then I remembered I had an appointment with a real estate agent that afternoon, and it tempered the mood, and I remember thinking, when was the last time I had an afternoon of nothing but joy?

~

He and Emily are holding hands, and turning back to my Bible, I give him a smile and a nod.

"The pure in heart shall see God."

I ask for a show of hands of all the pure hearts in the class. It's a mean beginning to the lesson, but I want to reassure myself I'm not the only one struggling. No hands are raised.

I ask what a pure heart looks like.

Bill raises his hand, and Richard Bauser does the same. Bill goes first with just what I'd expect from him. Don't drink, don't smoke, don't cuss, don't sleep with women other than your wife, don't kill, don't steal, don't think bad thoughts, whatever. Think on excellent things. Praise. *Voila.* Pure heart. See God. Done deal.

That's right, and now what else is there to say? Richard waves at me.

Richard and Maxine have been here a couple of years. I'm ashamed to say I don't know them very well. He's a free-lance photographer, and I think he shoots mostly portraits and weddings (he wanted to do Corey and Molly's, but they went with a guy from Dallas). Maxine runs a day-care in her home, and they still act like newlyweds, which is a pleasure to see anymore.

Richard says he thinks he knows what a pure heart looks like, that his dad had one.

He says his dad died in '83, of leukemia. Richard's from the south somewhere, and his nasal, tenor voice reminds me of Huckleberry Hound Dog. But it's a good, slow voice, easy to listen to, never in a hurry.

He says his dad's name was Joseph Bauser. He was an older dad, forty-five-years old when he came along, he said, and he pretty much raised him by himself. His mom died when he was two. She drowned on a vacation in Florida, got caught in an undercurrent of some kind. It was sad, he said, I'm sure, but I don't remember her.

Richard paused, and we waited. He took his time, and I wondered how long this was going to take.

He went on to say that his Dad, who most people called Ol' Joe, or Joey, grew up in Florida, with six other kids in a two bedroom house. But that it helped that Ol' Joe's pawpaw and maamaw lived next door. Richard said his grandfather and great-grandfather worked at a watch factory, while the two women raised the kids. Only problem was, they didn't know much about how to do it. Richard called them tough old birds, and said they were all as mean as the devil, or at least that's what his Aunt Burma told him.

"Aunt Burma was the youngest of the six kids, and she's the one who told me about my dad killing a man."

Roman's over there choking on his coffee, and Tom just sat his chair down. Heads swivel toward Richard.

Oh, he wasn't a bad man, and I guess that's my point, he tells us. He's a little surprised at our reaction, but frankly, that kind of news is both horrible and a welcome addition to the morning. It's certainly more interesting than anything I have to say. I mean, I don't know anybody else whose dad is a killer. Cassandra wants to know if he went to jail, and suddenly the room is buzzing, swarming over a bit of honey-sweet scandal, even though it was years ago, and has nothing to do with them or any part of Ruin.

I have to raise my voice a bit, saying hold it, hold it, let him finish, let him finish.

The room settles down, and Richard goes on to say that in my Dad's house, when he was growing up, discipline pretty much meant beating the kids. Ol' Joe got his share, he said, and it was amazing he didn't turn out worse than he did. Richard speculated for a minute on why his folks had been that way, saying maybe it was the squalor, though his Aunt Burma, now that she's thought about it, thinks they were probably a little low IQ, and just didn't know any better. But Richard says, and I'm not exactly sure why he's laughing about this, but he says that Aunt Burma's husband George says the IQ business is a crock and that they were just flat bad people. Ugly folks.

Why is he laughing?

But now he's getting to the good part of the story, saying his dad was 17 when he robbed the grocer. That he and a buddy did it on a lark, on a dare, and they both had guns, which his dad told him was just plain foolishness, that he'd never shot a gun in his life.

By this time, the class is rapt, listening intently, and I'm jealous, wishing I had a tragic story to tell.

Richard says the old grocer knew they were just kids goofing off, and wouldn't give them anything. Well, he says, his dad's friend got mad and shot the guy in the arm. And his dad, wanting to be like his friend, like dumb kids do, shot his gun, and he hit the guy square in the head. Killed him on the spot. The buddy ran, but the police found Ol' Joe sitting in the corner of the store over by the milk, crying his eyes out.

The class is still.

"He got 20 years."

∾

Pure in heart is hard to talk about. Hard to define. It's easy to say don't think bad thoughts, stay away from R-rated movies and pornography and CDs with foul language, but even as I listen to Richard's story unfold, I think he may have something else in mind.

∾

Richard's dad got out five years early on probation, and he said his mom came into the picture about a year later. He said they met at a bowling alley, married after six months, and moved to North Carolina when his parole was up. Then—surprise, surprise—I came along, he said. But then his mom died, leaving just the boys.

Bill wants to know how his dad got work after he got out.

He was a good church-goer by then, Richard says, a Catholic, mostly because of a priest that used to visit him in prison. After he got out, he met a Catholic in Jacksonville who was a cabinet maker, and he didn't care about his dad's record, and took him on as an apprentice. His dad discovered he had a real gift with wood. Making things, like wooden boxes, he said. Jewelry boxes, and recipe boxes, and what he used to think of as miniature hope chests, just to stick stuff in. Richard said they did pretty well, that there never was a lack of money. Truth is, there'd have been more money, he said, but Dad gave a lot to his parish, and there were always two or three widow women chasing him, and I think they got half his money before he died. Richard was smiling, but his voice betrayed him. He wasn't happy about the loss of the money. He said those ladies practically killed him with their roofing projects and plumbing projects—that sort of thing.

Roman says we've got some widows like that.

Richard's lost his way, but he plods on, saying he always wondered how old Joey had learned to be a dad. We played lots of catch, he says, went to I don't know how many minor league baseball games. The smell of hotdogs still makes me think of him—he could eat five at a game and still be hungry. Richard's talking softer now, more to himself than to us. Or he'd come home dead tired from work, lots of times after seven, and I'd be all over him, jumping on him, wrestling with him, kicking him. I was just a kid. Richard stops, runs his hand through his thick, dark hair. He says his dad never put him off, never told him no, just got down there with him, and it seems like to him they rolled in the floor from the time he was 4 'til he was 17.

The class respects the pause. We sit silent, looking at our shoes.

He says it was when he was 17 that he found out about everything. That it was Thanksgiving, and he makes the point that he didn't even know his dad had any brothers or sisters. He guessed that was his dad's way of putting his past behind him. But we were watching Detroit and Chicago play football on the TV, he says, around one o'clock when the doorbell rang. I answered it, and there was a little woman standing there, bundled against the cold, her eyes big as saucers. She said, who are you, and I said, who are you. She said her name was Karen Bauser, and that if my dad was Joseph Bauser from Florida, she was my aunt.

Richard's fully in the memory now, saying his dad came up behind me and said, in a real calm voice, hello Karen. And he stepped down—he was lots bigger than her—and they embraced, him bending way down over her, right there on the cold porch, and they both cried. It was the first time I ever saw him cry, he said. He stood up and said this is my sister, son. They hadn't seen each other in over thirty years.

"I heard the whole story that night."

The next day, Richard's saying, his voice starting to wind down toward the end of the story, the next day the three of them got in the car and drove all day, got a hotel, and the next day around noon pulled into the little town of Lawley, Florida, south of Jacksonville, a little inland. He says they pulled up to a grocery store that wasn't much bigger than a 7-11. That his dad said it hadn't changed much in all those years, and Aunt Karen said no it hadn't.

He says they walked in the store, and there was an older woman, maybe a little over fifty, working behind the counter. She said can I help you, and his dad said his name was Joseph Bauser. The woman said, you killed my grandfather. Ol' Joe took a big breath and said, yes, ma'am I did. And I'm here, he said, mostly to tell my son what a stupid thing it was to do. It was a mistake, and I've done my best to put it behind me, and live my life different than that. But since you're here—and Richard says he will never forget his dad's words or the look on his face—I must ask you, he said to the woman, if you can . . . and then he fumbled a little, and said, not look past my wrong exactly, but . . . maybe . . . somehow maybe . . . I don't know. Finally he took another big breath, and said I'm sorry ma'am. Please. Forgive me.

"The lady told him to go to hell."

≈

There wasn't much to say after Richard's story. I didn't know what the point was, except that pure hearts might be harder to see than we think, but Richard's face told us he knew his dad was a pure heart. We got through the rest of the hour, though coherency chose not to make an appearance, and I'm sure I don't know anymore than I did about what Jesus meant. But now class is over, and I'm shaking hands with Richard, thanking him, trying to head for worship. Mike waits for me, though Emily has gone on to the sanctuary, and we embrace, knowing well enough we're anything but pure. The three of us chat in the doorway another minute, then I have a thought, close the door, and we pray.

≈

God,

Pure in heart seems impossible. Miraculous if anything. You command these things that lie only in your hand to give. And we fail miserably. But you, O God, have promised that you will be our God, and that you will not test us in ways that will only destroy, and that you will be with us always. David was an adulterer and a murderer, and his heart was like yours. Pure might be a way to say it. Lord, if 1 sin like David, make my heart like his, so that it might be like yours. Help us to choose. In the moments of temptation, when money is needed and stealing is possible, when loneliness is my name and sexual sin is a real but fleeting comfort, when faithfulness seems impossible, and the hope of holiness a mockery in the face of real life, help us to choose you. We want to choose the pure, the righteous, the good.

God, we are blind, but we want to see you. Forgive us, and let us sin no more.

We receive your forgiveness as the free gift it is. We raise our eyes, and you are in the faces of our friends, our family. Blessed is your heart, O God, for it is pure, and it is only through your heart that we can see your face, and the face of your Son.

In faith,
In Jesus,
Amen.

. . . *obscenities I couldn't live with* . . .

My stomach's better, and it's dark now—it's after ten. I'm on the porch with a pint of Häggen-Daz and a cup of coffee, trying to fend off the tickle in the back of my throat. The boys are asleep and Sara moved to the couch where she's watching funny home videos on TV, though I'd bet by now, she's snoring. Connie said she needed a break and went to town to catch a movie. She asked me if I wanted to go. I said, uh . . . no.

~

Sara stayed in bed most of the day, and Connie was true to her word. Wayne and Richard like Connie, and they played misery all afternoon, running her ragged with requests for Seven-up and Ritz crackers. She read to them for hours, it seemed; first, a series of Arthur stories, then *Robinson Crusoe*, then *Black Beauty*, and a couple of Superman comic books. The boys ate it up, and so did she. Around five, Richard drifted off to sleep, and I stood watching Connie as she sat by his bed. *Black Beauty* lay across her lap. Her right arm was tucked under his, captured in a successful attempt at keeping her by his side. She was singing a lullaby I didn't recognize. I never knew she sang. It's a lovely voice.

~

I met with Jack and Roland for a few minutes after the evening service, and they asked me how I was doing, and I said fine, and they both said it was remarkable. I said what, and they said how I kept it up, the optimism and the attitude, what with my counseling schedule, and my teaching load, and the stress of . . . well, you know, they said. It was no wonder I was sick, and Sara and the boys, too, and I said thanks, that I was fine.

But I broke down, and cried, on the way home. It's been happening to me lately, though if Sara were to ask me why, I don't know that I could put my finger on it. I'll be lying in bed, or standing in my office, tears streaming down my face, and my mind is blank, not thinking dark, depressive thoughts, really—just crying. I know I'm in the process of losing something, and I know I don't want to lose it. But it's more than this job, this pastorate, and though Connie comes into my mind, I know there's nothing serious there, just an average, irritating distraction, a run-of-the-mill temptation, though its close proximity is getting under my skin. But I love my family, so that's not it, either.

Tonight, instead of going straight home, I went to the park, working back through my memory, back through the years. Losing feels like chaos, and often, the past is as hazy as the future. I couldn't sit still, so I put the car in drive and went wandering through late evening Ruin. I saw Francis and Joy going into the Baskin-Robbins, actually laughing together. Joy was holding the door for her mom, and I smiled, and my mind cleared just enough to let memory through. I went by the two-story hospital, such as it is, where Wayne and Richard were born. I remembered Sara getting broadsided on the corner near Second and Pine, and the guy wanted to sue, but didn't. A bookkeeper's office front reminded me of that terrible audit four years ago. I drove by my favorite coffee shop, the Grape Inn, where I went with Alex that first time, and the Eckerd's next door where Francis works. It got late, but I circled around and came back down the road we came into town on, laughing at that silly flatbed, and the damage to the old sideboard. The story's endearing now, because it reminds me of a beginning time. As I made my way back to the house, I saw that beginning time and a coming ending time melting into each other, and when I pulled into the drive, I imagined that house again with candles, and a couple dancing on the porch.

~

Now, alone out here, I'm thankful that God is dealing with me kindly, with miraculous softness.

But I have to say—I sure hurt.

My pint of chocolate is half gone.

I wonder what flavor Francis Moore got. When I saw Joy, I almost stopped, but I know how rare it is for the two of them to share these kind of moments, and there was a pint of good stuff at home, so I figured I'd just leave them alone.

One more tablespoon, and I'll stop.

Joy Moore. The name makes me laugh. I tease her, call her More Joy. On her 33rd birthday, a few short weeks ago, Joy found Jesus for the first time, or he found her, which is closer to the truth, of course—or better yet, he's still finding her, and a measure of that emotion that is her namesake is beginning to take root. When she was in my office that second time, several weeks ago, she said she wasn't terribly interested in learning about religious things, though she wanted to know did I know anything about praying with icons and candles. I said, not really. But we prayed together anyway. Joy has actively fought her church heritage for a decade or more, and almost physically gets ill when she walks into an assembly. But she said that sometimes, lately, when she's heard me talking about Jesus, I sounded like I'd met the man, like there was a real guy out there somewhere. I told her that was the idea, and she said she would love to meet him. We prayed that she would, and I told her to sit up and open her eyes and just imagine him in the chair across from her, however she wanted to imagine him, and talk.

She did, for almost thirty minutes, though she said she could never really picture him sitting there.

I'm no mystic, and in my mind, this exercise was nothing more than imagination, nothing more than an attempt to move Joy closer to the idea of Jesus' reality. She only got frustrated when she wanted him to answer questions, like where did God come from, and was it almost the end of the world. Then she got to giggling, and I said what, and she looked at the chair and wanted Jesus to give her the lottery numbers for the week. It got quiet, and I was hoping to hear something, too. We both busted up, and she actually slapped her knee. I'd never seen anybody really do that, and I laughed 'til I cried.

But the silence came back in the room, and her face descended into a mean frown, long and drawn. It made her look a bit like Vincent Price. She looked at me finally, and said Amen. We talked another twenty minutes about listening to God, and Jesus, and did they ever say anything, and how did conscience fit into it all? Maybe it was a combination of things, I offered. But what should she do about her mother, she wondered, and this hate she had for her? And what did I think Jesus would say? We sat still for another ten minutes, with a word here and there, at which point Joy's face cleared a bit, and she said, it's pretty simple, huh? Simple maybe, but hard, never easy, and she said, yeah. But I'm pretty screwed up, aren't I, she said, and I said, so am I. We sat for a little longer, and she said well, she'd see me next week. She gathered up her bag and coat and cigarettes, thanked me for letting her smoke, and got up and went to the door. But then she turned around and walked back to me, and hugged me. I thought she'd probably cry, and I could feel her tension, her wanting to—but she didn't. She said thanks, again, and laughed, and said, I'm a sad story, huh? I said no, you're a real story. She cocked her head like she wasn't sure she believed me, and then she left.

Joy came back the next week, much happier, and determined to get through whatever process was beginning with her and God. She told me hard stories of her and Francis, stories that made me wince inside, and stories that made me buckle over laughing, but this morning at church, and tonight at the Baskin-Robbins, are the only times I've seen her since.

∼

When I saw Joy this morning, I grinned, and got on her, and said stop avoiding me. She had clear eyes, and they twinkled, and I thought for a moment she was flirting. She told me she hasn't been avoiding me, but I said it's been a couple of weeks, and what happened last week? She teased me and said a good pastor would've checked up on her by now. I said I did, but you didn't answer. She said it was nothing, that she just got upset, and that it was no big deal. I said I'm not sure I believe you.

She smiled, pushed her hair back, and said she's been busy with her new job down at the Marston Office Supply, that the manager there's been really nice to her. I accused her of going out with him, and she said yeah, she has. She got embarrassed and I told her I think that's great, but that I've missed her. Surprisingly, she said she missed me, too, and I thought how rare to just enjoy a person. I'm glad for her new hope—it's all over her face. Her young girl smile has returned, though she's still nervous, and fidgets, and rubs her right hand. She didn't even sneak out at the altar call to go smoke. Her drawled-out stories of her mom and her knock me over. Their lives could be a sit-com, a southern all-in-the-family. Francis is a tight woman who loves to banter, with certain prejudices she does-n't bother to hide, at least not much, and Joy is intelligent enough to keep her going. Joy went to college in Denton, at the University of Texas at Arlington, and majored in communications. That's funny, too, because she and Francis still can't get anything across to each other.

I wish Francis could like me. But I have this image of her face, red and eyes popping out, veins in her neck thick with anger. Every family that's left this church in the past two or three years, she goes and asks them if it was me they were leaving. She's convinced it's always my fault, my liberal fault that this body of Christ . . .

But car lights are suddenly pulling up the driveway, and a car door opens even as the engine shuts off, and I'm shocked to see my friend Dirk step out, and he wonders if we can talk. I stand up and say okay.

The ice-cream's gone, and my throat hurts for sure.

~

The dust is settling, and his red tail lights are disappearing now. Walking back toward the porch, I can still hear Connie crying inside. Though she'll be sore tomorrow, I think she'll be alright, but it's one of those deep, wring-out-your-gut cries, and it'll be a few minutes before she gets her breath. Sara's with her.

Dirk didn't expect to run into Connie.

He said he'd been driving most of the day, meandering down I-20, wondering whether he should see me or not. But he said I'd been a good friend to him, real at least, most of the time, and he thought he'd at least come see me before he screwed his life up completely. But just then, Connie pulled in behind him, and when she got to the porch, she went to a corner and leaned on the rail like a prizefighter, and I excused myself.

~

I don't suppose families fighting, and marriages breaking up is just a big city problem; people yell in Ruin, too. Sara finally got out of bed and came in the kitchen, where I was holed up, trying to ignore the strident voices out in the yard. Sara asked me what was going on, and I raised my eyebrows and told her to go look. She waddled over, peered through the blinds. She ran back to the bedroom, saying she'd get her clothes. I said, there's nothing to do Sara, just let 'em work it out.

But the fight escalated, and I've never enjoyed listening to people swear, and curse God, at the top of their lungs. I was praying it would stop, or at least slow down, but no such luck. I was at that disorienting moment where a man wants to get involved, has to decide what to do, if anything.

I paced. But as I finished my third lap of the kitchen, Sara yelling at me to go out there and stop them the whole time—Dirk's voice changed, lifted a couple of decibels, shouting some obscenities I couldn't live with. I crossed the room, my head about to explode from the blood pumping, and opened the front door just in time to catch a glimpse of Connie hitting him across the face, every muscle in her body behind the blow. I hollered at Dirk, and ran into the yard, but he was too livid now to pay any attention to me. Before I could get there, he slammed her against his car, hit her in the head with his fist.

∽

Connie's asleep in our bed, and Sara and I sit on the porch. Stunned at it all, I guess. Connie said she's fine, that Dirk had just been telling her about his affairs, and that he was glad about them, cause at least he'd get some satisfaction, which is exactly what he'd never get with her. Sara had put her to bed, and we sat in the kitchen for awhile, but it was too upsetting to listen to Connie weep, not to mention the fact that we felt like voyeurs, so we came outside.

∽

"I'd kill a man if he ever hit me like that."

I wryly observe that it looked to me like she hit him first, and Sara glares at me, wanting to know if I'm serious. I'm teasing, I tell her. Bad joke.

I knew what she meant. When Connie's chin bounced on the gravel driveway, I wanted to kill him too. I managed to get between them, standing over her, and I thought he'd probably pummel me, but I shoved him, hard as I could, and screamed so loud it scared me. But he stopped where he was. He didn't say anything, just stood there, sweating, panting, but oddly, looking like he might fall apart any minute. He finally leaned against his fender, staring out across the field, while Sara took Connie inside. There was blood on her face, especially on her chin.

I didn't move.

I believe in letting people face themselves on their own terms, standing next to them while they do it. But finally, I walked over and leaned on the fender, joining him.

The crickets made the night pulse, singing that monotonous tune, while I tried to slow down my heart. Dirk's breath steadied, and we stood there together, quiet, probably looking like we just finished a double date, neither of us pleased with the outcome of the night. He took one more deep, chesty breath, his shoulder heaving up, and dropping. Then he was completely still, and I turned to him. Not a muscle on his face moved. He stared. I looked away.

"I don't know."

It's all he said. He dug his keys out of his pocket, walked around the front of the car, opened the door, started the engine. He leaned back in the seat, and I came around to the driver's side. His window was down, but his eyes were on the house. Connie stood in the door, looking at him, her thin frame draped between the doorframe and my wife. She held an icepack to her cheek.

The smell of exhaust was strong, and before long, Dirk looked up at me.

"See ya, Cyrus."

~

Sara's asleep on the couch, and Richard just wet the bed. It's been that kind of night. It doesn't happen too often anymore, and I always hurt for him, hurt for his embarrassment while I change his underwear and his sheets. I never tease him about it, though, never fuss at him. Everybody's different, we tell him, and his body'll catch up one of these days.

But now, after the bed's dry, and Richard's safely tucked back under the covers, I sit stroking his little back, thinking that Dirk used to be a little boy like this guy. Innocent, full of young energy, sleeping peacefully at night while a mom or dad looked at his clear face smashed on a pillowcase covered in trains.

O God, how do we lose our way?

October 9

He sure knows what to say when people die.

Mattie Mae Jones to Roland Minor
at Alexander Townsend's Memorial

. . . tragedy in the towering sublime . . .

Thursday night, late, Sara snoring next to me, the air chilled and still. Soft padding footsteps, then I hear the bathroom door shut. Sounds like Wayne's having trouble sleeping. Ever since Connie moved into Richard's room, Wayne's been restless, irritated by his little brother on the top bunk. Richard sleeps hard, but flops back and forth; he fell off twice Monday night, waking up the whole house. Scared Wayne to death the first time, made him mad the second. But Connie's exhausted, and says having a room to herself is heaven. She's been going to bed by 8:00, out for twelve hours or more, says she feels like a lazy teenager.

The toilet flushes, and Wayne tramps back to bed.

The house goes quiet again.

I turn over, eyes tight, determined to sleep.

But a voice keeps talking to me, running in my head, a crazy little voice that should be still by now—at peace, I'm sure—but I suspect it may not go away for a long time.

~

I met him outside Eckerd's in May, I think it was two years ago, just after my birthday. He asked me did I have some money to spare for a cup of coffee, and I didn't tell him I had one of those new $100 bills with the big Ben Franklin face in my wallet. But I said I was about to get a cup down at the Grape Inn, this little diner just around the corner, and did he want to come? He grinned . . . an upsetting kind of grin, really, cause he hadn't seen a dentist in a long time.

But he said sure.

I was scared, frankly. We don't get many transients here in town, and if we do, I don't normally do that sort of thing, but as a minister, the homeless bother me, inside my clean little pastor hole, and I can't stand it to just go by every time, like a Levite or a priest. I think I'm supposed to help. The church doesn't have a ministry to those sort of folks, and we're doing good to post a couple of volunteers at the Christian Service Center once a month. The whole problem makes me nervous, and I generally avoid it. But what possessed me that morning . . . well, I'm not sure, but as he and I shuffled down the side-walk toward the diner, I kept my distance, and wondered what in the world I was doing.

~

When Hubert called me Tuesday and told me Alex was dead, I was surprised. And today, there at the gravesite, standing next to his wife Jerri, whom I only met for the first time yesterday, I learned about this man I most often thought of as a ministry. She hadn't seen him in over six years, and she told me at the funeral that she had gone to work one day, and he kissed her good-bye, and handed her a sack lunch he had made, of tuna and apples, with a Ding Dong cup-cake, like she liked, and she told him he should go get his hair cut. Then she drove away with him waving in the door, and that that was the last time she ever saw him alive.

I called Jerri—she lives in Austin—after they found her name and picture, and a phone number in his pants pocket. When she answered the phone, she paused, said she had always been afraid of this call. How did I know Alex, she wondered, and how long would it take her to get to Ruin?

~

The day I met him, he and I sat down at a black vinyl booth that had these fake pink flowers in an ugly white vase next to the Tabasco, and I was struck by the presence of the man. He filled up his side of the table with a vitality that was missing on my side, a kind of raw energy that, on the one hand, was a little shifty, his lanky body constantly making little adjustments, like he couldn't get his clothes to feel just right. But on the other hand, he was focused like a beam, with a kind of awareness that made me think he lived inside my own brain. His brown hair was matted, like you'd expect, and long, down the middle of his back, and his beard was a Rip Van Winkle. But his eyes—they were awake like bats in the night, and the waitress was clearly not happy with me when she dropped the white, plastic, one-page menu in front of us.

I watched this lean giant—he was at least 6' 3" or 4"—eating the breakfast special—two eggs, white still a little runny, hash browns, toast, grape jelly and coffee—and at least four glasses of water, and he still hadn't really answered any of my standard lets-get-to-know-each-other questions. But he seemed a little more at ease after awhile, and finally he said he'd been a plumber once, and then thought he might be an actor, at which point he misquoted a few lines of to be or not to be. But something about "when we have shuffled off this mortal coil" coming out of his mouth was disturbing and real. He stopped, and said these eggs were sure good, and he had to go, cause he had an appointment down the road and thanks, mister. Maybe I'll see you again, I said, and without warning, he was gone. Driving home, I felt funny about it, and it wasn't until a couple of weeks later, outside the same Eckerds that I saw him again, bought him some cigarettes and found out his name was Alex.

Jerri was a handsome woman, a freckled red-head with thin lips, and though not as tall as Alex, she had presence, a broad-shouldered physique, and a great, clear look in her eye. I could easily imagine them together, because she didn't mind that she was a little undone, hair mostly askew, in her face, and she handled it with a quirky habit of kicking her head to the right to keep the red bangs out of her eyes. I liked her the minute she got to the church. We hugged like old friends. Her crying was slight, and muted, and I realized that Alex—to her—had died a long time ago. Her first words to me were of how hard he had worked to be a plumber, and she wondered what he'd been doing here in Ruin. She let out a startled cry and wept in earnest when I told her Alex was homeless for several years, living hand to mouth. They found him dead out by the railroad track in his lean-to, I told her, and she said, oh Tommy, several times and I wondered if that was the baby.

∾

That second time I saw him, I was about to walk on by, saying see you later, but something possessed me again, and I sat down next to him on the sidewalk. We leaned on the wall, watching the cars, him scratching his ears like a dog. I listened to him, trying to make sense of it. He talked swiftly, with animation, and in his raving, he was trying to get out a story about Jerri. That bitch Jerri, he kept saying, and it turned out to be a woman, his wife of his high school years. They'd had a baby, it sounded like, and lived in a trailer park while he learned about . . . plumbing. But as I was asking him about plumbing, just to see if I might trigger a coherent thought, he said but the baby got into some stuff under the sink, and Jerri never really knew what their little Tommy got hold of, but the emergency room didn't help, but they tried and did I know if babies went to heaven or what God did with them.

It was twenty minutes into the conversation before I put all that together, and I remember the whistle over at the meat packing plant went off. It was five o'clock. That whistle cut him off, like he'd been unplugged. He drifted, and was quiet to the point that I started to take off, but he suddenly grabbed my arm. He looked me dead in the eye, and he said that never really happened, it was just a story he heard, just a story he made up, but if there was a Jerri, he loved her, pudding and pie. His grip on my forearm backed up my blood, and my heart pounded in my shoulder, but after a minute of that stare, he let me go. I got up in a hurry as his eyes went away. But then he put his head down and started this weird keening, and though he didn't have any tears, it was as hurtful a cry as I'd ever heard. I sat back down and put my arm around him, and he instantly raised his head and smiled, quiet as the night. He pulled out his cigarettes, and we sat there for five more minutes, him quoting Edgar Allen Poe, saying nevermore, nevermore, nevermore.

≈

Clorox, Jerri told me, was what Tommy got into, and it had been a devastating loss. She showed me a picture, and Tommy was cute, 19 months, and walked, and was talking up a storm. Alex was proud of him, she said, and played rough like you think a dad should. I've heard it helps their brains develop, she said. She said Alex was so determined to be a good dad, because his own father had been lousy. Abusive, and drank. Slept around on his mom. Alex wanted to do better. But after Tommy died, Alex went limp inside, she said. He'd sit for hours in the yard, reading Shakespeare, memorizing, and though he was nearing the end of his plumbing apprenticeship, he stopped going one Monday. It was just over two months later when he vanished. The police looked for him, but after six months, she gave up, and had worked all these years as a waitress on Sixth Street. Once she hired a private detective, and he thought Alex had gone to Cleveland, and she had been hopeful for about a week, but the detective was wrong. She never got another lead.

Jerri said she couldn't cry much anymore, cause she'd lost Alex before, but he was a good guy, smart, and did real good in school. He used to take me to the park, she said, flicking her hair out of her eyes. He'd put me on a low tree branch, and he'd say you're Juliet . . . and then she sobbed, and told me she'd always wanted a real wedding, with the lace white dress and all, and they had meant to, but couldn't afford it, and now he was gone, he was gone.

≈

I told Jerri I saw Alex a bunch over the couple of years I knew him. He lived down by the railroad tracks, kinda, in a lean-to of various materials depending on whether it was June or October. Mostly refrigerator boxes with some odd boards he came up with, but they came apart when it rained, and he was always looking for better. He'd learned some construction in the city, he told me, but I could never talk Mr. Gunston, the local builder, into hiring him, and old Hubert Mulberry who had a little moving business used to go out and get Alex—he called him "Grinner"—and they'd go move a couple of stoves or refrigerators up and down stairs, or go clean some mattresses for the used furniture place down on Pine. Hubert would swear and cuss at him and give him 20 bucks, and somehow, between the good people of this town and the God that made it, Alex got along.

Alex had some cobwebs in his head for sure. But he could be lucid, downright brilliant if I held him to the sun just right. If I listened, unexpected bursts of poetry broke my heart, not so much with the words, but with the timbre of his voice, which was like a reed blown by an autumn wind, brushing up against a child running by. He sang, too, and often mumbled profanities, and had a habit of saying crude things whenever he saw Betsy Carter walking her black lab along 2nd street, which happened nearly everyday. Betsy was a drop-dead gorgeous blonde who was a cheerleader up at the high school. She reminded him of Jerri, he told me finally, and he wished he had a dog. One day in July he stopped Betsy on the street with some stolen flowers, half-dead yellow roses, and told her she was beautiful, that he wanted her to have them on account of a girl he once knew, but that nobody really knew what happened to her. Betsy walked away from him pretty fast, him calling out that he wanted to thank her for . . . well . . . for being there with her dog most days. Betsy kept the flowers, though, and her mom told me just the other day that last week at the dinner table, Betsy prayed for the nice, crazy man who gave her roses.

I told Jerri about Betsy, and she said it sounded just like him, and that he loved flowers, especially yellow ones. He was romantic, she said, and an artist of a kind, who liked to make odd collages from found objects, and that she still had on her wall a mask he'd put together out of bottle caps and crushed cans with bits of slick magazine covers that he used mostly for color. He was always doodling, she told me, drawing, singing, and that one of their favorite things was going to movies, or down to Sixth street to catch a new local band. I told her I bet he could dance, and she said like a demon.

～

When it was time for Jerri to go, we stood at her car, an old Chrysler that she said was on its last legs, with over 120, 000 miles, and no air conditioner. Thank you so much, Cyrus, thank you for calling me, she said. I told her I was glad Alex found his way here, that he was one of the reasons I believe in miracles. She asked how so, and I told her that he and I were in my backyard one time. He'd been out walking, and came down Curtain Street. I was just getting home, and I asked him if he wanted a coke, and he said sure. We walked around back, and he got to swinging on Wayne's swing, nearly tipped it over. But he stopped after awhile, took a big swig of the coke I had for him, and looked at me. It was cool that day, and his hair and beard made me think of God.

But this time, looking at me, something happened. That artist, the one Jerri told me about—the guy that came before the lunatic—showed up. That artist talked to me for almost two hours. Gone was the craziness, gone was the despair, gone was the rambling profanity, and in its place was someone I'm glad I saw, someone I wish I'd known. He talked of his parents that day, and how his mom had raised him to know Jesus, though his dad failed him, and how in high school he loved acting and art. But he was never good enough. He said how much he believed, and that God was the great God of Heaven, and of the oppressed, and how hopeful he was over the prospect of life for most of the world, that God would surely not leave his people—or him—to despair. He talked again of Jerri, and said he wished he could see her, because he still loved her, but he hadn't been strong enough to take his baby's death. He wondered if I ever found her, to tell her he was sorry. He said he loved to read, but it hurt too much, and that Shakespeare and Wordsworth had been his favorites, and that he hated it that Hamlet died, that tragedies had to be tragedies, but then he guessed that's what made them great, and did I think so?

And then, would I mind if we prayed together? I said no, sure, and Alex prayed our father who art in Heaven, thank you for Jerri, and Tommy, and Mom, and even Dad, and Hubert who lets me work, and Silas, and bless little Wayne who usually swings here. Dear God, I can't stay, he said. The clear sight of my life as it really is is too, too hard, too much, and please forgive me, but I don't know how. Amen.

After a long silence, he finally started swinging again, quietly, and then rambled, and swore, and the old Alex was back, making a final journey.

∾

Now, just past 2:00 a.m., I'm roaming through the kitchen, debating whether toast or cereal is best for my mood. As I slide the two pieces of bread into the toaster, the image of that kind, crazy man from Austin makes me smile. How just like you, I think, to just decide not to wake up anymore. No real sign of trauma, the fireman said, no heart attack or stroke, the doctor said, no reason to die, everyone said, but still, the rain found him dead on Tuesday.

I got there just as they were taking the body away. I watched, the drizzle beating my bald head. I wondered where he went, and guessed he just decided to go on about his business in the next world, maybe still looking for where God took babies when they die. I missed him then, and now, two days later, I miss him more, and I will never forget or dishonor the epic that was Alex. Alexander, an Elizabethan tragedy played out in the towering sublime of living, and his lost heroine Jerri, who played Juliet, who's back home now. Maybe she'll have some closure, and some peace, though she told me after all this, she didn't know what to believe about faith anymore.

∾

Dear God,

Sometimes we don't know what to believe. Bless the people who live there, with their loss, and their dark days of wandering. We don't know what to do with our weakness, our pain—too much to bear—but we know you are faithful, the God who is more powerful than all the hurt of the world combined. Heal us, lift us, hold us together when we come apart, and use us to heal, as we have been healed. May we know your grace, and know that what life we have is of you—indeed, the very touch of your hand. Bless Alex, Lord, and take his soul to be at peace. And thank you that his despair, his pain, became a treasure in the hearts of his friends.

And for Jerri, Lord. Send Jesus, and let him meet her, and may he tell her just who he is, so that she may be sure in her faith, and rest.

In Jesus,
Amen.

∾

The toast pops up, and I grab the butter. Two minutes later, toast in my tummy, and feeling warmer than I did, I saunter back down the hall. The door to Richard's room is cracked open, and I see Connie's face, slack, mashed against her pillow. She's lying on her side, and her hair half-covers her mouth, running along the line of her jaw. She looks warm, a hodgepodge of blankets wrapped around her, but a twitch runs through her body, and she turns over, lies face up, her dark hair falling over her face like a soft beard.

A flash of recognition.

Everywhere I turn, it seems, there's Alex.

Sitting on the edge of my bed now, saying a simple prayer, finally falling toward sleep. The voice still there, though. I sigh, my eyes closing.

'Night.

October 12

Maybe the next guy will give us ser-mon outlines. And better yet, maybe his sermons 'll have a point.

Bernie Hand to Jack Simons,
Administrative Committee

. . . *knowing already the answer is no. . .*

My office seems strange today. 6:45 a.m. Strange. It's bright, in an odd way. There's a gift here. I can feel it, an unexpected lightness to the air, as if my window was open. An out of place freshness that doesn't line up with the pain of the week.

Alex is still with me. In my mind, my coffee, my prayer, my quiet. I brought the Sunday paper along with me, which I never do, but I chuck it on the desk and refuse to look at it, not wanting to sully this morning gift, this gift left by God.

~

We took the quarantine sign down. Sara, the boys, and I are all better, though Connie caught whatever the rest of us had. Her ordeal with Dirk left her in bed all day Monday, more depressed than hurt, and the flu got her while she lay there. She spent most of the week woozy on over-the-counter stuff, and finally saw Dr. Elkins on Friday. He gave her some medicine and she was better yesterday, though she hasn't said much except that she'll be heading home soon.

~

Yesterday morning, while Connie was still sleeping, I sat at the kitchen table. The dishes in the dishwasher were clean and Sara was putting glasses and cups away up on the middle shelf. I asked her if she knew anything more about what happened last Sunday night.

She started in on the forks and knifes and spoons. She said Connie told her that Dirk had hit her twice before, once in a fight over money, the other time over sex, or lack thereof. Both times, he'd been repentant, especially the second time when she actually got the police on the phone. Connie was not a woman to mess around. But the next night, Dirk, ever pragmatic, met her at the door with a dozen roses, though she said she knew it wasn't because he loved her. Sara said he manipulates her all the time. They apparently went out for dinner, the whole nine yards, but Connie told Sara Dirk was only interested in—I won't repeat the word Connie used, the one Sara savagely whispered under her breath—and though Sara left out the details, she said by the end of the evening, with Dirk asleep at her side, Connie felt like she'd been raped.

Sara slammed the drawer shut. We heard Connie stirring in the bedroom.

Sara said that was three months ago, just before Dirk found the other woman. Sara spat out the words, her face puckered, obviously disgusted. Finally, she stopped with the dishes, and looked at me, a serrated knife in her hand. She said—kind of joking, kind of not—don't you have anywhere else to be?

I put on my sweats, and ran.

$\sim$

We were supposed to do one of our once-a-month special family nights last night, but it was a bust. It felt awkward with Connie at the table. She worked hard to fit in, be a normal part of the family, jousting with the boys, tickling them, teasing about girlfriends, setting the mood for a boisterous evening, which is not at all what I wanted. I had in mind a time of reflection and rest, maybe with candles, a Sabbath time, with strong, meaningful talk, full of religion, full of scripture and chanting.

We settled for the Lord's prayer and a movie.

We rented one of the talking pig movies. Connie and the boys sprawled across the floor and howled all night, though I couldn't get into it, and Sara fell asleep on the couch. I got the guys to bed, and Sara followed, waving at us, saying she was beat, and she'd see us in the morning. Connie lay down in Sara's spot on the couch, and I stuck to my TV chair, an inexpensive, shallow, green wingback not built for comfort. After a minute, I jumped up and made popcorn, put it in our plastic measuring bowl, and offered her some. She sat up and said, sit here. I said do you want a coke, and she said diet. I grabbed the cans, a couple of Dallas Cowboy coasters, and sat next to her, the plastic bowl between us. We stared at the news, chewing popcorn so we wouldn't have to talk. Finally we ran out of popcorn. I asked if she wanted more. She said sure.

When I returned with a second batch, the Pentecostals were on. I wanted to watch, but Connie won, and changed the channel.

∾

Saturday Night Live, a football highlight show, Connie flipping back and forth between channels, catching middles of jokes, never punch lines, neither of us laughing. The popcorn and coke ran out, and finally I took the clicker away from her and turned it off. It was 11:15.

I asked Connie if she wanted to talk. She reminded me I'd asked her to leave me alone. I said, yeah, well, a lot's happened between then and now, with Dirk, and then Alex, and that talking might be good for both of us. She looked down, her long fingers locked in her lap, thumbs touching. She said maybe. She cocked an eye at me, glancing through thin strands of black hair, grinning like a kid asking permission, knowing already the answer's no. She wondered if we could go out on the porch. I smiled, and hesitated, and she quickly threw up her hands, withdrawing the request, but I said no, no, that's okay, that I'd grab a couple of jackets. She protested, and got up, but I grabbed her hand, stood up beside her, and repeated myself. It's okay, I said. I'll get the jackets. She walked to the door, her hands stuffed in her jeans pockets.

∾

I left the light off.

It was brisk, out on the glider. Maybe just above fifty—I can never tell. But the wind gusted off and on, and that kind of air, that fall, snuggly air, takes me back to high school football games, with bands blaring, and the snapping sounds of shoulder pads as young men pound across the turf in pursuit of touchdowns and glory.

Connie and I were in love for exactly three days. But we kept dating for a week or two after that Friday night after-the-football-game dance, and it was at the next home game that we officially called it off. Well, we started the process at the game, though the final showdown was at her parent's house.

On their front porch. As she sat in their porch swing.

∾

"Can I hold your hand?"

Connie's voice quaked, shaking with that slight chill that just won't go away. I smiled and said, Connie, and she said, it's not like that. She was on my right, and she held out her left hand. Her ring was still on it. She said please.

Her hand was warm.

She said she felt so unreal. Like she was nothing. The days were bad dreams, she said, and that she was hanging on minute to minute, hour to hour. That she had lots of friends, and that her family loved her, but that she felt so sick. Her folks moved out to the West Coast, to La Jolla, after she'd finished college, and Connie said she was thinking of going out there for a few months, that she couldn't stand the idea of being alone. We listened to the wind, and she scooted over, closer, her voice softly reaching me.

Disconnected, she said. She felt apart from the rest of the world, like her pain was a planet, and she was the last survivor. Like the Connie she used to be was gone, like death.

Did I understand, she wondered?

∾

Do I understand . . . what?

Being disconnected? Lonely walks with myself, down dusty roads with fences on either side? Hollow prayers and silent gods? Youth conceding to age? Unfilled dreams lost to foolishness, to impossibility? Vast walls built to protect me, even as I ask worshippers to open their hearts? Basking in family love, drifting away to solitude of soul?

~

I nodded.

Her hair swirled around her face, slapping her cheek. She awkwardly pushed it behind her ear several times, but finally gave up and let it blow. She let go of my hand and pulled her coat closer, tighter. The tweed collar was turned up, and her profile said nineteenth century romanticism, and I wanted her to speak poetry. I asked her if she knew any poems, and she turned to me, and said, what? We both laughed, and she took my hand again.

She said holding my hand was a real thing, that it reminded her of being young, it made her feel like herself. Not so alone. Is it okay, she wanted to know. It's okay, I told her, completely unsure.

We chatted after that, of old acquaintances we hadn't seen in years, and teachers we both had and liked or hated, and other yearbook images, and for about an hour, Connie and I were a pair, cloaked in old intimacy. Bundled shoulder to shoulder, my hand in hers, and both of them tucked away in her coat pocket, we laughed, stifled tears, and finally, rocked in silence.

Connie finally squeezed my hand, and stood up, releasing me, saying she needed sleep. I started to get up, but she got in front of me, said no, no that she wanted to go in alone. Just sit here a couple of minutes, she said. I want to keep this image of tonight, and that feeling of holding on to you, she said, feeling not so . . . apart . . . for just a little while. She said if we just go in and turn on the lights and brush our teeth, she just knew it would suddenly be as if her life had never happened. I need this memory, she said. I need to nail it down. She leaned over me, and kissed my cheek, whispering thank you, you good man, you.

At the door, she turned back to me.

"Does Sara know about us?"

I said, you know the answer to that. Connie said she never told her. I said no, that I'd never told her either. She asked me if I ever thought about it. You mean, that night, I said, and she said, yeah. Only on nights like tonight, I said. She said yeah—me, too. She told me of all her memories, being in love for the first time was one of her best. I said, yeah—me, too.

"Cyrus? Was that love real?"

"Absolutely."

Then goodnight, and she was inside. I slid back and forth, back and forth, watching silvery clouds hurry by in the dark, wondering why God made such things as love, and youth, and loss.

~

I couldn't sleep, and was up by 5:15. I left a half-hour later, while the house was still dark, still silent save for the creaks in the wind. But as I backed out of the drive, the front door snuck open. I stopped, and Connie stuck her head out the door, pulling her short robe close. She stepped out on the porch, waved a small wave, mutely saying good morning.

I waved, and kept going.

~

I should be disturbed, distraught, torn apart by indecision, rejection, and looming temptation. Not to mention that perhaps a month from today I will be gainfully unemployed. But no—instead, there's this gift. I'm in my office, reading, and almost two hours have passed. 8:20. That lightness is still here, shacking up in my chest, wooing me into a peace that passes all my understanding.

Perhaps today will be my day to see a vision of the Christ.

~

Time for class, and as I head out the door, several Shakespeare titles are just to my left, in the bookshelves. I see there's a space next to *Hamlet*. Alex's worn *Romeo and Juliet* belongs there. Jerri found it among the things gathered from his cardboard house. She felt like he'd want me to have it. It's in my car, and I'll bring it in after class. I saw Alex in my dream last night. He didn't speak, but—and this was the odd part—he was clean shaven. Short hair. Standing with a woman I didn't recognize. He was yelling, as in celebration. I wanted to understand, but I never did, and finally he and his lady friend ran off down the road—I'm sure it was a road, but it looked like water—playing catch with a football. He wasn't the only one, though, and lately—all week long, in fact—faces have been stopping by in the sleep hours, some mute, some speaking.

There was the dream of my junior high girlfriend who had a funny lip, an alto named Toni. We fought a lot, but she always smelled nice, like an autumn rain, and I hadn't thought of her in years. And John Paul, my best friend when I was just thirteen. His right pinky finger was shattered in a freak bicycle accident, and he faded just as I was asking him if it still hurt. Friday night a kid I spent a few days with two years ago showed up—a little black boy named Delvon who started coming to church after we knocked on his door on an evangelism campaign. During vacation Bible school, he and I got to be buddies, and we played football catch at lunch. Delvon had a luminous smile, with one front tooth a little turned out, and loose, and what happened to him, and why don't I know?

I dreamed about my boss at my first job, at the corner grocery. His baggy neck, and dark, circled eyes were so real, almost hovering over my bed in the night. But he faded into my dad's face—long, but puppy bright—smiling like he was glad to see me. Mrs. Rutherford went by, a crack-up of an old lady who I shopped for, years ago. I never liked it much cause she had 5 dogs at her house, and it was filthy, and standing at her door with the groceries, the smells would knock me over, but she always hugged my neck and told me thanks. Then there was the kid with red hair. I'd never seen him before.

But Jesus never came.

~

I turn to the desk to get my Bible, and I'm still asleep, I guess, cause there's another face. It's Joy Moore, but it's her whole self, and she's saying something—thank you is what it looks like. She's flirting again, and I laugh, grabbing my Bible, shaking my head, waving off all visions. I need more sleep. I shut off the light, close the door behind me, and mosey toward the water fountain, then the gym.

Lapping at the fountain, gulping more than my share, ever careful not to put my mouth on the silver, I mull over Romeo's loss. Hamlet's, and Lear's. How can tragedy fill us up, I wonder. How is it that sadness, blood, and death, and all their cousins, told in stories, lift us up, point us to the eternity inside? I stop and watch the liveliness of the gym. Eight or nine boys run up and down the court, screaming, their high voices bouncing off walls, and finally the poor kid with the ball disappears underneath arms and legs piling on, his protests shut out by the rousing chorus of "dogpile, dogpile." Such joy.

Suddenly, an ache makes me bend at the waist, breathing hard. Something hurts—there's a bursting, erupting squarely out of my chest—my God. I straighten up, mouth agape, eyes wide, trying to walk, trying to breathe deeply again. What is this urge to crumple, to sit right here at the foul line, and bawl my eyes out? And what's this . . . wonder . . . this . . . this promise . . . I . . . will . . . not . . . get . . . more . . . than . . . I . . . can . . . bear. But this feels like the edge . . . I don't know if I can bend . . . anymore . . . but there's the wonder again, and . . . yes . . . I will stand again . . . the promise . . . go on . . . go on.

My vision clears, and Sara's at the door of my class, waiting for me. I take her hand, and her eyes search me. I know my eyes are shining, teary, but throbbing with a kind of wonder, as if I've seen a ghost, and she wonders if I'm alright. I can't think of how to respond. Finally, I say what seems most true.

"God."

Blessed are the peacemakers
for they shall be called the sons of God.

It's 8:35 a.m. Roman and Serena are still getting the coffee, and Jeff and I stand by the door discussing our wives, and their snoring. He says Bobbi snores a lot these days because she sleeps on her back, with the baby and all, and I say you should hear Sara. Sara and Bobbi can hear us—they're talking, ten feet away—but thankfully, they ignore us. What I don't tell Jeff is that while I love Sara's mouth, when she snores, it puts me off, hanging open, completely ajar. That chopping sound she makes, that hopping grunt of a snore, is cute at first, and funny, but it gets old. Of course she denies it, says she's never snored a day in her life. So I recorded her once, and to my surprise, it hurt her feelings. But that was years ago, long before I learned that being right can sometimes be dead wrong.

∾

Blessed are the makers of peace, I'm saying, when the Bubers come in. They're making their apologies, hovering at the corner table, getting their refreshments situated. Now they sit next to Tom, and wait for me to go on. Perhaps "to make peace" is what I'm seeking, I continue. To make peace. God, in making creation, made peace. He made it with great dynamics, and though I don't think so, really, perhaps it took a really big bang to get the whole thing going. Again, peacemaking is an act of war on war itself. The Big Bang blowing the hell out of chaos and separating the dark from the light, the sea from the land, order from confusion, and making the peaceful turning of a blue planet among a billion stars. And then came the garden on the planet, the new man and the woman from and at his side, lovemaking alongside peace, and God hovers over a new world. As we join in, we are called the sons of God.

That sounds okay, though the blank stares concern me.

I go on. Make peace. Can we not see the wars in the faces of our friends and neighbors? What are we but ambassadors? What are we but an army of warriors? We are the makers of possibility, the ones who bring hope to a world of eyes constantly looking away. We seek to bring an atmosphere of peace into the bristling hostility of civil war. A civil war inside. Me against me. Us against us. Brother and brother. Love against love.

Roman's eyes are getting heavy. Bill and Roxie are obviously fighting, and Will Sorendon's playing tic-tac-toe on his napkin right in front of me. Sara's reading her Bible. I might as well be teaching chess.

I tell them there's a man I know (barely—just enough to call by name), whose smile testifies to the audacity of faith. He smiles like the sunlight in the high mountains, for no reason, just seeing each person. I tell them the light in his eyes is no sales job, but real, that it beams straight from his deep place, a solid joy, as if an earthquake couldn't move that smile from his face. And though I rarely see him, it's always a pleasure, and though he's not handsome, his rugged demeanor . . . .

~

Jack is motioning me to come outside, into the gym. I excuse myself, and Jack is visibly upset. What, I say, and he says it's Joy, and that they tried to call, and what is Francis going to do, and I say wait, slow down . . . what?

"Joy had a heart attack, or something, they're not sure, and she's dead, Cyrus. She just . . . died . . . not twenty minutes ago."

~

My God. Joy Moore, age 33, died suddenly, just now, on a light morning in October, at home, with her mom in the other room.

~

When I was in college, a casual friend of mine was killed in a boating accident in Lake Austin. He was skiing along, and fell, and the driver of the boat was clowning, and turned quickly, too quickly, was thrown from the boat, and the boat circled around and caught my friend Adam underneath, and sheared him. The emergency room doctor said it was like being back in Vietnam, and Adam died there on the table. I was shocked when I heard. A dark, hispanic girl who was falling in love with him didn't hear it until the next day in class. I remember her hysterics, and now, with this news, I think, I should be hysterical, too. I want to be hysterical. I want to fling my body into space, grappling with air, denying death.

∽

Jack, handle the class, get people to pray, do communion, and then dismiss, because I've got to get to Francis' house. I grab Sara, yell at Mike to see about the boys, and thirty seconds later, I roar out of the parking lot, my jaw set. Sara's eyes are scared, locked on my face, searching me, wondering at my anger. I see white stripes flashing by. The radio is on, blaring out a snatch of "Angie" before I can snap it off.

∽

My tears sit just on the edge, and Sara's weeping is the only sound in the car. I'm at eighty now, on I-20. One more off ramp, and we'll be there. I'm unconscious, and I think I'm shouting, maybe obscenities, and Sara's hitting me, banging on my arm, saying stop it, stop it, stop it. I barely hear her. I slam on the brakes, slowing down, and roar through the stop sign. A kid on a bike watches me round the corner, frozen. Sara's gripping the car door, and we're there, we're here. The car stops, and I kill the engine. It's silent, except for my heart pounding, and Sara's whimper, and her saying, Cyrus, Cyrus. My mind returns. I breathe, open the door, step toward grief.

∽

The porch is tiny, oddly small, with one post, and there are extra cars around, including a police car with lights just going off, and a blue and white ambulance with back doors open. It's a chaotic scene, bustling quietly, as if something can be done. Joy often told me of the chaos in her house, with shouting and slamming pans, and all this seems appropriate. But the crowd clears away from the door as the crackle of a police radio cuts the air. Hushed voices reply. The gurney is coming out, a covered body hauled away. I hear crying from inside, but it doesn't sound like Francis. I want so much to see Joy's face, and the stretcher slows as it passes me, but I don't make those kind of scenes, and she's gone. Sara takes my arm. I hear myself ask how do I get through this? This young woman's face won't come to my office again, but why am I so upset?

~

Joy's hands always hurt from arthritis. I remember one of the stories she told me, of her old elementary school just across the street. There was a sixth grade spring program when she was twelve, and afterwards, just as the sun was going down, she came home, and walked in the door of her living room. Francis had been there—to the show—she said, but hurried out right after, and Francis hit her when she came through the door, shouting and grunting, something about a daughter being too embarrassed to be seen with her mother. There's that chaos again, Joy said. She said I get this chaos inside when I'm with her. The fist is always in my face, she said, and I hit her. Joy said, I hit my mother when I was twelve. We fought to a standstill in my living room, and I remember panting, and thinking my mother wore ugly bras, because there was that strap, and her puffy red-face was wrenched, but so sad. We're standing there still, and I'll be there when she dies, she said. Her last breath will kick me out the door, and I won't have anything in the world, because there'll be nothing left to despise.

~

I'm calming, digging my hands into my pockets, looking for the wisdom I keep there. Sara's already in the house. Can't I go home? But no, and I think, the lawn needs cutting. I drift toward the door. There's an old rock here on the corner of the drive, a rock that looks like glass melted on glass, sharp, glinting slightly in the sun, with a touch of white in the middle. Another car is pulling up, a young man and his wife, not in my class, and I recognize the ritual of the church descending on the family of the dead, everyone terrified, but coming anyway. A policeman comes out, brushes by. He's Hispanic, a square-jawed, good-looking man, in a Jimmy Smits way. I stop him, and he turns his big, strong face to me. I ask him what happened, and he tells me he went to school with Joy. Officer Ramirez says he even went out with her once, to see one of the Godfather films he thought, but he didn't know she was still around. I could tell he was shaken by meeting this old friend again, and I knew he thought Joy was a good girl. How did she die, I ask, and they weren't sure, but it was probably a heart attack. Certainly no foul play.

~

There's crying just inside the door. I hesitate, remembering how Joy regretted that she smoked unfiltered cigarettes, how she said she wished she didn't like the wild things. But she did, and it was hard to give them up. She told me on that second visit that as a teenager she had once taken up a friend on a bet that she couldn't shoot tequila. She took five shots, and in the aftermath, wasn't sure she won the bet.

I enter the house. The mourners clutter the living room.

Beatrice Thomasen catches my eye. She can't really dislike me right now—she hurts too much. I walk to her, speechless, an idiot. She holds me, I hold her, her old body shaking, and in that pose, our status as brute enemies ends. Is Joy all right, she asks me. I know what she means, and I think of Joy's description of anxiety attacks and constantly getting lost, and the trauma of learning to drive, and god, how hard it was to live. If she ever found someone to love, she'd said, it would have been easier. I remember seeing a memory there, a love she lost, maybe, but I didn't press it—I figured she'd tell me next time around.

I tell Beatrice Joy is very much all right, and will be from now on. The kitchen is full of people—local family, churched and unchurched, and of course, the chicken fried steak girls. The quiet noise that guests in a death house make calls me to the center of the grief. I turn the corner into the dining room.

A lone figure sits at the table.

Francis is still, her back to me, gazing out a sliding glass screen door into the backyard where Joy had first played with Casper, the dog who came to the door one childhood night, and stayed. One of Francis' few acts of kindness, Joy told me once—in front of her mother.

Francis is alone, now, nobody too close. I go to her, but she doesn't turn. But there's no malice in her stillness.

I kneel at her side, quietly take her hand. Her eyes turn to mine. I say nothing, my eyes taking in hers. A long moment passes between us. No anger here anymore, just regret, and confession, all spoken with eyes only. She looks away, but her hand is tight in mine. She squeezes, like it's the end of a prayer, but the strength doesn't let go, and I'm as lost as she. An impulse comes, and I follow it, placing my head in her wide lap. What I mean by it, I don't know, but she strokes my hair, and now it's me sobbing, and she joins me.

I'm wishing for a new life to take over this ugly earth, wishing that death would end, and that all of us stuck here stood together.

Finally, I'm quiet. Red in the face, I'm embarrassed, afraid of what I'll see if I look in her eyes. I sneak to my feet, and she stands alongside. My arm rests on her shoulders, and she leans on my chest. I hold her for a time, as we talk.

"Joy told me to make peace with you, Cyrus Manning."

~

It's seven o'clock. I'm standing outside the Barwell-Risor funeral home. Mr. Risor died years ago, of old age, with no sons to carry on, so the Barwell's handle it all now. Dale Barwell, 53, his toupee slightly askew, hovers in the door—thin, gaunt. His chin isn't nearly as large as he's making it, and I wish he'd stop pulling down the corners of his mouth. I suppose he thinks he looks sympathetic, but he's ghastly. Barwell points grotesquely down the hall to "viewing room two," where Joy's body has just arrived. Francis and the rest of her family will be here soon, but I hope to steal a few moments alone with her.

The softness of this hall, and these rooms, with lush carpet and burgundy drapes, is false, a damn lie, in my view, and I wished for a shovel in the rain, so I could just dig a hole and throw in the body. Such harshness would be more fitting, more real, than the pseudo-comfort of this eerie place.

∼

I enter the viewing room, bearing down on the moment.

I realize a certainty, something sure.

My head spins. My world is changed now, and I am, this moment, passing through a door in my life, a section of what it will mean for me to live on the earth. A massive door swings behind me, and I swear I physically jerk with the impact of its slamming. Now I am at the body, and I know that my time as a pastor, preacher, Sunday school teacher is almost gone, and that it hurts like hell to think I will not be needed—perhaps ever again—to publicly speak grace into the face of death.

And now, leaning over her, there is that moment, when in utter stillness, the heart explodes, and grief bludgeons the face. I can't ignore the details—how simple her mouth was, and her nose. She died gently, with no bruises. Your hand doesn't hurt anymore, does it? I say the words out loud, with tears. I stand cemented, eyes glued to the made-up face of a dead girl I was only starting to know. I want to dive in, to shove her aside, to see behind her eyes, and follow her trail to the ether world, to that unseen paradise I'm always imagining, always praying for, always aching to find.

∼

I could raise her, you know.

Yeah, yeah, I tell him. Funeral parlors are never the same when

Jesus walks in. Remember Lazarus, and I say I'd like to talk to her, to Joy, and see what's over there. He says the family is coming, so let's walk, and I say, what about them, and he says, don't worry, I'll be there, too, and my Spirit.

~

I step out the back door, but not into Ruin. It's a different world, and the air is stunning. I can't describe it, but it's sugary, sweet to the tongue, sweet to the touch, and the skin. I stop, and behind me is a landscape of wooded darkness, a Tolkein or Lewis landscape with beauty to break the heart. Clouds of pink climb against blue, and gradations of orange hang to my right. Stars crawl from behind the day's curtain, and as he and I walk, my body is unfamiliar to me, like it's been replaced, renewed. I am nothing like I was before—perhaps a different man, with a different name, and soul.

I open my mouth, but no words come. There are no words that fit. To say heaven is to slander the shattering pulse of these unknown, never-before-seen colors, the searing rapture of the dense comfort of this . . . air. It thrills my arms and legs, and its wetness is a spooky mist, but, again, sweet and clean, a light on fresh night snow.

Does this place satisfy, I ask him. His answer is to point to a place ahead of me, where a woman walks. It's Joy, and I run, an easy stride. Wind is blowing, and I am a thought, light, without weight, springing toward her. Jesus runs at my heels. I stop at her side, and he at mine. I grasp her hands, and we three sit in the grass. I miss Sara, but there is a gift here, and I will take it.

No, Joy says, there is no place that satisfies. I doubt her, because here, my soul runs like a clear stream. Breathing is easy, muscles and memory lying back, letting deep rest in. It's a fine rest. Joy touches my arm, and it's like silk, but it isn't love, it's not eros. I take her hand—*awed*—it has the stuff of very being in it.

But she says it's not the place. It's him.

I sit up, and look at the guy next to me. She's right. It is him. He is the power here, the stuff running through all the rest. He is Heaven walking, bounding along, spraying forever with God's inventions called love, and art, and beauty's grace. It's all right here—in his eyes, in his chest, in his sly smile. He winks, and says there is no desert here, and better still—here . . . you are known.

Known.

Now we walk, and there's another man. Dad's here, but he's young, and strong, his arm chiseled, and around my shoulder. His hand slides to my neck, and scratches my head, gruff, like I was ten, or eight. Joy's hand takes mine, and Dad laughs, and now I know what the air is like—it's like music. Like walking through "Ode to Joy," or a favorite love song. This air is youth, new born, but wise, like the ages, and our strides are long, like running, but without hurry. Breathing is smooth—a long, sweet drink of everything possible, everything a heart has ever wanted, everything lying in the deepest places of being human. A figure is ahead of us, almost flying, and long hair tells me it's Alex, and again, we are *known*, and free.

∾

But suddenly, I'm too tired to keep up, and Ruin breaks in. The truth is, I'm leaning on the light pole out by the street. It smells of creosote. I'm getting dirty, but I don't care. I'm full of Alex, and Joy, and death, too aware that the ache hanging here is not satisfied, is never satisfied.

My hands fumble with keys, and I wake up in my car, moving slowly, headed back home to my porch, and the glider, and the family. A pit stop at Allsup's. Get a coke, buy a pack of Camels, and light up just as I run the stop sign at Curtain and 42nd, a few blocks from home. My car squeaks a feeble squeak as I pull into the drive. My brakes are probably shot. There on the gravel, I walk around the car. I walk around again, and again. Absurdly, I smoke, coughing up nothing, and finally, after three cigarettes, I light the whole pack, and watch it burn at my feet.

Connie and Sara watch the whole thing from the porch. Afraid to speak, I suppose.

Thank God the day's over.

~

The funeral will be Tuesday, at the church, and I will preach it. I will say goodbye to Joy, and much more besides.

~

Dear God,

I know death is without victory, but it is winning tonight, pressing down on me, like a slab, the execution of old where rocks pile on until the witch is crushed. We all die, and it terrifies me, but more, my life without Joy, without Alex, and Mrs. Eric, and without Ruin, or without Sara, or one of the boys, terrifies me, and who will it be tomorrow? Death stalks me like a predator, cutting down my life, memory by memory, chance by chance, and though I may live forever, right now I am dead inside, all feeble, and wish to simply lie in the road and fade into nothing as cars roar by. If I open my chest to you, O Lord, and to life, it is too much, too much, and I will die too much to ever return.

Job said though you slay me, yet will I trust you, and I'm working on that, but it's hard. All death is foul murder, and slays, and I am slain as well, and I'm not Job. I'm just a guy who can't grasp the meaning of so many loves, so many deaths, so many cruel good-byes, and so much hateful life.

Forgive me, God, as I lie here, sinning, perhaps, in my distrust, or is it anger? Lonely, self-pitiful, and like a two-year old, mad that Daddy can't fix it.

I wish I could praise you tonight, and sleep well, nestled in a deep faith, but I can't. Maybe trust will come again with the morning.

Jesus.
Amen.

~

Sara and I are awake. It's way past midnight. We lie side by side in our bed, mattress sagging in the middle, and we roll together, thigh to thigh, and hold on. The making of one flesh is a gift from God, but it is little comfort tonight. After, Sara cries, and sleeps.

I wander down the hall, looking in on the boys. Richard sits up. I kiss him on the forehead, and push him back down, under the covers. His eyes grow into mine, and I sit quiet, our hands locked together. Finally he turns over, dropping off, releasing me, and I go toward the living room, headed for the porch.

I pass Connie in the hall. Seeing my eyes, and my mood, she decides to turn in, slipping off to bed, saying goodnight, and I'm sorry.

I get to the front door, put my hand on the knob.

But I stop.

I can't go out there. I can't go out there anymore. It's too dark, too cold, and I can't be that alone anymore. I have to retreat, find a way to remake myself. All the lights are out. No candles, no music. A floorboard creaks, then the walls.

I need these walls.

My knuckles are white, gripping the handle.

Finally, I give up, sit on the couch.

Just sit.

I'll wait for the day, chewing on my tongue without knowing it. Who knows what happens in tombs when the dead are patient, just waiting, hoping. Wondering if it's true, if there's a God to save them? I eventually close my eyes. My sleep is blank, and hollow, with no dreams, anymore.

October 14

He's my preacher. He baptized me.

Lynnette Armstrong, age 14, to Jack Simons
Notes on interviews concerning preaching
at First Church

. . . such a large request. . .

The funeral is over, the graveside memorial is over, the potluck dinner for the family is over. I'm standing at Joy's grave, where there's fresh dirt, deep, dark brown, mixed with red, like beauty bark, and I'm holding two blue balloons by white strings likely to break with the slightest breeze.

Wayne stands next to me. His balloons are red.

~

The mood was somber at breakfast this morning. The boys wanted to go to the funeral, and we decided to let them miss the day at school, so there were five of us around the table. I made pancakes. We gorged, taking our grief out on our stomachs, and we barely had enough syrup to go around. Connie felt out of place, apologizing for overstaying her welcome. Sara and I both said no, no problem, but Connie said she was going to Odessa for a day or two, that she had a friend there, and wanted to do some shopping. She'd be back toward the end of the week, she said. I told her she didn't need to do that, and I know she listened for what I might have meant by it, and I found myself not wanting her to go. Sara got up from the table, washed off her plate. She told Connie she was welcome, but that she should do what she needed to.

Sara banged her plate into the dishwasher, too loudly, and abruptly said she was going to shower. She left the room, obviously in a foul mood, which is not what I needed from her today. Connie smiled at me, pulling her hair back behind left ear, shrugging her shoulders, wondering what to do. I said—pointedly—will you come back Thursday or Friday, and she said okay, that she guessed she'd be back Friday.

She got the message.

But an hour later, as she stopped at the front door to say bye, I gave her a hug, and she hugged me back. There's a truth the body tells that reaches past necessary silence, and that embrace was a comfort in my grief, and a warning to my soul. It lasted too long, felt too good. Her eyes caught mine as we moved away from each other, and her warmth helped me, though I fought it. Her hand touched mine as she left the porch—an instant only—and it was hard to watch her drive away. I leaned on one of the porch posts at the top of the stairs, following her car with my eyes, silently, not wanting to break away until she was out of sight.

Sara missed all this—she was on the phone in the bedroom—but Wayne didn't. He sat on the couch, watching, curious, not smiling. Finally he grinned a little, and asked if she was coming back. I told him I didn't know.

~

Sara's moody these days, and I don't blame her. But she doesn't speak to me much, and it irritates me. But it also makes me nervous. I went back to the bedroom, and by this time she was in the bathroom spraying her hair, getting ready for Joy's service. I grabbed my blackest tie, and stood next to her, avoiding the mist, facing the mirror, starting on my half-Windsor. She finished the hairspray, and started on her teeth. Two minutes of quiet, shoulder to shoulder, catching each other's glance off and on, and I finally asked her what she was feeling. She spit out the toothpaste. Nothing, she said, rinsing. I pressed her. She wouldn't look at me, but said she was sorry, that things were on her mind.

She left the bathroom to get her dress. I got the tie squared away, and followed her. I asked her what things were on her mind. She stepped into her black skirt, and stood up straight, zipping the back. Her face told me she thought I was an idiot.

Oh, not much, she said. The future, her having to find work, what I was going to do—or not do—how the kids would transition, what everybody thought, everybody dying, the vote coming up, Connie and Dirk—that sort of thing. She stood there, glaring at me, and though I was embarrassed at my stupidity, what I really wanted to tell her was that she looked great in that black bra—especially with the long skirt and black heels.

But I figured it was not the time.

Jack's was the first face I saw when I got to Francis' house. I wanted to be there with the family before going to the church for the service. His face screamed fatigue, and stress, and I don't know how much longer the First Church of Ruin will have two elders to serve them. Yesterday, Jack came to my office and said he wanted to resign as an elder. It's not the first time he's offered, but Roland never lets him get away with it. But these days, Roland's fading as well, and who knows, I think they might both walk if given the chance. They're tired men. Jack and Roland are like brothers. They've known each other over forty years, and like brothers, they bicker and fight, mostly over dumb things. Last week, Jack walked out of our meeting—stormed out, really—upset over Roland's idea to let Beatrice speak at the church meeting on the twenty-eighth. Roland said he already promised her, which sent Jack through the roof, and lots of old, unfinished business came spewing into the room. At one point, Roland stopped just short of calling Jack a lying SOB, but I shouted him down, telling them they had to stop it, that they were going to have to get past this petty stuff—jealousies, turf issues, whatever—before God could do anything with this church. Jack grabbed his coat and hat, furious, tears right on the surface, and walked out, saying over his shoulder that he resigned, and to go on and let Beatrice be pastor, that we might as well let her preach on Sunday, and make her an elder to boot. He was still hollering when he hit the parking lot.

Roland and I sat there, exhausted, not stunned at all, and this morning, standing there in Francis living room, shaking hands with Jack, I worried about the little church in Ruin, sad for what might happen if and when I had to say good-bye.

≈

The funeral was open casket, as all these things are in Texas, and as people filed past, viewing the body, I watched their faces, most of them fixed solid, scraping against the mystery trying to swallow them up. A cheap recording of the "Hallelujah Chorus" blared over pitiful speakers as they closed the box a final time, and I knew the version Joy was hearing was probably much better.

Francis didn't cry much before the service, and held herself together at the church, though the last moment with Joy at the casket was tough. It's the moment in any funeral. Mom saying good-bye to the girl she birthed thirty-three years before, and now she's alone again. I'm told Francis finally broke down in the limo, weeping long and hard.

She and I had a long, miraculous talk yesterday evening, over apple pie and milk, after reminiscing with other family for a couple of hours. She said she takes great comfort in the fact of her daughter's conversion, and though we talked about God, and death, and the love of Jesus, the subject of church hardly came up. She was stunned when I told her about seeing Joy as I was leaving my office, that she seemed to say thank you, and that I'd blown it off as an imaginative fancy. But we figured the time, and the time she died was about the time I was leaving the office for class. Neither of us knew what it meant, but it gave us a welcome sense of awe, and an unexpected comfort. Right then and there, we were friends, lost in that strange, pleasant territory where palpable memories sparkle, and departed loved ones take on a charm and loveliness they probably never had.

≈

I spent the afternoon looking for helium.

Francis said Joy somehow knew her time was short, that not too long ago, while they were watching Seinfeld, Joy had made a passing remark about the soul. She'd been to a funeral of a friend's parent in recent days, where they let balloons go to say good-bye to the man's spirit, and that that would be a cool thing for her funeral, if she ever died. But such circus pageantry was too lightweight, too odd for Francis, and she couldn't do it, though I think she wanted to. But I like circuses, and after stopping by Baskin-Robbins on the way home today, I went in the drug store and picked up a packet of balloons. Richard blew one up, a green one, and Wayne let it out the window. It floated to the ground, and in the same instant I realized I needed special air to make it rise. I couldn't think of what that air was called, and Sara said helium. Now where was I going to find helium, and after dropping Sara and Richard off at home, Wayne and I ran around for over an hour.

Wayne's been watching me all day, staying close.

~

He can feel it, too.

He can feel the change coming, that unsure imbalance that comes with God's quiet. Since Connie's arrival, and more so since Alex died, he's been hanging around me, staying close when I'm at home, even going so far as to ask me to tuck him in, which he hasn't wanted in several years. I've lain beside him in bed every night for a week, sometimes talking over school, and plans for the tennis season, though I know he's got a different thing on his mind. I know he wants to talk, wants to get to what he's feeling, but he can't form the questions, and I ask the wrong ones. He makes comments like, Connie's been here two weeks, and Alex went to heaven, didn't he. He's asked me several times if we'll be moving soon, and if we do, will I get another church to preach to. I tell him both answers are up to God. He says how will I know what God says, and I can only tell him I'm listening as best as I can.

When we drove away from the graveside service, I told Sara I wanted to do the balloon business, and asked her did she want to come. She declined, but Wayne heard me talking about it, and when I stopped at the house to drop them off, he said he wanted to go with me. I told him no, but the longing in his eye looked familiar to me, and I knew I needed to say yes.

Who knows? Maybe God will use my son to tell me the plan.

≈

No one had helium.

We finally stopped at Nancy Popper's Floral Shop. She said sure, right back here. She blew up four of our balloons for free, saying what a shame about Joy, though she didn't know her, and wasn't I impressed with all the flowers. What was I going to do with the balloons, she wanted to know, but I lied, and said they were for some kids I knew, and she said what a good minister you are. We grabbed the balloons and hurried out. Wayne climbed in the car, and I felt his stare. Fighting off the balloons as I backed out of the parking space, he wondered why I lied, and I didn't have an answer, except to say that I thought that we should keep this secret, that this was a ceremony, kind of, or a prayer, and I wanted it to be just him and me. That maybe it was like going into the closet to pray, and not letting the left hand know what the right was doing. I asked him if he understood.

He said, not really.

≈

It's past five now, and Wayne's chilly out here in the wind, though he's trying to tough it out.

I say, it's a nice cemetery, and Wayne says yeah. Elms line the north edge of the plot, and give us a bit of a windbreak. But still, easy swirls tug at the balloons, bouncing them against each other, and I panic, not wanting to let them go until the right moment. Wayne asks if we should let them go, and I say no, not yet. When, he says, and I say soon, that I'll tell him.

I've never done this before.

"Daddy? I'm scared."

Daddy? He hasn't called me that since before school, since kindergarten—at least, that I remember. I say sit down here with me, and we settle in the grass at a corner of the grave. What are you scared of, I ask him, picking up a clod of red clay before I realize what I'm doing. He says he doesn't know, that things just seem not very sure right now. He says he's been thinking about Christmas, and the kids in school he wants to give presents to, especially Mary (she knows she's the girlfriend now) but he gets kind of a sick feeling when he remembers that he may not be here in Ruin to give them out.

"Dad, I don't want to move."

⁓

When Wayne was four, he lost his blanket.

My son's never been good at keeping up with things. Even now, toys tend to live in the back yard grass, though I make him clean up as often as I think of it. We constantly search for GI Joe's and tennis balls, and Legos are buried in the cushions of every chair in the house. "Have you seen my . . . " is a common question in our home, though I confess I probably ask about my keys and wallet and belt as often as he does about toys and shoes. But, the constant process of searching for lost goods can be, and often is, infuriating.

We never found the blanket. We turned the house upside down, discovering items we'd lost years before—a Junior League of America sweatshirt from my college years (I thought I'd sold it to my room-mate), a brand new daily planner I'd bought after landing the job at Ruin (it was packed in a box titled "old things to do"), several books on the Holy Spirit I'd been missing, and—thank heavens—Sara's first wedding ring—which, by the way, is a whole 'nother story.

But no blankey.

We checked Safeway, Wal-mart, the local day-care place we took him to maybe once, every inch of space at the church, the trunks of our cars, the parks, the lost and founds of several movie houses, and the homes of every friend Sara had before we called off the search, finally giving up the blanket, admitting it was gone for good.

I remember sitting on the porch with Wayne in my lap, giving him the bad news. He was brave, but the tears got him in the end, but the harder part for me was that when he went to bed, he'd lie there for a minute at the most, then get up and simply stand by his bed, then point at his sleeping spot, looking at it, and he'd say it didn't feel right, that his blankey was wanting to be with him in there.

He stopped that ritual after three weeks, but, even with a pooh bear to help, we mourned the blanket, off and on, for almost six months.

About a week after our porch conversation, Wayne and I were wrestling on the living room floor just before dinner when he suddenly stopped punching me. He said Daddy, and promptly sat on his bottom with a thump. I said what. His thoughtful face told me he was gathering up the question. He said he been thinking about it, and he kept wondering if I knew why his blanket had to be gone.

"Why did it have to be gone?"

∼

As I made notes for the eulogy, that's the question that kept floating around my paper. I tried to ignore it, because there's no answer, but it wouldn't go away.

I guess people die every day. Businesses go up in smoke, and life savings melt away in foolish investing. Married people meet single lovers, and affairs bring solid marriages to their knees. I could destroy mine if I wanted to. Easily. Nothing new, I suppose, to lose things— friends, wives, parents, dreams, lovers, calls of God. But I must say, I'm tired, and would like to know, like my son, why does it have to be gone?

I had my Dad's Bible with me this afternoon, praying for that silent counsel of eternity, when the thought struck me that maybe I should consider why did it get to stay as long as it did, "it" being whatever good thing I have or will enjoy. Why did I get to meet Joy? Why do I get to have Sara, and children, and the blessing of knowing God for one moment of my life? What about bread, and water, and the simple act of swinging on my porch with a book and coffee? The truth is, blessings rain on me like monsoons.

But these days, that thought doesn't help.

It doesn't replace a blankey.

I remember hearing a preacher say that every blessing of God is grace, that we deserve nothing really, and though I knew what he meant, I was a little miffed at the idea of deserving only bad things, especially since I've never felt that way about my own son.

Wayne deserves the best I can give him, though it's true enough I can never give him what he wants most. The gift of no suffering.

∾

I ask Wayne if he ever prays. By himself, just because he wants to.

Some, he says, but not too often. Though he's been asking lately not to have to move.

I never know how to do these conversations. I have visions of being a great spiritual leader in my home, but to instruct a young soul in pursuit of God always makes me think of the guy with the millstone at the bottom of the sea, the one Jesus said would be better off there than to make one of these little guys stumble. I teach my sons with fear and trembling, knowing it's my own salvation I work out, as well as theirs.

Why do we pray, I ask Wayne, and he gives me that I-don't-want-to-have-this-conversation silence, and the look that goes with it, but I say come on, let's talk about this. He frowns, and says mockingly that we pray to get God to help us, like he's heard it a million times and it's so beside the point, especially sitting with balloons at the foot of a fresh grave.

I ask him what do you do when you need me? He shrugs, and says, I don't know, I guess I come see you. You come talk to me, don't you? He blinks, peering up at me. I guess so, he says. Do I give you what you want? Sometimes, he says, but lots of times, no.

I say let me ask you another question. He interrupts, complaining about the cold, wanting to know when we can let the balloons go, and go home. I say, just a minute, and we will. I say, do you know me? This catches him off guard, but he guffaws, saying, Daaaaad, of course I do. That's a stupid question. How do you know me, I ask. Daaaaad. No, really, how do you know me? I don't know, he finally says. He's grinning. Okay, okay, he says, how do I know you?

The same way we know anybody. Spending time together, talking, being honest about what we feel with each other, having special moments when we cry or laugh together. I ask him if he remembers losing his blanket and he laughs and says yeah, how mad he was that day on the porch. I say it's a good thing to have a dad, huh? He says, yeah, I guess so.

I say that's why you pray. God is the dad, a much better dad than me, and you're the son. I'm the son. We spend time there, with him, to ask why it has to be gone. Even if he can't tell us just now. I tell him there's lots of big things happening in our family, and he says yeah, he knows. These are the times to pray, Wayne. The times when we need to take long walks with Jesus. Talking, listening, doing all the things friends and dads and sons do together, that the help we ask God for might be real things he does, like making things work so we don't have to move. Things like that. Or healing people, or helping someone find a job.

Like you might need a job, he says.

Yeah. Like I might need a job.

But I tell him most of the help comes not from those kind of things, but from just knowing him. Knowing how to feel him standing close, how to feel him speak, to learn to hear what he says. And learning that he really does know what the deal is with us. What we want, how we hurt, what we long for, what we dream. What we fear.

Wayne says, he knows?

Oh, yes, I say. He knows.

"That's good."

A gust of wind rips one of the balloons from his hand. His eyes dart to mine, wondering if he'll be in trouble. I tell him it's okay, no big deal. He smiles, says thanks.

"Still scared?"

"Yeah, a little, but . . . I'm better, I guess."

I stand and tell him it's time to say goodbye to Joy, time to let go. He stands, grateful, ready to go home, ready to be warm. I say, let's pray. He says, okay.

"But I still don't want to move."

~

Wayne sits in the car, waiting on me, while I take one more minute alone with Joy. After our short prayer, Wayne let his red balloon go, and I let go one of mine. It was odd to watch his go straight up, while mine made a jagged line up and down, falling behind. Wayne's balloon was lost from sight long before mine. He said, mine won, and ran to the car. I said I'll be right there.

~

I'm supposed to know that God understands this death business.

Joy, come forth, I say out loud, and the dirt lies still, nothing but dense dust. How many of us have stood out here, a living man or woman standing over a dead man or woman, talking to the day, or the night, the wind and stars, wanting nothing more than to feel their skin one more time on our fingertips?

~

I can't let go of my balloon.

I'd like to imagine Jesus standing next to me, maybe holding a gold balloon bigger than mine, with a basket underneath, to take us both—Joy and me—to skies I've never seen. Or maybe God standing next to me, or at least an angel of His, like the guys who came to see Abraham, announcing a coming child, and a coming fire from heaven. Or maybe Jesus with a sword sticking out of his mouth, like John saw. Heck, I'd settle for the three guys in shining white on the mountain, and I, like Peter, would idiotically offer to build a tent, falling on my face in worship.

But there's nobody here but me, and the sun's gone down.

❦

The balloon's still wrapped around my pinky, cutting off circula-
tion. I unwrap it, one small string circle at a time. There's a bit of dust
blowing across the field just beyond the border of the memorial park.
I stop the string. The temperature of the wind eases its way into my
memory, and the up and down roaring of the wind in my ears . . . it
feels familiar . . . like *deja vu,* like clocks reversing, years spinning
away to yesterday.

I rewrap the balloon, remaining still, every nerve tuned to something coming.

The lake. The wind on the lake. That day on the water, years
ago, when I felt the call of God. Wind rustling in the trees, trees all
lined up like emerald soldiers standing guard over the unknown. This
time it's grass instead of water, as green as can be expected for this
time of year. Brown patches litter the ground, but in the distance, tall
weeds make waves heading toward the horizon.

Perhaps if I asked now—this right now, he would hear, and reply.
Can it truly be such a large request, to simply hear a sound? A voice?

❦

Perhaps this is the moment.

The moment I've been looking for. The moment when a new
thing is decided for my life. The wind is right, feels like it could carry
a voice, a word with my name written on it, if I can be still enough.
Like a cloud it comes, perhaps on the back of that dust, perhaps rising from the place where dead people reunite with family from centuries past—better yet, from that part of the unseen where they
reunite with the lost part of themselves. The part of which they said,
"why does it have to be gone?"

Yes. Perhaps. Perhaps, such a moment.

A good time to die.

So be it.

I will change my life—here, now. God will do it. I will give up my longing, give up my questioning heart. God will free me. This moment. As he freed Joy, he will free me.

I'll close my eyes, pray God to give a sign, a vision, a noise, a grunt, an aural how-dee-do. Just a pin dropping, a pea-size notion of an echo, any old thing will be fine. I need an understanding I don't have, and I'm asking you to do it now. This now.

When I open my eyes, I'll be a new man. Not to test God, but to simply say please, ask for a little help.

∽

Wayne honks the horn, two short blasts.

I wave him off, closing my eyes, forcing concentration on the wind, the dark, and the unseen force swirling round my head.

Now.

Now.

There's a slight throbbing behind my left eye, a headache's unexpected arrival announced.

Nothing more.

∽

I've stood here long enough. Time to open my eyes.

There's the grave, and the trees, and the brown patches.

I let go of my last balloon, saying goodbye Joy, not bothering to watch, not bothering to pray.

To this silent God, I have nothing to say.

October 18

*Patricia: I don't know how . . . or why
. . . Sara does it. Honestly.*

Tahnee: Oh, mother . . . I do.

Patricia and Tahnee Cubstead, as told to
Jack Simons, Administrative Committee

. . . *to wake the gods* . . .

Connie left this afternoon, for good.

Sara took the boys to the grocery store around ten, leaving me to help Connie pack, or to ready myself for tomorrow's sermon, or for whatever else I might do on a Saturday morning. Cartoons distracted me for awhile, but listening to Connie rummage around in her bedroom, getting her stuff together, made me antsy, and I couldn't stop my knee from bouncing. I gave it up, clicking off the tube, and went to watch her pack. Leaning on the doorframe, I couldn't help but notice the tousled strings of dark hair hanging over her eyes, her fresh, not-too-heavy make-up, and the fact that her bra was in her hand, not on her body.

I smiled at her, and she smiled back. I didn't even try to look away.

I told her Richard's room liked her, that it wouldn't be happy if she left. She tossed the bra into the suitcase, making note that I hadn't shifted my gaze. She picked up a white cotton blouse, laid it out on the bed flat, face down, and turned her back to me, folding, taking care to get the creases in the sleeves just so. She said the room would have to get over it. She said tell Wayne thanks for letting Richard take his top bunk for awhile, and tell Richard thanks for letting me borrow his room. I said no big deal. She tossed the shirt in the suitcase, and taking another look around, shut it, closed the locks, yanked it off the bed. Now she was standing in front of me, waiting for me to move. I held my ground. She peered at me through her bangs, grinning, leaning under the weight of her luggage, and said, what?

I said it's just that . . . you know, sorry you have to go. She looked at the floor and said I know, I know—me, too. Then she told me to get out of the way.

~

Her trip to Odessa did it, I suppose. She spent almost two hundred dollars on clothes, after which she realized she probably had to get a job, which meant going home. She'd said she'd made plans with Abby, her Odessa friend, to get an apartment in Tyler. Yesterday, I said who's this Abby person, and she said they'd known each other at Southwest Texas State, and learned to drink martinis together. I asked her if that's what they were going to do in Tyler, just drink martinis, and she said if that's what it takes.

~

"I have to go, Cyrus."

I smiled and said okay, but I didn't mean it, and I knew this standing in the door stuff was simple flirting, a game I didn't mean to play, and didn't really have the stomach for, but she was leaving, and I was lost, so why not? She looked toward the window, eyes shining again, frustrated, then came on through the door, managing to slide by me, face up, body closely square to mine. As she headed out to the car, I looked for her other suitcase, the older blue one, but it wasn't ready to go, so I followed her empty-handed. I got to the steps in time to see her set the suitcase down on the passenger side of the truck.

What are you going to do, I said, coming down off the porch, and she said there'd be secretary jobs there, she hoped, temp work to get her started, and that maybe she'd try to figure out a way to finish her degree in business at the UT Tyler branch. Fumbling for her key to the door, she dropped her small ring in the gravel. I bent down, grabbed it, found the right key, and opened the door. I picked up her suitcase, but she said I can do that, grabbing the suitcase out of my hand, tossing it up into the cab. Why don't you put it in the back, I asked, and she shrugged and said, might rain.

She pushed the door shut, ignored my hand on her arm, and ran back inside.

∾

She took off about 2:00 p.m.

She was certainly in better spirits than she'd been three weeks ago—less desperate, less destroyed—and there was lots of laughter that last five minutes as the three of us stood at her truck. She hugged Sara, and climbed up behind the wheel. But just then, we heard the phone ringing, and Sara said that she was expecting a call from school. It's about Wayne, she said, and she started to take off, but I stopped her, telling her I'd get it. As I ran in, she was yelling thanks, that she'd been playing phone tag with this lady for three days.

I was running from the good-bye.

"Hello?"

It was Sara's mom, calling long distance, and I tried to tell her that no, Sara couldn't talk right now, that she was busy, and now that I think about it, I should've just lied and told her Sara was gone to the grocery store. But my mother-in-law hassled me, and finally I said hang on, I'll go get her.

When I hollered at Sara from the porch, she groaned and told Connie to wait, not to leave just yet. As she ran toward the house, I ambled back to the truck, getting there about the time the screen door slammed. The yard was quiet.

Connie closed her door, but the window was down, and I stopped there beside her, leaning on the truck, my hand resting on the door. I picked off bits of white paint already peeling from the truck. Her fingers were long, slender lines, cool against my skin, moving slowly across my knuckles, like feathers, and she stared at our hands together. She raised her head. Her fingers stilled, as did mine, and they interlocked in that ancient grip. She had trouble looking at me.

"Thank you, Cyrus . . . I'm sorry . . . last night . . . "

She stopped, lowered her head again. I nodded.

"Yeah . . . me, too."

"Take care, Cy. Take care of Sara. And the boys."

"I will."

For a couple of minutes, we stared at the curb line of the empty street, listened as a horn honked blocks away, felt the pressure of our palms and fingers. Finally, I raised her hand to my mouth and kissed it. Then back to silence, back to staring at the curb. She wanted me to look at her. I felt some part of her reaching for me, and I knew it was time to break it, break away, let it go.

Sara came out of the house, onto the porch. But she was too far away to hear the tremor in my voice.

"Goodbye, Connie."

I stepped away from the truck, and Sara curled under my arm, and we stood there together, watching the truck back away from us. We followed to the street where we waved and waved, until Connie was gone, the truck out of sight.

∽

I grabbed a cup of coffee and sat on the porch while Sara went to get Richard and Wayne from a birthday party. When they got home, the boys grabbed a football, and I watched them throw it around screaming I'm Troy Aikman and I'm Michael Irvin, neither of them doing decent imitations. Sara sat down next to me, wanting to talk, I suppose, but we were out of sync, off the track, and I didn't know how to get back on. She said her mom had called just to check on us, worrying, wondering what new news she had. I said that it was sweet of her to care. Sara said yeah, she's a sweet lady.

Sara kept staring at the low clouds. The sun was already leaning that way, arcing down.

Sara said it's too bad—that Connie was such a beautiful woman, too beautiful to deserve the kind of man she got. I agreed. Sara thanked me for being so hospitable, for letting Connie stay so long. I said sure, no problem. Sara wondered out loud if I'd slept with her.

I blinked.

"With Connie?"

She nodded.

"No."

She said, did you ever?

Think, think, think. Like Pooh Bear, but quick, because I couldn't afford a pause. But seeing her face, I knew she knew the answer. To lie would be crazy, not to mention disastrous.

"Years ago, before I knew you."

She took a big breath, and then wondered if I'd ever wanted to. Sleep with her. With Connie. Since back then.

I sipped my coffee, opened my mouth to answer.

But the pause nailed me, and Sara got up and walked inside. I heard her keys rattle, and drawers rustling as she hunted down her purse. She let the door hit the frame as she took the distance to the car at a fast clip. She ducked into the car, calling out that it was okay, that she'd be back, she'd be fine.

But her tires dug into gravel, and she backed off the curb, bouncing, as she whipped the car into the street. She roared off, going west, which meant toward nowhere, and I should've been upset—and maybe I was—but it felt to me like I just didn't have the energy to care.

∾

It's been a hellish week.

Tuesday night, Wayne and I walked in the door from the cemetery at 6:30, and I went to bed at 7:00. Sara wondered if I was sick, and I said yes, that I felt like I had the flu, with achy body and chills, to which she said I'm sorry, and promptly went back to her book. It was all a lie, of course, though I did feel sick to my stomach, sick of giving up my life in pursuit of what apparently wasn't there.

Oddly enough, I slept immediately. Ten hours of rock hard, no-dream snoozing, never wanting light again. The clock said 5:09 when my eyes finally snuck a peek at the world, but thankfully, the house was dark. My mind was blank, a white rage layering the top of my consciousness, and I knew that to move would be to explode. I lay mummy-still, sheets up under my chin, for over two hours, cringing at the faint glow touching the edges of the blinds. I finally hit the floor at 7:18, just as Wayne padded his way down the hall to the shower.

I didn't brush my teeth, didn't shave, didn't eat breakfast. Slipped on a pair of old jeans, a tee shirt, that old super hero sweatshirt I found in the blankey search, white socks, tennis shoes. Grabbed my wallet and checkbook, ran past Sara and the boys at the breakfast table, said not to look for me 'til they saw me coming. Said I love you as I walked out the door.

I'm not sure Sara ever looked up.

~

I skipped Shady Oaks.

First time in ten years to let it go. Sorry, Geyser, but no excuses, no guilt, no nothing—I just didn't go. Nor did I call the office to let anyone know. Finally, around 12:30, knowing she'd be out to lunch, I called Jan, leaving a note on her machine that I wouldn't be in at all, that I wouldn't be at the evening midweek service, and that some other preacher would have to do the talking. As I got to the end of the message, though, I heard someone pick up the phone, and I rattled out a quick thanks, hanging up before they could stop me.

I stepped out of the phone booth, went back to my table, my lunch spot, a truck stop with a fake oil derrick standing like a dumb colossus just outside. I was ten minutes from Abilene, in the middle of a driving day, killing time, just doing I-20, looking at nothing, thinking of nothing but how much gas I had, whether my tires were still good, and whether I would ever bother to turn around, ever bother to go back home.

It didn't help that coming across, two hours back, on the eastern edge of Midland, I got a ticket for doing 92 in a 65. I'd beaten a ticket once before with the I'm-a-preacher business, but when I tried it on this guy, he just laughed and said he was sorry to hear it. Funny, but I felt the blood rush into my face, and I guess he knew I was ticked off, because he apologized. Writing down my license plate number, he said he didn't mean to laugh, but I didn't look like a preacher. No offense, he said.

I told him I'd been thinking the same thing.

He asked me where I was headed, and when I told him I wasn't sure, that it was just a day to drive, to get out, that business had been tough lately, he smiled and said he understood that. He tore off the ticket, and tried to muse about the difficulty of selling God in the market, but in the end, he did nothing but make my profession seem absurd. Out of curiosity, I asked him if he believed.

"In God?"

He chortled, a mean little laugh, showing his teeth. He shook his head as if to say he couldn't believe guys like me existed, and waved me off without committing one way or another. Have a nice day, he said, and be careful. I watched him turn his car, cross the median, and when his taillights got lost in the glare of the sun, I hit eighty again, daring God—or anybody else—to come get me.

~

Abilene, Texas. Nice place. I'd been there off and on over the years, stopping for meals on the way to Dallas, attending various religious functions at one of the three Bible colleges there, or preaching on rare occasions in one of the zillion evangelical churches in town. There's a mall to the south, a few restaurants nearby, good bar-b-que downtown at a local joint called Harold's, and a railroad track cutting the city right down the middle. There's even an airport. Streets are clean, people are friendly, clerks helpful, crime rare, and though liquor is abundant, everyone has the decency to frown about it, saying they wouldn't touch the stuff.

I spent the afternoon driving up and down city streets, stopping at antique stores, at what I call hobo shops—stores selling junk—nasty, dusty goods sitting on tacky floors in piles, piles that have been there for years, if not decades. I walked the mall, sat through a kid's soccer game in a nearby park, ate a damp cheeseburger at a Sonic—the soggy burger due to a spilled cherry coke, courtesy of the sock hop on skates.

I picked the tomatoes off my burger, considered my options.

~

Simply put, my heart was splitting, cracking like rotten timber, and I was running.

The silence of Joy's grave was the hammer that did it. God was coming. I had felt him coming, knowing—*knowing*—he would speak to me—in my head, through my son, through a vision, through a scripture remembered, through a renewed sense of call and service. Maybe I'd catch a glimpse of an image, two trees touching, a jackrabbit scratching his back, a pair of swallows mating, or a big flock of Canada geese lost, moving that giant V to Mexico. Something, anything, to suggest that his presence in my world was active, and personal, and that he would not, after all, give me a rock when I stood with open soul asking for bread, the one bit of food I needed to survive.

But all I got was a dull pain in my temples. In that moment, a piece of me broke away. Wayne knew I'd changed the minute I sat foot in the car, but he'd known better than to breathe a word.

Sara hasn't noticed. She has her own crisis. Or so she thinks.

~

My burger disgusted me—wet bread always does. My mood was foul, and possible sins hung around my windshield, around my eyes, begging me to choose them. I didn't exactly want to go to jail—I was clear enough to know that—but suddenly all the sins of the early Cyrus seemed petty, kids play, paranoia masquerading as a desire for perfection. I wanted to do something wrong.

I figured I'd feel better.

I pulled out of the Sonic, sloshing cherry coke on my right leg. Wiping at it, I thought about murder, but that was out of the question, and beyond that, I couldn't think of anyone to kill. Adultery was a possibility if Connie was willing, but how much trouble would that be, and I barely had energy to live my life with one woman, much less two. Assault and battery seemed silly, and reading about old lechers exposing themselves, the dumbest of dumb activities, always grossed me out. I had no one to embezzle, no tax return to cheat on, no fraudulent scheme to perpetrate, and pornography was boring. The idea of a prostitute came to mind. Too scary. The chance of disease, not to mention getting knifed by a pimp or arrested by an undercover guy in drag, put me off. I guess I've seen too many movies.

Maybe I could rob a Seven-Eleven.

It was 6:20 p.m. I stopped at the first Seven-eleven I came to, trying to imagine it all. I left the cherry coke in the car, and went in. I got a sixteen ounce hot cup, and as I poured the thick, black goop this place was selling as coffee, I scoped out the joint. Approaching the counter, I imagined waiting for the 12-year-old girl behind the register (she looked about that, with her Pippi Longstocking pigtails) to open the cash drawer, then I would leap over the beef jerky and the dill pickles sitting by the corn dogs, shove her aside in my best Clint Eastwood bravado, and empty the money into a grocery sack (she'd have to give it to me), and run silently into the night—richer, happier, feeling more alive than ever in my life.

I smiled and asked her how she was doing. She said fine. I smiled. She smiled back, huge—but it was fake, her eyes absolutely on vacation. In fact, I'd never seen anybody smile that big without opening her mouth.

I took my change, and my cowardice, and left.

~

It was almost 7:00, and I kept wandering through the town, gently making my way west again, and north, back toward the interstate. I tried to ignore the churches, but they were on every corner, and as I passed by, I noticed parking lots filling with the midweek faithful. I'd always heard Abilene church people were serious about this Wednesday night business.

Just before I hit I-20, I saw a Christian Church quietly going about its business. I pulled into the parking lot, and stopped. It was about 7:15. I sat in the lot entrance, thinking I might go in, either to be saved again, or to disrupt the worship with a hostage threat. I couldn't decide.

Suddenly, I honked.

A whim, an impulse, but with the first rush of sound, I knew this was an absurdly good thing.

I leaned on my horn for maybe fifteen seconds, an eternity in the midst of soft praise and prayer. I stopped and waited. Nothing. I hit it again, another ten to fifteen, shaking my head, silently mouthing, cursing in gibberish, waving first one arm, then the other, making sure passers-by would know I was having car trouble, trouble out of my control. I stopped again, still nothing. This time I held it for thirty full seconds, counting one-thousand-one, one-thousand-two, one-thousand-three . . .

aahhnnnkk . . . aahhnnnkk . . . aahhnnnkk . . . aahhnnnkk . . .

Finally, after three or four minutes of this off and on, off and on honking, a gray man in a gray suit stepped out of the gray church front door and brought his gray hair over to my car. My horn quit just as he started to speak. He yelled DID YOU NEED HELP? I hollered back NO THANKS, and he jumped out of his skin. I said, sorry, I guess there's no need to shout, and he said no, there wasn't. In a calm voice I told him I was really sorry, that I was having trouble with my horn. He said he didn't know much about it, but if I'd pop the hood, he'd look. Of course, unfortunately, as soon as he put his head under the hood, the horn blared again, though the blast was no more than a blink. (I didn't want to hurt his hearing.) But of course, he jumped again, staggering backward, and looking back on it, I suppose I could've hurt the poor man. He got away fast, hobbling toward the door of the sanctuary, saying he'd see if he could find someone to help. I followed at a snail's pace, blaring away at what I calculated were regular intervals. The sanctuary faced west, and a floor-to-ceiling plate glass window stood at the front, so that the congregation could see the sunset and the interstate. I rolled my car slowly past the window. *Aahhnnnkk.* The preacher turned around, frowning. *Aahhnnnkk.* Heads were craning, stretching, trying to see the noisemaker.

I got to the main entry of the building, and the congregation's mechanic came out to the car. Miraculously, my horn quit. He looked under the hood as I stood next to him. He said it looks like it's all-right, said it could be a short, that I should check it out. He shut the hood. I said, thanks, and that oh, it probably wouldn't do it anymore. I grinned, and he narrowed his eyes, catching on, getting the gist of my smile.

"Mister, do you have a problem?"

I climbed back in the car and started the engine. I rolled down the window, and told him I did indeed have a problem, that I was complaining about the silence of deity, and that come hell or high water, I was determined to make enough noise to wake the gods. He clearly thought I was a loon.

He said there's only one, you know.

Preachers, preachers, everywhere. He was witty—I'll give him that—this six foot guy with a goatee, with enough dirt under his nails to make me think he knew his cars. But he thought he knew his people, too, but with me, he missed by a country mile. Only one god I said. He handed me a tract outlining what appeared to be the five steps to salvation.

I laughed out loud. Yeah, well.

I crept out of the parking lot, feeling silly and hot-faced, but amazingly better for a time. I felt juvenile, foolish, cut free from the lousy grime of having to be grown, of having to sit in a corner paying bills, paying dues, paying respects.

I hit the road, expecting to get back to Ruin around midnight.

But just on the other side of Midland, not far from the spot where the patrolman laughed, I had to pull over again. But this time, I did it on my own. Sick to my stomach, throwing up burgers, coffee, and cokes, and then dry heaving, mostly sick with grief and anger, and the thought that I was no longer the Cyrus I knew. I kept shuffling sideways, moving down the road a few steps at a time so I wouldn't have to look at my guts lying on the ground. Finally, it was over, and I straightened up, gasping for the air that was turning cool again, again coming from the north.

Getting back in the car, speeding down the on ramp, I thought to pray. I turned the thought down flat.

～

I got home at midnight, watched TV until three, and some forty-five minutes later finally said goodbye to the day.

I slept 'til noon.

~

Thursday, I called in sick, hoping for the message machine, but Jan picked up, saying thank God, that she was worried about me. I said I had a bug, that I'd thrown up the day before, leaving out the fact that I'd also driven around four hundred fifty miles. She said the Shady Oaks people called, wondering about me. Then she waited, not talking, expecting to force an explanation. I coughed a few times, and said thanks, that I had to go. I'll see you tomorrow, I said, hanging up before she had a chance to say bye.

Sara was out, at lunch with one of her Monday night prayer group friends.

I snooped around my bookshelves, looking for a book to read, settling on a piece of fantasy I'd read years ago, about an unbelieving leper, though I couldn't remember what he didn't believe. I wrapped myself in a blanket on the couch, and made it through about twenty pages, before I put it down, and went back to bed.

I couldn't stay there either, though. I threw off the sheets, and decided to clean the house. I started in the kitchen, digging crumbs out of corners, hand mopping the floor, rinsing out the garbage pail. I attacked the bedroom next, putting clean sheets on the bed, scrubbed out the shower and the toilet, got the mirror crystalline. Even emptied my chest of drawers, folding my sweaters and shirts into tiny squares and cylinders. Then I quit and watched Oprah, munching on my usual toast and butter.

The boys made me sit through a kid show about animals, and Sara came home just as the cheetah ran down the antelope. She didn't mention my cleaning. She also didn't ask me about Wednesday, saying she figured I was a big boy, and that I knew what I needed. After five, I made hamburgers for dinner, played catch with Richard, yelled at Wayne for not respecting me, read the paper, read a bedtime story, took a hot shower, kissed Sara once while we watched the news, and unbelievably, the house was black again. Night had come back already.

But this time, no sleep.

≈

Now, Saturday night, after the pause on the porch, hiding out in my office up at church, ten o'clock, with a single light on, I'm wondering what Sara thinks. What she thinks about Connie. When she got back from wherever she went—and I gave her as much privacy about where she went as she'd given me—I told her nothing, really, had happened between Connie and me.

She said that wasn't the point.

≈

Connie had come back to town from Odessa Friday afternoon, around 3:30, just as the boys were coming through from school. She'd had a great time, she said, and then she modeled new clothes, showing off in a classy tan and white linen jacket and top (a fly-away tunic, she called it) with matching patterned rayon pants. Sara oohed and aahed appropriately, and I said "nice pants," referencing the Docker commercial (I think it's Dockers), but the girls didn't get it.

Then Connie took a big breath and announced that she'd made plans. She was going home, getting an apartment with Abby, getting on with her life. She had, in fact, made up her mind.

She was giving Dirk the divorce.

Divorce. She smiled bravely, but the tears were threatening to spill over. I said maybe the boys and me should find a place to go. Sara nodded that that was a good idea.

≈

I took the boys to Burger King and to see *Space Jam*, though we didn't have the money for it, and I guess the girls jabbered the whole time we were gone, grousing about men and money, and the way times have changed, that the white horse didn't ride anymore, that princes were all turned to frogs. At least that's what I gathered from talking to Sara. But as I brushed my teeth, watching her brush hers, we smiled at each other, and I couldn't remember the last time I'd gotten one of those open smiles. After I got the boys to bed, I told her I was going to read, and she said she needed to sleep, that Connie was wearing her out. Sara was upset, but okay, and for her, sleep was the best way out.

∾

I kissed her, and went back to my books.

Connie had gone on to bed, and after looking over my shelves for something to distract me, I decided against reading, and turned off all the lights.

I like to sit alone in the dark, in the kitchen or the living room, or maybe even go for a walk in the backyard. When all the lights are out, it feels like breaking rules to be up, wandering, sitting, watching street lamps, or the shadows they make. Last night, it was the kitchen, though after ten minutes or so, I had to walk, had to futz around. I wandered into the backyard.

It was cool, but there was no wind to force the chill. Clouds were high and scattered, and the moon's fullness tinged the yard with a silver hue, which I thought was pretty for exactly one second, a feeling immediately giving way to a cynical distaste for all things monochrome.

I love full moons, but last night I wished for deep black, thinking again how those kind of nights hide—and birth—a multitude of sins.

Perhaps even the sin of giving up.

∾

I'm not sure how it happened. I'm not sure I want to know.

I was about to turn the northwest corner of the house, headed for the front, when I heard the sliding glass door open. I stopped and watched Connie step into the yard. She was still dressed, and the steam rising from her hands made me think she was carrying cups of coffee. But the kitchen was still dark, and I distinctly remembered that I'd turned the pot off, though there were several cups worth still in the carafe.

When she handed me the cup, it was indeed hot coffee, and she read my surprise.

"Microwave."

She went back to the door, slid it shut, and came back. She wondered if it was okay to join me. I said sure. I led around the corner, heading for the porch, thankful for the large spaces between my house and the neighbors.

≈

Connie held the coffee close to her face. She savored the steam, and the warmth, and as I watched her mouth sip at the edge, I felt the need to talk, to blabber, to get the words started. Too much silence might undo me. If I waited for her to lead, I might follow, and that path might take me far, far away.

≈

I sat on the porch steps, while she sat cross-legged, shoes off, on the walk in front of me, her face raised toward the stars, which were especially bright along the western horizon. We were fully encased in shadow—the moon was not yet in the west. I wondered if she'd want my hand again. She sat her coffee in the grass, and lay back, flat on the ground, her hands a pillow behind her head. She seemed happy, I thought, but hard—deadly attractive, prone like that, her upraised arms lifting her tee shirt to reveal a slim line of skin just below her navel. I was chilly, but she looked toasty, and I supposed it was that warm feeling that comes with making decisions, right or wrong. Connie was pleased, proud that she'd done the hard thing, made the decision, moved on, determined to be a powerful woman in the world. A finality sat in her body, in her gesture, even in the way she moved her eyes, certainly in the hard, sure lines of her mouth, and I knew it must be true that there was no longer any hope for Dirk and Connie's life together.

But there was also a mystery about her, a deeper something, and I had a hunch there was a secret lurking around, and I wondered if I'd be the one to hear it, though I figured Sara already knew.

~

I asked her what divorce felt like. Not a sensitive question, and I immediately regretted it.

She sat back up and looked me in the eye. She wondered if this talk was going to be with a pastor or an old friend. I said just a friend, a guy, and she said a guy I used to sleep with, and I said, well. She said sorry, that she was feeling sassy, and strong, and that she very much just wanted to talk to the guy she used to know, though the tilt of her head told me there might be more to it than that.

I said, that's me, I'm the guy.

She let her head drop back, and said this divorce thing was crazy, that inside she felt kind of crazy: strong, tough, sick, like a brick hit her in the head, like she'd been stained, like she knew who she was for the first time in her life. She said her emotions were right on top, so raw, so intense, that it made everything in her sight burn with a kind of brilliance. She paused and I could see her searching, figuring out how to put it. She said it was like there was a life, or an aliveness, behind everything—the clouds, the neighbors' house to the west, her truck, the field, the street lamp—I can almost see the air, she said. Your face, she added. And that what we usually see is only a reflection of that life underneath, but that right now, she could see clearly, clean to the core, to the place where the life underneath lay, waiting to be seen.

She got up and joined me on the steps, snuggled up against me, put her arm through mine.

She told me she could see me. Clearly. Clear to the bone. And that it terrified her, but she liked it. That she liked feeling it, liked being close to me, or at least, feeling like she was. She leaned in, but her voice didn't waver or go soft.

"Kiss me."

Maybe I do know what happened.

God knows I wanted to kiss her. Her face couldn't have been more than two inches from mine. She was lovely, hair lightly touching her forehead and cheeks, a strand in her mouth, which looked lush, though in truth, her lips were always thinner than what I preferred. Kissing was never her strong suit. But her pale skin was smooth, and clear, and she'd obviously found a perfume she thought I'd like, a subtle, dark scent, with a touch of floral sweetness. I don't think I'll forget it.

But car lights appeared just up the road, heading toward us, and I used the break in the moment to stand up and move across the walk, across the grass, heading for the mesquite. I didn't want to run, exactly, but I needed room, room to dance, if a dance is what I was to do. I had to be standing to face the music, to face my life.

She caught up with me as I leaned against the tree, street side, saying she was sorry, that I probably thought she was a slut or something. I didn't reassure her, but instead asked her what she wanted with me. She shrugged and said she loved Sara, that she wasn't asking for anything, certainly didn't want to mess up my home. She said you have great boys, and I said yes, I do.

"I didn't get any boys."

~

Connie once dreamed of having a vastly different life.

Honestly, I haven't thought of that night we spent in bed together for years, but last night, standing at the mesquite, watching emotion play across her face under the full moon, I couldn't escape the image of these two youngsters curled together under sweet, sinful covers, sleeping, and of the dreams we painted for each other as we whispered things of ourselves we were only beginning to apprehend. It wasn't the sex I remember—truth to tell, it wasn't terribly satisfying, and nothing like the Hollywood pictures. What I remember was Connie's face tucked into my neck, her mouth occasionally lifting to tell me her dreams of Europe, and traveling on so little, seeing the mountains of

Switzerland, riding the trains, flirting with foreign waiters, and eating cheese and bread in the morning, and washing it all down with a luncheon wine. How she wanted a family, with a strong man like me, she said back then, with children—lots of dark haired boys and girls playing chase over green schoolyards, but especially boys, with their crazed energy and bounding sense of life. How she'd walk in the afternoons to pick them up, and chat with the other moms, trading stories of men who adored them, who fought wars on their behalf, genuinely believing they were special people, with special gifts and destinies, and that moms chatting would lead to women knowing women, and that that knowing would birth friendships worth dying for.

≈

Her strength started to fade. Crying came like a night cloudburst, and she knelt on the ground, weeping silently, her back shaking, and she finally fell onto her side, taking a fetal position, knees pulled into her face, breaths coming rarely. I knelt beside her, then sat down next to her, my hand on her head, then her shoulder, down along her arm, patting, rubbing, wanting to comfort her, knowing I wasn't even coming close.

I've thought more than once how little men know of grief.

Finally, I had to join her, and I wept, too, though not nearly as hard as I might. Mine were gentle tears, next to her sobbing: my dam wasn't ready to break. But her silence came apart, giving way to sounds, keening noises, heart-tearing, though soft, and low. I echoed those sounds, and pulled her up and into my chest, and we wept together, in tandem, our lost cries mingling, rising from the earth all mixed, bonded. Our grief was prayer, a calling for salvation, or a new world, a new understanding of love, and of God.

I wished for someone to hear it. I doubted anyone did.

≈

I don't know how long we sat there, arms wrapped around each other, heads leaning on shoulders, quiet, with simple aftershocks still coming. We kept wiping the tears off each other's cheeks, and we even managed a laugh or two. We tried to speak a couple of times, but both times the need for peace overwhelmed us, and prayer kept raising it's head. I'd discover I was in the middle of a prayer, asking God to help Connie, to take care of her, to hold her like Dirk never could, but then I'd stop, realizing it was just a habit, this praying, and I'd drop it cold. Then two minutes later, I'd be back at it, asking the nothing for help I no longer believed in.

I guess the intimacy of it all is how it happened.

Two kisses. The first, short, simple, inquisitive, magic. The second, full of passion, urgent, digging for what we needed, long, and longer, not breathing, knowing this would be the only kiss, the only time ever in our lives that we would revisit the intimacy between us. Our mouths clung to each other, wanting to go on, but I knew such going on was suicide, absurd, not possible, whether there was a God or no. She knew it as well. A last touch, lingering, the center of our lips finally stretching apart, separating, and a last waft of her breath and perfume moved on my face, and it was gone.

We walked back to the house, not speaking, her hands in her pockets, my hands limp at my side. The front door was locked, so we went around back. The glass door screamed as it slid open. I locked the door as Connie moved across the kitchen toward the hall and her bedroom. I stood at the kitchen sink, staring out the window, absently listening to Connie changing her clothes, brushing her teeth, brushing her hair. The dark remained throughout. Her door lightly closed, and the bed squeaked as she lay down. Finally, the house was absolutely still.

I went to her bedroom.

I pushed the door open and peeked in. She was under the covers, lying on her right side, her face looking up at me. I could see her dark eyes, and I moved toward them. I knelt by the bed, brought my face close to hers, and her eyes filled, making them shine, catching what specks of light there were. I kissed her forehead—a long, held kiss—and stroked her hair. She took my hand, pressed it against her face, and pulled up her shoulder to snuggle me.

She released my hand, turned over onto her back as I stood up. She looked beautiful, caught in the shadows, her face revealing both peace and terror, and I wanted to paint that face, capture the eternity I saw there, for I knew such a face I might not see again until an angel took me home.

I said goodnight, watched her close her eyes, and left, closing the door behind me.

~

It's past 2:00 in the morning now, still in my office, and I suppose I should go home. But I won't be getting up at 5:30, coming in early. Why should I, except to get my doughnuts?

I suppose I should talk with Jack or Simon about my state of mind. Maybe Mike. About my crisis, if that's what it is. But I don't want to, preferring to sit in it instead, waiting it out, fully expecting that it will, after all, all come out fine in the end, as even the worst events seem to do. Digging the heels of my palms into my eyes, scratching my head to stay awake, I mumble that this too, shall pass.

Tomorrow's menu includes the face-off with Sara, lecturing on the persecuted for righteousness' sake, preaching a tired sermon on praise in the morning, and another on Hosea in the afternoon, and in between, trying to figure out what to do with the rest of my mad, mad days.

For inside, in a deep place beyond my usual reasoned thought, is an ancient, sacred knowledge that this is indeed madness, this unbelief I have let in the door. But, if it is madness, this silence of God is madder still, and perhaps I will hold him accountable for his crazy decision to keep his wisdom for muteness only.

How hard can it be for a God to speak?

October 27

Now, Jack, what 're ya asking me for?
Yer just gonna do what ya want anyway.

Weeper Cagle, told to Jack Minor
Administrative Committee

. . . *the blurring of my vision* . . .

Two more Sundays gone. Nine days since Connie left. Thirteen days since I've prayed. Four days 'til Halloween. Eight days 'til the church decides.

So why am I here, Monday night, at the Down Under, thinking of ordering a frozen margarita from this waitress with sculpted calves?

～

Sara's not satisfied with my explanation of Connie and me, but what's to explain? Old friends, old lovers caught in a warped sack of time, a pocket of raw emotion shared, grasping at straws while their respective worlds fall over with brick-wall heaviness. An unexplainable mystery, a touch of friends one step beyond what's appropriate, all of which to most folks is little more than poetic shinanigans masking the truth, which is of course, that I'm a flirt, a philanderer, a guy with no character, and that I might as well have done it with Connie right there in the grass, since I already wanted to in my heart. But of course, though no one would believe me, I didn't want that at all. The kisses were unexpected, and though sex is on my mind every six seconds, as it is with all us guys, that was not the deal with Connie. Of course, Sara keeps saying, so what is the deal?

I don't know.

It happened and I'm sorry for it, and God will deal with me on those terms. I told Sara about our conversations on the porch and out at the tree, though of course, I left out the kisses, and true to form, she cried, and wondered about us, asking if I wanted to be with Connie rather than her. Of course not, I said, and it was an easy thing to say, because it's the truth. I don't want a different wife any more than I want a different God.

~

It's Monday night, the Monday before Halloween, and I'm sitting at a back table in that old bar of mine, the Down Under. I'm tired, needing alone time, time outside my universe, time outside my pain, and driving always seems like a good idea. Sara asked me where I was going, on edge, and I truthfully said I didn't know, but not to wait up, cause I might go over to Odessa. She wondered if I'd met anyone over there, and I said no, not to worry, that I loved her, that I might not even go anywhere but to the store and back. Her eyes clicked back and forth as she stared at me, as if secrets were written in code across my pupils, and she searched for those codes. I felt bad, said I'd just stay home, and truthfully, that would have been okay, but she recognized the truth in me and relaxed, and said, no, no, to go ahead. She kissed me and said sure, it was fine, that she'd get the kids to bed. I left, and wound my way east, not thinking, tired of thinking, and my car zeroed in on the Down Under like a missile. I pulled in the lot, which was surprisingly full, and I knew this was the place I needed.

~

The waitress with the calves is Marci.

I tell her I don't drink, but she knows that, having served me nachos and coke on more than one occasion. But my heavy plate is empty, as is my glass, and now she's recommending a margarita, saying nothing's better with Mexican food. I smile and tell her that's what I've always heard. Marci wonders if she can take the plate, and

I say sure. As I watch her clean the table, I smile again at the fact
that if I'm seen here by anyone from Ruin, during Halloween week
of all times, I'll be the great pumpkin in nothing flat, and none of
this will matter.

~

Marci's small, but built sturdy, and I've thought several times to
ask her if she lifts weights. She leans over me reaching for an ashtray,
and I can't help but look at her collarbone. She's tan under her yoked
black cotton shirt, and though three of her pearl buttons are open,
from my angle there's nothing to see. She's got the ashtray now, moving to another table. Her tight jean skirt shows off lean legs, muscles
in thighs and calves marked by clear lines. I blatantly watch those legs
walk away, and absurdly, I call her back, pushing my luck, flirting with
a disaster I want no part of, but I've gotten better at ignoring things.
Those legs turn around, return, and stop in front of me.

She's caught me looking. I should stammer, I guess, but instead I
ask her why she's not in costume. She says she came on at 4:00 in a
Peter Pan outfit, but that she'd misjudged its decency, and the reactions of the men were raunchier than she wanted, that it was the
back that did it. She says the boss didn't mind her changing, which
was good, and I reassure her, telling her she looks nice, if not beautiful, and that I'd rather see Marci than Peter Pan. She sits down at the
table, hovering on the edge of the seat, and leans toward me. She
lowers her voice, mocking the sultry voices she's no doubt heard
around these tables, saying you didn't see the costume, that if you
had, you wouldn't be saying that. Maybe not, I tell her, but I like you
just like you are. She leans back in the chair.

"Should you be flirting?"

She's looking at my ring, and I tell her I don't believe in flirting.
She stands, smiling a curly smile. Her cowboy hat sits slyly off center,
and shifting her weight onto one hip, she swings her tray in her hand
behind her back. She's rocking now, side to side, heel to heel, impa-
tient, a bit flattered, pleasantly annoyed. She eyes me, like she can't
decide who I am, then breaks the look, turning her face off toward

another table. A long moment, and her face is back to mine.

I decide, and ask her to bring me a margarita.

At that, Marci lets out a barky laugh, and kneels down next to me. She says, you want a margarita. I say yes, please, and as she puts her hand on my leg, she says what about coke, I say no, a margarita. Through giggles she manages to ask if I'd like it frozen or on the rocks. I tell her frozen, and she's up, turning with a twirl, still smiling. She bounces away, but after three steps, she stops, turns and walks a bee-line back toward me. She's modeling, laughing, knowing I'm watching, wanting me to, I suppose, and I do, without regret. Great legs, I think again, wondering why I like it, knowing I should stop, but as she disappears behind the bar, I flatly refuse, deciding to enjoy the moment, alone, amazed that God made such feelings, such beauty, such potential trouble.

Again, I wonder, did Jesus ever see a pair of legs like Marci's?

∼

Since Joy's funeral, I go to my closet to pray, and say dear God, and then my soul shuts up, sits in a stupor, not as if God has abandoned me—it's not like that—it's just that . . . for me, all the old concepts are dying. The wise old man, the policeman with the big stick, even the shepherd and all those great metaphors Jesus gave us; the door, the way, the truth, the life, the vine, the gate. God's exploded on me. Gone bigger than I thought. He's all those things, I know, but if he won't speak to me, if he won't answer my one ache, the one ache punching its way out of my stomach, and if it remains true that he still loves me, then there must be something here I don't know—something I can't know. Something larger than my petty need to be good, to be successful, to be acknowledged as having enough worth. And if there is a larger thing, then why ask him for money? Why ask him to help me find a church? Why ask him to make sure Sara knows I love her? And why ask him to save me from temptation that may take the form of woman, and sexuality, but that really has something else to do with my soul I can't name, and can't resist?

~

I've been here since 7:45. The cowboy and the girl aren't here
tonight, and I miss them, but the bar's lively, a few meager costumes
adding color to the already boisterous air. Tonight, it's Monday
Night Football, almost Halloween, and though a costume will get
you a free drink and appetizer, not to mention a $50 prize for the
winner, less than a third of the maybe twenty five or thirty patrons
bothered.

My favorite is the Lady Napoleon playing pool in the back with
what looks to be a Cowboy Julius Caesar, complete with chiton, gar-
land, and black boots. Napoleon is short, as he, or she, should be, hair
combed forward around chipmunk cheeks, with a bald piece barely
hanging on in the middle of her head. She's got a cigar in her mouth,
and when her turn is over, she straightens up, standing with classic
eighteenth century affectation, reaches into her waistcoat to hide her
hand, and without fail, scratches earnestly. Subtle, discreet, but she
is—no doubt about it—scratching her belly.

There are a couple of angels, one with halo, one without, and the
obligatory devil, though he's not serious at all, at least not about the
costume. He's got a red tail attached to his back belt loop, with a
pitchfork not even painted. He won't win, but I'd give him extra
credit for the look in his eyes. To complete the contestants, there's a
bad Marilyn Monroe, not well endowed, her red hair peeking out
from under her skewed platinum wig; a slick-haired fifties guy sport-
ing a Fonzie motorcycle jacket, pointed shoes, and a pot belly of serious proportion; an older gentleman with a fedora and suitjacket with
a hastily written sign saying Tom Landry pinned to his back; and last-
ly, Santa Claus, sitting alone at one end of the bar, beard hanging
down, red and white cap on the surface in front of him. He's bombed,
and Marci told me he'd been here since before she got there. It's now
past ten, and for some reason, I can look at Santa just so long before
I get a strong urge to run to the men's room and there, in the privacy of a locked stall, bawl my eyes out.

Lots of smoke in the room, too, and it's starting to irritate my
eyes. The decor is All Hallows Eve deluxe, with witches' hats and

miniature pumpkins serving as centerpieces, while skulls and plastic jack-o-lanterns sit with patrons at the bar. A paper skeleton here and there, along with ouija boards and goblins of all shapes and sizes, and a few latex masks lurk about the walls wishing they were scary, ashamed of being no more than grotesque.

∼

Here comes Marci with the margarita.

My table sits along a back wall, about fifteen feet from the dance floor, which is on the south end of the room, to my right. I'm facing the bar, where the haloed angel and the devil trade jokes between occasional kisses, enjoying shots of something clear, both of them tipsy and happy. I try to calculate the money these poor folks fork out for booze, but the language of highballs, cocktails, and liquors is Greek to me, and I have no real sense of what anything is, much less what it costs. Tom Landry and the bartender watch the game on the monitor over the bar, talking over the Cowboys no doubt, while Marilyn and Fonzie play cards in the north corner with two other men. Five or six other tables are filled with threesomes and foursomes, and two older couples are moving toward the dance floor, responding to the pulse of a new Garth song I haven't heard before.

Marci laughs at my surprised face—this drink is as big as a bowl. She wonders if I've ever had a Margarita before. I say no, and she says she wants to see what I think. She steps back, throwing her weight onto her back leg, tucking her chin, grinning, watching intently. Bending toward the table, I gingerly touch my tongue to the salt on the rim. It tastes clean, sharp, and lifting the glass, I sip. The bite of the drink makes me pucker, and Marci says see, I knew you'd like it, but I shake my head, waving her away, saying thanks, but bring me some water. She's stomps her foot, laughing, saying okay, okay, and that she'll bring me some more chips, too, on the house.

I say thanks, and sipping and puckering, I watch her legs again, but this time absently, because now I've slipped over to this problem of mine called preaching, and my life's call.

∼

I've been thinking about it, about preaching. On a planet of four or five billion, to think of standing in front of less than a handful, and proclaiming the word of God, as if I was sure, is no less than shocking, and tonight, it seems miraculous that God might entrust his words to us. To me, certainly. What have you to do with me, O God, I think, taking another slurp of the gold drink, though I am certainly more believer now than I was when I stepped into the pulpit for the first time. But back then I was simple, and clean, and knew doctrine could save me, if I could just get it right. Now the world seems madder than it did—as in crazy, loony—and Jesus, thankfully, terrifyingly, has risen not only from the grave, but from the pages of the book as well.

∼

My first sermon was in Elgin, Texas, not too far from Austin, just before I left college. It was a bright morning, with Disney-like promise, and there were forty or fifty believers, all over the age of 85, it seemed, except for one young couple with a smarmy baby that crawled on the floor in front of the pulpit for almost an hour. Nervous, mostly unprepared, I spoke off the cuff, but quoted lots of passages from John 1 and chapters 13, 14, and 15, which I had been memorizing on a lark. I convicted them, though, and one old man cried and came forward, confessing sin, and we solemnly prayed that he might be forgiven, redelivered into the fold. Afterwards, I stood at the door, shaking old hands, acting the role of pastor as the elderly filed out into oblivion, and I was certain God sat on my shoulder, proud and impressed, though of course now I know it was a different presence at my shoulder, and the only one proud was me.

What impresses God, I wonder?

Probably not much.

∼

"Jesus wept!"

A voice spits an oath, crackling with irritation, as if it's been in

the business of hate for decades, and I look up. The non-haloed angel
drops into the chair across from me, her flimsy wings falling around
her waist. I grin. This gnarly cherub is an old woman, a tree-stump of
a woman, seventy if she's a day. A cigarette dangles from her mouth,
a mouth stretched with frowning, and it looks like the rest of her face
followed. Ears sagging, nose drooping, turkey skin under her neck.
Sun baked wrinkles crisscross her face, with cheeks pockmarked in
crevasses etched in childhood. Her chin is a round moon, and dark
circles under black eyes frighten me, scaring me into thinking this
could be me someday.

This woman, straight out of Arthur Rackam, was never pretty.

Her right hand even fingers a cane—plain brown wood, drug-
store variety—her twisted digits clinging to its handle like tree
roots. That hand moves constantly, gripping the cane, letting go,
gripping, releasing, over and over, and the handle's glossy finish is
worn clean. Now she turns her face to me, sets the cane on the table,
keeping her grip. Her black, round eyes stare over the droopy nose,
which arches up and out, like a beak, making me think of an eagle,
or a hawk, which, instantly intrigues me, makes her difficult to
resist. She barks at me.

"I want a coke."

Marci's here with the free chips and I ask her to bring my friend
a coke. Marci says she usually takes whiskey, but the old woman barks
at her, too, saying with clergy around, she never drinks. Marci says
where's a clergy, winking at me, and the old woman stabs her cane at
my chest. A coke, she says, and bring him one, too, and get that
liquor outta here. I tell Marci that's fine, that I don't like the margarita anyway, and the legs take off again, leaving me with Loreen.

Loreen, she grumbles, sucking on her cigarette, mumbling how
she didn't know what the point of having a TV was if you weren't
going to turn up the sound. She says people are damn stupid around
here, and I say, yes ma'am, I guess so. She glares at me, her head jerking every couple of seconds, a small twitch, but her eyes never waver.
She says the Cowboys suck, don't they.

I ask her how she knows I'm a preacher.

She clears her throat, bellowing at Marci to bring an ashtray with the cokes. Several heads turn as Loreen leans over, coughing, hard and quiet, her vocal chords blasted. The spittle rattling in her throat gives me the creeps. She tries again to clear it, raking her throat, working to get the crud up and out, but she ends up chewing a little, swallowing it back down. Her eyes are watery, her cheeks damp when she glares at me again.

"First Church of Ruin."

I've never seen this woman before in my life.

"You see the wings, don't you?" It hurts my legs to hear her talk. Now she's laughing, and that's worse.

"Cyrus, God tells us these things."

~

Two hours later, Loreen's forehead rests on the table, comfortably asleep on a miniature pillow of napkins.

About ten minutes into my conversation with Loreen, Marci slipped me a note saying she belonged to Jim Bob, the bartender—she's his mom, the note said. Jim Bob, fortyish, a chubby lug of a fellow whom I'd never seen not smiling, came over not long after, wondering if Mom didn't need to head on to bed. She stood up and swore at him, loudly, whacking at him with her cane in earnest. At least half a dozen people whistled and cheered, and I felt oddly privileged to see their routine—which it obviously was—him lurching to avoid blows that would no doubt crack his skull, the crowd saying "wwh-hooaa" if she ever came close.

Jim Bob asked me if I was okay. I said I wasn't sure, but maybe.

Now, as I pull out bills to pay for the night, I watch him pick up his old mother, gently, like a child carrying a butterfly, afraid to break it, afraid it'll fly away. Marci runs ahead, opens a door just off the bar. They disappear, and Marci returns. I hand her two twenties, saying keep the change, and thanks for watching out for me. She says thanks, and that not many folks tolerate Loreen the way I did, that she was impressed. I tell her preachers have to take care of angels, and she says she always thought I was pulling her leg about the preacher thing.

"But you really are a preacher, then, like she said?"

I tell Marci maybe not anymore. Angels tend to clarify things.

~

Loreen said a gift is on the way, a gift to die for.

I expected to hear her story, that maybe she got abandoned by her husband, her and Jim Bob scraping out a meager, impoverished living by running brothels and bars, and that she'd suffered abuse, miscarriages, and cancers, and mean cousins who bilked her out of property, lockboxes, and what little love she had. And no doubt Loreen had indeed suffered atrocities of one kind or another, but there was no getting them out of her. I'm good at questions, but she'd have none of it, wanting to hear from me, what I was preaching on, what book I was studying, and whether or not I was still being good to that pretty girl who put up with me, raising my kids, washing my shorts, her being the only thing standing between me and God killing me dead like Eli's kids, she said. She smirked, knowing I was impressed.

"I know my Bible."

I asked her if she was mad about something, and she said hell, yes, she was mad, mad-as-a-hatter's what everybody told her anymore. Folks shouted at her like she was deaf, and hell, like she was senile, which she sure as hell wasn't, she said, emphasizing hell over and over, like it was a place she really hated, hated it like she'd been there, seen it, seen its blood in the streets, and never wanted to go back. She paused, her lower jaw hanging down to the right, out of sync with her upper teeth, as if she'd gritted them since her twenties, but then she shut her mouth, stuffing in the cigarette, leaving it there, pulling on it, breathing it in. Smoke emerged from her nostrils, as if her heart was burning, and as she drug the coke up to her mouth, sipping as quickly as she could, which wasn't fast, I thought of Geyser, of my broken promise, regretting, wishing I could apologize in person.

~

Loreen wouldn't tell me how she knew me, only that she'd been to First Church lots of times, knew lots of people there, and that if I wasn't nice, if I didn't behave and do what she said, she'd get my butt fired, and quick. All of which I knew was a lie: I'd never miss a face like hers. I told her she better tell me the truth or I was going to quit anyway, to which she replied that she didn't give a damn what I did, that God sure as hell didn't need me to stand around talking about him. I told her somebody's got to talk for him, and she practically yelled, the hell he does, and she spat out that most preachers ought to just shut up, just shut up like the lions in the den, that maybe then they'd hear something worth saying.

I frowned, and she pointed her forefinger at me, the bone curving toward me like a claw, her eyes slapping my mouth shut like a mother's quick haymaker. I froze, my heart gearing up, going faster, my tongue locked against my front teeth. She kept pointing, and I couldn't move, couldn't speak, couldn't break her grip. I got scared, thinking, my God, this woman's a witch, a demon, and that claw's a curse, clamping my mouth shut, and when she speaks, my heart'll rip from my chest, and I'll be dead, a murdered casualty they'll report as the victim of a mere heart attack.

But her hand lowered onto the table, slowly, drifitng like a cloud, and I relaxed, relieved to still have my sanity.

That's when she told me her Christmas story.

~

"Christmas is coming."

I thought, wrong holiday, but she went on. But it's hard to see it in here, she said, flicking her cigarette ash. She growled that she hated Halloween, though not for religious reasons, but that it was just ugly, with the Frankenstein masks, and vampire teeth, and to demonstrate, she made a face at me, scowling, kicking her false teeth slightly askew as if she was a skeleton, a ghoulish waif bent on terrifying God believers. Putting her mouth back together, she said, hell, we don't need any more ugly on our faces, and that Christmas was much better. She punched at me, saying at least it's happy paganism, hey preacher, and I said uh-huh, diving into the chips for refuge, testing my sore jaw.

"You think God likes Christmas?"

I told her I hadn't thought about it. She said the man upstairs likes gifts, doesn't he, doesn't he like shopping? I chugged more coke as she cocked an eyebrow. She said you're on his list, that he's the real Santa, and that he was going to get you something. I said really, and that I wished he would. She said in fact, he already got it, and it's on its way. I smiled, amazed at how lucidity and dementia mixed in old folks: Loreen sounded like she was talking to a grandchild about a gift from Neiman's that she'd ordered herself.

Marci stopped by to check on our cokes, and caught me telling Loreen I needed to get it before Christmas, that by then it might be too late. Marci laughed and scolded Loreen for getting excited about Christmas too early, that she knew it was her favorite holiday and all, but Jim Bob had already told her that she had to wait to tell Santa what she wanted, and that if she wasn't patient, Santa might not find her at all this year.

I stared at Marci. Loreen was right: she was talking baby talk, as if Loreen was four. It annoyed me, and I curtly told Marci we were fine, that we'd call if we needed her. But Marci persisted, and wondered, scolding the four year old, if Loreen had been telling Cyrus she was going to get him a present, that that was Loreen's favorite story, and she told it all the time, any time of year. Marci was looking at me, smiling knowingly, thinking to explain the craziness, but I didn't want the craziness explained. I didn't smile back, and Marci got confused, saying she was just trying to help. I said thanks, but we're fine, and she wandered off.

Loreen didn't mention Christmas again—in fact, she pretty much stopped talking at all, as if she'd been unplugged. Her head started to nod, but she wouldn't let me get her son, so I grabbed several napkins. I stacked them up maybe ten deep, and told her it was a pillow and that I'd be leaving soon, but if she needed to go on to sleep, that'd be fine with me. Scooching around in her chair to lay her head down, she complained that she couldn't get drunk anymore, that the doctor said yesterday it'd kill her if she did. She told me to get drunk while I could, that maybe a little wine would be good for my stomach.

She rested her forehead on the napkins. I got up and got next to her, kneeling down so I could see her profile. I asked her if she was all right and she said, see, I know what the Bible says. She closed her eyes, and muttered again, see, I know.

I went and got Jim Bob.

~

Back home now, lying in bed next to Sara, lights all out, dark as a dungeon and awfully cold outside the covers.

Driving home, it felt like Halloween, and I thought about poor Jack wandering the earth with his turnip and hot coal. Not much light, I thought, and again, I tried to imagine the unseen, what angels and devils might really look like if they ever showed their faces.

I haven't imagined Jesus in a long time. It's a game I learned when I was small, and it's always served me well, although in recent years, those imaginings come on me unannounced, tricking me, and more than once I've caught myself believing in them. Or they come in dreams, like the dream I had that Sunday afternoon a few weeks back, just after Connie arrived. I don't know what Jesus would say to me, or think of me, or what he would do if he were me. I've seen tee shirts and hats bearing the initials WWJD, which I'm told means what would Jesus do, but frankly, I've never known what he would do, and being the unpredictable guy he is, I've never thought to peg him. But it's helpful to think about him, talk to him, wonder what he might say, what he might laugh at, what might make him angry, what might thrill him beyond words.

But the game's been impossible lately. Even *that face* seems to elude my memory, and I think I am perhaps growing tired of imagining what I can't see. I know the book says that's what faith is, the assurance of what we can't see, but it's all so fatiguing, so unsure.

According to James, I guess I'm the double-minded man, the one who should expect no thing from God, certainly not a gift, not at Christmas or otherwise. Out on I-20, I almost imagined such a thing, that Jesus rode next to me, holding a package with paper made in heaven as a wrapping, and that when I opened it, it held the secret, the key to all I'd ever wanted, all I'd ever longed for. But even as I tried to tug at the ribbon, pulling apart the bow, the box and the Jesus who held it vanished, fading in the face of my fear, and I made a small promise to myself, a simple yes that I would do no more imagining of such unearthly things.

Pulling into my drive, I realized I had just answered my question. The question of my call. What is the work of the preacher/pastor if not to constantly re-imagine his life, and the life of the people of God? What is preaching but imaginatively spinning the unseen world into stories and tales children can grasp and hang on to, tales that are truer than true, but forever incomplete so that faith might take root and lead them all the way to death, where they perhaps will hear the final telling, the telling that completes our journey toward the real, the very presence of God.

I hurried into the house, hurried into bed.

How strange, to find an answer. In my world of questions, I know one thing. Lying here in my bed, my wife at my side, warming me, I know that if I can do no more imagining of Jesus, or heaven, or hell, or faith, or healing, or other unearthly wonders, then I am done with preaching. If I can no longer imagine this Jesus I follow, then I must be silent. I will remain a quiet believer, but my voice will be still.

I will truly enter the silence of God, and be done with it.

November 2

You watch. He'll dump her someday.

Doug Goods to Jack Simons
Administrative Committee

. . . *the face of God* . . .

Sunday, November 2nd. The morning's church bulletin lies in front of me. There in the upper right corner, "Insights with Cyrus" offers a dry, brief discourse on John 17 unity. But what interests me more is the announcement across the bottom of the page:

Business Meeting / Tuesday Night / 7:30 p.m.
Topics: Budget / Elder Selection / Preaching Ministry

Oh, boy—here it comes.

My foot is tapping, uncontrolled. I catch a reflected glimpse of myself in the glass of a picture frame sitting on the desk—a picture of Sara and the boys. I hunker down, look closer.

There's no excuse for the light in my eye.

I've been up a long time, since 5:13 a.m., scared I'll miss something, scared a different call will come at the last moment, scared I haven't heard correctly. Two hours later now, my office crackles with an energy it hasn't seen in months, maybe years. I know I'm grinning, but it's hard to stop. I type furiously on my computer. A letter to the church, full of hope, brimming with a new sense of having something strong to do, something worth being a fool for.

Fear's still hanging around, running along like a kid nobody wants to play with, hiding in the shadows, hoping I'll forget he's there, so he can nail me when I'm not looking. That fear has a name, probably, a personality, and he'd like me to believe I've lost my mind, thrown over reason for a fool's mysticism, but for the life of me, I can't go along. I can only know what I know.

Besides, at six o'clock this morning, Sara got up, showered, and joined me in the kitchen, her clean arms looping under mine in a hard embrace hardly routine, not what I'd come to expect of old shoe husbands and wives. The strong taste of my coffee mixed in our mouths, and as we peered through bleary eyes at the sky's easing dark, as I listened to a soft I love you, and returned it, my teeth tugging gently at her lobe, I knew this morning was not imagination, that Friday night had been actual, real, as real as the cold under my feet, as real as the warmth of her breath on my neck. We leaned against the counter, her shoulder under my arm, gazing at our table, at a chalice newly come to our house. Last night, weeping in her arms, the dam fully broken, she had not understood, but she knew that to me the goblet on my table meant the world, meant that perhaps . . . perhaps . . . God had not left me, after all.

∾

Friday, on a crisp Halloween morning, my rebellion finally settled on its course. That restless urge to commit a crime had resulted thus far in a serious, but misguided misdemeanor, though by no means unhurtful, and with that bit of folly behind me (or so I hope—we haven't heard from Connie), I set my sights on a better thing. A simple kidnapping would have to do.

I hijacked my wife.

∾

The table was as nice as I could hope for in a place like Fort Stockton, some forty-fifty miles south of Ruin. Thankfully, The Stockade—the best place in town, according to the front desk man—hadn't gone orange and black with harvest pumpkins; Sara and I had been looking at crepe paper witches and cardboard ghosts all day. But this was white tablecloth, and a single, strawberry-size red rose in crystal greeted us as we sat. Tall heavy goblets cut in cascading glass sat like opposing pawns, and the wine bottle's label flourishes framed words that said romance is ever possible, even when lovers aren't speaking.

The day to this point had been a mixed bag, disaster followed by bliss, and back again.

~

Historically in our marriage, surprises, especially relating to things romantic, have not always been welcome. My plan was a breakfast date, after which we'd skip town—Mike and Emily would get the boys—but when I told her about breakfast, she declined in favor of plans to get with her girlfriends. I said maybe we could meet for lunch, and when she hesitated, I knew she wasn't interested, but I pressed her and she grudgingly agreed to meet me at Furr's cafeteria at 11:30. I told her no, that she needed to come home so I could take her some place special, that it needed to be a surprise. She said she wasn't interested in surprises, that if I had something up my sleeve, to forget it. No presents, no candlelight, certainly no dancing, that she was still upset, still needing some time.

But I said please—twice—and she relented.

She got home at 11:15, at which point we got in the car and drove, heading south. When we passed the "Ruin" sign marking the city limit, she didn't speak, didn't look at me, didn't move a muscle. But five minutes later, she opened fire, saying she didn't appreciate being manipulated, that she didn't appreciate being ignored, as if what she felt didn't matter. When I told her I thought it was important for us to get away, she got louder, saying *what about what she thought*. I pulled over to the side of the road and got out, slamming the door, figuring I should just give it up, have it out right here, and go back home.

The weekend was lost, but at least we'd save the money on the hotel.

Sara sat in the car while I stood in the breeze, looking over the burnt brown plains. A Cadillac slowed down, thinking I was having trouble, but I waved him on. Sara finally eased her door open, and stepped out.

Getting out of a car on a highway, even on a backroad, wakes me up, what with the wind blowing, cars going by at sixty-five, and the crunch of gravel on the shoulder. I rarely walk on highways, and it seemed like a movie as Sara and I stood at the back fender, ready to get after it.

Her arms crossed as she stood there, the car door open, her face a stone. The wind gusted, catching her skirt, and she grabbed it, pushing it down, holding it, palms clinched against her thighs. She turned to the west, to the wind, and her dark hair flew back in long, whipping lines, exposing her taut jaw line. Her eyes squinted against the force of the bluster. The sun was high, but brought little warmth, and goosebumps rose on her arms.

She said she didn't know what she wasn't doing. What was I not getting from her that I had to get from Connie? I told her nothing, and she wanted to know if I was in love with her. With Connie. I wasn't, so that was easy. I had certainly felt odd about her, but I wasn't in love. I told her simply, deliberately avoiding the few romantic tones I had, that Sara Manning was the only woman I had ever loved, the only woman I ever would.

It was true, but she wasn't impressed. She said what does that mean.

It's a fair question, a good question, but not one I had a good answer for. I've been thinking about it, of course, because at the moment, I didn't feel particularly in love with anybody. I was in crisis. Sure, there was a spark, a touch of romantic notion with Connie, and had I been wiser, I would have recognized it as a wisp of scented wind in the long, long stretch of desert that life can be. But wind does little more than parch the skin in the heat, and standing out on state highway 18, using metaphors of wind, and water, I tried to explain.

I started with that desert analogy, and said you are the water for my journey, sometimes a river I stumble across, sometimes a drop from my canteen, sometimes a crystal lake I immerse myself in. That your water gives me life, the strength to move in the world, that it sustains me. That it's the relief I cannot live without, the substance of washing, and being cleansed. That I did not need sweet smells, or wind, but that without water, I would die.

I didn't say it just like that, exactly, but I tried to, and we talked there on the road for about fifteen minutes, and after that, things got better.

~

I should learn to keep my mouth shut.

When we got to the hotel—a Best Western called the The Big Bend—we immediately went upstairs, tore off our clothes, climbed into the first of the double beds gracing the pale room, and made love for half an hour. Passionately, wonderfully, husband and wife again, and as I dressed for the rest of the afternoon, no doubt looking for what dismal tourist shopping there might be, I was hopeful that all doubt about us had been removed.

As we shopped Halloween wandered through the town. We passed various costumed characters: a Dorothy with red slippers and a real Toto, a couple of heavier guys doing Tweedledee and Tweedledum, an Elvis. In the middle of the afternoon, kids started to show up here and there, running about in flimsy plastic masks, mostly Darth Vaders and rabbits. We finally bought a sack of Kit-Kats, handed them out as we went.

We poked around antique stores, walking quickly to avoid temptation, only once getting stuck in front of a nineteenth century mirror, gorgeously beveled. We checked the price tag, and immediately moved on. Though all this was pleasant, our closeness waned. We talked, saying nothing, both aware that we were keeping to ourselves. I knew Sara wanted to hear more from me, but I didn't know what exactly, or where to start. Finally, lightly fingering the shade of a bluish Tiffany lamp, Sara said to tell her more about this water business. I quickly calculated her desire for honesty, and told her the difficulty was that though water was the best, the most needed thing, the primary source of survival and health, it wasn't meant to be all the intake we needed.

Pretty dumb.

The further the conversation went, the worse it got. I tried to talk about diversity and variety, that God had made us complex beings, that we had many needs, emotional, aesthetic, romantic, intellectual, physical, and that he had made provision to take care of them all—I could see her brain jumping ahead, looking for logical conclusions—but that such a burden was too heavy to place on the shoulders of one person, that marriage was not meant to bear the full weight of responsibility for our panoply of needs, and that the metaphor of the body of Christ fit this idea perfectly. We needed each other, everyone did.

None of which Sara was interested in hearing.

Was I suggesting men might need mistresses to fulfull them, she wondered, chewing on the chocolate bar I'd bought her. I took the clerk's change, twisting my neck around to see if she was kidding, which she wasn't, and said, no I wasn't suggesting that, but that I understood why it happened.

She threw the chocolate at me, and stomped off toward the street.

∼

From my vantage point on this Sunday morning, it's easy to look lightly at the craziness. As we sat there at the table with the rose, finishing off an unexceptional helping of shrimp cocktail—this is West Texas—waiting for marinated chicken, rice pilaf, prime rib, and mixed veggies, it became obvious to me that even though I was not going to win intimacy immediately, our love was still solid, that we were indeed lifers, committed to better or worse, whatever that might mean, which of course we would never know until the moment was on us.

The waiter poured the wine: first Sara's, then mine. Anything else, he asked. Sara fiddled with her fork, tapping the bread plate, when she looked up at me and said to bring her a cup of coffee. I said, make that two.

When he was gone, I picked up the wine and asked her to toast with me. I knew this was no time to showboat, or to rattle off sweet nothings to make her feel better. I needed authenticity, and it wasn't hard to find. I held up my glass.

"To grace."

She answered me.

"To loyal husbands."

Her eyes weren't smiling, but they had light in them. My turn.

"To Sara, and coffee, and her willingness to live with a stupid man."

She gave little quarter.

"To me, that I'm willing to live with . . . and love . . . a stupid man."

I said so you love me then. She said it was to her detriment, but that she did indeed. We clinked and drank, and she made a face, that foul I-still-don't-like-wine face, and I mirrored her. Tension eased, and we laughed.

The waiter arrived with coffee and we leaned away from the table to make room. She kept her eyes on me, and though the worst of the storm was past, I knew it wasn't quite over. When the waiter left, she leaned over, motioning me to come closer. She whispered.

"If you ever touch another woman, you lose me. And the boys. Do you understand that?"

I nodded, my throat too tight to speak. She sipped her coffee, then sent me one of those open, all too rare smiles, and scolded me gently, asking me to wake up.

"Cyrus, I need your words. When are you going to start talking to me again?"

~

So Friday night, Sara and I talked.

We gave up the white tablecloth for red and white vinyl checks at a truck stop about five miles east of Fort Stockton on Interstate 10.

It was a bright place, overhead lamps stuffed with hundred watt bulbs, supported by a large cast of flourescents. People were milling through every inch, suits and ties and classy country women strangely mixed with the more usual array of rough truckers, with a few festival costumes and square dance petticoats thrown in for color. It was as if the Halloween nine o'clock hour was truly magic, a time when truckers shut down rigs and overalls, and dressed up, holding harvest

gatherings to show off their strength, their women, and their great
hands, made especially for gripping giant wheels. I asked one of the
suit and tie guys what the deal was, and he asked me if I might be
interested in a business opportunity.

That explained it. We'd seen this Amway bit before, and though
I wanted no new business—or at least not that one—I was glad for
all the distributors, because they brought additional energy to an
already festive world, a Texas world, with boots and hats and
Peterbilt caps, though it was unnerving to see a scruffy, toothless
smile dressed in frumpled suit and power tie. (Sara whispered that has
to be a costume.) But the crowd exuded joy, and hope, chattering
noisily over eggs and pancakes, coffee pouring constantly, and the
only downside was a red-headed trucker obviously piqued over this
invasion of his sacred haven. There were about ten distributors in the
booth next to his, and the rise and fall of raucous laughter, not to
mention the two young guys wanting to climb into the unoccupied
seat in ol' Red's booth to get a better look at whoever was holding
court, finally got to the driver. As Sara and I plopped into a corner by
the emergency exit, I saw him throw down his fork and stand up. He
grabbed his baseball cap, broke through the irritating mound of people, stuck his face into the heart of the discussion. I didn't hear what
he said, but the jerking of his head and body said it wasn't pleasant.

The Amway booth went silent as ol' Red stomped out.

But that lasted all of fifteen seconds, and the room exploded
again, laughter and frothy talk re-lighting the festive din, and the staff
joined in, as if such Friday night madness was normal, and welcome.

~

Four hours we talked.

How long had it been since we giggled together, poking an occasional rib, wiping a bleary eye, plotting out plans on napkins, believing that life had special days ahead? Here our lives have been unrav-
eling—all familiarity pulled from under our feet—and it's been weeks
since we sat down to trade notes. We had lists and lists to cover:
Wayne's growing anxiety, Richard's foul moods and deteriorating

schoolwork, our feelings of grief, our guarded hope and excitement about whatever was about to happen, any plans related to a move if there was to be one. Sara reminded me that she had mentioned all this numerous times, but that I'd been too preoccupied (she leaned on the word) to pay her any attention. I crawled.

But finally she got to the question I was looking for, wondering if she'd ever ask.

"What about God? What are you thinking these days?"

～

She knew nothing of my imaginings, my vision of Joy, my struggle at the grave, my hunger to hear from God. Nothing of my despair at his silence, of my honking in Abilene, my excursions to the Down Under. She had, all these years, in faith, respected a kind of privacy in my spiritual walk, and even now as she asked, I knew she simply wanted to know where I was, what I prayed for, how I saw it. What did I think of the way God was dealing with us, and what was the plan?

Our coffees were cold. It was just after 2:00 a.m. Amway had left the place, and now there were just a sleepy few. I opened my mouth, dreading having to put my despair into words, but I started in by saying I'd let Geyser down, that I'd skipped Shady Oaks. Then the story of seeing Joy the morning of her death, then the balloon and the moment at the grave. I told her about Francis, and the horrid conversation with Sam. She thrilled at my talk with Wayne, but even as I went back in my mind, trying to explain that next feeling, that knowing he was coming, I felt again the wind, seeing again those weeds moving like waves, and a wall rose in me. I shut down, backed off, focused on Pat—the waitress—pouring more coffee. My hands started sweating—just barely—and Sara's gentle kneading, intended to comfort, didn't help. I tried to let go, but she gripped harder, holding on to me, demanding to hear, begging me to go on. I smiled, said I just want my coffee, and she relinquished. I sipped, sat the cup down, then tucked my hands safely beneath the table. Our magic four hours evaporated, and an odd film stood in my eyes, that I've-gone-away look Sara claims is all too familiar.

∽

To break the mood, Sara said she'd been thinking.

I raised my eyes, and tried to reconnect, but it was like looking down the wrong end of a telescope: she seemed small and far away. But her next words smashed the barrier between us, and I roared back to reality.

"I saw God—or maybe Jesus—in a dream."

I looked at her like she'd just announced she was pregnant, which means I was thrilled, but didn't believe a bit of it.

In her dream, she said, she saw a series of pools hidden in crevices of a steep, white place—a glacier, maybe. We were hiking, she said, walking along, cold, slowly frozen, no coats or backpacks—in fact, in short sleeves and shorts. She remembered looking at me, because I was leading, and I was scared—lost, she thought, though there was a paper in my pocket, a napkin she knew had directions, and a man some twenty feet in front of us. But you fell, she said, and it was so real. Then she was falling, too, and we hit one of these pools, and it was like a rock, and we both died, but didn't. I wondered what that meant. She went on saying that underwater, there was a cavern, underneath, and she paused, reaching for the words, or the image . . . she said it was lit with torches made of nothing—nothing but air, and she passed her hand through one of the flames and wasn't burned, but it wasn't wet, either.

I said cool.

She stopped and stared a bit, absent-mindedly playing tick-tack-toe in the red and white squares. She said she had the feeling we were following—just following. Following the man, I asked, and she just shook her head, said no, no one was there, but that in the water, a shadow went by, and she grabbed it, and it was my leg. We swam back to the surface of the pool, and when we broke through, the next thing she knew we were walking again on the white, on the glacier, cold, uncertain, but not wet at all. But now it was night, and the napkin was gone, but the man remained, but bigger, like a giant.

But we fell again, she says, longer this time, further down, and we watched the pool get closer. It was black, and beautiful in a mountainous way, and though we didn't feel pain, she knew all our bones were broken at impact. Down we went, and I told her I imagined us limp, floating, but she said no. She shook her head again. We were still falling, she said, being dragged down, bumping rocks and bleeding, but (and she started laughing here) there was music, a high-pitched children's choir singing "Holy, Holy, Holy." Then she said she saw Richard and Wayne playing, naked, and they were five and two again. I said you're kidding, and she said no, they were there, and we swam toward them. But they headed down, and she wanted to follow them, but I was leading and swam for the surface, and though she cried and fought me, we finally found the surface again, and presto—again, we were walking on the glacier, and this time both sun and moon were in the sky, and it was gray, like ash. She said she knew she would never see her sons again, and in the dream, she wept like a baby.

But she said when she stopped crying, she looked up and, this time, the man was turned around, facing her. But he didn't speak, didn't say a thing about her crying, just turned around and kept going.

I asked her what he looked like. She said she didn't know, that for a moment she'd thought he had on a parka, or a polar bear coat, but then she remembered the muscles in his arms, so he couldn't have worn a coat. Was it God, I said. She rubbed her nose. No, at least not yet. What about his eyes, tell me about his eyes, I threw at her, but she said they were normal, just eyes, maybe blue, maybe brown, nothing really. He was just a guy. She rubbed her nose again, then sneezed.

She excused herself, ran to the restroom.

She came running back, and said this time we were walking on the same plain of ice, the glacier, and we fell again, this time a much longer time, and there was no bottom, no surface to see, but that falling, we were clasping hands, trying to stay together. But then, there was a bottom, black water, and she lost me when we hit. But instantly, she was suspended in light blue, a silent place, with no walking to be done, and no dreams. I asked her what she meant, no dreams, and picking up her cup, she said no dreams. It was . . . well . . . like being inside an idea, or the place where dreams were made, and she was no more than a thought of God.

There at the table, my wife and I were holding hands again.

Sara got quiet, touching my ring, spinning it slowly around my knuckle. She said nothing happened for a long time, and we hung there, so still. So still. Her face told me she was back inside the dream. She remembered feeling afraid, she whispered, afraid of just . . . fading away, and being . . . nothing. Nothing at all. But then, blue shifted, and became all colors, like real life, but more like rainbows, like rainbows were the air, suddenly—and now Sara smiled, and I could sense her coming excitement—and we were walking again, she said, talking faster, this time on a new mountain, a small hill, really, among larger peaks, and though there was nowhere to really go . . .

She came out of the dream, focused on my face again.

She said just before she woke up, she looked at me, walking beside her, at my face . . . and it was my face . . . but not like any face she'd ever seen. Sara's eyes filled, and she touched my chin, my lips, fingertips only. Lightly tickled my cheek. As she felt my skin, I felt exposed, naked, but without fear, without shame. Sara was flesh of my flesh, and she said that in her dream, streaming from my face in great shafts was . . . emotion . . . a raw, stark sense of that . . . something . . . that she knew was related . . . to what we call . . . joy, she said. But it was new, godlike, or godly, and it staggered her, and she was overwhelmed, full of panic until she realized—she didn't know how—that she, too, had this face.

Her face contracted. I don't know how she kept from crying.

But she inhaled, and said it was the only time she'd ever wanted to die. She said she didn't want to wake up. That that face was the face of the man on the glacier, that on him, it had seemed normal, but on us, it was the face of God. And the face was just beginning to speak, but dawn came—in the dream, she said—and she knew she had to wake up.

Now she cried. Briefly, she bowed her head, hiding that deep body shaking that comes with quiet, public tears.

But it passed, and Sara went on, ignoring the glistening lines on her cheeks. She said she prayed and prayed, and when she heard me in the kitchen, she snuck down the hall, and I was at the kitchen table, sitting alone, and sad, she thought, just so sad. She said my dad's Bible sat in front of me.

"It was your dream, wasn't it? Meant for you."

I told her I had no idea.

She said she wished she'd never seen that face, because since then, it was all she could think about—who it was, what it meant. What it meant that it belonged to both of us.

"It was beautiful. You and I . . . so beautiful."

~

We pulled into the lot underneath the vacancy sign. I put it in park, pulled the door handle, triggering the dome light. I pulled it shut again to make it dark. She reached to me, turned my face toward her. What, she said, her eyes telling me it couldn't be any safer to speak. But I turned back to the dash.

"I think I can't do this anymore."

What, she wondered. Preach?

I thrust the door open, stepped out. Puff clouds rolled over the moon, and we walked in the cold to the door, bumbled up the steps to room 216, and undressed. All in silence. I met her under the sheets, where we held hands, and stared at the ceiling, while the TV sold us juicers. I asked her if I should turn off the tube, turn off the light.

She said please.

In the dark, Sara covered my body with hers. We lay still, and now, 36 hours later, I remember a small spot in my heart opening, like a tear in a seam, and whether emotion was rushing in or rushing out, I can't say, but I wept into her shoulder, over nothing, over everything, heaving pain at her I hardly knew I had.

Repentance and fatigue, uncertainty and fury, despair and hope all stuffed into a single release, a multi-grained fit of crying in pity, like all those children in grocery stores protesting stroller straps. I wanted to run and play in God's glory—just so tired of sitting strapped into my teeny mind, so inept, so incapable of seeing the wonder in front of me. I whispered in her ear through the sobs.

"I want to see *him. I just want to see him.*"
Sara assured me I would.

~

I remember waking up, the sun pushing against the curtains, Sara on the other side of the bed, lying diagonally, managing to keep one leg on mine. The clock said 7:42, and it was morning.

All my life. Waiting for something to happen. Even last night, riding the wave of our lovemaking, again, I could feel something of a Godly presence, but it only made me stop and look for more, a feeling more transcendent, more divine. A breakthrough was on me, and I was trying to catch it, trying to hold still, let it catch me, but with every breath, it was gone again, and after Sara rolled over and slept, I knew yet one more time that it—God, holiness, transcendance, an actual glimpse of heaven—would never come, never stay, never reveal itself. At least not for me.

I said a two word prayer just as Sara stirred.

"God. Please."

Maybe pessimism, maybe reality. I don't know.

~

Sara dressed slowly, for my benefit, I'm sure, but my thoughts were on her spirit, her loveliness of soul. Her face was aging a bit, lines marking the skin around her eyes and mouth, neck not quite so firm, gray starting to flicker here and there in her hair, a few extra pounds around her waist. But I didn't care. She smiled at me, and I went to her, held her, knowing I would never leave her, never intentionally dishonor her again, and I told her so, and asked her forgiveness for losing sight of her. She said sure, that she did indeed forgive me, and that she was glad we were okay, and that she was sure I meant all the things I said.

But she teased me—or was it scolding—saying what happened to the "we need more than water" bit.

I rarely make the same mistake twice. I told her I didn't know what she was talking about.

. . . *I will find all I need* . . .

Oh, my wife.

Together again after weeks apart, worlds apart. Driving home, I gave her the wheel, and we sat holding hands, or me leaning on her shoulder, my hand beneath her thigh, making her nervous, jabbering about nothing, playing Sara and Cyrus trivia, listening to the radio, and I knew that if I had to be in crisis, this was the woman to be in it with.

I didn't know what to make of her dream. Still don't, although the themes of journey, and Jesus inside of us, and our someday rebirth, are all clear enough. But whether God spoke to Sara, or her subconscious merely threw up her secrets, I can't say. But our experience as she told it and the intensity of our sharing, led us to believe that it was, at least, a kind of gift—certainly a blessing. We decided to leave it at that, thankful for its coming.

We got home before 1:00, grabbed the boys from Mike and Emily, and the four Mannings thought to try a picnic in the park downtown, but after ten minutes of tossing a football while Sara unsuccessfully fought to light a fire in one of the public grills, wind and cold forced us home. The Black and Blue raced up just as we pulled away, following the car for almost a block. Then he turned back, limping along, pretending, all haggard and bent, as if to die of rejection. When he saw we weren't coming back, though, he kicked into a canter, then tore across the park full bore.

Faker.

Ignoring the weather, we turned Saturday afternoon into a family special after all. Wayne and Richard beat Mom and Dad in a game of two-below, Richard won at Skipbo, Sara cleaned up in our truncated version of Monopoly, and the Ohio State/Michigan game came down to the wire as always. We popped popcorn around 5:00, and gathering around the kitchen table, we draped ourselves over the

morning paper, digging for the movie page. We decided to hit the
video store instead, but I told the boys I was hungry, and we'd go right
after we ate. I gathered up fixin's for grilled burgers and fries while
Sara entertained Richard, who was mad cause Wayne wouldn't play
with him. Wayne lingered at the grill with me, wanting to know if he
could light it. We piled on the charcoals, and were just dousing them
with lighter fluid, when the doorbell rang.

I heard Sara say come in, and the front door closed. I set down
the lighter fluid, wiped my hands on the dishtowel sticking out of my
pocket, and wandered through the kitchen, poking my head into the
living room.

Weeper and Rhody Cagle, standing in our doorway, a shoebox
hiding under Weeper's left arm.

I smiled broadly, and to my shame, lied through my teeth.
"Welcome!"

~

Not that I don't like the Cagles. These folks are good folks,
ancient like the earth, and just as strong.

Sara and I exchanged glances while they made their way to the
couch. Richard slinked to his room, and Wayne hid in the backyard,
and soon I heard the squeak of the swing.

So much for family night.

We don't know them terribly well, but stories about Weeper and
Rhody are among the best First Church has to tell. Eons ago, they
begat many children (six? seven?), mechanics all—even the girls—
because Weeper Cagle was the best carburetor man this side of El
Paso, and could coax a dead Ford back to life in less time than it takes
to spit. Especially trucks dated before '59. He was just that kind of
man: if you were his kid, you wanted to be like him. When he was
62, though, his hands stiffened up, and now, at 85-plus, they're gnarly
and barely open.

But he still drives his only car—a brown, early-model Mustang—
like a night sandstorm, and Rhody begs him to sell the rusted thing
and stay home. Off he roars, though, a couple of times a week, and

she won't ride with him unless he swears to keep it under thirty-five. His skinny face smiles with a limp, his stubbled skin wrinkling like a wadded shirt. His eyes are light, though—mischievous, tough with survival.

Rhody, on the other hand, is a flower, a gentle old art teacher who paints wretched still lifes anymore, though from the looks of the watercolors on her walls, she was quite good before her stroke ten or so years ago. Her speech slurred, but got better, and the Bell's Palsy the year after that permanently changed her face, giving her a funny, droopy droop in the right eye. Her hugs at the church door, though, after a poor sermon, are holy, like rain in the heat, and I always said if God ever chose a wife, he would most likely choose sweet Rhody Cagle.

Lights of the world, salt of the earth. Just what Jesus described.

I said what are you doing here, and Rhody patted Weeper on the knee, saying it was his idea to come, that he'd been feeling funny lately, like he wanted to tell me something, and he'd be mad if he died before he did it. Weeper smiled at me, nodding his head, then Sara, still nodding, and back to me. He finally squirted out a word or two I didn't catch, cleared his throat, said he was sorry, and began again.

He said he didn't know much, but that he'd seen lots in his time. I said lots of what. He ignored me, or missed it (I'd forgotten about his hearing aids), and said he'd seen state of the art engines go bad with no oil. I could see Sara drawing a blank, and I didn't have the foggiest. Then Rhody broke in and said there was this child—years ago—this kid in her class at—oh, Weeper, help me here, she said, slurring along—oh yes, at Rungston Junior High back some 40 years ago. A young flaxen-haired sculptor—I could tell she loved that word, flaxen—a young artist named Scottie, who just sat in talent, she said, with brilliance running out of her hands, but like the car, she'd had no oil and no tune-up and her soul died young. Weeper said he thought her name was Brenda Mae, but Rhody said no, it was Scottie, Scottie Booler, and turning back to me, she said Scottie Booler didn't do nothing but work her whole life in a cloth store—a blame cloth store, she said. And that last she heard, the poor woman was a widow at 56, lonely as an unpicked pumpkin.

It was a good story, but I still didn't get it. Sara smiled, though—

a secret little grin that said she enjoyed being smarter than me.

Weeper cleared his throat, gurgling more words. I heard him say they were afraid for me. Rhody pitched in that they knew a good heart when they saw one, and that they loved me.

Weeper stood up. Told me to do the same.

Rhody held the shoebox.

He put his right hand on my shoulder, and I was surprised— thrilled, too—to feel the strength in his closed hands. He looked up at me with those clear blues. His white brows touched in the middle, just over his nose, threatening to make one single hedge of hair above his eyes. This man's long life moved into mine as he tottered there, holding on to my shirt, my arm, my soul.

"Cyrus, like Rhody says, we love you, and I don't know why exactly, but we've come over here to bless you, to give you a blessing."

A special moment, a blessing at the hand of an old church father. I thought how sweet, how moving. Sara stood up, helped Rhody to her feet.

"Cyrus, we brought you something."

≈

The room disappeared, blanked out by shock. My heart rate surged while disbelief battled a desire to run screaming from the house. I fully expected to hear an unimagined Jesus walking on my porch, knocking on my front door, angel legions at his side.

Loreen had said it.

The gift to die for.

≈

I looked at Rhody. She crinkled her nose at me, smiling blandly, as if Weeper blessing me, bringing me a prophesied gift, was an every-day affair. Sara, on the other hand, saw my shock, my panic, and came up behind me, patting my back, wondering if I was okay. I'd for-gotten to tell Sara about Loreen. I didn't want her to miss the moment, but I couldn't speak, couldn't explain, trapped in another of those warped sacks of time I was talking about, where God climbs out of obscurity, declaring with all lucidity that he is there, and not silent. I tried to shout *the box, the box!* but Weeper leaned on me, and I listened.

Weeper said not to forget God's name was Love. That right and good were okay, but that love was it. I had done what I could here, he told me, and now that there was a new thing for me to do, I shouldn't get concerned if it didn't feel like much at first. I said what new thing, but Weeper said that that was up to me to know. Then he told me God said that I was too nervous, too restless, with too much wearying. God said too much wearying? Weeper laughed.

"Rhody, Cyrus needs the box now."

It was a shoe box, simply wrapped in brown paper—a Safeway sack. "For Cyrus" wiggled along the edge, marking the box as mine. The weight of the rectangle made me think of a book, and I was glad, but when I opened it, pushing aside the tissue, I realized there were no words here.

It was a goblet, a simple chalice.

Holy Grail or not, it was spectacular.

I lifted it from the box, feeling its dense weight. It's plain, austere bearing made me wince inside, as if it belonged to a less greedy age, a less tawdry time, but as I held the chalice upright, it felt solid in my hand, as if the drink from such a cup could indeed heal, raise the dead back to life, offer ascension to the holy, the blessed. The gold was tarnished, almost to brown, its bowl smooth, with no ornamentation. It stood some ten to twelve inches high, with the central girth of the deep bowl maybe three to four inches in diameter. Not a big space for the blood of Christ.

I looked at Weeper, and he stood quiet for awhile, shifting his weight now and then. Old years sat heavy on him, his small feet barely enough to hold him up, and I asked him to please sit down, but he stood straighter, pushing his fingers into my shoulder for balance. He said no, that he didn't need to sit, that he was going to do this on his feet. His left hand wiped at his bald head, scratching just above his ear.

He finally told the story, brief and curt. The cup belonged to his great-grandfather, a crusty elder in a frontier church back in one of

the Carolinas in the middle 1800's. And that from that man's family, since then, there had been eight pastors and preachers, and not a
few elders, deacons, and evangelists, though none in recent years.
This chalice blessed most of them, he said, though it's been a long
time out of use. But back then it lived in no telling how many sanc-
tuaries, blessing believers with the presence of Jesus. He said when he
was a boy, they were one-cuppers, and not ten minutes after his baptism, his first taste of Jesus had been with wine from this cup.

Though, of course, it was grape juice, he said. But still—fruit of
the vine.

Weeper said when his Daddy died several years ago, he'd gotten
it from his old things, that none of his four living brothers and sisters
wanted it. Then Rhody interrupted, saying they'd wanted the old
church pew, too, the one Weeper had slept on whenever the family
had company and there weren't enough beds, but that his sister Berta
Mae got there first, and stole it right there before they had a chance
to say boo or kiss my foot.

Weeper said, Rhody, and she said go on, then.

His arm finally gave out, and he let it drop from my shoulder. I
held the chalice in my right hand, gripped his hand with my left. He
said I was a good man, though not a great preacher by any stretch. I
raised my eyebrows, but he went on to say he knew I wanted to be
honest and humble though I couldn't always do it just right, and that
someday—and this made my knees shake—that someday, I would be
holy like I wanted to be holy.

He said he didn't believe much in the Lord talking to people, but
that it's been in his mind for some time that I should have this cup.
His kids didn't need it, being mechanics, and he figured that whether
I came or went, I was still going to want Jesus, so Rhody and him
brought it on over, because who knows how much longer either one
of us will be around.

At that, his eyes went watery, and Rhody put her hand on his
checkered woolen shirt. He took a quick wipe at his tears, but missed,
saying shoot, that he wasn't done. As he bowed his head, finding composure, he gripped my hand as best he could. Then he raised his head,
and his eyes still shone, but this time with clarity. He was passing

something on to me now, his spirit maybe, and in that moment, he prayed, suddenly, eyes open, looking right into mine, as if to pour some ancient knowledge, and I thought, this man is Elijah himself. He prayed quietly, though to me, it seemed like shouting.

O holy God take this man, this son of yours, and this cup, and may he find your Jesus. Press his heart with the love of that Jesus, O Lord, and let that wine that is your blood cover him, nourish him, and give him your presence all his life. And don't let him think this stubborn bunch of folk around here knows what's what for your servants. O holy God, have him drink from this old cup often, and may the Spirit flame up whenever he does. You told me—I guess you told me—that you have something to do with this young man, and now I beg you, O holy God, go out and do it, and don't let the devil have him. I bless him, holy Lord, and Rhody blesses him, and may you go with God, my son, and in Jesus. Amen.

I pressed the old man to my chest, saying thank you, thank you.

We didn't get the video, but went on with the burgers and fries, inviting the Cagles to join us. They did, and after dinner, we all sat in the living room with cokes, coffee, and iced tea. Surprisingly, the boys had warmed to these old folks, and they listened to their stories, laughing at Weeper, at his crusty tales of early automobile Texas, and falling in love with a woman named for Rhododendrons. The boys sacked out on the floor after awhile, while Weeper kept talking, and Sara and I held hands, watching Rhody nod off at his side. But still he talked, telling one slow story after another, and finally he and I were the last awake. We wandered into the kitchen and talked into the early night, mostly of wine, and Jesus.

After they had gone, with Wayne and Richard tucked in, Sara said she wondered what I was feeling.

I told her the story of Loreen and the gift. Her expression didn't change. I said it might be a miracle of a kind, and Sara shook her head, but whether she meant she doubted the miraculous, or was

awed I couldn't tell. We readied ourselves for bed, mulling over the
night in Fort Stockton, the chalice, the future. We brushed our teeth
quietly, and she went on to bed while I flossed. I switched on her
bedside lamp, stacked up my pillows to read. I climbed in and
grabbed my Dad's old Bible, thinking to read Ezekiel, or Revelation,
but the masonite flipped open to the inside cover, and I read again
the old inscriptions.

Sara was dozing, but when she heard my sobs, felt the bed quaking,
she sat up and held me. I doubled over, face toward the covers, abdomen
screaming from the force of it. What, what she said, her hands rubbing
my back, but I couldn't make a sound, couldn't get a breath.

It had swept over me unannounced. The words had broken my
heart, and all the walls besides.

There, in my dad's humped scribble: *"If I ask God to give me the
things I need; then I must assume that I have the fulfillment of my prayer
in whatsoever cup he gives me to drink."*

For better or worse, I took it to mean my God had spoken.

∼

Sara and I talked until almost two. We planned, we agreed, we
prayed. We sealed it with love, then slept.

The morning came early, rousting me out of bed with an unfamiliar passion matched only by a concurrently running giddiness. Little
sleep, but no fatigue, and today, Sunday morning, I turn a corner, welcome a year of chosen quiet, fully intending to be useless and still,
except perhaps for a job, a northern blue-collar enterprise with an
hourly wage, a place in the midst of roaring machines I can't yet name,
quietly laboring, watching in the rest for what I know will come.

Peace will come, and in his cup I will find all I need.

Simply put, I give myself to God's voice, and he has called me
to quiet. To communion. I will follow as best I can. To honor him
. . . I quit.

I'm leaving Ruin.

November 23

I swear he had wine on his breath.

Velma Washington, to Roland Minor
Administrative Committee

. . . the season of Christ's appearing . . .

The Sunday before Thanksgiving. One last lesson, one last mini-sermon, a small, late afternoon goodbye gathering, no evening service. By six o'clock, all will be said and done.

We pull out tonight, headed across the desert and the mountains, hoping to get to Sandpoint, Idaho, and the in-laws, by Thanksgiving.

∾

I'll miss my morning donuts.

I stopped at Tastee Donuts on the way into the office about 6:00 a.m., and grabbed three plain glazed from the morning's first batch. Doris said she was sorry to hear we'd be leaving, and that she'd have voted the other way, if she went to First Church. I said they didn't vote after all, and she looked funny and said why leave, then. I didn't explain, but said thanks, anyway. I teased her, saying for the hundredth time how she ought to come to hear me preach once, at least. She made a face, and stuffed two extra old-fashioneds into my sack. Doris said she knew me, knew I liked donuts with substance.

"No charge this morning, Mr. Cy."

Doris' eyes were wet, but I knew better than to notice. When I said see ya, and thanks again for everything, I stepped around the counter, gave her a little hug, and thought how I hate goodbyes, hate

that the day will be chock full of them. Goodbye to friends and rituals, and the early hour Tastee Donut run. I touched her shoulder, said
to take care.

"I'll pray for you, Mr. Cy."

Thanks, I mumbled, and through hazy eyes, I somehow managed
to find my way out, find my way to the car. I turned the ignition,
punched on the headlights, blasting the shop's dark glass. My radio
blared, tuned to oldies, and Jim Croce made me think of Dad. I eased
onto the dark street, singing "Bad, Bad Leroy Brown" at the top of my
lungs, relishing the flaking sugar of an old-fashioned.

∽

I announced my resignation three weeks ago, on Sunday, November 2nd, at the end of my sermon, and the whole sanctuary audibly
sighed in relief.

We broke the news to Wayne and Richard early that morning,
before church. The minute the words spilled out, I knew I'd made a
mistake, not talking to them, not having them involved in my
process. Before he stomped away from the table, Wayne said he
wished we'd at least asked him, but we obviously didn't care what he
thought, and *a lot of good prayer does, Dad!* The door slam punctuat-
ed his frustration, and for once, I let it go. Richard cried, head down
over pancakes, still eating, but managed a smile at the end, even
throwing an I-love-you-dad over his shoulder as he headed for the
comfort and privacy of his room.

Even in seemingly miraculous times, doubt always has a face.

∽

Sara sat on the front row that morning. I glanced at her again
and again, charmed, in love, needing her eyes, her assurance. She
wore warm black and white, a high waisted outfit, and her hair was
pulled away from her face, that tough and gentle face. She held it
high, toward me, as if to say, go on, go on, though her hands were
rarely still.

After the altar call (yet one more time, nobody wanted Jesus), I called her up to the podium with me, read my letter, and afterwards, walked hand in hand up the short aisle to the foyer, waiting for the chaos. We heard Jack tell the congregation he loved us, that he was proud of us for making this difficult decision, and on and on, but the last part we didn't hear. We were necking in the cry room, reveling in freedom.

I had hoped someone would jump up, protesting, shouting *No, he has to stay! What a raw deal! We'll never survive without him!* But most folks nodded like they knew already. After church, people said thanks for everything, wished me luck, and asked lots of inane questions like what kind of man did I think Ruin needed now, had I heard Jack Nebley from Abilene preach, did I think we needed to get a woman deacon or not. Pretty soon, though, the commotion died, and the Mannings climbed in the car and came home. The roast was done, Richard complained that he liked ham better, and when the rolls were brown on the bottom, the iced tea was poured and sugared, we sat down and prayed, then dug in, feasting in an odd state of shock and euphoria.

After chocolate pudding, I cleaned up, comforted by sounds of home. I relished simple tasks—sudsing up plates, scrubbing potatoes off the pan, pouring Cascade in the dishwasher, sweeping. By two o'clock, the kitchen sparkled.

I felt like I'd never pastored a day in my life.

The Cowboys had a bye week, but we watched football anyway, drowsy, and Sara said it was all so anti-climactic. I'd changed our lives forever, but as usual, Sunday dinner ended, John Madden raved, my wife dosed. The boys romped in the yard, fighting and shouting, each earnestly taking out their grief and fury on the other.

That afternoon, Francis called to say sorry, and Mike came by, offering brief solace. Other than that, it was quiet, though we eventually got a few cards during the week.

Eleven years, *and we got a few cards during the week.*

∼

The following Sunday, two weeks ago, I gave a short sermon calling the church to meditation and silent worship, to a deeper seeking after Jesus, a quiet sense of listening for his presence, for his word. I wondered about the poor and the oppressed, and how to serve them, publicly repenting of not doing much on their behalf—or anyone else's, for that matter. I called my sin self-absorption, and prayed a long prayer to Jesus. At the amen, I looked up, feeling wholly refreshed, and almost burst out laughing at the solemn chagrin of my stuffy brothers and sisters in Christ.

But an amazing thing happened. Maybe a miracle. Time will tell.

There were three baptisms after the service that morning. The last was the young daughter of a new family in town named Nye, and the dad, Jonathan, heard his girl's confession of faith. Jonathan Nye spoke to the congregation for ten minutes, convincing us again of Jesus' love and forgiveness, eloquently describing Romans six and the process of dying. He said burial was a big deal, that his dad had been a prisoner of war once, that he'd told him that even as confinement taught love of freedom, so burial taught the glory of new life. He lowered young Bretta into the water, his firm face concentrated, as eloquent as his words. She was underwater maybe 20 seconds, maybe 25—much longer than usual. Women leaned forward, hanging on to the pews, and two men stood up, as if they were going for the baptistry, but then he brought her up out of the water. She sucked at air, spitting and coughing, grabbing on to her daddy's strong shoulders, gasping. There was a stunned silence, then a sudden outbreak of applause and cheers. We knew she'd been buried, and saved, and though we don't often act this way, we spontaneously broke into "Jesus is all the world to me, my life, my joy, my all . . ."

I spoke with this intense baptizer just after, and he said he and his wife Gail had come to Ruin because the Lord told him to come. Period. At which point I stared and stood there with my mouth open, dumb. Speechless, I excused myself, and ran to find Jack and Roland.

Two weeks of interviews and negotiation, and Jonathan Nye is Ruin's new pastor. He starts January 1.

He also bought my house. We closed three days ago, on Friday. Tuesday, they move in.

~

8:00 a.m. Not much time.

This time yesterday, thick U-haul boxes stacked four high crammed my office. Mike and I made two trips in the church van from the office to my garage. Fifty-four boxes of books.

Now blank shelves line the room. Five books occupy the middle shelf formerly holding my Shakespeare. I'll take them home today. Alex's *Romeo and Juliet* , my *Jerusalem Bible*, a copy of Emily Dickinson poetry. Also an old copy of Merton's *Seeds of Contemplation*, and Beuchner's *Telling the Truth*.

It's desolate in here. Expansive, bigger than usual. Haggard walls, random holes all over. Family pictures gone, Christian posters gone. Sunlight's faded the paint in spots. "Silent Night" echoes as I hum.

My new chalice sits on the empty desktop, telling me the season of Christ's appearing is almost here.

The phone rings, and Sara's checking on me, crying a little. I ask her what's wrong, and she says nothing, it's just her period, but I know better. She says she wants to go, but she loves the old house on Curtain Street, with the south porch, and the lawn, and the mesquite. Wayne broke his ankle in that house, she says, and remember that old floor furnace, and how one winter, little Richard burned his feet on it, his soles red with markings that looked like black lines on a grilled burger? She says I love you. I say I love you, too, and are you going to be all right, and she says of course.

"I love you."

"Love you, too."

We both hold the phone, silent, needing each other, but I tell her I have to get ready, and she says okay, love you once more, and bye.

Quiet again, and light peeks in the window, announcing a crisp, near-winter day.

. . . *a participation in mystery* . . .

Class in seven minutes. Buster shoots baskets as I meander through, and I'm sad Mrs. Eric won't be here. She called the office, citing a bad spell at breakfast, but she wanted me to know. It's uncanny: I feel her absence, like the floor's lopsided, the stars out of whack.

I wonder if she remembers her husband's last day.

Roman's here already, lumbering around in his Pillsbury Doughboy tee shirt, lugging a black/silver airpot he bought in Abilene, saying it'll be nice to have hot coffee for once. Serena lays out four dozen assorted donuts from Tastee, and I yell, and run over, because Doris is here, laying out the sprinkles and the raspberry filled. I scold her, hugging her, saying I'm mad that she didn't say she was coming. She squeezes my hand and says well, make it good, preacher, it may be your only chance.

Skipper McKinnon slips in. Lacey's not with him, and his eyes are red, hidden. He knows about her. I hear him tell Brett she's sick this morning, and his eyes catch mine, dart away. Why won't he tell me he knows? Lacey says he won't come see me. She told me he caught her in the bathroom after a dinner out, and devastated, he didn't sleep, but drank instead. It was the only time she'd ever seen him drunk. I move to him, taking his hand, but he can't look me in the eye, even as he wishes me well, saying he's sorry we're leaving. I want to tell him to look at me, and surprisingly, the words come out. I can't cry here, he says, and I say maybe we can talk later. He mumbles maybe, maybe, it would be good, maybe. I watch him wander off toward the men's room. Mine is not the only loss this morning.

A little smatter of applause breaks out, and I think it must be for me, but Goose Anderson's coming through the door. He just got back from Houston with Kari, and it's good news: she's in remission, and the docs say it's beatable. There's no relief like death pushed back, and for a moment, I forget. Goose and I bear hug, and I can't wait to hold Kari and her bald head—if my last day will let me.

My God. The last day.

Francis comes in, and she has a friend in tow, her walking partner, she says, one Rose Gonzalez. She's a lovely lady, really, and Francis is stressed, smiling through heavy make-up, trying to hang in, and I take her hand. I'm sorry for our sour history, sorry that there's no time to fix it. Her friend Rosa is a talker, and with my arm around Francis, I turn back, listening to her tell me about her five boys, that she worries about them, with all the talk about guns and safe sex. Francis watches me listening, and as I catch her eye, she smiles, and I see just a bit of Joy.

I smile back, and head for the lectern.

~

Twenty-four people this morning, and prayer requests take awhile.

Praise for Kari, welcome to Rose, and Skip vaguely mentions Lacey, barely audible. Brett Mitter's department at the city is downsizing, and he'll know next week whether he keeps his job. Brett's daughter Angela got accepted to UT, but he's worried about the morals there, and please pray for all of us. Maxine Bauser's mother just had a pacemaker put in and she's better, but Sharon and Dusty Jones are breaking up, Maxine says. Dusty's moved out, and we all hurt for Sharon and Dusty, and little Baylor, their 6-month-old.

Anybody else, and of course there's more, always more.

Reggie's back is out, and the McCowans, Donna and Katy, are headed for a family reunion that'll be concrete hard. Will says Cassandra's having problems with the pregnancy, that she may have diabetes, and nobody knows anything else about it, so Will's gonna check it out with Jeff and get back to us. Any more, I ask, and the room stops, waiting, and suddenly, I miss Joy, and Connie, too—a little—though Sara is sitting right in front of me. "Weather's nice" comes from the back and I say sure, and finally, the requests are over. But Tom raises his hand.

"You, Cyrus, and your family."

I guess he had to say it.

I write *Cyrus' family moving* on the deposit slip, next to the other requests. I start with Dear God, but follow with a long pause. Clearing my throat, I start again, but I motion at Mike. He joins me, and I hand him the deposit slip, asking him to say the prayer, please.

~

10:00. Groceries enter the sanctuary, reminding me I don't have to preach.

On the Sunday before Thanksgiving, every year for the past six years, First Church gathers food for the local food bank, a festival tradition I picked up listening to a guy over in Abilene. Families bring one or two bags of groceries from Safeway or Food Lion, stocking up on canned vegetables, Bisquick, and pasta. We clear away the pulpit, making a flat clean floor, and parade the sacks to the front, piling them onto the stage. Several usually break, dumping Rice-a-Roni, Wesson Oil bottles, Campbell soups, and all manner of non-perishables onto the carpet, sending men in suits crawling, desperate to stave off breakage or spills. A stunning reminder of God's bounty, these Christians piling their gifts at the front, though I worry about parading our generosity before men.

Jack and Roland and I stand at the front, accepting the bags, supervising their placement, while the piano plays improvisations around the doxology. The children bring decorated bags, all smiles, clamoring onto the stage, making messes, giving hugs, and just now Buster approaches me, hands me his sack. It's from an athletic supply house, and I peer in. A basketball. I bend down, squeezing him, and he throws open his mouth, pointing to his new tooth, and wonders if maybe me and Richard can play next week. I rough up his hair, send him back to his mom.

Watching the eyes of the people going by, dropping off their food, I see both thankfulness and pity. They wonder about what will happen to us, I suppose, thinking they'll write, maybe, but they won't. Maybe a letter or two before five years passes and they realize they haven't heard from us in who knows how long. Every hand I shake is a parting, a farewell, and though there's to be a small party this afternoon, I know that my good-bye is really here, here in this sanctuary, my last worship in Ruin.

≈

Two columns of men approach, walking in step down the center aisle, flanking to my right and left. Four men on each side, now settling in, facing the people, hands crossed at belts, or behind backs, chins down, looking gravely religious.

Fifteen more minutes, and it's over.

Instead of preaching, I've opted for communion, presiding over the Lord's Supper, as they say, the final item in our worship. Silver trays hold down the table in front of me—thin ones on my right for the unsalted crackers, thick ones on my left for the plastic cups of grape juice. Between them is my chalice, and a loaf of bread. The loaf is dark, and brown, a grainy bread without yeast, rich and dense, hard to chew. The chalice is regal in its simplicity, glad to be of service once more.

I can see Weeper and Rhody, four rows back. Weeper's smiling, nodding his head.

I quickly hand out the metal bread trays, swiveling first to my left, to Mike, then to Jason Carpenter on my right. They pass them down the row, two trays per man, and now they're still, ready to go. I lift the bread, break the loaf in half. Crumbs litter the table, and I hold the halves high.

"*I am the Bread of Life. This is the bread which comes down from heaven, that a man may eat of it and not die. Unless you eat the flesh of the son of man, you have no life in you. He who eats my flesh has eternal life, for my flesh is food indeed. This is my body.*"

Father Rosey would wave incense now, or make a sign of the cross. I've watched him offer the Eucharist twice, and I envy his sense of weight, his sense of presence, the real presence of Jesus.

I pray that God will live in the bread, live in our bodies as we eat. Amen, and the men take off, still grave, and one by one, the people break off a snip of cracker, stoically munch the body of Christ.

~

I lift the chalice, presenting it as if to propose a toast. Several arms cross, and I catch at least one set of eyes rolling.

I grin. The chalice holds half an inch of blood red wine.

"Unless you drink my blood, you have no life in you. He who drinks my blood has eternal life, and I will raise him up at the last day. For my blood is drink indeed. He who drinks my blood abides in me, and I in him. This is my blood."

Holding this chalice is like holding the hand of God. I pray for Jesus to live in this cup, in this blood, and that after we drink it, he will be in us that much more. Amen, and the men move away again. I close my eyes, bring the chalice to my lips.

Jesus' blood. I drink the wine, first a sip, then another, taking Jesus in as best I can. The sweet bite helps, its warmth moving down my throat, opening my chest, my senses. More than metaphor, not miracle exactly—a mystery, a participation in mystery, his blood and body mixing with mine.

"Come, Lord Jesus."

~

I open my eyes, and there's *that face*, lingering along the back wall.

I left my imaginings behind. I'm not seeing Jesus—it's the Sunday night only man, lifting his cup of juice, swallowing it like a shot of whiskey, wiping his mouth on a woolen sleeve. Gripping the chalice, I briskly walk the center aisle, watching him slip out the old antique door. Just as it closes, I hit it, throwing it open, and the force of the noise bangs like a shot, but I don't care.

He's jogging now, and I give chase, catching him out at the edge of the lot, just in front of Harry John's new BMW. I grab the man by the sleeve, turn him around. We trade stares, but he has far more composure, far more levity. I'm breathing hard, and I'm surprised to see him leaning toward me. I glance over my shoulder. Several people mill around on the church steps, watching us.

"Drinking?"

I show him the chalice, tell him it's just communion, and he says
. . . oh. I tell him I've always wanted to meet you, but you keep slipping out on me. I ask him his name.

"Folks call me Hanner. First name's Paul."

We shake hands. I'm not surprised by his grip, nor his calm. He
wonders if the wine's gone. I hesitate, stalling him with it was just for
communion, just for today. He backs off, says fine, that's fine. I ask
him if he drinks, and he says no. Then why do you want it? He says
wine just makes more sense to him than grape juice. I say sometimes,
handing him the chalice. He smiles, takes it.

"The blood of Christ."

He says amen, and drinks the few sips left. Handing the chalice
back to me, he says thanks. We're staring again, not having anything
to say, but I can sense he's in no hurry. I fumble, assuming I need to
go now, explaining that it's a busy day today, but maybe he'd like to
meet some of the other members here . . ?

"You're moving today?"

I say yes, astonished.

He takes a breath, thinks, not finding the words. Now he recon-
siders and says, that's okay, that he'd see me another time, but just out
of curiosity, where was I moving to?

I don't answer him.

The day's sunny, a perfect day, maybe as much as sixty-five
degrees. Texas clouds can be white as angel robes against that rang-
ing blue sky, and Paul looks away, squinting at the sun.

I invite him to lunch, saying it'll probably just be McDonald's,
but we'd be proud to have him. His lean face breaks into a smile, and
he says that'd be fine, fine, that he'd like that.

~

Paul helped us load the last of our stuff into the truck. He's a
strong man, carrying two and three book boxes at a time, and between
him and Hubert, and me and the boys, we got the second half of the
truck loaded by 3:00. That left enough time to vacuum the house and
sweep the garage before heading to the church at 4:00 for the party.

At McDonald's, I told Paul we were going north, to live in Idaho or Washington, depending on where Sara could get a teaching job. He wondered about my work, and I said I'd just have to see, that it might be a paper route, might be a factory thing, or delivery. But that thankfully, the church was going to continue my salary for six months while I transitioned. But that I wanted to do some writing, maybe some volunteer work, hospice, meals on wheels, maybe—that sort of thing.

Hanner shook his head, wiping special sauce from his stubble. I said what, but he kept laughing and chewing, working on his second Big Mac. He took a long drag from his coke straw.

"You are one funny man."

He said he'd been listening to me preach for years, that First Church was the only church he ever bothered with, mostly because of me. He said he didn't even believe in Jesus really, but that he kept thinking I might convince him, though in his travels, he'd found that most folks who said they believed in him, didn't. He said he thought I probably did, and that he liked that about me.

I asked what he did. For a living.

He laughed again, and said you know better than that, that his living was just getting by, getting guys like me to give him McDonald money. He changed the subject then, and got to chatting with Wayne about wrestling in school, saying he used to wrestle for his high school, and once got to the state tournament. I asked him what high school, and he said a western one. Before I got any further Wayne was talking, saying he'd never seen wrestling in school, and Paul said well, you will now.

After we finished loading, while I was fussing over the vacuum bag, I noticed Wayne and Paul out on the swing. Paul was getting his knapsack together, his loaves of bread, extra sets of clothes, and the few books he carried. He'd told me books helped on the road—the pulp fiction to escape it, the poetry to wake him to its beauty, and an occasional verse of scripture, maybe Proverbs, to remind him it's all a mystery anyway.

I saw Wayne reach in his pocket, hand some bills to Paul. Paul's hand reached out, though it seemed reluctant, and he didn't speak as he stuffed the money into his torn corduroys. But he shook Wayne's hand—a good, hard pump—and went back to his knapsack.

I got the vacuum squared away, and ran it through the house, scarfing up pennies and pins, stopping now and then to retrieve rubber bands and safety clips. Twenty minutes later, I figured good enough, and stepped on the off switch. Wayne was standing on the empty porch, feet spread, a thumb in his belt, eyeing the west. I stepped over the vacuum, joined him outside.

The porch seemed strange without the glider.

We could hear the easy swish of Sara's broom in the garage. Richard leaned on the mesquite, his Pooh Bear securely under his arm.

"I don't get homeless people."

Wayne's face was blank, but his eyes were tired, and I didn't know what he meant. He said, you know, like Paul. How did he get there, out on the road, just wandering like that? He told me Paul was gone, heading west. He was going to El Paso, and that he probably wouldn't be back to Ruin anytime soon.

We both turned to the west, trying to catch a glimpse of our stranger friend in the distance.

I asked Wayne about the money he gave Paul. Wayne shrugged and said he didn't give him much, and that Paul hadn't asked him for it. He said watching Paul eat at McDonald's just hit him funny, and he got a thought that he should share what he had. He said, so I did.

No big deal.

I wondered where that left him financially, trying to buy the bike. His answer made me push down an unexpected urge to sob.

"I guess I'll have to start over."

. . . *such gifts* . . .

We got away.

Wayne and Richard are asleep in the double bed next to the window while Sara and I stare at the eleven o'clock news. Carlsbad, New Mexico, where my mom and dad brought me to see supposedly spectacular caverns when I was a kid, maybe seven, maybe eight years old. I don't remember a thing about it.

Might as well sleep on a pine box, she says, throwing her head against the mangy pillow, pulling up the pseudo cubist brown-orange covers. Brushing my teeth, I lean over the bed, looking at the factory made paintings. Flick-of-the-wrist-seagulls high over see-though waves, a fantasy of oceans in a desert hovel.

Time to spit.

Sara turns off the bad lamp by the bed, leaving the TV to light the room. She's on her side, facing away from me, but her hand reaches over to give me a squeeze. She says thanks for talking to me, and I say sure, and soon she's dropped into soft snoring. I flip through the channels, come back to the news. I hit the mute button, watching closely, playfully reading lips, catching a phrase here and there— murder, men and women of the jury, we'll be back after this.

～

This trip isn't going to be easy.

I'm driving a twenty-four-foot U-haul, pulling our Corolla, while Sara drives the Taurus, back seat stuffed to the ceiling. Tonight, it's Motel Six, as it will be throughout, and Sara's not exactly perturbed about it, but close. I told her we're on a budget. On the other hand, I spent twelve bucks on a bottle of wine as we came through Pecos, thinking we needed to mark our departure with what romance we could muster, forgetting, of course, about the boys in the next bed.

But still, I'd packed the Waterford goblets in the Corolla just behind the steering wheel so I could get to them, and when I poured the wine, Sara smiled. We plopped down on the edge of the bed and clinked our crystal together, toasting all things uncertain, and whatever it is we're doing with our lives.

We sat there, stooped shouldered, hoping to chat, but a monumental fatigue kept us still. Sara slipped off her shoes and stood, slowly stretching, unwinding, moving toward the suitcases in the mini-closet. She undressed, said thanks for the wine, plodded into the bathroom, shutting the door behind her, and I heard the shower. I knew she'd stand there under the hottest water she could stand, and cry as if she would die.

Sure enough, when she came out, her eyes were red and swollen, but she said she felt better, that the hot water was glorious.

It was my turn then, and it was glorious, indeed.

~

Talking, snuggling under covers, laughing in the dark.
At least we're together.

~

Sara wondered if I'd had a chance to get with Mike. I said yeah, that after he'd helped me move my office, we'd grabbed a coke, and headed over to the park, where we spent the better part of two hours watching the Black and Blue chase leaves. Mike had never met the Black and Blue, and was wary at first, but when the dog offered him a paw, a trick he's known ever since I met him, Mike warmed right up, wondering who'd let such an animal go.

Sara said Emily was making him swear they'd come to see us. I told her Mike said they'd try, but no promises.

Then I said oh, yeah, and grabbed Mike's present. I said look at this.

When it was time to leave the park, Mike placed a small box in my hand. He said he wanted me to have it.

I hand Sara the ring box. She opens it and gasps. A simple gold ring shines like hope finally realized.

"A wedding band?"

Mike told me he'd proposed to a rather plain girl years ago, before Emily, and while they were engaged, he'd slept with another woman, a blonde who would eventually introduce him to Emily. The plain girl broke the engagement, returned the ring, and went on to marry a double-A baseball player from Houston. Emily doesn't even know I have it, he said, but he kept it because . . . well, he didn't know why. He said he always wanted to do something good with it, though, and now he wanted me to have it. I told Sara he gave me the box, saying keep the ring, and let it be for fidelity.

My God, I thought. Another gift. A ring of promise. A poet for a friend.

~

Lights out. My family softly breathing, shifting under covers, getting legs just right for the night's sleep. Car engines rumbling in the distance, barely audible. Shadows from the motel sign slice the wall in thin stripes. Lying on my side, staring at the blinds.

Ruin's gone, and our plan for tomorrow is sketchy at best. But how gentle God can be, uprooting our lives, our very souls, filling our emptiness, our panic, with such gifts.

Sara, my children, the eleven years at First Church, and now, a new coming of his voice into my life, though not like I expected. And Joy, Francis' kindness, the chalice, Mike's ring, even Connie, and a chance to remake my life, perhaps yet finding the me he calls me to. So many gifts in my upheaval.

For now, his call is to quiet. My imagination wants to run wild, calling on what I think Jesus might say, what he might advise me, but the message I've heard says that it is indeed Jesus I am to meet, but that his new coming will not be an imaginative one, but one bearing the blood and bones of his humanity.

I liked Alex, and Paul Hanner, and the Black and Blue. Connie, too. All of them cast-offs, thrift-store material, soiled and broken, but not used up. I find myself milling over Wayne's question. How do they get there? Perhaps I'd like to know, and perhaps communing with God in this silent place will open me, let me find out.

I suppose I, too, am cast-off. I am not homeless or poor—yet—but I am certainly adrift. Bitterness will be tempting, in the loneliness of it all. I don't understand the past few months—what it means, where it's leading—but I am leaning into the faith I have, into the shoulder of Jesus, hoping he will hold me up.

I have asked God to give me the things I need. I must assume that I have the fulfillment of my prayer in this cup he gives me to drink.

I rest in his grace.

Which is not to say I can sleep.

December 24
the next year

You should see him dance.

Sara Manning
to Jack Simons and Roland Minor,
Elder's meeting

What gift, I wonder?

There's not a porch anymore, and it's cool now, and Sara and I have graduated from plain coffee to what they call lattes here in Washington, and it's a Christmas Eve with rain.

It's late again, after 11:00, and the boys are sleeping, but lightly, ready for the first sounds of Santa. Richard coughs now and again, and Sara and I lie on the couch in front of the fireplace, her cheek on my chest, and she's asleep as well. The pre-fab log's about gone, though the last embers are far from dying.

It's a full house, with Sara's mom and dad staying through New Year's, and Paul Hanner here indefinitely. Paul showed up about three weeks ago, standing on the doorstep with his knapsack, saying Seattle was his new home, and could he get a bite. We said sure, and now he's doing chores, looking for work, sleeping on the floor in Wayne's room. Paul had a thrilling night, what with the carols and all, and hanging his stocking on the mantel. All through the singing and storytelling, he sat right in front of the fire, not four feet away, now and then turning his back to us, staring at the flames. He said it was his first Christmas in a home with a fireplace.

But Paul bit the dust an hour ago, and Grandpa just headed upstairs, saying Merry Christmas to all and to all a goodnight. An astronaut GI Joe stares at the treetop while Christmas lights flash, making ceiling patterns, just like when I was a kid. I used to lie for hours watching red, green, white, and blue lines, and balls and stars and washes dancing on walls and ceilings, calling out for Santa to come, come here.

~

The transition hasn't been too bad on the boys, though it's hard to tell. Richard's blossoming at Shorecrest , a gorgeous elementary school featuring fifty foot evergreens towering over long, lush playgrounds. Most beautiful playground I've ever seen. He's got a girlfriend, a smiley angel named Nikki who skates over to our house several times a week. He's doing well in math and language arts, and calls himself the king of wallball, a game of choice among pee-wees in the know.

Wayne struggles. The rebel years are beginning, I suppose. His school work is fine, though not exemplary, except in math, which has proven to be a strength, at least the way they teach it here. He seems to connect with numbers and sequence, and his bent toward logic shows itself in a non-interest in the arts, and a general scorn for anything I say. He won't talk to me, talks to Sara less, and we're getting concerned, not knowing how to help him. I've tried to talk to him about his anger over the move and about his growing attitude about God and all things religious, but I find talking to eleven-year-olds about grief and loss, and other mysteries of God, difficult, if not impossible. He still doesn't pray.

~

It was hard, leaving Ruin. Jonathan Nye never panned out, and they got a new preacher about six months after we left, and they liked him, but then his daddy died, and he had a breakdown. Francis wrote that it was a bad fit all the way around, so now there's a new search committee, with few resumés coming in.

I was back in Texas in July for a Bible conference they hold annually at one of the Christian colleges in Abilene. I flew into Midland on a Tuesday, rented a Taurus and drove out to Ruin, arriving in the late afternoon.

Curtain Street was the same, but the old house was vacant, the for sale sign barely visible, hidden by the weeds. I stood on the porch, looking at the empty space along the horizon where the old mesquite stood. I couldn't imagine why it was gone.

I went to see Francis, to thank her for her letters, and Weeper Cagle greeted me at the door. Francis told me he came over for supper most days by 6:30. I said, you're kidding, and she said that after Rhody passed on, he just decided he needed company, tearing over to her house one evening, asking could he have some dinner, and that he's been there ever since. I told him the chalice was still safe, and in use, and that while I hadn't found the church my family really needed, we were attending a small Bible fellowship in the southern part of the city. He said, south is good, and I told him I was reading the minor prophets these days, and he said, minor prophets are good. He wasn't quite there, not like he was, and while Francis and I talked about Joy, he sat silently staring at his plate.

Francis said she found a letter going through Joy's chest of drawers, in the top drawer, tucked inside a small paperback of Emily Dickinson's poetry. I told Francis we'd talked about Dickinson, Joy and I.

Francis handed me the envelope. It said "Mom."

The tone of the writing was warm, and forgiving, speaking of her conversion, her baptism, her growing curiosity about this new Jesus she'd come to know. But there was also her regret, and the letter became an accusation, a confession. Bitterness over neglect, an unknown abortion at 21, and the shame she wanted Francis to feel about ignoring her only daughter. She needed to say these things on paper, the letter explained, but now, they need never come to light, because forgiveness and newness were real, and she wanted to be part of the living grace in the world.

And a final sentence, asking Francis to mend things with me, which Francis said she'd tried very hard to do. I reassured her, thanked her. Our healing has been miraculous.

∾

The day after Thanksgiving, I got another letter from Francis. On Monday of that week, Weeper followed his sweet Rhody to heaven. I bet Jesus and Weeper are up there trading stories, and Weeper doing most of the talking, maybe even telling him the story of the guy who got the chalice.

∾

The year's been tough, but good. An expensive move, Sara's new job with an impressive little school in the southern industrial district, a new home, new schools for the boys, new work for me, and traffic that reduces me to a screaming lunatic at least once a week. I've done a couple of different jobs, neither of which fit well, and right now I'm driving for a courier service, putting over a thousand miles a week on a used white Toyota Tercel so bottom-of-the-line that I couldn't put an air conditioner in it even if I was so inclined. I answer to number 86 on the dispatch radio, delivering one-, two-, and four-hour packages to busy exectives, and I know the insides of almost every downtown elevator. The work gives me lots of time to think, and I've been surprised to find, though it's been a year, the folks in Ruin travel with me still.

∾

Mike and Emily were here in September, and good news— they're hopeful about adopting soon. We took them on a ferry to Whidbey Island, and Emily's radiance was thrilling. Obviously taken with her husband, she laughed at the sharp winds coming in off Puget Sound, wrinkling her nose, hanging on to her wide hat, and I could see why Mike loved her. Emily also thanked me for introducing them to the Black and Blue. I gaped, and Mike shrugged, sheepish, saying he couldn't get rid of him.

Sara and Emily went for coffee, and Mike and I leaned on the rail, watching gulls with still wingtips swing back and forth above our heads. He asked about the ring. I still have it, I told him. He smiled. Watching the gulls, he said he didn't know fidelity could be so sexy.

∾

They caught us up on news and gossip at the church, and the biggest relief was that the Manning family wasn't in it. Katy McCowan has a boyfriend, Emily told us, and they'll be married just after the new year. Brett and Mindy took a second honeymoon last August, and Angela made all A's at UT, but came home pregnant, and isn't sure she'll go back to school for awhile. Doris still comes to church, and Tom Martin moved to California after falling in love with a bank teller from San Francisco, and his divorce was final about this time last year. What about Skipper and Lacey, I asked him, and he said he thought they were good, doing good, and it occurred to me Mike was unaware of her disorder.

I need to call them.

It looks like Sam Cooser will be a new elder, and I asked Mike about Harry Johns. Mike said one of Harry's business partners had taken Harry over to Dallas for Promise Keepers, where Harry apparently recommitted his life to Jesus. Emily said he and Edna gave a testimony to break your heart, that everyone cried, and that their son was back on the wagon. Mike said he gave Harry my address, said Harry was going to write.

I hope he does.

~

Back on the couch by the Christmas tree, and Sara's body shifts. Sitting up, she groans, says she wants to go to bed, so I guess it's time. I crawl under the blue spruce (I've got one that looks just like it in the front yard) and unplug the lights. At the foot of the stairs I realize Santa hasn't eaten the cookies or finished off the milk, so I kiss Sara and send her on while I linger in our cramped kitchen. Chocolate chips don't fit the night as well as the green Christmas tree sugar cookies my mother used to make, but a cookie is a cookie, I guess, and the milk is still cold, though this non-fat business is like drinking white water. But we're getting used to the changes, and God lives here just like he did back home.

~

The mystery's pretty thick around Puget Sound, like the fog, and they say the suicide rate's high. Nobody goes to church much, and the New Age and grunge happened here first. Multiple tattoos and body piercings make for interesting pedestrians, and neo-pagan bookstores selling gargoyles and witches handbooks still boggle my mind. But driving all these miles lets me taste the full range of humanity, from the million dollar Eastside to the homeless dotting downtown, and I'm thinking of volunteering at Union Gospel Mission or for Big Brothers or something. But mostly I'm quiet, grabbing an occasional cup of strong coffee at a dark, cagey cafe called the Mecca on Queen Anne Hill, near the Space Needle. One of the other courier drivers, a squatty guy named Frankie, sometimes joins me, but mostly I read there, alone, jotting notes on napkins, musing over what I think listening to God means, and though the city roars in my ears constantly, cause I mostly drive with my windows down, my inner ear is much calmer. I hear God calling me still, with an ever stronger voice, though nowadays it's not the hearing that concerns me.

What concerns me is the coming moment when all is clear, and it's time to obey.

~

Climbing into bed next to Sara, a touch of old anxiety sneaks in, and a familiar feeling, largely absent for almost a year, catching me off guard, swirls into the room, a neglected demon coming for one more shot. Like so many former nights, I don't want to sleep, am afraid to sleep, though why, I don't know. "Oh, come let us adore him" floats through the room, and it's me, singing to ease the strain of my nervous stomach.

The word says he inhabits the praise of his people, and on the third time through, after "Christ the Lord," my breathing eases. The virgin birth and the resurrection surround me, invite me, calling me to give up whatever I am trying to be, to give up whatever I am afraid to be, saying God is enough, he gives enough, and by the way, more gifts are coming.

The window's open. Sara likes the bracing air, and the tinkle of rain has changed to a soft patter. I'm cold, and pushing back the covers, I cross the room to shut out the wind. But oh—the evergreens have a touch of white now, and though I'm shivering, I can't close it, wrapped as I am in my new life, my new world where snow on Christmas Eve is not impossible, and holiness may yet be true.

I want to sleep, but thoughts jostle me, asking for a walk in the snow.

Hey.

It'll be there tomorrow.

～

I scurry back to bed, skidding my feet on the carpet, hoping friction will thaw me out. On my side, the sheets are frigid, and I pull into a tight ball, knees at my chin, covers up over my head. I rub my legs together, fast, cricket-style, and Sara rolls over, her body seeking warmth. Gradually, my muscles ease, relaxing into drowsy, and I peek out, into the dark. My eyes have adjusted, but they're heavier, sliding shut, and I have no desire to resist.

Thank God. I burrow into the covers, faintly smiling, the last smile of the day. Nothing left but rest.

One more yawn.

Funny, in Ruin, I roamed through years of midnights and early mornings. But sleep rarely comes late anymore.

Tonight, it's right on time.

The Author

JEFF BERRYMAN is a writer, actor and director whose original one-man performances have been seen across the United States and Canada. He has toured the stage version of *Leaving Ruin* extensively, as well as *The Little Guy, When Comes the Way*, and *Postmodern Art*. As a playwright, his other works include *Arthur: The Begetting* and *The Christmas Cafe*. *Leaving Ruin* is his first novel. A former professor at Abilene Christian University, Jeff lives in Seattle, Washington, with his wife Anjie and their children, Amy and Daniel.

For information on the stage version of *Leaving Ruin*, including booking information, go to www.jberryman.com or email Jeff at jeffberryman@attbi.com